IN THE NAME OF THE FLAME

IN THE NAME OF THE FLAME

ALEXIA MUELLE-RUSHBROOK

Cover design by Pantelis Politakos

Chapter artwork by Hannah Zoey

First paperback edition 2024

ISBNs:

Paperback: 978-1-0687416-0-9

Hardcover: 978-1-0687416-1-6

eBook: 978-1-7392662-9-5

www.alexiamuellerushbrook.co.uk

For readers who would like a pronunciation guide, there is a glossary at the back of this book. If you wish to decide for yourself, that is absolutely fine.

The Flame cares not for precise pronunciation, only your enjoyment.

TECTA
HALO
VIRISINIGNE
THE MAGMA ISLES
THE WESTERN ISLES

PYRALEM
SABYLOA
BRENTON
OLD EMBERBVRG
DYANA
EMBERBVRG
VAPYOS
FORT FVUEGO
LJEKKE
LJEKKE VALLEY
THE OUTER ISLES
BENEGNYEM

For Carol,
In loving memory of Peanut and Wichita—Fyre Dogs in
heart and spirit.

And for all who are willing to see new worlds with an open
mind

ONE

The only hint of home was a faint orange glow on the edge of the horizon, but the scent of death and ash was still firmly fixed in my nose. The sea seemed unnaturally calm, or perhaps it just felt wrong to have smooth sailing when those we left behind were subject to such torment, yet their screams filled our sails, sending our meagre ship towards the jagged rocks of the World's Divide.

Songs were sung about treasure hunters carving out great riches from the grey-green stone face, but no one had purposely docked against the almighty wall for centuries. My father forbade it, as did his father, and the many more fathers before that. Respect for ancient text and decree compelled obedience, but so too did the shimmering wave of colour that rippled throughout the rock the moment anyone or anything approached.

The thought of climbing an enormous inanimate mass would have been daunting, but the World's Divide's surface moved akin to a reptile's scales, and I, along with my friends, could sing the morbid sailors' lyrics off by heart. We knew that those unworthy of the optical delights found themselves and their cargo dashed into a watery grave and I am sure those words were racing through our minds as the ship illuminated under the glow of the looming wall.

Fifty-three fearful faces turned to me and I reached for the pendant that my father had placed around my neck saying, "Go, my son. You must break the Divide and seek help from our neighbours. Beg them for mercy and appeal for assistance. The evil we face will not stop for rock nor water."

As my hand wrapped around the pendant, a flame filled and burst between my fingers like I was holding a fiery sun. The flame hit the wall, propelling its colours into a racing circular formation, producing an arch of multi-coloured light. My fingers were instantly forced open by the speed of the pendant's white-gold ornamentation as it rotated around the shining emerald. Ribbons of green flame struck out, eating into the red before a beam shot forward, cutting huge cracks into the stone wall, causing it to groan like thunder with each fissure.

Suddenly a great gust of wind lurched the ship towards the wall and we all cried out in fear. With no chance of changing course, all we could do was watch as we were flung into the cracked, but still very-much solid arch of light. I tried to stare and meet my maker without grimacing, telling myself that I would die with dignity, but a sense of self-preservation—however fruitless—grasped me at the last moment and I dropped to the deck and hid my face in my arms as impact seemed unavoidable.

Disbelief that death, or at the very least significant pain hadn't immediately ensued, froze me until I heard the confused grunt of Marino, my first mate, and I uncurled myself to find we were smoothly sailing away from the cliffs undamaged. As we picked ourselves off the soaked woodwork, Alun pointed to the sky and swore.

"What is it?" I asked, wondering how the sky was the most fascinating thing at a time like this.

"It's the wrong direction, Captain," Alun grunted.

"What is? Can you be more specific?"

"The rising sun. East should be behind us, not in front."

Marino laughed in that tone that people use when there is nothing else to do but find humour in uncertainty, disbelief, or fear. "Well, I'll be," he said, turning to me. His grin explained what sense could not.

"We went through the wall?"

"Aye, Captain, we went through the wall."

TWO

Being at sea with no land in sight had never bothered me until that day. The thrill of passing through the wall might have given us hope, yet we all knew that our mission required the discovery of new lands and sympathetic people—neither of which were going to be found floating in the middle of an unnamed sea.

Perched on high as a lookout with his spyglass almost glued to his face, Raine was the first to spot land on the horizon. The call of *land ahoy* was met with a rapturous cheer and it wasn't long until even those on deck could see the cliffs of a new settlement as Marino pointed *The Leviathan* straight for the port.

The wind was pleasantly warm and we all hoped that was an omen of things to come. Meeting new folk never worried us before. In the past, our crew were either welcomed or attacked and we were ready for either, but this was different. We didn't even know if civilization existed beyond the World's Divide, let alone whether anyone had an advanced army. A small fishing village or backward town would not help us any more than bumping into a pirate hideout.

"There's a massive wall up there keepin' somethin' in, but that port looks abandoned," Alun said glumly, shielding his eyes from the sun with his weather-beaten hand. "The ships aren't big—nor numerous enough. Maybe there's another port around the cliff. I think we should keep sailin'."

"I don't." Raine's voice drifted from above as he continued peering through his spyglass.

"What?" demanded Alun.

Raine waited for my signal, then slid down from his lookout post to my side. "Alun's partly right, Captain. It is undoubtedly a city stronghold wall overlooking the cliff, but there's also a lot of civilian activity in and around those buildings below. That's no frightful, forgotten ghost town." He passed me his spyglass. "See."

The rocks were plain to the naked eye, but through Raine's spyglass the unfamiliar white stone now shone clearly in the morning light along with the movement of a thriving community. Neat rows of houses poked out of the rock itself and rose from the shoreline up the cliff like a perfectly carved staircase. All were constructed from the same gleaming stone—including the almighty wall that towered over them. Small windows were dotted along the wall, but I doubted whether they had any greater purpose than to provide natural light for those treading the otherwise dark halls. The only window of size was on the round tower that stood on the corner of the wall, almost hanging over the cliff into the sea. Seeing it gave me hope of an army, yet to my disappointment, no one seemed to be on watch.

"What kind of defence is this?" Alun chuckled disparagingly as we approached. "Even with our measly cannons we could make a mess of this bay and they couldn't do anything to stop it!"

"Then it is a good job we have come in peace, looking for help, not trouble, *isn't it*?" I replied, gritting my teeth as the fear of Alun's ignorant voice travelling over the calm waters increased tenfold.

Alun understood but pouted, nonetheless. "Just sayin'. I'm not sure what use these people are gonna be if they have such crappy defences."

I didn't reply. I needed Alun to shut up, even if I shared his concern. The bay was the most open I had ever seen. The extensive dock was exquisitely designed using a mixture of stone and iron, yet such beauty seemed foolhardy when any ship, regardless of size, could sail unhindered straight up their harbour with zero resistance. It seemed too fantastical that this world had no looting. Back home pirates would ransack the boats, stores, and general city within days—maybe less—if it wasn't for our complex canal system and constant sea patrol.

Alun clicked his tongue. "Well, let's hope their security is maintained by a thriving, yet amicable army."

I scoffed. "There's only one way to find out."

An alien dry heat and sandy air greeted us as we docked at the front of the ornate jetty. Marino raised an eyebrow at my order but knew better than to openly question me. I had to hope that someone was watching, and in that case, perception was everything. We had to look humble and at their mercy. Anchoring safely out of harbour or the far end of the jetty would send the opposite message. All of our eggs were in their proverbial basket and they would either let us sail out or not—assuming they had an army because I still couldn't see any signs of one.

Unwilling to leave the ship unmanned, I instructed all but Raine to stay onboard. Marino would take charge if I failed, and as two guards approached us something told me that I might benefit from Raine's calm demeanour, not Alun's undiplomatic sarcasm.

"Would you look at them?" Alun declared as I jumped onto the jetty. "One will take your head while the other your ankles!"

I turned to appeal to my crew member, but Marino was already mid-swing clipping Alun around the ear. As usual, Alun had a point, even if he shouldn't have voiced it. The oncoming guards were identically dressed in exquisitely designed leather and iron armour that shone with each stride. Their shields depicted a flame that seemed to be leaping out of the metal and as they approached, I could see the same, equally realistic flame bursting from their silver breastplates. Both men walked with a hand over the hilt of their swords, but the main difference between the two guards was size—and it was no small difference. In fact, if someone told me the larger man had been copied and they had forgotten to feed the replica, I would have had difficulty denouncing it.

My father had always told me to maintain a sense of self-important presence but also speak to people with equal kindness. He didn't tell me how to do this when one was seven feet tall and the other only four. My eyes naturally went upwards.

"Good day, sirs," I said when the men were twenty paces from me.

Relaxing his arms, the larger guard chuckled and gazed down at his companion.

"Business or pleasure?" asked the smaller guard—neither politely nor impolitely.

"Business, I suppose, though I—"

"What you trading?"

"Nothing. I'm not trading. I need to speak—"

"No trade, no business."

"Robyn, let the man speak," said the larger guard, still chuckling. "Forgive my brother, he likes to keep on point."

"For good reason, Cuykoo. We'd still be unloading the first boat if I left you in charge!"

"Too true, too true." Cuykoo shrugged. "So, who do you wish to see?"

"Your ruler. Whoever is in charge of your people—namely your army."

Suspicion spread across Robyn's face. "Why? Surely you are not stupid enough to threaten our great city?" He peered around me to our ship. It was on par with those in the bay but clearly it didn't impress.

"No, not at all. I come looking for help, not trouble. We have travelled through the World's Divide as our home, the world as we know it, is under siege and if we do not find assistance then all will be lost."

Robyn narrowed his eyes and stared at me. He was testing my patience, so I chewed on the inside of my cheek to stop me from barking an order at him. Remaining stern faced, he quickly glanced up at his brother before saying, "You'll need the king then."

"Yes, please! Where can I find him?"

"In the City Keep—*if* he'll see you."

Cuykoo pointed to the top of the cliff. "Follow the road up the hill until you reach Brindley Meadow. The path will lead you to the Kennel Gates."

"Surely we should go through the main entrance? It is essential we get there quick—"

"*Everyone* goes through the Kennel Gates."

"Even those seeking—"

"Everyone."

"Can you not escort us?" Raine quietly spoke for the first time. His request was pronounced as clearly and respectfully as possible, yet both the brothers' faces cracked with laughter.

"What?" I asked, feeling frustration rise as they failed to sense our urgency while Raine stepped back in embarrassment.

"Where do you come from, really?" Cuykoo asked, nudging his brother in the head with his elbow. "The fisheries at Pyralem? Did the old man put you up to this? You must have practiced those accents for months!"

"What accent?" I resisted commenting on *his* quaint speech. "I have no idea where Pyralem is—in fact I do not know where *this is*." I said seriously. "What is the name of this town?"

The amusement dropped from Robyn's expression. "*Town? Town?*" He tutted. "You come to Emberbyrg, the greatest, most illustrious city in all of Benegnyem, and call it a *town*?" A chortle preceded spit on the jetty. "Go, see the king if you want to try your luck—or insanity—maybe he is curious, but *we* are busy."

Robyn strode towards the nearest ship without looking back.

Cuykoo paused for a moment, silently eyeing us up and down before stepping to follow Robyn.

Confusion hit me. "Are you not going to impose rules on docking—or a fee?" I had limited gold and had no idea if they used it as currency, but my father had supplied a few cases of treasure to plead with (which I had hoped would not be used, confiscated, or stolen by these inconsistent twins).

"No," replied Cuykoo. "No trade, no rules—*yet*."

Raine and I exchanged a look of disbelief.

"Are you not worried that we'll—I dunno—attack or something?"

Cuykoo shrugged. "They don't see you as a threat—or at least will speak to you first."

"*They?* This place has no defence. How could you know if—"

Staring up the hillside, Cuykoo heartily laughed, yet there was no mirth in his words. "I don't know where you have been hiding. I don't believe for a second you've come from the Divide, even with your funny clothes and funky accents, but I assure you, if you were considered to be a threat the dogs would already be here—and you'd already be dead."

THREE

Despite years at sea visiting numerous coastal towns and cities all over the kingdom, the heat of Emberbyrg was set to a completely new level—and the light sea breeze did very little to lessen it. The sun bounced off the white stone making it difficult for Raine and I to open our eyes fully, yet for the sake of credibility and pride, I forced myself to walk into the foreign city with a sense of command.

Directly off the dock were several buildings, one of which looked like a stable. Securing transport to the king seemed like a wise move, so when a man confidently strode into the building, we followed.

"Good day, sir," Raine said as the man checked over his shoulder. "Do you hire out carriages perchance?"

His eyebrows rose sharply but his voice remained steady as he extended his hand to an open-top carriage. "I do."

"Fantastic! Would you be so kind and deliver us to the king, we have urgent—"

"Not today. Tomorrow."

"We're in quite a rush..."

The man's steel-grey eyes rolled. "Best walk it then."

"Is there no way—"

"Do you see any animals?" He thrust his arms out. "No. No, you don't, do you?"

The presence of a carriage had, I admit, blinded us to the lack of horses. "Are the horses all—"

"No horses in Old Emberbyrg."

Raine and I exchanged equally baffled glances. People tended to instinctively like Raine. His tidy brown hair and soft blue eyes set off his quietly handsome, trustworthy face, whereas I—whether I meant to or not—with my long dark-brown hair, trimmed but rustic beard, and tall, muscled frame looked like I was ready for a challenge. This made for an excellent captain and law enforcer, not so much an asker of favours or polite enquiries. For this reason Raine was supposed to do the initial talking, yet as I could see Raine was running out of momentum, I stepped in. "Just today, or ever?"

"Ever. Up there," he jolted his head towards the clifftop, "in the main city, sure, but not here."

"What pulls the carriages then?"

"Hinnies, they're stronger on the steeper roads."

"What's a hinny?"

"A donkey cross a horse."

"A mule?"

The man sighed, rubbing his giant hands over his two-day stubble. "*Hinny.*"

Fearing I was losing his already vague interest, I returned to our original request. "Is there not a hinny available today? You see, we're—"

"*Tomorrow*. Today is their day off. They worked late cleaning up last night. No hinny in Old Emberbyrg works today, so unless you're going to corner a dog or pull a cart yourself, you'll either need to wait or walk." A sarcastic grin spread across his face as he pretended to hitch himself to the cart.

Were I on my ship, I would have drawn my sword, or at least threatened to. A little reminder of who I was and who they were not. But I was not at home and to him I was not a prince—or even a captain of note. Staring in his eyes at that moment, I was just an ignorant fool looking for a fight in his stable. We'd probably have made a dent in his pride in a physical fight, yet truthfully, even though both of us were well-muscled from years of manual labour, we were no match for that guy. Against him, we'd have needed Marino. Neither Raine's slight-build nor my thick-set body could compare to Marino's towering mass. Together we made a strong rank of command, but without space for a sword fight or Marino to bail me out of a fist fight, making jokes about pulling carts or responding to his smirk seemed unwise.

We left without another word.

Quickly finding ourselves in a market, we gladly mimicked the locals by keeping under the multitude of canvas as we wandered around the stalls. So many things were the same, but not, and only our looming sense of duty stopped us from exploring every inch of the place. The familiar smell of fish and sea water—which was more homely to us than any castle comforts by then—was interrupted by spice and perfume that was as new to our senses as the temperature. One man called to us, trying to sell us fish. Of course, I had no immediate need, but the sight of the large red and orange coloured fish laid out in salt stopped me in my tracks.

"What species is this?" I asked.

The man stared at me as though I were asking if the sky were blue, but eventually said, "Fyre Fish."

"Are they common here?" Raine asked, obviously understanding the man's expression.

He snorted. "Like the sand in Sabyloa."

"Is that a lot?"

The man on the neighbouring stall laughed heartily, nudging his partner so hard that I thought she might fall over, however, she simply started laughing herself.

"My apologies. We're not from here. Could you be so kind as to point us to—" Raine gave up. Each word he pronounced just increased their mirth.

Frustration hit me and I hit the table. All eyes fixed on me, but any chance of gaining directions was gone.

Jolting my head, I signalled to Raine to keep walking and internally sighed with relief when no one retaliated with more than a sneer. Passing new stalls, we glanced at the faces hoping to find a sympathetic smile, but those in earshot of our exchange blanked us and those further on had no interest when they realised we were not looking to buy.

Robyn's words came to me. *No trade, no business.* Without knowing their currency, and not wanting to risk further ridicule and ask, I felt at a loss. Dipping my hand into my trouser pockets, I rolled the few gold coins I had there through my fingers.

"Perhaps we need to buy something?" I whispered to Raine.

"To gain their interest?"

"Yes. It's worth a go. Look for someone humble, you know, someone—"

"The opposite of Alun."

"Exactly," I laughed. I couldn't help it. If he liked you, Alun was as loyal as the day was long, but he wasn't known for his patience nor his humility. Had either trait been practiced before I took over *The Leviathan*, he might have been granted a ship of his own. However, despite his undeniable experience, his hot temper made him difficult to follow and no captain would promote him—or keep him on board longer than a year or so. With a keg of beer in hand and a few curse words in his mouth, he once informed me that he preferred to guide from the side anyway. He wasn't lying, he loved nothing better than to tell me when he disagreed with a command, but regardless of his harsh tongue, after a decade together I wouldn't have changed the old man for anything.

"How about there?" Raine nodded to a stall on the edge of the market where a middle-aged man in a light brown tunic stood in the shade selling nets. In the sun next to him, with no more than a head scarf for protection, a girl of about eighteen sat weaving rope into exquisite patterns. I felt ten degrees hotter just looking at her, yet she didn't appear to be sweating—which just made me feel hotter.

As we approached, the man smiled and hope raised within me—or at least fought against the knots in my stomach that had become so tight I wondered if I would ever be able to eat again. "Good morning, sir. I wonder if you might help us?"

He squinted as Raine spoke, and for a moment I expected him to break into laughter, but instead his smile widened and he proudly waved his hands over his nets. "Certainly! What are you interested in? I have a net for every occasion."

"We're searching for the king, actually, and hoping you could show us the fastest route—"

The man fake-coughed, waving his hands over his nets again.

Raine picked up an ornate fishing net in front of the girl and for the first time, she looked up. "How much for this?" he said, glancing between the two.

"Two discs."

The girl stared at the man but he ignored her.

"I only have gold coin..." I said, pulling two pieces out of my pocket.

He grunted and extended his hand for me to drop the coin. "Huh." He shrugged, tapping the two coins together. "Deal."

The girl continued to stare and I began to wonder how much I had overpaid by. "Could you deliver to our ship? It's called—"

"I know your ship."

"Oh?"

"Everyone has seen it. Looks a bit experimental to me. A fancy net suits it, I suppose." He grinned. "Yes, I'll see it delivered. So, where you from?"

"We've come from the World's Divide seeking assistance."

"Yeah, right," he chuckled, walking away rubbing the coins between his chubby hands. "Good luck with whatever you're up to." He waved to the girl. "Oryana, I'm off to the bank. Get your brother to deliver the net."

"Please," I said in earnest, fearing the number of people dying back home while we stood there buying a net we did not need. "We desperately need to see the king. What is the quickest route? We were given somewhat vague instructions at the dock."

The man kept walking, but called over his shoulder, "Oryana can answer any questions."

Staring at my lips, Oryana narrowed her crystal blue eyes as though she was waiting for me to complete my sentence—or give the punchline to a joke—then quizzically turned to Raine.

"He wants the king?" she asked.

"Yes," Raine replied. "We need an audience with him urgently, but no one will take us there. All we've been told is look upwards for Brindley Meadow and the Kennels?"

"We need the king, not the kennel," I added.

Again Oryana stared between us, focusing on our lips, not our eyes, and suddenly it dawned on me that she could not hear.

I turned to Raine. "She cannot hear us."

"If you look at me, I can understand your words perfectly well—I'm just unsure of your request. You have been told where to go, but still seek an answer." Her words filled my ears in the most curious way and it was clear from Raine's expression that he was no less touched. It was almost like she was singing—even if she was ultimately telling me off.

"Oryana!" a man shouted as he approached, clicking his fingers in her face as soon as he was close enough. "Stop pestering people. I just saw Dad. He said you have to deliver a net while I watch the goods."

Reading his lips, Oryana screwed up her face. Her brother—who was a younger version of the man who just left, only with blue eyes to match his sister's—immediately lost his temper and turned his hand to slap her.

Raine repelled his swing like he was swatting a fly.

"You ain't paid enough to touch me, pirate!" he barked, turning red, preparing to swing again—this time with his fist clenched in Raine's direction.

"Enough!" I shouted, knocking him back with one push, simultaneously throwing a gold coin at him.

He grabbed it like Alun grabs mussels—greedily.

"There, I'm sure that compensates you for your time and any offence. We won't keep you any longer. Oryana just kindly said she would deliver us."

Three sets of eyes stared at me in confusion.

"Shall we go?" I gently waved my arm, inviting her to lead the way.

"Fine. Go," he grumbled before chuckling to himself as he slumped into his father's chair, biting into the coin.

In that moment, he reminded me very much of my elder brother, Baran.

Oryana rose from her stool, only briefly stopping to tidy the net she was working on. She pointed towards the one we had just purchased, but I nodded up the hill. Understanding that she was to literally deliver *us*, not the net, she glanced at her brother. Feeling her gaze, he met her eyes but only scowled before dismissively waving his hand—and the fact that none of us had a net in our possession when we left somehow escaped his notice.

"I'm only going to take you to where you could find yourself," she said once we were out of earshot.

"But you'll do it so much faster."

"I suppose."

Following Oryana in silence, we took in the unknown architecture, travelling through a few side streets which were connected by staircases cut into the cliff.

When we arrived onto a much wider, main street that curled and curved into the rock in front of the ornate houses, I gently tapped on Oryana's arm, causing her to turn to me. "Why are the roads so wide?" I asked. "Surely it was a lot of extra effort to carve so much rock back when no hinny needs such a wide path?"

"No, but the dogs are clumsy sometimes, so space is better." Oryana shrugged. "Are your roads narrow?"

"Compared to here, yes."

"Huh." Gauging from her expressive, short response, I was sure she wanted to call us primitive.

"Have you always lived in Emberbyrg?" Raine asked as we continued past row after row of white houses.

"In Old Emberbyrg, yes. I don't go to the main city anymore."

"How so, when it's so close?"

Oryana twisted her lips and stared at me as though I should know the answer. Whether she thought I had caught on or she simply gave up, I'm not sure, but after a short pause, she shrugged, saying, "Da keeps me busy down here anyway."

"But do you want—"

"No."

"Why not?"

Oryana's face flashed somewhere between disgust and irritation. "Judgement comes quicker in the city. I've seen enough of it for a lifetime."

"Oh?"

"You didn't pay me for my story—in fact you paid everyone *but me*." Her lips twisted into a grin.

"Ah-ha, good point." As I dipped my hand into my pocket, her smile dropped.

"No, keep it," she said, briefly laying her tanned hand on my arm.

"It's only fair—"

"No, no, let's just call this a freebie. I'd not be able to spend it anyway."

"You can exchange it, I'm sure?"

Oryana looked uncomfortable. "It's not that."

I waited to see if she was going to explain, but she didn't. "What then?"

She sighed. "Conley, my brother, has *sticky fingers*."

"*Ah.*"

"And flying fists." Raine gritted his teeth. "Maybe *he* deserves judgement."

"Maybe, but Ma paid enough for him. I can't see that again, no matter what," Oryana said sadly. As we turned a corner, I opened my mouth to question her but stopped as she suddenly pointed, saying, "I'll take you as far as Brindley Meadow, but that's it. From this point it's a simple ascent to the main city because you just follow the curve of the road as it climbs the cliff. The meadow is at the top. It will be empty today, so entry should be quick."

"Oh?"

Oryana rolled her eyes. "Judgement Day was yesterday. No one will be queuing—and the dogs will be quieter."

"The dogs?" I felt myself scowling as a woman walked past with a dog trotting next to her. It wasn't a breed I was familiar with, but it looked like a regular dog, nonetheless. "Why do people talk so much about dogs here?"

"Do you *really* not come from this world?" she raised an eyebrow, alternating her gaze between Raine and me, but lingered on Raine as though he was the most likely to speak the truth.

Raine grinned like a lovestruck puppy. "Really—"

"Oryana! Oryana! I told you to answer questions, not take them on a tour! Get back to work!" Raine and I grimaced at the sight of her angry father.

Seeing our expressions, Oryana turned back in time to see her father repeat his demands. I am sure she stifled a groan before whispering: "Gotta go. Good luck."

FOUR

Although sorry to lose our guide, we were thankful that the road ahead was now clear, so Raine and I pressed on, ignoring the passive invites from sun-and-drink relaxed locals to enter bars and restaurants.

The higher we got, the hotter it became, and my normally trusty hat began to feel like it had melted into my skull—causing me to lament not stopping in the market to buy two head scarves instead of a net that we left behind.

Just before the verge of the cliff, the houses stopped popping out of the rock, leaving a section of road bare except for the copious amount of sandy stone that lined every surface and strange spiky plants which protruded through rockeries and cracks alike. Some were in full bloom, attracting an array of insects who paused to smell our foreign flesh. Although intrigued by the new species before me, having experienced more mosquito bites than I cared to count, I hoped that foreign blood wasn't on the menu. However, being conscious of maintaining some degree of dignity, I refrained from irrationally waving the critters away or jumping when the tail of a sandy-orange lizard flashed near my right eye as it darted into a sizable hole in the rock.

Rising over the final lip, Raine swore under his breath and we both paused to appreciate the size of the city wall as it stretched before us. From below, or even at sea, it was clear that it was large, yet now it spread inland further than the horizon and loomed with omnipresent authority.

My heart skipped with admiration and hope—and, honestly, fear. Such a great nation was precisely what we dreamt of finding—what the very lives of our loved ones relied on—but it was as though the enormity of the task was being depicted in stone before us and I doubted if I was up to it.

The road led straight towards a gate on the corner of the wall. Despite its size, it was cleverly concealed from anyone at sea by the curvature of the lookout tower—which also seemed to have increased its magnitude now that we were approaching it. An ornate iron archway displayed the name *Brindley Meadow*, but back home, a meadow meant a lush-green pasture for animals, so without the sign I would never have thought to name the stony dustbowl between us and the wall in such a way.

In my mind, I had expected to find the stable keeper's hinnies gently munching under a few fruit trees—or some other, similarly idyllic scene. What we actually saw was an elderly, yet very stern man overseeing a dozen youths as they raked stones.

"You missed a print!" shouted the man. "There'll be hell to pay if anyone trips up because of your laziness!"

The group ignored us as we made our way down the road, but as the shadow of the wall loomed nearer, Raine and I realised they were raking around the entrance to a massive pit which was surrounded by black rope.

"How many people have stumbled into that in the dark?" I scoffed.

"Is that seating?" Raine whispered—although no one else would have heard had he raised his voice. "It looks like seating... It is, look, there's people cleaning it."

Descending into the ground was a kind of auditorium with a flat oval pit carved out in the centre. Just as they were above, people were raking the ground in addition to sweeping the rows of stone benches.

"Is that a viewing gallery?" Raine pointed up at the wall. From the ship I innocently thought they were hallway windows. From this angle, positioned above the pit, the windows did seem perfectly placed for viewing without descending into the throng of activity below.

"Maybe."

"What do you think they watch from such a distance? Tournaments?"

"We don't have time to find out," I replied, pushing my curiosity aside. "Let's go."

Approaching the city entrance I thought it was possibly one of the most oversized, ridiculous structures I had ever seen. It was clear that the residents of Emberbyrg wanted to impress anyone who visited their city—regardless of whether they were friend or foe. I understood the sentiment, my own family had built an empire on a similar principle. However, this door was beyond any normal statement of wealth and power. It dwarfed Raine and me. It dwarfed our ship—literally.

The door was made of two almighty leaves, both forged from iron and beautifully adorned with murals that danced around a fire. Patterns from the left appeared to be racing to meet their twins from the right, and where they met, they combined and wove into a flame that seemed to be living. Simply raising the doors into place must have taken an army. Certainly, no one was going to be stupid enough to attempt ramming into it—even the significantly smaller carriage and pedestrian admittance doorways in the far-left side were as solid as the cliff itself.

"Who has three doors in one?" I scoffed. "Unless they plan on sailing a fleet of ships up here, why make such a large gate and then have to cut two smaller ones out for daily use?"

I didn't expect Raine to answer, but even if he had one, he had no time to give it as the pedestrian door opened and two guards stepped out. Adopting the same stance as Robyn and Cuykoo, the guards approached with their right arms crossed against their flame-depicting breastplates as they gripped the hilt of their swords.

Guessing by the tufts of grey hair and wrinkles by his eyes, one guard was a good twenty years older than the other, but no less athletic. "Good day," said the older guard, staring intently between Raine and me, holding out his hand. "Papers."

Raine stepped forward. "I'm sorry, we have no papers—"

"You wanting admittance?"

"We are, yes. Quite urgently." Raine spoke in a tone that I almost didn't recognise as he tried to hide his accent in the hope of being taken seriously.

The guards' eyes boggled as they exchanged glances.

The older guard shrugged. "You *need* papers."

"But we have none—"

"Where are you from?" The younger guard didn't say, *because your accent is weird*, but it was clear from his face that was what he meant.

Raine cleared his throat. "We have come through the World's Divide seeking an urgent parley with your king."

The guards laughed.

"Well, that's a new one!" the older guard chuckled.

"Our ship is in the harbour, flying the white flag, we—"

"Ah, it's *you*." He looked us up and down. "Figures."

"What does?"

"Strange ship, strange clothes—*strange request*." He scratched his head. "Pity you had to arrive today. It should be a simple day, but I sense you're going to mess that up."

"Not intentionally."

"That's not a *no*, is it?" The older guard rolled his eyes before turning to his colleague. "You best call Lord Byrne."

Stepping inside the gate, the guard shouted, "Lord Byrne, sir, the white flaggers are here."

The sound of a bucket being placed on stone rang out, then the head of a grey-haired, weather-beaten man appeared around the door. If Alun cared to dress in an elaborate silver tunic, they would have looked alike—except Lord Byrne had red eyes. "Papers?"

"They say they have none, sir. They ask to see the king—they *say* they've come from the Divide."

"We *have* come through the Divide. Our world is in peril and we come seeking—"

Stepping out of the door, Lord Byrne waved his hand, stopping Raine in his tracks. "You, young man, can seek all you want, but you have been marked by the dogs so will not step foot into our great city. Not unless you wish for eternal damnation here and now?"

"I've not been marked by any dog! Sword, sea, and fist, maybe, but never a dog." Confusion and pride cut across Raine's face.

"Your eyes say differently."

I took a step forward. "My companion is loyal and true, Lord—"

Lord Byrne's eyes cut into me. "And who, exactly, are you?"

I had two titles of note. My attire should have spoken of both—back home my hat would have screamed *captain* and my jacket, decoration, and stance declared *prince*—yet this man, this glorified gatekeeper, sneered at me from underneath his greybeard. "I am Prince Niall Beckett of Virisinigne—*from beyond the World's Divide.*"

Lord Byrne narrowed his eyes but didn't take them off me.

"What do you think, sir?" the younger guard said.

"Call the Kennel Maid."

"Excuse me," I interjected. "We need the king, not—"

"If you wish for your request to be considered, and wish to walk unhindered through the Kennel Gates, you *must* be granted access by the Kennel Maid."

Arguing seemed fruitless but standing silently took every inch of myself control. Such grandeur seemed bizarrely offset by being forced to wait for a maid to admit us. As the sun spun round, the guards allowed us to stand under their canopy, but that was as far as their hospitality went. When Lord Byrne finally returned, I jumped forward.

"*You*," Lord Byrne said, holding my stare, "may come in. The Kennel Maid will see you now."

"What about Raine? He must come with me—"

"No, he *must not*. He is free to stand there or return to your ship." Lord Byrne saw me open my mouth and scowled. "This isn't a debate. It is you alone or no one."

I didn't understand their objection to Raine, but we both knew what we had to do. Watching Raine walk across Brindley Meadow alone was an almighty blow to my confidence. Even if I had planned on doing much of the talking myself, he was to pick up where I failed—to be the soft, amiable touch if my edges became too rough.

"Shall we?" Lord Byrne gestured for me to walk through the gate.

Dutifully stepping inside, I found myself in the strangest room I had ever seen. The path ahead led to a series of decoratively roped lines and iron-clad kiosks, but my eyes tracked right, identifying a short hallway that led to the lookout tower as it rose above the enormous room. Following the line of the tower, my eyes naturally pivoted in the opposite direction, marvelling at the exquisite roof that seemed to be as high as any cathedral at home. A beautiful iron framework weaved from the roof and it was impossible not to be impressed by the elaborate design. Everything appeared to have precise order except a woman who wandered the lofty walkways. Her unkempt hair and water-stained clothes seemed out of place, however, fascinated by the grand, swirling display, I ignored her and visually tracked the iron stairway to the ground.

The sound of giant bolts shutting behind me coincided with my eyes reaching what I could only describe as a gigantic, ornate animal stall. Then, and only then, as my stomach dropped into my shoes, did I see the dragon staring at me—and instantly the oversized door justified every single inch.

FIVE

The sound of laughter snapped me out of my stupor, but I couldn't bring myself to look away from the dragon. Any hope that it was a monument quickly sank when the creature blinked and I followed the double eyelids up and down with absolute terror.

"You'd think you'd never seen a dog before!" The guards laughed heartily.

"D-dog?" The word tripped on my tongue, refuelling their roars of laughter. Suddenly everyone's obsession with dogs made sense, even if the misnomer did not. "That's because, up close, I haven't seen a—"

"*Everyone* has seen a Fyre Dog." Distrust rang through Lord Byrne's voice. "Just as *everyone* knows to show respect to them."

"Well, I'm not about to challenge one, am I?" I blurted. "If my people knew how, I wouldn't be here—"

"What nonsense are you trying to bring before our king?"

Panic rose within me. For years, I had been the one to command, yet the beast had frozen my confidence, my wits—my ability to form any kind of coherent sentence when it mattered the most. Just as I opened my mouth to protest, the dragon extended its neck towards me, keeping its gleaming amber eyes on me while the strange black strip in the centre acted like a hypnotic chasm for me to fall into.

The sound of me gulping echoed off the walls, yet Lord Byrne's amusement had turned to cemented suspicion. He glanced upwards, then turned to me, sneering. "Enough of this farce. Return him to his ship and ensure his men are on it when they leave. If they cause any trouble, Wydgitta, please sink them."

The dragon tilted its dark green-grey, scaled head in Lord Byrne's direction before returning its gaze to me. By now it was so close to me I could feel steam coming from its nostrils. Every inch of me dripped with sweat as a memory of my little sister echoed in my mind.

Bees and dogs can smell fear, she declared when our mother asked why she was sitting uncovered amongst the hives in the castle orchard. *I am not afraid, so why should they be?* There and then, I wished that I could channel her confidence, but something told me this dog was above caring whether I was afraid or not. They rested in the confidence that I should be.

Fingers grasped around my arms and my voice returned. "Please, I beg you, let the king hear me!"

Lord Byrne turned his eyes upwards for a moment, nodded, then tutted at me. "It is my job to save the king from someone such as you. Liars and pretenders—leeches on our great nation. No, we are done. If you have come post Judgment Day in the hope of you or your devious plan living longer, you are mistaken. Our guard does not sleep." He waved his hand and turned away. "I have seen enough."

"Please! My people will die if you do not help us!"

"*You* will die if you don't immediately get out of this gate," snarled a guard as another unbolted the door.

The dragon stretched its neck again, leaving no more than an inch between us. Immediately the air shifted, like the dragon was absorbing me—breathing me in—seconds before the guards proceeded to drag me towards the enormous gate.

Fearful of retribution, but suddenly more fearful of returning to the ship a failure, a name sprang to mind. "The Kennel Maid! Please, you said I would see her?" I still failed to understand how it would help, but I clung to the minuscule slither of hope that someone would listen.

"I thought you were too good for her?" a commanding voice rebuked from above.

Immediately all below stood to attention.

"Not today, I am not," I babbled—instantly knowing that Raine would have grimaced had he heard me. My eyes panned the iron framework, searching for the owner of the voice, only to find the dirty-looking young woman I had dismissed moments earlier.

Hearing my words, she scoffed and began to walk away, higher into the framework.

"Forgive me!" I called. "Please at least hear my plight fully before condemning a nation to ash due to my inadequacies!"

Whether from conscience, curiosity, pity, or what, I could not say, but she stopped. Without a word, she descended the iron staircase, carefully placing each footstep as though floating on a timeless cloud. Her relaxed, methodical heart rate couldn't have been any further from my irate, desperate beats. Once on the ground, she carefully placed a bucket and thick cloth to the side of the steps, gently caressed the dragon's cheek, and then stood regally with her hands together in front of her. As the woman's piercing, emerald green eyes examined me, it struck me that her expression was as set and unreadable as the dragon's.

"You are in charge here—the Kennel Maid?" I asked, trying not to show incredulity.

"I am." Her voice spoke with a confidence that her ill-fitting beige clothes could not. "You claim to be the spokesperson for a troubled nation beyond the World's Divide yet have no evidence to support your claim. This—" She waved a hand in my direction. "is unusual attire, I grant you, but is hardly proof of what you say."

"I understand your reluctance, I—"

"He is more likely to be a spy from the Eastlands, my lady, then from the World's Divide." Lord Byrne dipped his head respectfully towards the Kennel Maid as he spoke.

"Quite." She narrowed her eyes at me.

"He'd not be the first pretender, even if his ruse is more impressive than some."

"I have no ruse!" I declared. "I come unarmed on a mission begging for mercy from a city I have never heard of by means I thought impossible, but my people's plight will not stay beyond the Divide. He who attacks us could attack you, and—"

Lord Byrne's fist landed in my stomach, sending me to my knees. "How dare you stand before the Kennel Maid and threaten her with attack?"

Again, I internally lamented Raine's departure. Diplomatic Raine wouldn't have been on his knees coughing his guts up.

"I'm not threatening," I spluttered, standing. "Have you never heard of not shooting the messenger?"

The Kennel Maid turned to the dragon as though in conversation with it, then said. "Wydgitta is right. He has green eyes. No Easterner is likely to have green eyes."

Lord Byrne's red eyes peered at me. "Huh."

"How did you get here?" The Kennel Maid said.

Realising that my words were failing me, I decided to use the only available prop I had. Pulling the chain that held my father's pendant from under my shirt, I laid the jewel in the palm of my hand and angled it towards the Kennel Maid. Since opening the wall, the pendant had been dormant, yet when she stepped forward the emerald seemed to flicker as the sun reflected in her equally green eyes.

As the Kennel Maid slowly reached out her hand, gently caressing the pendant, I noticed the intricate tattooed dragon scales which ran from her fingers up her arms. "Where did you get this?" she asked in a reverent tone.

"My father, my king. He gave it to me and sent me sailing towards the World's Divide in search of assistance."

"Then I agree to your request," said the Kennel Maid, standing tall. "You must speak to the king."

SIX

The guards led me through the iron kiosks into a courtyard. Were it void of life, I would have been amply struck by the artistry as my eyes surveyed the foreign architecture which rose layer upon layer before me. But the courtyard was not void. People moved up and down the beautiful walkways and ornate balconies in lazy, carefree splendour, happily oblivious to the multiple dragons of varying size that laid sunbathing in the sand.

Glancing backwards, I caught sight of a beige shirt as the Kennel Maid disappeared through one of the archways followed by a dragon. Instinct compelled me to shout a warning to her but I bit my lip, reminding myself that she was literally washing one a few minutes ago. These people did not share my fear of fiery beasts. In my heart, I knew these people were the salvation my father—my world—prayed that I would find, but I doubted my ability to form an alliance with a civilisation that had built their cities to accommodate what our world would undoubtedly shudder to contemplate, let alone champion.

"Can you ride?" Lord Byrne asked as we walked under the welcome cover of a canopy. Unsure of the species he was referring to, I stared a moment too long. "Do they have horses in your world?" he asked sarcastically.

Relief hit me. "Yes, yes, I can ride a horse." A nervous chuckle left my lips. "Sorry, I thought you meant a d—"

Lord Byrne scoffed. "Don't be ridiculous."

"Sorry, of course not. How would anyone—"

"Only the bonded ride Fyre Dogs—and a spy is not going to be worthy of that accolade, *is he?*" Disdain oozed out of the old man but I found myself respecting him, just like I respected Alun. Alun was equally prickly until you truly got to know and trust him and he you. Not that I believed Lord Byrne had any more interest in bonding with me than his dragon did.

"I'm not a spy!"

"We'll see."

A guard appeared with a casually dressed stable hand holding four horses between them.

"I was told the horses don't work today?"

"Who said that?" As Lord Byrne narrowed his eyes, I felt like I was going to burn under his suspicious gaze.

"A man I asked for a ride from the docks."

Lord Byrne rolled his eyes. "*Hinnies* don't work after Judgement Day. Some horses do. Today should be a day of rest. *Should be.*"

As I opened my mouth to speak, a guard pushed me forward. "I thought you were in a hurry? Get on the horse."

In truth, it had been a while since I had ridden anything other than waves but the grey mare patiently waited for me to climb onto her back. They had clearly given me the slowest, least likely to misbehave horse they could find, yet they tethered her to the horse in front anyway. Where exactly they thought I would try to run to in that almighty, foreign, dragon-laden city, I do not know.

Our equine train had travelled no more than one hundred yards down a sandy road when a shadow skipped over us. No one looked up—not even the horses—despite the sun seemingly departing for several seconds. Awe struck at such an anomaly, my eyes darted upwards as an enormous, scaled beast skimmed over the rooftops. Whether it was luck or skill that prevented its tail from sending the tiles flying, I couldn't say.

Civilians stared at me as I rode past them but I didn't mind because I was as fascinated by them as they were me.

"How far is it to the king?" I asked after a few minutes' silence.

"The palace is on the northern edge of the city," replied a guard.

"How far is that?" I asked, trying not to sound irritated by the man's half answer.

"Can you see the palace from here?"

"No?"

"Then it's far."

Disheartened by their cold attitudes, I returned my attention to admiring the architecture. Obviously, the dragons were expected to appear on every corner because there was not a narrow road in sight. The potential passing of scaled monsters didn't stop them putting ceramic pots along the walls though, nor did it detract from the beautiful gardens that bordered many of the streets. One bush with red blooms the size of a dinner plate seemed to be on every road. I wanted to ask what they called it but pride stopped me from voicing my question. Well, pride, and fear that it would be a top-secret plant that only Emberbyrg grew and I would be accused of trying to steal it somehow.

As a cool breeze suddenly wafted onto my left ear, I caught sight of a sandy-orange creature hovering next to me. Sensing my surprise, my mare tensed underneath me as I turned to view the miniature dragon. Had I not been petrified, I might have thanked it for its fanning services, but instead I stared, hoping it would fly away.

"You're overdressed," the guard behind me said. "You will overheat as you are."

With my sweat-drenched shirt clinging to every muscle, it would have been more accurate to say *you are overheating,* but I simply agreed. My humility was rewarded as the guard trotted his horse to my side and passed me a water bottle—inadvertently encouraging the winged beast to move on.

Feeling the fresh, almost sweet, water touch my lips, I felt invigorated. "Wow," I said without thinking. "This water is amazing. It must come from a special spring?"

"Nowhere that you can swim in or out of our great city, if that's what you are thinking," Lord Byrne said brashly.

Exasperated, I said, "Do you have a problem with spies breaking in?"

"What?" Hearing Lord Byrne's reply, the guard behind me sucked in their breath.

"You keep alluding to me being a spy. That makes me think this city has security problems."

"The greatest city in the world is such because of our unfathomable security. Maybe your city wouldn't be in peril if you took better care of it, *Prince of Virisinigne*."

Raine's voice echoed in my ears, telling me not to retaliate to the Lord's ridicule. I'd been in enough brawls over the years for less, but ultimately I had the weight of the crown and a loyal crew on my side and had proved myself a formidable protectorate and member of both.

Now I had nothing.

My horse turned left, heading on a northern road. It was as wide as any other and just as sandy, but there, stretched before us in the distance was the palace in all its glory. Great white pillars rose out of the ground marking the vast sections of the building, each as rich and splendid as the next. Whether I liked it or not, I had to admit it was the grandest building I had ever seen.

When we finally reached the end of the road, ornate iron gates marked the entrance to the palace. Guards saluted Lord Byrne with their right hand while the left held the hilt of their swords. They didn't speak, but they both eyed me with the same curious suspicion that their colleagues seemed so happy to display. It wouldn't have helped, but I found myself wishing that I hadn't left my sword on *The Leviathan*. My reasoning was sound, I wanted willing friends, not foes, yet under the weight of their stares, the idea of going down fighting felt a lot more appealing than being cut down by their ill-placed, unsympathetic wrath.

Along with palace stable staff who appeared like clockwork to claim our horses, a tall, burly, red-eyed man in his early thirties presented himself. His armoured uniform matched the other guards in cut and design, yet he was heavily decorated with honours and set with an ornate emerald-green leather sash woven into his breastplate.

"Commander," Lord Byrne said as we approached. "Have you been updated?"

"Indeed, Lord Byrne," he said proudly. "The Kennel Maid has just informed me and is now speaking to the king."

"Excellent. Prince Niall, this is Uryah Ashley—Commander of the Royal Guard." Lord Byrne pronounced my name correctly, but the undertone of mockery was thinly veiled at best. I let it pass, instead shaking the hand of the commander, hoping, if not believing, that his frigid expression could be befriended.

Lord Byrne, Commander Uryah, and two additional guards escorted me through the palace. The inside was no less glorious than the exterior as staircases, doorways, and arches lined and spiralled in different directions. Everything shone with white marble and white gold with colourful tapestries hanging alongside splendid paintings and artefacts, but although grand, the scale was human, not dragon. *A palace fit for a king, not a beast*, I thought to myself. As with every assumption I laid, I was quickly proven wrong, because when an enormous door was swung open I found myself outside in another huge courtyard.

"The king will come to the Throne Room, shortly," a servant said. "He asks for you to wait here."

"Very good," Lord Byrne replied, resting on a stone bench.

"*This* is the Throne Room?" It was impossible to hide my surprise.

"There is a throne, is there not?" Lord Byrne pointed towards the opposite end of the sand-filled courtyard where the ground rose to a platform. In the middle were four richly decorated red chairs under a printed canopy. A gentle breeze flapped the canvas, yet it clearly bore Emberbyrg's flaming emblem. Rows of seating lined both sides of the courtyard. Some were protected from above by a balcony, others by a canopy, some by nothing at all. Back home, the central positions would speak of power, yet I couldn't imagine that many of Virisinigne's nobles would consider being subjected to the elements as an honour—not that the sun seemed to be bothering the dragon sitting to the left of the throne.

"It is rather open, that's all." I quietly remarked.

"What greater throne is there than that which sees the sun and stars?" Lord Byrne said proudly. It was the closest thing to a smile I had seen from him.

Suddenly a drumbeat filled the courtyard and particles of sand bounced with the rhythm, but as another, larger, dragon appeared, I realised it was the creature's footsteps that compelled the dust to dance. The drum was just announcing what the earth already knew.

"All rise for the king!" declared a herald in a grass-green tunic marching beside the dragon—which positioned itself on the right side of the throne and fixed its amber eyes on me.

Wearing a crown and elaborate dark green tunic, the king gracefully made his way to his throne with the queen by his side, followed by a younger man and woman who sat on either side of them. Once all were seated, the king beckoned Lord Byrne with a simple flick of his wrist.

Poking me into motion, the two lower guards trailed behind while the lord and commander flanked me. Hoping the protocol was similar to home, I planned to stop at a respectful distance from the throne steps, yet three strides before my mark, two hands yanked on the back of my jacket, halting me and my already faded dignity.

The herald stood in front of the larger dragon, puffed out his chest, and declared: "Presenting His Majesty, King Inygo, of Emberbyrg, the most illustrious city, ruler and overseer of all of Benegnyem, defender of the Flame—Her Majesty, Queen Brydget, and Their Royal Highnesses Prince Aydan, and Princess Enya, crowned and sworn defenders of our esteemed kingdom and the almighty Flame." He paused, both for a breath and dramatic effect. "Your Majesties, Lord Byrne presents Prince Niall Beckett of Virisinigne, beyond the World's Divide—*or so he claims.*"

Ignoring the snarky herald, I held the king's eye, bowing slow and low, making my humility plain. Having done it since birth, meeting royals and nobility had never bothered me until that moment. Back home the number of crowned offspring outnumbered these four to one, yet these people knew how to inspire admiration. So did the dragons.

"I am told you are from the World's Divide?" the king said, doing away with any further formalities.

"Yes, Your Majesty, I am. I—"

"Do you realise how improbable that is?"

"Yes, Your Majesty. Until I travelled through the wall, I thought all who touched it died."

"Precisely. Yet, you wish me to believe you anyway?" He waved his hand, stopping my response. "You say your kingdom is called—?"

"Virisinigne, Your Majesty. My land, my people—the entire kingdom is under attack and I have been sent by my father, King Ennis, to beseech you for assistance before it is all turned to ash."

The king held my gaze, weighing every word I said. My heart raced as I anticipated his response. I was desperate to speak and provide more detail, yet my head told me to wait. It struck me that this man was like my own father, slow and deliberate. If pushed into a hasty response it would be a rash, intolerant one. Sadly for me, patience was not my virtue—a point so well discussed by my family that it was one of the leading reasons I had been sent to sea full time aged sixteen. Not that I regretted that decision for long.

"Show the king the amulet," a female voice commanded.

All heads turned to the princess.

"The Kennel Maid?" I said, staring. Had she not spoken, I may not have recognised her. The humble, beige work clothes had been replaced by a purple full-length silk dress which loosely hugged every curve and dipped seductively towards her chest, revealing a necklace with a matching purple sapphire, while her long dark-brown hair shimmered in waves to the pit of her back. Seeing my confusion, her eyes chuckled where her mouth did not. She enjoyed my ignorance.

"Ah, yes," said the king, gazing at me whilst gently patting his daughter's hand, showing off their matching dragon scale tattoos—simultaneously drawing my attention to the fact that all four royals had the same marks on their hands and arms. The only difference was the king and princess had scales to their shoulders, where the others stopped just above the elbow. Having only ever heard of one other having such marks, I wanted to ask their relevance when King Inygo snapped his fingers, saying, "Yes, this amulet. Show me."

"Stop gawping at Her Highness, and do as you are bid," Commander Uryah snarled when I didn't immediately react.

It was hard not to stare. She had been baffling before but now she was positively spellbinding. "Forgive me. I was surprised to see the Kennel Maid in—"

"*Princess Enya*, the anointed Kennel Maid," Lord Byrne corrected.

Desperately wanting to shout, *If no one bothers to announce names fully, how am I to know?* I forced my tongue into silence, reminding myself that he believed me a spy. Nodding, I produced my pendant.

"Here, Your Majesty," I said, holding the jewel in front of me, keeping the chain around my neck.

The king's expression dropped. "Approach."

Gulping, I climbed the stairs under the suspicious gaze of two dragons plus the shadow of Commander Uryah and Lord Byrne. The king held out his hand, clearly expecting me to pass him my pendant. My head told me to comply without reserve, yet a sense of sorrow hit me as I slipped the chain over my head and placed it into his palm. Regardless of my curiosity for the people around me, I couldn't take my eyes off the emerald. For twenty-eight years I had seen it hang around my father's neck and it felt wrong to see it in the hands of another—even if it did seem to react more to me and this world than it did back home. Not once had I seen it shine, produce fire or light, nor thought it might one day belong to me and invoke such interest from the ruler of a nation whose name had never passed my lips.

"Surely, it is a fake, father?" Prince Aydan said. "Only you hold the Amulet of the Flame, so how could this man have it?"

The king didn't answer but did hand my pendant back.

"The design of the Amulet is no secret," reasoned the queen. "Although illegal, a jeweller from Brenton or Sabyloa could have produced this as a trick to gain access to you. It wouldn't be the first time a Sabyloan has tried to fox us with an artefact, my love."

"True, but I've never seen them dress like this or speak in such a dialect," the prince said, almost laughing.

Prince Aydan looked to be a similar age to me, maybe a couple of years younger, just without the scars from weather or war. His athletic stature suggested he was prepared to rise to a challenge, given the right occasion, so I instantly wanted him—and his perfectly poised creatures—on my side. Allowing myself to be mocked seemed like the first step to achieve this.

Having always heard it referred to as a *pendant*, I had never considered calling it an *amulet,* however, I could not deny that it had earned that name. Yet they hadn't witnessed its abilities, so why they held it in such reverence puzzled me—until the king slid his left hand under his chin, collecting a chain of matching platinum, revealing an identical jewel.

"Who threatens you?" the king said.

Shaking off my surprise, my heart skipped, telling me to answer quickly. "A man from the north. He has gathered an army and is using them—and fire—to pillage or subject all the towns and villages in his wake. When I left their army had breached ours and Tecta, the capital city, was next. If I do not hurry, all will be lost."

"Why did you not squash them when they were small?" asked the king. "Do you not have security?"

"By sea and land, but not—"

"Then perhaps the wiser rule, a new age, is your destiny?" said Queen Brydget.

"You would not sit there and say such a thing if the lives of your family, your people, those you have sworn to protect were under threat, Your Majesty." I checked my tone, eager to keep myself on the right side of humble. "You are right, the scale of the threat was underestimated for too long. My father believed the Magma Isles too barren, too weak, and left them to their largely independent ways unchecked. He—we—therefore failed to notice when surrounding tribes and towns who were once sworn enemies united under one reign. The impossible became a—"

The king waved his hand, furrowing his brow. "Sir, if this is true, then I am sorry for it. You will hear much of this being the greatest nation—*rightly so*—but it is also a just and benevolent one. We too have unconnected tribes, groups, and nations to our east. Most live by their cultures peacefully, yet some are jealous, fool-hardy enough to challenge or attempt to pilfer from us, but none are strong or wise enough to breach our unfathomable, Flame-anointed defences. Because of this knowledge, this fact, I neither favour nor subject those who do not wish to live with the blessing of the Flame. We do, however, unyieldingly protect our own. This Amulet is a symbol of the Flame's protection. I will not—*cannot*—risk the peace of this mighty nation on the words of one man. I am sorry."

My insides felt like they were being crushed. The screams of my people rang in my ears. I was failing them.

"Please, Your Majesty," I begged. "If you acknowledge the Amulet as a symbol of the Flame's protection, surely two such jewels being united is significant?"

My eyes darted from one member of the royal family to the next, hoping, praying, that one would speak for me. The emerald gaze of the princess held mine. "Did your father not tell you of the Amulet's history? You say *if* as though you yourself are unsure of it. As a royal, an heir to the throne, surely you should know?"

Her words cut me. My ignorance cut me. All I had was honesty. "He did not, Your Highness. His command to send me on this mission was hastily given. If he knows fully of the Amulet's power or was simply sending me out with a last prayer, I cannot say. Were circumstances different, I am sure my brother, Baran, would have inherited the—"

"Why?" the princess cut in. "Are you not the heir to the throne?"

"No. My eldest brother, Prince Baran, holds that position."

The king scoffed. "Then why is *he* not standing before me?"

"As crowned prince and leader of the City's Guard, his presence was required, Your Highness. He will rise or fall with Tecta."

"How many siblings do you have?" asked the princess.

"Seven."

"*Seven?*" The queen looked genuinely shocked. "So, there are eight princes and princesses?"

I acknowledged her with a simple bow of my head.

Princess Enya eyed me suspiciously. "What ratio of boys to girls is there?"

I knew she would jump on my answer. "I am the seventh son. I have only one sister."

A triumphant smile crept over her face as though I had confirmed all of their distrust. "Where does your sister rank in order of birth?"

"Muriel is the youngest."

The princess barely stifled her mirth. "Your mother *really* wanted a daughter."

My little sister was the only sibling who didn't make me feel like a spare part. My brothers all had rank or purpose nearer to home and in court. I didn't conform with royal life and was cast away, so I found family at sea. Despite accepting my path, I loved my country and the princess' glib comment cut me worse than any sword. By then, I would have said I was good at burying my pain, however, it must have flashed in my eyes as Enya's amused grin dropped.

"Forgive my little sister," Prince Aydan said. "That was—"

"True, Your Highness, very true." Grateful for his intersection, I bowed my head at the prince. "But no less beside the point to why I am here instead of my brothers. I am captain of *The Leviathan*, Virisinigne's most renowned and effective sea defence vessel. My crew and I were recalled from the west because we are the best fitted for sailing at speed into the unknown—"

"Sea defence against…?" King Inygo cut in. "Disrespectful tribes? Pirates?" I could see the anger rising in his face but I couldn't think of anything to put out the fire. "You're telling me, that throughout your kingdom, all your king could spare to invoke a treaty is a *pirate hunter*?"

"A prince—"

"For all I know you could be the bastard son of a noble who just happened to inherit green eyes, heard a vague story of fortune, stole the Amulet, and now seeks riches—*or mischief*—on the other side of the world."

"Please, Your Majesty, that is—"

"Enough!" boomed the king. "Commander, please escort this man to his ship and see he returns to whence he came."

"So you acknowledge the existence of Virisinigne?" Fingers wrapped around both my arms before I realised the soldiers had hurried up the steps to collect me. "Please—"

"I acknowledge nothing. You could be a Sabyloan with a speech impediment or an Brentonian actor for all I know. If your world is truly under siege, then I pray to the Flame your fate be true, honest, and swift."

The soldiers dragged me backwards down the stairs but I refused to look away from the king. He would have to turn his back on me. "We'll all burn! You condemn us all to burn!"

"No," stated the king. "I ensure *my* people live. That's all any ruler can strive to do."

"That's easy for you!" I screamed. "*You already have dragons!*"

Instantly, the soldiers and I were knocked to our knees with a bone-cracking thud. Whether the force came from the dragon's tail whipping over our heads or it landing on the ground, I couldn't say. Yet I do know, my face was inches from the enormous spiky, scaled limb of a dragon who didn't want me to leave.

SEVEN

"What did you say?" the princess said reverently, resting her hand on the neck of the dragon whose tail closely wrapped around my position.

A strange hush came over everyone and I didn't dare open my mouth.

With her jaw set in determination, the princess rose from her seat. "*Repeat your last sentence.*"

I gulped, wondering if these were going to be the last words I ever spoke. "I said, *That's easy for you. You already have dragons.* I only meant that—"

"How do you know that word?"

"Which?" I stared in confusion. "Do you mean *dragon?*"

"Yes. If you are what you say you are, how do you know the sacred name of our protectors?"

My face must have been the definition of dumbfounded. With one on either side of them, their knowledge of dragons was clearly greater than mine—although as the beasts stared at me with their heads tilted in eerie parallel, I felt like they were boring into my soul.

"What makes you worthy of voicing the Fyre Dog's sacred name?" bellowed King Inygo.

The dragon flicked its tail, sending dust into the air.

"If I have caused offence, forgive me," I said, wiping my face with my sleeve. "I confess to having heard them referred to as dogs—as Fyre Dogs—during my time here. I also confess to having been confused by this name. I—"

"Why?" demanded the king.

"Because back home, dogs are mammals—hairy mammals. They are loyal companions and defenders of home. They are—"

"Do they not have the same characteristics here?" King Inygo sounded genuinely baffled. "Do you not see my glorious friend beside me? Does Seraphyna not watch over and protect everything I and my family does?" He gestured towards the dragon beside Princess Enya. "As Wydgitta also cares for my daughter and vice versa?"

"It would seem so. It is just I have seen creatures that resemble *my* definition of dog here, so I don't—" Not knowing how to continue safely, I cut myself off.

"*Don't what*?" asked the king in frustration. "Understand why we use the name *dog* for both?" Agreeing, I bobbed my head. "You just answered your own question! You described their comparable traits but don't listen to your own words! The word *fire* separates species. That is enough."

I repressed the desire to say, *If you say so.*

"You have not answered my question. How do you know our sacred word?" demanded Princess Enya.

It felt like the already scorching temperature had risen as all eyes—human and otherwise—waited for me. "In Virisinigne, that is the only name we have for—" Afraid of angering anyone by repeating the word *dragon*, I waved my hand at the tail beside me.

"Why? Be specific," Prince Aydan said irritably.

His request had verbally backed me into a corner. "He who attacks my country rides a-a dra—*a Fyre Dog* and calls it *Dragon*." Gasping, the four royals stared at one another.

"It cannot be," whispered the queen. "Can it?"

"No," said the prince. "It's impossible."

"This man must be as you say, my love. Surely he is an actor or spy?" Addressing the king, Queen Brydget glanced at me nervously. "What do you think the goal is?"

"Lord Byrne, Commander, please approach. Leave *him* there." King Inygo's olive skin looked pale as though he had seen a ghost. Actually, they all did.

The two lower soldiers remained by my side while Commander Uryah and Lord Byrne made short work of the steps. They huddled around one another speaking in hushed tones and I waited as long as my patience would allow, but each minute seemed like an eternity and I knew that my people were facing harsher terms than the roasting sun that I was experiencing.

I had to call out.

"Would it not be better to question me further?"

Lord Byrne turned to me, scowling, but it was Princess Enya who spoke. "This man, the one who rides a Fyre Dog. What is his name?"

"He calls himself King Gryer, leader of Simulinigne—not that my father will acknowledge his authority or new nation."

"*Together in fire*," said the king sadly before closing his eyes, grimacing. "It is him."

"Who?" No one would look at me. "If you know this man, please tell me!"

"How could he be on the other side of the World's Divide?" asked the prince. "I thought there were only two Amulets of the Flame?"

King Inygo shook his head. "I don't know, Aydan. The knowledge that is passed through the Fyuego clearly states the First Empress only forged two Amulets—one for either kingdom."

"The Fyuego?" I was tired of all the new terms being thrown in front of me.

"How is this man a royal but knows next to nothing?" said the princess, seemingly talking to herself as she didn't wait for an answer. "The *Fyuego* is the holy order of the Flame. All who are anointed by the Flame—royal, noble, or civilian—are sworn to protect and honour the divinity of the Flame, obey its decrees, and commit to the sanctity of life, our great nation, and our hallowed companions. I *assumed* you would have such in your world."

"Did you not hear the name of their world, my love?" said the king. "Virisinigne—*green without fire*. They, similar to our neighbours to the east, live without the blessing of the Flame."

Baffled, I asked, "How is it you understand our ancient words more than we do?"

"The same way I know of the Amulets, I imagine," replied the king. "Before we divided, all nations spoke the same language. When the World's Divide was created, your world turned its back on the Flame. We embraced it—and continue to do so through the commitment of the Fyuego."

"We thrive because of it," said Queen Brydget proudly.

My heart raced and my head buzzed as I tried to absorb the information before me. It would not save my home, yet the question that crazed me was *how much of this does my father know?* Surely he knew something—or certainly enough to send his son headed towards a wall famed for its lethal touch and impenetrable mass. Regardless, I *had* travelled through it and, it would seem, so had Gryer.

"Who is Gryer? You clearly know him and his dragon." As the D-word came out of my mouth, I watched their faces grimace. "*Fyre Dog*, sorry."

Lord Byrne looked at me with continued suspicion. "What colour is the Fyre Dog on your side of the world?"

"The one that I believe matches Seraphyna's size," I said, cautiously pointing to the largest dragon as it reacted to its name, "is black, but there are at least three smaller, dark grey ones."

Horror struck their faces.

King Inygo pinched his forehead, displacing his crown momentarily.

"Four Fyre Dogs? You said there was one?" Lord Byrne said, narrowing his eyes.

"No, I said there was one called *Dragon* so we had come to call the species *dragon*."

"Now I know you are lying!" declared the Lord. "Black Fyre Dogs don't breed!"

Facing her dragon, Princess Enya bowed her head before turning back to me. "Do you have volcanoes?"

It seemed like an odd question, but I answered anyway. "In the Magma Isles, yes. That is why the lands in the north are so difficult to inhabit—or they were until about ten years ago."

"What happened then?"

"Mount Halo stopped erupting."

"*Flamma vobiscum,*" the queen whispered emotionally, bowing her head.

Hearing her, the hair stood up on the back of my neck as everyone repeated her words.

"Excuse me, Your Highness?" I said. "What does that mean?"

The queen looked at me with tears in her eyes but did not speak.

Enya stepped forward. "She said, *Flame be with you.*"

A tender degree of hope had crept into my mind until that moment, but seeing their reaction, sensing the meaning in the words, and feeling the sorrowful tension in every silent second, I knew it was fast disappearing. Deciding I had to keep them talking and having no better place to go from, I started where they finished. "What is the relevance of a dormant volcano?"

"Although the power and blessing of the Flame is omnipresent, volcanoes are outlets for holy energy—hubs, if you will. Fyre Dogs are the Flame's greatest, most sacred guardians and as such are blessed there beyond all others."

Enya held my gaze, waiting for my response. All I could manage was, "*Okay...*"

Sighing, she added. "Fyre Dogs nest in volcanoes—their presence focuses the energy, ceasing uncontrolled eruptions."

Inside, I felt the coin drop—hard, like an almighty rock. For twelve years I had sailed the western seas. Ten of those years I had been captain. For at least nine of those years I had been hearing tales of a man and his beast, a lizard type creature, preaching to the newly lava-free Magma Isles. I had reported to Admiral Remi, my second-eldest brother, and King Ennis, my father, asking permission to investigate. *We have crews sailing the area, it is nothing*, was the reply. Reading their dismissal, I decided I had satisfied my conscience. Ignoring the fanciful tales of pirates, merchants, and fishing villages under our law and surveillance, we kept to our own business—until villages started emptying and the news of an army marching on Tecta landed on my deck alongside a note from my father, begging for my immediate assistance.

Attempting to swallow the knot in my throat, I asked, "When was Gryer last seen on your land?"

I knew the answer before Enya spoke.

"Ten years ago."

EIGHT

Aptly describing the crestfallen countenance of King Inygo in the following moments is almost impossible. Hearing the name *Gryer* had truly left him bereft—although no one would tell me why. When King Inygo walked towards Seraphyna's giant dark green-grey head, the queen quietly ordered a soldier to send for refreshments but left her husband to silently stare into the soul of the beast. It was a strange, unsettling sight. However, when I was placed under the welcome shade of a parasol, my astonishment increased because at my newly adjusted angle, I witnessed the king's animated eyebrows and realised that he was not mindlessly gazing.

He was in deep conversation—*with the dragon.*

When the king finally turned around, he looked at me with regret. "Thank you for waiting so patiently. My trusted advisor and I have been discussing our options. I am sorry to tell you that our position remains unchanged."

"What?" My eyes darted from one person to the next, trying to read their faces. Whether it was from practice, agreement, or simply having predicted her husband's decision, I do not know, but stone would have been easier to decipher than the queen's expression. Her children were not much better—although the prince's eyebrows raised for a split second and the princess side glanced at her dragon before returning to her statuesque status. With no help coming forward, I turned back to the king. "You cannot be serious, Your Majesty?"

"I'm afraid, I am."

"We do not expect your assistance for free, Your Majesty. We have gold. Some I have here, but there is a mountain to be had in Virisinigne, should you help us."

"Prince Niall," the king said through a sigh. "Does this great city strike you as being in need of gold?"

I grimaced. "No, Your Majesty."

"Then why would we risk our peace, our lives, for what we already have plenty of?"

"Because our invader is obviously one of yours!" Desperation once again made my tongue act faster than my brain. "Do you not have some sense of duty to right the wrong of one of yours?"

"We cannot be absolutely sure he *is* one of ours, but even if he is, our people are not prisoners. They can leave our great city and start afresh in another land if they wish—"

"This is not *starting afresh*! This is wiping out a way of life and destroying a kingdom!" His denial was infuriating. Every piece of evidence I presented was pushed aside. Every glimmer of hope I found dashed into the sand. Again I searched the royals, hoping for an advocate. My eyes settled on the fidgeting fingers of the princess as they laid in her lap. *The tattoos...* "Princess Enya, may I ask about your tattoos?"

Enya looked bewildered. "What about them?"

"As you are the only people I have seen with scaled tattoos, am I right in thinking they are a mark of distinction?"

Enya smiled. "Correct. Only anointed members of the Fyuego are blessed with scales."

Commander Uryah proudly removed his vambraces, showing off scales which wrapped around his lower arms like skin-woven accessories. "It is the greatest honour."

"Why the different positions?" I said, addressing the princess as she seemed the most willing to share.

"Only royals receive scale sleeves from the elbow. Most have scales around the wrist like a cuff. High Fyuego have gauntlets, like Lord Byrne and Commander Uryah." As reality hit me, I scoffed silently and Enya noticed. "Why? What difference does this make?"

"Because the man who attacks Virisinigne has scales up his arms to his shoulders. It was told as folklore by many—*the man with marks like his beast*—yet my father confirmed it."

Both dragons snorted, causing me to jump out of my skin—and make a mental note not to call them beasts out loud.

"So you didn't see it for yourself?" Lord Byrne seemed as eager as the king to discredit me.

"No, my lord, I have not seen Gryer or Dragon up close. They were a great distance from me, but when I was on route to meet my father, I saw them through my spyglass flying in the opposite direction. Shortly afterwards, I was ordered to sail to the Divide—*to you*—without delay."

"He lies, Your Majesty," Lord Byrne said without irony—just cold disbelief which I found more disheartening.

"Why are you so convinced of that?" I asked, trying to control my tone.

"Because the Gryer we know doesn't have scales up his whole arm."

"What was true ten years ago and what is now are not necessarily the same thing, surely?" No one answered me. "Is there no way to earn more scales?" I hoped my choice of words was correct. The restraint was killing me.

King Inygo sighed. "There is."

"In theory only, Your Majesty," Lord Byrne gently added.

"Indeed." King Inygo stood up. "But it is of no use to discuss its likelihood. Prince Niall, my answer is still the same. I am sorry. My people must come first. I cannot help you."

The king rested his hand on Seraphyna's side, shaking his head sadly. All words left me as failure rained on me more heavily than a thousand suns.

"Father, forgive me," said Princess Enya, "but should we not consult the E—"

King Inygo spun around. "Have you forgotten she is in mourning?"

"No, of course not, but this is rather—"

"She does not want to be disturbed. Not even for—"

"A black Fyre Dog breeding? I think she would want to hear that."

"Princess, black Fyre Dogs cannot produce eggs alone—they are all male. Parthenogenesis is only possible with females. You know that," said Commander Uryah softly.

"Yes, but I also thought my uncle was dead, yet it would seem that isn't true!"

"Enya!" Queen Brydget gasped, hiding her face with her hand while the others grimaced.

Knowing the princess had unwittingly given me a gift, I was about to jump in with questions when the sandy-orange miniature dragon I saw earlier returned. Instead of hovering in front of me, it landed on my left shoulder and stared at me through its piercing amber eyes. Seeing its brighter, pocket-sized friend settle on me, the head of Wydgitta curled to my right side, giving me a perfect view of every intricate scale that covered her skull.

"What are they doing?" I asked, barely daring to open my mouth.

"Hmm," said Enya.

"Curious," whispered the king.

"Anyone care to help me?" No one moved. *"Really?"*

Aydan laughed. "If Wydgitta wants to roast you, there is very little we can do about it."

"Aren't you reassuring," I said sarcastically. Had I dared to move, I would have scowled at him. "How about getting this one off me?"

"Keep still," said Enya. "What is he saying to you?" Had her tone not been so solemn, I would have thought she was mocking me like her brother, yet a simple glance told me she was serious.

"Saying? He isn't saying anything?"

"Only because you are not listening." Enya patted Wydgitta's leg and she recoiled her head, leaving me with the smaller, but no less freaky version.

"I think it is more likely to bite me than talk."

"Not really. They tend to burn before they bite," the princess said matter-of-factly. "*Listen.* If the Fyrewowwa wants to bond with you, he will tell you his name."

"The what wants to what? Does he breathe fire?" Panic rose in me as I envisioned my earlobe being bitten or scorched off.

As if on cue, the orange creature shuffled closer to my ear and opened its mouth. I froze, waiting for a word, then felt ridiculous when it didn't come. I needed a mighty army and giant dragons, not their blackbird-sized cousin. If I didn't have an audience who seemed to revere the creatures—regardless of magnitude—I would probably have taken my chances and pushed it away with my hat.

"Hold out your hand," commanded the princess.

"Why?"

"It's pointless, Your Highness. He isn't worthy," Lord Byrne said in earnest.

Enya scowled at him and repeated her command to me. It seemed like an absurd waste of time, but any communication was better than none—better than eviction—so even if it literally got me burnt, I raised my right hand as she directed.

Without hesitation, the creature flew to my outstretched hand, grasping my fingers with its powerful talons whilst holding my gaze. As all else seemed to fade away, it felt like staring into a soul—beautiful but impossible to describe in worldly-words.

Suddenly, the Fyrewowwa adjusted its weight, arched its back, and stretched its wings, whipping up a burst of air that sparkled with thousands of floating embers. Somehow I knew the embers would not hurt me, so I had no fear as they rushed around my face. Then a voice unlike anything I had ever heard spoke inside my mind. It was just one word, a name, yet I was humbled to hear it. *Pynyt.*

"Pea-nut," I sounded the word out. "Pynyt," I said again with unfathomable certainty. "His name is Pynyt."

Princess Enya and Prince Aydan smiled in amazement before turning to their father.

King Inygo swallowed hard, raised his chin, and said, "The Flame has sent a sign. Convene the Fyuego. We must try to consult with the Empress."

NINE

Resting was the last thing I wanted to do, but I was escorted away from the Throne Room and shown into a bedroom draped with fine cloths and dragon imagery. My body was tired, yet my mind raced with information, rerunning conversations, trying to make a plan for whenever I was next called before the king. He was obviously still reluctant, I could see he would have been much happier to have seen me sail away—or never show up in the first place—but Pynyt speaking to me was apparently a sign he was not willing to challenge, and I wasn't willing to walk away.

So many questions plagued my mind. *Who is the Empress and how does she out rank the king?* was my most leading question yet no one would answer it. *In good time,* was all Lord Byrne would say before he disappeared with the royals.

Eager for information, I tried asking a servant, but he was baffled into silence—either by the ignorance of my question or my foreign accent, perhaps both. His bewildered face had rattled me so badly that when a female servant appeared with clothing, I didn't dare ask again.

Pynyt, the miniature dragon—Fyrewowwa—had perched himself on my shoulder after our introduction and, despite the servant informing me I could wash in a hot spring in the adjoining room, he seemed in no hurry to leave my side.

"Your fresh clothes are laid on the bed when you are ready. I will ensure yours are washed and returned to you. Do you require your back scrubbing, Prince Niall?" the servant asked, standing in the steaming doorway.

I wanted to laugh. No one had scrubbed my back—or offered to do it—since I was a boy. My nursemaid often gave up trying to keep me clean, and when my brother took me on sailing trips, he'd throw me into the sea, declaring *sort out your stink* as I hit the water. By the time I was sixteen and a full-time sailor, I threw myself in. Bathtubs were luxuries in merchant towns and hot springs were rare gifts from nature in some of the northern isles, but even in such places I had no desire for someone to scrub me—or question how or why I had so many scars and bruises. Alun or Raine sewing me up was probably the nearest I'd come to what that poor woman felt compelled to offer.

"No, thank you. I'll sort myself."

"Very good, sir," she said, bowing her head, stepping to leave.

"What do I do with him?" I said hastily, pointing to Pynyt.

She smiled, pointing to a large black-wood dining table by the window. "I've left your spirit guide a plate beside yours."

"Spirit guide? I thought he was a Fyrewowwa?"

"Yes," she said patiently with a smile, "but they can also be sacred messengers of the Flame—and yours is hungry."

The servant paused again, waiting for me to respond or dismiss her. Lifting the carved wooden lids from two plates, I found a cooked dish of rice and fish beside one of two whole, raw fish. I didn't need to ask whose plate was whose. Seeing the food, Pynyt hopped from my shoulder to the table and flame grilled his fish with a single burst of fire from his mouth.

A noise crossed between a scream and a chuckle left my lips, causing the servant to giggle. She instantly looked guilty for mocking me, but as I doubted whether anyone would be able to remain straight faced hearing such a ridiculous cry from a man my age, size, or rank, I let it pass. Besides, I was too amazed to be truly embarrassed—plus Pynyt had started to eye-up the contents of my plate. Deciding I was hungry, and afraid Pynyt would steal or charcoal my dinner if I bathed first, I sat down on the green velvet lined chair and marvelled at the quality of the meal.

"How long do you think I have until the king returns for me?" I asked between mouthfuls.

"My apologies, Prince Niall, I do not know. I was simply instructed to feed and bathe you. Can I get you anything else?"

I thanked her and she left me to my thoughts—and my dragon. "Spirit guide, huh?" I said, staring into his eyes.

My little sister's voice hit me again, as it always did when faced with the natural world. *You shouldn't stare into the eyes of a dog, especially an unknown, angry, or frightened one. It will see it as a challenge.* I knew Muriel's advice was sage, but gazing into Pynyt's eyes was fundamentally different. Until that day, the name *Fyre Dog* or *Fyrewowwa* had not crossed my lips, yet there and then I felt like a piece of me had been found—even if I had no idea what it meant.

Like the food and bath, the towel I dried myself on was heavenly. Captain or not, if I tried to keep such luxury on my ship, the men would have stolen, begged, or eternally borrowed such comfort—or thrown it overboard in a drunken fit of comedy. The castles in Virisinigne had underfloor heating and steam baths and communal hot rooms, but individual hot springs were an undoubted perk of Emberbyrg's location and climate. Wandering back into the bedroom, I picked up the clothes I had been given and couldn't decide if they were simply giving me what they had available, were claiming me, or hiding me from the general population.

"No pomp or finery for me," I muttered to Pynyt, who seemed content to silently watch me as I pulled on the beige leggings. "Huh," I said, realising they were incredibly light and comfortable—and hoping the servant didn't feel the need to return my hot, heavy clothing anytime soon. The light brown top was somewhere between a shirt and a gambeson. It looked thick and padded, so was clearly designed to go under armour, yet it was actually light and breathable—as were the matching socks despite appearing thick and woolly. The strapped boots and jacket surprised me. The people I saw around town had simple sandals or flat shoes with no form of coat, yet I had been given robust, tall boots and a military style armoured-jacket plus accessories. The craftsmanship of the combined iron and leatherwork was stunning. Each stitch, strap, pocket, and fastener was completed with precision. Each stroke of ornamentation meticulously etched. Each inch perfect for my size. The only thing missing was the flame. It was the armour of an apprentice.

Out of the window, I watched the sunset over Emberbyrg and witnessed the expanse of a great city as it transitioned into night. *The Leviathan* was way out of sight beyond the walls and down the cliff towards the ocean, but I hoped my crew were okay. I knew they would be anxiously, faithfully waiting for news. I knew the people of Virisinigne waited for me to bring them salvation. My heart cried to them. *Hold on.*

Pynyt flew to my shoulder, somehow managing to land with gentle precision instead of digging his talons into my flesh—which I was extra grateful for because I had just left the jacket on the back of a chair. For a few minutes we watched the city lights, but then Pynyt flew to the bed and called out, making a low-hissing sound.

Hours earlier, I would have been afraid, but instead I laughed. "Why do I feel like a five-year-old boy being told to go to bed?"

Pynyt hissed again, whipping the pillow with his tail.

"Fine," I said, running my fingers along the Amulet's chain, "but my mind has a million questions running through it. I will not sleep."

Pynyt hissed and it almost sounded like laughter.

He was right.

Exhausted, my body switched off within minutes—maybe seconds—after laying my head down.

It was the first time I'd been lulled to sleep by the breathing of a dragon.

Although I didn't know my future, something told me it wouldn't be the last.

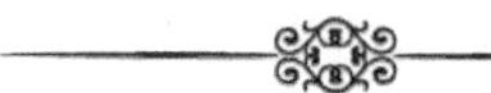

My mind had barely registered the sound of someone knocking on the door when my eyes were affronted with a burst of light as Commander Uryah stormed into the room with a lantern filled with flaming coals.

"Time to go," he said gruffly. If he said my name, I missed it in my groggy state, but I am pretty sure Uryah had already decided he'd had enough with formalities—and me.

"Where are we going?"

"In five minutes, you'll find out. Come on." He placed the lantern on the table and walked out, leaving the door ajar. "Drink up!"

Beside the bed was a thick, frankly unappealing liquid in a glass tumbler. "Breakfast all in one?" I asked Pynyt. Unlike my meal last night, he didn't seem interested in sharing. Neither before nor after drinking it did I blame him.

After splashing my face with water, I strapped up my clothing and went in search of Uryah with Pynyt on my shoulder. One white-washed stone wall looked like another and no one seemed to be waiting for me as I stood at a four-way junction in the corridor.

"There you are," said Princess Enya, striding out of an archway wearing armour that curved and protected her strong, feminine form. The scales on her arms were largely hidden by vambraces and pauldrons, but somehow they seemed more prominent between the shining silver and dark brown leather. Her hair was twisted into a bun, revealing flame tattoos which licked up the back of her neck to the base of her skull like a fierce, yet regal collar. Knee high boots and tight leggings covered her feet and legs, and a thick belt clipped with weapons hugged her waist while a sword hung from her left side as though she were born to wear it. "Ready?"

"Morning, Princess," I replied, trying to catch my breath. "Er, yes, but for what, exactly?"

"Your pilgrimage." I couldn't tell whether her grin was playful, hopeful, or spiteful. I chose to believe it was one of the former, secretly fearing it was the latter.

"Pilgrimage?" I said, skipping a step to walk by her side. "I was hoping the king was going to help me—to introduce me to—"

"The Empress. Yes, precisely." Enya stopped under a hanging lantern. "King Inygo and the Fyuego Council have voted that Uryah and I escort you to Mount Liekke to the start of your pilgrimage."

"Can I not complete this afterwards?"

"After what?"

"After you help my world."

Uryah approached, chuckling coldly. "It is not yet certain that we *will* help."

Ignoring my desire to hit Uryah, I turned to Enya, trying my best to channel Raine's calm, soft voice. "Please explain this process. Your customs are clearly different from mine."

Uryah snorted. "Clearly."

"You seek help. My father is not inclined to give it, however his presence—" Enya nodded at Pynyt, "suggests the Flame is at least willing to listen—"

"Which I am eternally grateful for—"

Enya held her hand in front of my face. "Which means you must prove yourself worthy by completing your pilgrimage before being granted a meeting with the Empress. She will then decide your fate."

"How long will that take? Time isn't something I have a lot of right now."

"As long as it takes," she replied firmly. "Worthiness cannot be rushed."

"Nor guaranteed," Uryah said, grinning.

"Indeed," Enya replied seriously. "Come, we have a long journey."

"Can I just ask one more question before we go?"

"Yes?" Enya tilted her head in anticipation.

"Who is the Empress?"

TEN

Princess Enya genuinely looked like I had just listed every swear word, kinky sexual act, and heinous crime I could think of when she heard my question. Even Commander Uryah couldn't immediately muster a comeback, but it was he who spoke first.

"Can you really be so ignorant?" I honestly believe that until that point, Uryah saw me as an irritating traveller with questionable motives from a backward country, not another world with no knowledge of the past or the hierarchy of their way of life.

"I'm afraid so."

Enya's mouth gaped and eyebrows arched. "The Empress is the Guardian and Voice of the Flame. The Chosen One. The vessel through which our holy order flows. The most high. The benevolent keeper of the peace—nay, life itself."

"So your father, the king, is not ruler then? He takes orders from another?" It made no sense to me. "I thought Benegnyem is the greatest nation? Why—"

"It is. Benegnyem means *blessed by fire*. We stand proud because of it. Humans and Fyre Dogs thrive directly due to this blessing. It is only right that the almighty, final word or directive comes from—"

"Is the Empress a Fyre Dog?" In my mind I had been picturing a temple on a mountain with believers of some description with a large, probably uncomfortable, throne where some old lady sits waiting to bestow blessings—or judgement—on anyone who is stubborn or crazy enough to climb up there. With a miniature dragon on my shoulder, perhaps the involvement of one should have been less surprising. Possibly my brain was trying to save me from the petrifying knowledge that I was going to have to purposefully seek a dragon's mercy, and it wouldn't be the dinky, almost cute sort that gently grilled fish and told me to go to bed.

"She is *the* Fyre Dog."

"The one you're going to live or die by," Uryah said without an ounce of humour or regret. "The Fyuego agree. The Flame *has* called you. There is no going back now."

With all questions, words, and pleas lost in the pit of my stomach, I followed them in silence. Lord Byrne was waiting outside wearing full armour with a silver and green leather strap added across his chest. Next to him were a dozen soldiers, four people in silver tunics, and twenty hinnies. Each one had been tacked up but only four had packs on the sides of their saddles.

Guess how many people are venturing into the unknown, I said to myself, too afraid to ask questions I couldn't cope with the answer to.

Some of the soldiers looked at me with suspicion, yet the majority had adopted a new, more confusing expression.

Awe. It didn't make sense to me at first, but when one repeatedly gazed at Pynyt, I decided it had more to do with him than me.

The gentle creak of leather saddles and hooves steadily treading on the sand-dusted stone were the only sounds as we rode away from the palace. Streetlamps economically lit the darkened roads and I wondered how long it would be until the sun rose. Normally I would know without question. Years at sea had honed my skills meaning I could quickly calculate my direction or the time of day or night with impressive accuracy, but not in Benegnyem. It was as though a haze had been thrown over my senses.

With darkness around and everything feeling off, I opted to gaze ahead through the enormous, hairy ears of the hinny I had been assigned. Back home, I had seen mules but never ridden one. They were for dragging carts, cargo, and weaponry—should some new civil dispute turn into war. On my ship, I had no need for equine. On land, Father insisted on his family riding the largest steeds he could find, so this medium sized creature would never have been given to a prince, but I had to admit he was comfortable to sit on.

What if it's the last thing you ever ride? I asked myself as intrusive thoughts flooded in. *What if they are escorting you to your death? As a sacrifice to the Flame? It wouldn't be the first culture I had met who sacrificed to appease their deity...*

"What's my hinny called?" I asked, suddenly desperate for conversation.

"Calcibus—or just Cal," replied a soldier.

Commander Uryah laughed.

"Why is that funny?" I asked, nervously observing Cal's ear twitch to the side.

"His name means *kicks*."

I could happily have punched Uryah. I certainly wanted to shout, telling them that if any nobles visited my father, he would not treat them with such disrespect. Just as my anger rose to the point of reaching my tongue, Pynyt took off from my shoulder, causing my thoughts to flip. *That's not true*, I said to myself. *If Father wanted to, especially if he benefited from it, he would treat visitors with great care. If they turned up, asking ignorant questions, demanding assistance, he would test every inch of their resolve.*

Everything is a test.

Both Lord Byrne and Commander Uryah's red eyes were on me. They trusted their hinnies more than they trusted me. They were waiting for my fuse to blow. On my ship, I was in command. My fuse was supposed to blow. Those who crossed us were meant to fear that very response. Everything I had learnt was no good to me now.

Pynyt circled me. It felt like he was waiting for me to find my sense of reason.

Listen.

That's what the princess told me yesterday.

Listen.

I glanced in her direction and saw that she, too, was waiting for me to respond. She saw my frustration at her commander. They all did.

For Virisinigne, I had to become something else.

Raising my left hand from my body, I curled back my thumb and extended my fingers. Immediately, Pynyt landed on me and stretched his wings before tucking them against his back. As he looked into my eyes, I'm sure he smiled. The corners of my lips definitely bent upwards—and a hearty guffaw left them when Pynyt turned to Uryah and hissed loudly. Nineteen out of twenty hinnies pinned back their ears and threatened to run. Calcibus was the only exception and it felt like we were in a smug party for three—well, maybe four, because while everyone else pulled on their reins with haste, Enya simply chuckled and chose to trot on.

Finally we reached the city wall, passing through a massive exit they referred to as Pilgrims Gate. It was the same size as the Kennel Gate, but this one faced south-east—and seemed to open into yet another new world. The clearing around the city wall took at least twenty minutes to ride across, but the sand almost immediately gave way to grass which was filled with the sound of insects as the sun rose. Had we headed east, our hinnies would have been wading belly-deep through fields of waving grass. However, our party took a southern path, straight into an expanse of trees that was unlike anything in the whole of Virisinigne.

"You gaze at trees as though you've never seen them." Princess Enya sounded more curious than reproachful.

"Oak, elm, and beech are common where I come from. The western isles have different, hotter climates and ecosystems, but I have never seen leaves so large or felt humidity like it."

"Welcome to the jungle," she laughed.

"Is it like this the whole way?"

"No," Uryah replied. "It gets harder. Much harder."

I am going to die here. My people, my family, are going to burn to death, and I am going to die in a foreign jungle.

Pynyt bit my ear.

"Hey!" My fingers rubbed my earlobe, testing it for blood. Surprisingly, there was none.

Pynyt looked at me, unrepentant. His eyes dilated.

"Can you read my mind?" I whispered to him, staring in anticipation of an answer. The existence of magic or forces beyond my control hadn't really occurred to me until two days prior. The World's Divide was a known anomaly, yet it was also a barrier, a place you avoided, not a magic source to challenge or harness. Watching Pynyt's breath rise and fall, I understood it was all around, even if I didn't understand it.

He flapped his wings and a single word hit me.

Forward.

Confused, I checked in front of me just in time to see a soldier fall off his hinny like a sack of potatoes.

"What happened?" Lord Byrne sounded more irritated than concerned.

"A branch just swung out, my lord," the man said, dusting himself off.

Throwing his leg over the back of his hinny, Commander Uryah drew his sword, and thrust it into the tree before another word was spoken. As he stepped back, two halves of a snake the width of ten men's arms fell out of the canopy.

"Well caught, Uryah," said Enya.

Although he simply bowed his head and remounted, a beam flashed across his face.

"Indeed, thank you, Commander. I don't fancy being crushed by one of those things," said the soldier, staring at the corpse. "Mind out for those, Prince Niall. They're not called Pilgrim Punishers for no reason."

Late morning, we reached a clearing with a large stone fort in the middle. In such a remote area and surrounded by trees, a building made of logs would have been so much easier to construct, but they didn't seem to use anything other than stone or iron for their structures. Before I met the dragons, I might have asked why, but one rogue or careless dragon passing by was probably enough to educate a millennium's-worth of people.

Two guards in silver tunics and flaming breastplates stood to attention on either side of the entrance when we approached, but they were clearly expecting our visit as their red eyes immediately settled on me, not any of their ranking officers.

Obviously knowing the route well, the hinnies wandered without direction under the awning that ran around the building and waited to be untacked. I assumed we would all go inside, however, as the hinnies dispersed around their grassy paddock, two soldiers took up position to watch over them.

Enya must have read my quizzical expression because she answered my silent question. "It's not just snakes who will eat the unvigilant on this path."

"Wonderful," I said sarcastically.

Despite the looming wildlife, I would have been lying if I said I wasn't keen to explore this world or learn about the Flame. However, my curiosity ate at my conscience because every moment of rest, just like each footfall, seemed to be taken in the wrong direction. My world sought a hero, and there I was, setting out on a bizarre field trip *away* from a city filled with enough soldiers and dragons to challenge any army. With information so frugally given, I internally argued that the lines between coercion and free-will had blurred, making me closer to an untied prisoner than a guest or pilgrim, but it did not appease my mind. Nor did the realisation that that was truthfully how they saw me. They believed the Flame—whatever that was—had sent them a sign and as faithful followers, they would deliver.

Inside, the building was humbly decorated but none of the rooms I saw were small. Members of the Fyuego dressed in pale green tunics quietly bustled around us offering refreshments and giving the Princess and Commander updates on the likely weather and condition of the path ahead. None of the place names meant anything to me, but words like scorching-hot, landslip, and lynx didn't exactly fill me with joy.

With no discernible warning, the room hushed as seven members of the Fyuego—all with striking red eyes—formed a semi-circle around my chair and signalled for me to stand. Once on my feet, they turned, revealing Princess Enya who regally stood wearing a crown of silver flames. All seven bowed, then the person in the middle—an old lady with a bent back dressed in a platinum robe—presented Enya with an ornate glass jar. Enya didn't touch it, nor did she have anything in her hands, yet when she clicked her fingers over the jar, a spark flew to it, setting the contents alight.

Intense, sweet-aromas instantly filled the air and the seven methodically faced me. The elderly woman carefully knelt by my feet, waving the jar of incense while the others sang a chant—the words of which were spoken too low for me to understand, but they felt peaceful, nonetheless.

As she stood up, the intensity of her chant increased and she swung the jar closer to my face, making the cloud of fragrance rush across my cheeks. My eyes stung and the Amulet began to glow around my neck, but only for a moment as Pynyt suddenly flapped his wings, sending emerald sparks across the room.

Watching the embers disappear, the Fyuego gasped, then whispered, *Flamma vobiscum,* before bowing to the princess and exiting without another word.

After a period of reverent silence, the room slowly began to move and bustle again, but no one attempted to explain anything to me. The longer I sat there, the more questions raged in my mind, but every time I tried to raise them, my tongue either failed or someone butted in with an unrelated comment or quip to purposefully shut me down. Overwhelmed by the inexplicable smell that still lingered in my nose, and beaten by the numerous voices surrounding me, I settled on observation. In doing so, my eyes kept returning to the princess. So far, she had proven to be the most open-minded, yet her reception of me seemed to alter almost as often or radically as her outfits.

"You keep staring at me, Prince Niall," she said, smiling as we waited for water to be drawn from a well in the corner of the room. "I cannot tell if it is out of pleasure or disgust."

"I very much doubt anyone would look at you with disgust, Princess." My cheeks flushed as my mouth spoke before my brain. Quickly wanting to cover myself, I continued, "Forgive me. I meant you change appearance a lot, that's all."

"I dress according to the role required of me."

She replied without emotion and I feared I had messed up. A combination of Enya's curiosity for a foreigner and loyalty to the Flame had undoubtedly led me this far, so making risky comments on her looks seemed ludicrously stupid—and typically, the one time I wanted Uryah or Byrne to jump in and save me from myself, they remained silent.

With no one to check my tongue, it ploughed forward. "Are you a chameleon?"

"A what?" Enya rolled her eyes, signalling that she was not impressed with me.

To be fair, nor was I. I wanted to ask what was going on, not talk about lizards—or certainly not small, non-fire breathing ones. However, I'd started, so I would finish. "A chameleon. It's a lizard that changes colour and appearance according to its environment. Do you have them here?"

Enya chuckled softly. "Ah, yes, but we don't call them that."

"Let me guess, you call them rainbow dogs?"

"Yes!" she exclaimed with a cheeky glimmer in her beautiful eyes. "See, you *do* know."

Half seriously, half not, I shook my head.

"What?"

"Not everything is about dogs you know. There's so much—"

Enya's face dropped. "On the contrary. It's *all* about the Dogs." Turning her back to me, she filled up her water bottle. Still pushing in the lid, she stepped away, but then paused to face me, saying, "I'm afraid you'll either accept the truth of that before this trip is over or die denying."

ELEVEN

Continuous threats veiled as matter-of-fact statements were becoming as wearying as the climate by the time we returned to the hinnies. Close to thirty people assembled outside, so I assumed a large party was coming with me until I saw that only four animals had been tacked up.

"Rhys, there's no need to go as far as Fragile Rock," Lord Byrne said as he walked in front of me with a member of the Fyuego. "He isn't a tourist. Just take him as far as Pilgrims' Toe and come straight back. He'll either make it to Liekke's Peak or he won't."

"As you wish, my lord." Rhys bowed his bald head before they both turned to me.

"May the Flame's judgement find you swiftly," Lord Byrne said, obviously expecting me to fail whatever was coming.

Although I feared the truth in his assumption, my pride wasn't going to tell him that. "May the Flame's judgement be more understanding than yours."

"It's not the Flame's understanding you need to worry about," Commander Uryah said, swinging his leg over his hinny, looking down at me.

Any witty response I might have normally mustered was stuck in my throat, so as I was handed Calcibus' reins, I simply took them. Stepping to the side of the dark-bay hinny, I stared at his back.

"Where's his saddle?" Checking the other three hinnies, I saw they all wore saddles.

Uryah smiled without any warmth. "Where you are going, you don't need—or want one."

"I beg to differ. I—"

"A saddle cloth is perfectly sufficient. Here—" Lord Byrne handed me what I thought was a light-weight bag with straps. "This is yours."

"There's nothing in it?"

"It's a cape. You carry it like a bag on your back, then wear it in the cold or heavy rain."

My eyes instinctively went to the clear blue sky and I scoffed. "Very funny."

"You laugh now but come nighttime you might be glad of it. It gets cold up there," Uryah said seriously, jolting his chin upwards.

Avoiding Pynyt's feet, I swung the bag onto my back and strapped it on my shoulder. "Can't you give me more information? You know, prep me just a little?"

"A pilgrimage with a guidebook is rather useless—both in effectivity and predictability." Lord Byrne spoke with almost reverence. "The only guidance I can give you is to tell you to stay on guard and listen." He nodded to a soldier—who apparently didn't need words to understand the lord's order.

Linking his fingers together, the soldier stooped next to the hinny, bracing, ready for me to use him as a step. I would have much preferred a stirrup—no, I would have much preferred a saddle—but he had obviously given leg-ups before as he timed my boost perfectly.

"Are you at the front or back?" Rhys said, eyeing up my hinny.

"Does it matter?" I replied, straightening myself on Cal's back.

"If you don't want to fall off a cliff, yes."

"Excuse me?" Suddenly the meaning of Calcibus came back to me. "Oh, because he kicks?"

"Precisely. You either ride well up front or behind. Which do you prefer?"

On the way there, Cal had felt like a perfectly easy mount, but it seemed ridiculous to take an animal on a journey when they didn't trust his behaviour. "Can we see how—"

"No. Positions must be arranged *before* we leave the safety of Fort Fyuego."

If the regimental way Rhys spoke was supposed to strike fear into me, it worked. "I'll go last."

"Figures." Uryah snorted.

Enya rode in front of me. "Shall we go?"

Rhys took the lead, heading east away from Fort Fyuego on a new, narrower, and much less civilised pathway which was very quickly closed-in by trees. Lord Byrne's direction to stay on guard rang through my ears, but honestly I think it would have done anyway as everything around me—from the trees, brush, colours, smells, and even the texture of the air I breathed—struck me as new and fascinating but potentially lethal.

Cal's stoic pace impressed me and as the ground quickly rose, I could see why a smaller, lighter-footed hinny was preferable to a horse. Unlike me, Cal wasn't interested in sight-seeing though. His line of vision rarely altered, yet his giant ears were constantly on alert as they twisted and turned to take in the most minute noises.

Or at least I hoped they were minute.

Aboard my ship, my crew would laugh, sing, and swear, depending on the mood of the day, but either way, time rarely dragged. Even in the silence we had the song of the sea, our constant companion (and sometimes greatest foe when she was angry). All of those sounds were like family to me and I longed for them—any of them—instead of endlessly watching the backs of three strangers' heads as they gently rocked in their saddles.

For about an hour, the track wove around the mountain on a gentle, yet notable incline. I wasn't stupid enough to voice or test the theory, but even for a non-hiker like myself, the terrain would have been pretty easy if on foot. However, as we curved around a particularly large, jagged boulder, it became clear that it marked the beginning of a much harder, more treacherous path. Trees still remained to my left, but rather than riding beside the trunks, I was suddenly viewing them from on top as a great ravine opened up.

By then, the idea of falling to a watery-grave shouldn't have sent shivers through me. Climbing masts, nets, and lookout posts was second nature. *Just hold on and don't let go,* Remi, my brother, had told me with a smile when I was ten. After a few bruises, I made it to the top and never fell. I didn't think about it. Staring down through alien trees to a rushing river surrounded by boulders definitely made me think about it.

"You're fine! Just don't get off," called Uryah, obviously reading my expression—or my mind as his words were eerily close to Remi's.

My eyes panned upwards, hoping to find comfort, but as this new vantage point granted the most panoramic view I had ever seen, it also gave the most realistic view of how high the mountain range was—and we were not on the tallest mound. Peak rolled against peak, each one rising a little more than the last with what looked like tiers of trees and gullies of valleys spread between them.

It was impossible not to be awe struck.

As we carried on along the track, the others began to gently chatter. It was as though they had been waiting for the most narrow, most dangerous path so they could speak—relax even. The desire to ask if they were all mad was only squashed by my need for their help, especially when I eyed an enormous brown bear watching us from one of the trees below.

"How worried should we be about that bear?" I asked, running a hand around my armour in the hope that I had missed a secret knife, no matter how small. I hadn't.

"Rock bears are good, but slow climbers," called Enya. "Only worry if on the same level with one."

"Then what?"

"If you don't have a Fyre Dog or a weapon?" Uryah said. "Pray."

Rhys' bald head rolled backwards as he laughed. Even Enya's shoulders wobbled.

"Wonderful," I muttered.

"Relax!" Uryah called, still laughing at his own joke. "That's why we're here!"

"For now," Rhys added.

"Sure, why let me die until I get further up, right?" As the youngest of seven boisterous, over-indulged brothers, I was never particularly good at being the butt of a joke. Learning how to fight back as soon as I could, and however I could, had been a necessity. Two days in a foreign world wasn't going to change that. I didn't want it to. It had saved me on numerous occasions as captain—as had my crew. For the thousandth time, I lamented Raine not being with me. He would have calmed the frustration within that was threatening to turn to rage. Failing that, Marino would have backed me up and kicked their arses.

"You must appear before the Flame as you are." Enya twisted in her saddle to face me and a new anxiety raced through me as I pictured her falling. "If your body, heart, or soul are not humble, you will not be Charred."

Enya spoke solemnly, but it was clear that her definition of charred and mine were quite different. "And I want to be *Charred*?"

"Absolutely. Only the Charred join the Fyuego and meet the Empress."

Which apparently I also want to do, I said sarcastically to myself, but decided to vocalise a different approach. "So, I want to climb this mountain, complete my pilgrimage, be Charred, and then appeal to the Empress for help?"

"Precisely." Enya smiled, and for a moment I totally forgot I was on the side of a mountain.

"Whether what you want and what actually happens match up, is yet to be determined," Uryah said, grounding my thoughts.

"He'll make it to the top," Rhys said. "I am sure of it. The Fyrewowwa and Amulet of the Flame combining tells us so, for in the Parchment it says, *Hallowed be those blessed by the guidance of a spark or a furnace, for all are filled by the mighty Flame, just as hope of unification is contained within the emerald stone. They who seek both may find.*"

"Yes," replied Uryah, gazing at his friend, ignoring me. "But it also says, *woe is they who are unworthy or seek to divide, for they shall reduce to ash.*"

"I'm not trying to divide! I want to save my people!"

"We'll see."

My eyes found Enya's again but her expression told me nothing. "Rhys is inclined for me, Uryah against," I said, arching my chin at one man then the other. "Where do you stand, Princess?"

"Firmly in the middle. I am not your judge. For that, I await the Flame." Effortlessly flicking her leg, she spun around in the saddle again, facing away from me.

"The scale between two hammers," I muttered to myself.

Enya heard me and laughed.

Encouraged by her mirth, I decided to continue talking. "Is that why you don't ask me any questions about my world?"

"What do you mean? We have asked you questions."

"Not many. I expected you to be as curious about my world as I am yours."

"I am—" Enya sighed. "I am, but—"

"A Flame-less kingdom who cannot protect themselves—and who is likely burnt to the ground doesn't seem like a place to spend much time dwelling on," said Uryah.

"Gryer will not burn it all," Rhys said, "not unless he has to."

"Obviously not." Uryah scoffed. "There's little point in reigning over a bowl of dust."

"The wise move is to burn enough to make a point, then smoke out the rest."

"Four Fyre Dogs would make short work of that, even if three are smaller."

"There's more than four," Enya said sadly.

"What? How do you know?" Enya continued to look ahead but I badly wanted to see her eyes—especially when she didn't answer me. Even Uryah and Rhys turned to her in astonishment. "Your Highness? Have you been to Virisinigne?" The possibility that she wasn't asking questions because she had been there turned my stomach. Was all of this a game?

"No," Enya eventually said. "No, I have not. I do not need to, to understand his strategy. Niall, you say your city is under siege and one large, black Fyre Dog holds the front line?"

"Yes, Your Highness."

"One a similar size to Seraphyna, the Wings of the King?" She saw me screw up my face at yet another term I had never heard before. "The Fyre Dog who is bonded to my father."

"Yes, it is probably the size of my ship—like Seraphyna, but black, not dark green-grey."

"And the smaller ones. What size are they?"

"I have not seen them, but reports say they are the size of ten horses combined."

"So ten, maximum twelve to fifteen years old," said Rhys.

"Precisely." Enya gazed up at the clear sky.

"That doesn't explain why you think there are more than four, Your Highness," Uryah said, voicing my own thoughts. "Nor how he got eggs to begin with? Of all the Fyre Dog population, only Dreygon is unaccounted for."

"Dreygon—" Enya turned to me. "That's the *actual* name of Gryer's Fyre Dog, not Dragon. Your people either misheard or Gryer is making a statement. Probably both. Either way, *Dreygon* must have helped Gryer steal them from the Empress before he was exiled."

"It is a pity he didn't steal from her now," laughed Uryah. "It would have saved us a lot of bother because—"

"Enough!" Enya was suddenly angry. "Any and all such actions are not to be spoken about lightly."

"My apologies—to you and the Flame." Uryah humbly bowed his head. "So you think they have reproduced?"

"Niall says their volcano has been inactive for ten years, so the younger ones were born there—and will have been able to breed for the last few years. I have no doubt. To have a successful, prosperous army—both human and Fyre Dog—my uncle *will* have hatchlings."

TWELVE

The thought of my world being overrun with flying, fire-breathing creatures weighed heavily on me. A solitary conqueror was bad enough, but Enya's idea of Gryer breeding more dragons for his generals and turning Virisinigne into his version of glory made me sick. I wasn't naive enough to believe our world was perfect—including my father's reign, even if he was open to suggestions from his council and cared for his people. Perhaps that was the problem: he didn't regard those in the far west or north as *his people* enough and they sensed it, so the rhetoric of a newcomer who told them what they wanted to hear as well as showing them the unfathomable strength of a mystical creature—and possibly a life force they had longed for but did not understand—was welcomed with open arms.

I felt like I was reading a cautionary tale and I was the footnote.

These people had an air of smugness about them. Holier-than. It was both inspiring and frustrating as I refused to believe they had all of the answers.

An advantage? Absolutely.

Absolution? Absolutely not.

"You do realise it would be prudent to learn about my world as well?" I said after a few minutes of sorrowful reflection. "Is it possible we could learn from each other?"

"Did you miss the part where Benegnyem is the greatest nation?" Uryah grinned. "Others learn and copy us, not the other way around."

"And yet one of yours left—under some sort of exile. Presumably, that is because he did something here you didn't like? He had an ideal you did not share but others might. Ignorance isn't bliss. It left us unprepared and ripe for invasion. Do you think for a second that what happens on my side of the wall will stay there?"

"Why would it not?" Uryah scowled.

"Gryer calls his nation Simulinigne."

"And?"

"The king told me what that means, I assume you can translate it, too?"

Uryah eyed me suspiciously. "Together in fire."

"Precisely. *Together*. Surely, that's an ideal for world domination, not half. Four Fyre dogs will take Benegnyem. An army will take the world."

No one replied but as the princess halted her hinny on a wider ledge and turned to face me, I could see that she had already considered this possibility.

"The Flame would not allow that." Rhys spoke with reverent pride.

"The Flame gives guidance and strength to the faithful," replied Enya. "The righteous option is there. It calls to us. Yet the Flame does not enforce the path we tread."

"Are any of your people devout?" Rhys asked. "What colour are their eyes?"

The two questions seemed ridiculously unconnected. So much so, I could not find the words to answer.

Uryah stared at me—almost through me—with his red eyes as he waited for me to reply.

"None have red eyes, if that's what you mean?"

Rhys bobbed his head thoughtfully.

"My uncle will change that once he has an established order," Enya added. "He may encourage others to seek the enlightenment of the Flame and find his own form of Fyuego." She shuddered involuntarily.

"So, you're all brown and green eyed?" Rhys asked, apparently stuck on his original point.

"And blue," I said. "Mostly blue, actually."

"What?" gasped Uryah. "Then they are truly a nation of heathens!"

"That's hardly fair. I—"

"Yes, because Lord Byrne told me you tried to bring a blue-eyed soldier into Emberbyrg!"

"Raine is a good, loyal man, and a valued member of my crew. I count him as a brother—"

"Another one?" Uryah smirked. "That's a little greedy, don't you think, Seventh Son?"

Regardless of the altitude, I almost jumped off my hinny and threw him off the cliff. As I tried to contain my seething hatred for Uryah—and the nickname that had hounded me since birth—Pynyt stretched his right foot onto the base of my neck, just inside the armour, and nipped a nerve. The pain was unpleasant, but it also served to centre my emotions.

As if pleased with himself, Pynyt released the same, laughter-like hiss that he did at the palace. I wasn't calm enough to laugh back, but my heart rate slowed, allowing my thoughts to significantly simplify when I replied to Uryah: "For a pious man, you judge a lot."

"The Flame is the only way. I do not apologise for believing in my path."

"But you do not need to condemn others for theirs." My eyes spanned across the mountain range, resting on Liekke Peak. "There are many ways up this mountain."

"But only one to true enlightenment," said Enya.

"Precisely." Uryah's smirk dropped and suddenly I saw him in a different light. There was a sadness there. A belief that all others are lost if they do not follow, yet he masked it—coped with it—with his brash outer layer. I wondered who he had lost—or regarded as lost—in this belief.

"So, you believe those with blue eyes are—" I struggled to find any kind of words. "What, exactly?"

"Marked by the Dog," Rhys said simply.

"The Fyre Dog?"

"Yes. Blue eyes signal judgement being passed. Water extinguishes the fire from the soul."

"But for hundreds of generations blue eyes have been dominant in Virisinigne. Brown is uncommon. Green is almost unheard of."

"Green would be. Only the blood of nobility and royalty have green eyes."

I felt my eyebrows nose diving. "That's not so."

Enya's mouth gaped. "Have your siblings not got green eyes?"

As it wasn't something I dwelt on much, I found myself desperately searching my memory for the faces of all my family members. "Only my sister and the queen have green eyes besides me. Everyone else has blue."

A trio of gasps echoed across the valley and I felt like I was in some kind of comedy play. Then I realised they might consider Gryer's attack as just intervention on a heathen kingdom. I decided not to mention the fact my entire crew were blue eyed.

Seeking hope, I asked: "Can the soul be saved or is judgement permanent?"

Enya adjusted herself in the saddle, ensuring she was sitting up straight. "The mark is permanent. Where an individual's soul lies is between them and the Flame."

"Yet you still exclude them from your city?"

"Emberbyrg is the worldly display of the Flame's great blessing," Rhys said. "Having convicts walking amongst the great walls would be counterproductive."

I caught Enya's expression. She tried to hide it, but a slight wince flashed across her face. *That is a manmade decision, not a divine one, I am sure,* I said to myself.

Pynyt took flight, hovering in front of me.

Hold on.

"Hold on?" I repeated, staring at my winged friend.

"Did he speak?" Enya asked just as the ground began to rumble and shake. "The Empress! She is raging!"

The hinnies all pinned their ears back and I held my reins tight, hoping Cal would not bolt. Although the tremors felt unending, they only lasted for a few seconds. As I was about to ask Enya if she thought it was over, I caught sight of a group of boulders racing down the side of the mountain.

"Move! Avalanche!" I screamed.

The others glanced upwards and immediately set their hinnies into action—a notion that I would otherwise think insane, but it turned out that cantering up a wild mountain track was sometimes a good idea.

Pebbles, rocks, and boulders tumbled behind us, bouncing and crashing where we had just stood as the lumps of stone made their way to the jungle floor.

The sound was deafening.

With his ears flat back against his neck, Cal's focus was impressive. Realising I had no choice but to put my trust in my hinny's sure footing, I slackened the reins and just held on.

My ears rang, making it difficult to tell when the torrent of rock ceased, but when we finally reached an opening in the path and slowed to a halt, the ground no longer danced. At approximately seven metres wide, it was a good spot to catch our breath and take stock of how close the rubble had come to us.

Satisfied he wasn't going to be squashed by flying debris, Pynyt returned to my shoulder. I didn't understand our bond, but I was weirdly relieved to have him back with me—like he was part of me, somehow.

Ahead, Rhys pulled his hinny to a stop, blowing out his cheeks in relief as he glanced between the group. A smile crept across his face and he chuckled, seeming to release the tension that we all felt. Exhaling deeply, he opened his mouth to speak but was abruptly cut short by a stray rock flying over the ledge above. With no time to react, it plunged into him, knocking him off his hinny in one swoop, sending him sailing over the edge.

THIRTEEN

Although it would have been easy to sit in dumbfounded silence, the three remaining on the path immediately dismounted, and ran to the cliff's edge.

"Thank the Flame!" Enya called out.

For a second I thought she had lost her mind, but then I spotted a small shimmer of armour coming out of a patch of brush on a perilously small ledge.

"Rhys?" shouted Uryah. "Can you hear me, Rhys?"

"Get a rope!" commanded Enya, running to her saddlebag instead of waiting for someone to comply.

Securing the rope wasn't easy. In fact, it would have been safer if it had happened where we started our mad dash because there were a few robust trees and roots there. In our current spot we had almost flat rock.

"You two will have to hold me," Enya said without an ounce of doubt.

"What?" Uryah grimaced. "Enya, no. I will go down the rope. It is too—"

"I am strong, but I cannot confidently hold you or Rhys on a rope. Looking at you and Niall, you can." Her eyes flickered. Internally I am sure she said, *I hope.* "We haven't time to argue. Get on with it."

Wrapping the rope around our waists, then clipping it to Enya's armoured belt, Uryah and I braced ourselves. It would have been easy to sink myself into doomsday thoughts, having to return to the king and tell him that I had failed, and killed his only daughter, but I refused to let those thoughts in. Reacting to immediate need was my strong point. Sometimes I reacted too fast, but if our ship was in crisis, my crew knew that I would keep my head long enough to see the task through. Action was my friend. Words were where I struggled.

Enya made short work of reaching Rhys. When she called out, "He's alive!" we both sighed with relief. After a few anxious minutes, she shouted, "Pull!"

Uryah and I, despite our differences, made a good team. Hoisting Rhys over the final hump of rock was the hardest. Had he been conscious, it would have been much simpler, but trying not to bash his head into the cliff edge took skill and I'm sure Rhys incurred a couple of extra bruises while we worked it out.

Retrieving Enya was a comparative breeze.

I'm not saying she wasn't worried for her friend, but the glimmer in her eyes as she appeared over the edge told me in an instant that rising to a physical challenge set her on fire, just like it did me.

"What now?" Uryah asked. "I don't think Cyrus can land here—not without causing another rockfall." We all apprehensively looked up at the mountain, hoping not to see anymore boulders flying towards us.

"Well, if Cyrus can't, Wydgitta definitely can't," Enya replied.

"You mean your Fyre Dogs? You can *call* them?" I could only assume that was what she meant, but the fact they all had dragons to call upon seemed crazy.

"The Fyuego to Fyre Dog bond knows no limit. We cannot converse unless close, but we can call from anywhere." Enya smiled, then turned to Rhys in time to see his eyes blink back into consciousness. "Rhys! Oh, thank the Flame!" She knelt by his side, assessing his wounds. "Don't try to stand. I am sure you have broken at least one ankle."

"And a wrist, I think," he said, wincing heavily whilst trying to sit up. "We need to move though."

"We'll have to carry him to a clearing and call for a ride back to the Fort," said Uryah, standing tall. "If we go now, we'll have him in a bed and tended to by the Mederi way before dark."

"Can you ride?" Enya said to Rhys, ignoring Uryah. "If we sit you on your hinny, do you think you can stay on top?"

"Honestly, I fancy my chances on a hinny better than a Fyre Dog, right now. Cyrus or Brytt will mean well, but one false wind and I could fall. I can't sit in the talons and my hands hurt too much to hold the scutes." Rhys glanced at me and obviously read my confusion. "The large, horned scales that we hold on to—and climb up to get on board." He turned to Enya. "Forgive me, Princess, I—"

"Up here, I am just Enya, remember?" she replied warmly. "And there is nothing to forgive, old friend. Uryah will escort you back. Rest, heal. Be well again."

"Enya, no." Uryah was clearly shocked. "You cannot be serious? Surely we must all return?"

Panic hit me. "I must go on, even if alone—"

"Agreed, but you will not go alone," replied Enya. "I will accompany you."

Uryah stepped forward. "I cannot leave you out here with—"

"Do you doubt my capabilities?" Enya's eyebrows rose.

"Of course not."

"Then why do you question me? Have I not proven myself on this mountain?"

"You know you have. Many times."

"Then have you suddenly been anointed as the Kennel Maid and retire me from my Flame-bestowed duty?"

Enya held Uryah's gaze. Although she was not a short woman, he towered over her, however, his countenance yielded to every word she spoke. When he replied, he did not reply as the assertive Commander of the Royal Guard, he spoke as an awestruck, humble servant—and probably a man in love. "You are irreplaceable. You are the only true, anointed, Kennel Maid, crowned princess, and sworn defender of our esteemed kingdom and the almighty Flame."

Enya held out her right hand. Immediately, Uryah bent his knee, took her hand, and kissed it. "Then do as you are told. I will take Niall to Pilgrim's Toe, initiate his pilgrimage, and then call Wydgitta. You two must ride home with haste—and great care. My brother will never forgive me if you die, Rhys. See that you do not."

Making a cradle between our arms, Uryah and I lifted Rhys onto his hinny. Pain struck across his body, but the only audible complaint was a sharp intake of air between his teeth.

"Flamma vobiscum, my friends," Enya whispered, gazing into both men's eyes.

"Flamma vobiscum," they repeated before Uryah nudged his hinny into action, gently pulling Rhys' with him.

Cal had wandered up the path, grazing on small shrubs without a care in the world.

"Approach from the side," Enya called from the back of her hinny.

"Right, yeah. Thanks," I said, wondering if Cal was deliberately standing at an angle so I could *only* approach from behind.

I'm not getting kicked by you, my hairy friend, I thought to myself.

As if he heard me, Cal turned, nickered, then continued grazing.

Enya laughed.

Suddenly my sister's voice came to me. *Pull up some weeds and hand them to him.* She was always befriending creatures when we grew up. Actually, I think that's how she met her husband—talking to his horse.

Cal's ear twitched to the side as I plucked the ground, then curiosity got the better of him and he wandered to me. Slowly, I lifted my hand, collected his reins, silently thanked Muriel for her wisdom—and then realised I had to get back on.

Watching me unceremoniously roll onto Cal's back, Enya's roar of laughter was probably heard at the foot of the mountain.

Hovering above me, even Pynyt hiss-laughed.

"You should have used a rock as a mounting block!" she chuckled.

"Why didn't you say so?"

"What? And miss *that* display?"

"Haha. Ships don't exactly require great horsemanship, you know?"

She didn't reply—not with words anyway.

FOURTEEN

Until that day, I would have said that far out to sea was the only place I could experience a true state of calm, however, riding Cal up and across the Liekke mountain range, I felt a tranquillity unlike anything I had ever known before. The horrors back home and the concern for Rhys—who after all, wouldn't have been up a mountain were it not for me—hadn't left me, but somehow even they seemed less violent as I gazed across the canopy below.

Rather than the slightly uptight or serious versions of Enya who I met in Emberbyrg, the woman who now rode beside me relaxed. She already had when Uryah and Rhys were with us, but I expected that to change once we were alone. It didn't.

The mountain freed us both—if only temporarily.

"We'll reach the temple by nightfall, but I think it best to start your Pilgrimage at first light," Enya said after a few minutes of comfortable silence. She obviously read my expression because she quickly added: "I know you are in a hurry, but lynx and rock bears in particular hunt at night. If you are not used to them, you'll never hear them coming. Better to delay a little then get a lot eaten." A smirk spread across her face.

"I'm glad my death amuses you," I said, smiling back. *Damn, her eyes are beautiful,* I thought, before rebuking myself for such unnecessary observations.

"As we aren't rushing, would you like a mini detour to see into Liekke Valley?" Enya said, almost coyly. "The most impressive view is from Liekke Peak, but the Tailfeather is my favourite spot in the world."

"Then I would love to see it."

She smiled again and my heart skipped.

Stop it, I snapped at myself—openly smiling back.

When the path forked, Enya led us onto the right-hand track that narrowly squeezed between two peaks. Without a guide, it would have been easy to miss the path entirely as the start weaved around a large boulder. Even if I had found the fissure-like pathway, I would probably have turned back because the exit involved another loop around a massive chunk of rock, making it look like a dead end. It was as though nature didn't want this place to be found.

After trying not to scrape my legs against the walls as Cal worked his way out of the claustrophobic path, I could immediately see why this was Enya's favourite place.

Looming above like an almighty guardian stood Liekke's Peak with a gentle, non-threatening waft of smoke weaving into the clear-blue sky. Below was a quietly shimmering lake surrounded by white sand and lush green trees. It was the most perfect oasis imaginable.

Or it would have been, were it not for one, equally awe-inspiring and terrifying fact.

It was filled with dragons.

Lots and lots of dragons.

"Welcome to Liekke Valley." Enya's voice was barely a whisper as she gazed across the beautiful expanse.

As the sun kissed her cheeks and reflected off her armour, and the wind gently blew the loose strands of her hair, she could have been posing for a portrait. Even the ears of her hinny pricked forward with picture-perfect precision. So did Cal's to be fair, but I was not portrait worthy. I was a sweaty mass on a saddle cloth perched on a ledge waiting to be dragon fodder—or at least that's how I felt.

Seeking grounding thoughts, I examined where we were standing. It was a wide ledge filled with multi-coloured flowers sticking out of the cracks. At first glance, the plants appeared random, just growing wherever they could establish their resilient little roots, but then a chevroned—scaled—pattern became more obvious.

"This place should be called *Scale Rock*, not *Tailfeather*," I said.

"If viewing from above, you might see how it got its name," Enya replied. "With the mountains protectively wrapped and layered around the valley, it looks like a huge birds' nest. This ledge was formed by the tail of Dragana, the First Empress. It is said she slashed a vantage seat into the mountain for herself and all the rulers to come to meet in peaceful and gentle appreciation of nature's beauty. The feathered pattern of scales combined with the flora is truly breathtaking, especially at sunrise in spring."

"It is breathtaking now," I answered, gazing all around. "Is there a path to the valley floor?"

"No. Nor is there a safe route to climb down." Enya turned to me seriously. "You are either invited and escorted by a Fyre Dog or not at all."

"Have people tried?"

"Yes, and their burnt, broken bones lay as a cautionary tale to those foolish enough to consider it." Shaking her head, she pointed towards a waterfall cascading down one of the far peaks. "That ledge is Fragile Rock. Tourists love it, but too many people have tried to ride the water into the valley. There are rocks to break you and your fall almost every inch of the way down. Don't try it."

Picturing myself bouncing off the jagged edges, I grimaced.

"There are no shortcuts. Not even out. The streams are narrower than you and sift through underground tunnels. I doubt even a Fyrewowwa would survive it."

Pynyt's shoulders shuddered. Apparently he didn't like the idea of drowning in an underground stream. Funny that.

"Do Fyrewowwa's live here too? I cannot see one—or are they actually baby Fyre Dogs?"

Pynyt hissed.

Enya laughed. "You just offended your spirit guide."

"My apologies." I extended a finger to Pynyt's face, hoping he wouldn't bite me as penance. I think he thought about it as his mouth cracked open, but then he tilted his head to one side, signalling for me to scratch his cheek. His smooth but thick skin felt odd yet strangely satisfying—as was watching the sandy-orange scales ripple with each stroke.

"Fyrewowwa's normally live around hot springs. They hunt fish and other creatures that live in and around the rockpools and lay eggs high up the volcanic rock away from human activity. When harvesting dog grass or hibiyre, farmers have reported seeing them on the edge of fields or the jungle, but they are rarely seen in the city."

"Hibiyre?"

"The big flowers you have probably seen. They are the national flower of Benegnyem, thanks to the blessing of the Flame. They are extremely tasty and have many uses. The leaves and petals are plucked, dried, and mixed with dog grass seeds and stems to make a very nutritious feed or flour for people and animals—depending on the format." She rolled her eyes. "And some smoke it."

"I know I am going to regret asking... but what is dog grass?"

"Did you see the tall, hairy grass in the distance outside of Emberbyrg?"

"Yes."

"That is dog grass. We have many fields for grazing and fodder, plus grains, but those are not dog grass. Only grass fertilised by Fyre Dog's earns that name and therefore has extra value."

"You smoke grass that's been—"

"Fertilised by Fyre Dogs, yes."

Resisting using less regal sailor expressions, I asked, "Like, pooped on?"

She nodded.

My eyes boggled. Then I thought of my brother, Baran, who heavily smoked and decided if I ever make it out of here, I'd take him a pouch of dragon turd tobacco and see if he still wanted to smoke.

"Hibiyre is actually medical, too. The blue ones heal bones. The Mederi will be wrapping Rhys in them now. The green ones fight infection—and if mixed with the blue blooms, they make an excellent poultice, but green hibiyre can also be crushed for oral medicine. The purple ones are used by the Fyuego in sacred mixes for blessings and readings, as well as being presented to the Flame."

"Is that what you had in the essence jar at the Fort?"

Enya nodded. "They were part of the mix, yes."

"What about the red ones? I saw a lot of red ones in the city."

"Yes but be careful with them. They are *very* hot, so are rarely used in their pure, natural state. Red hibiyre flowers will chase away fever faster, but you have to be strong enough to take their full, undiluted, effects. If you understand the balance and use any of the hibiyre correctly, they are a blessing, but too many have died looking for a quick cure—or a cheap high."

"Oh?"

"Some *less wise* users bulk up their tobacco with red hibiyre. In low doses, mixed with dog grass it can have relaxant side effects."

"And if in high doses?"

Enya scoffed. "They call it *the vocal coach*—which is somewhat in dark humour because it paralyses the voice box for six to twelve hours." She shook her head. "Which is better than what happens to those crazy enough to inject it."

"Do they die?" It didn't have a directly comparable plant, but Virisinigne had its share of lethal-if-ill-used drugs, too. So, although the details of hibiyre fascinated me, the terminal price of abusing this wonder-plant was no great surprise.

"Often, yes, like I said, the wrong balance of anything with red hibiyre is lethal, but—" Enya paused, grimacing. "Let's just say that if help isn't sought out quickly, silent, painful, side effects are lasting, even if not fatal."

A little coyly, I sniggered. "Good job I don't smoke or do drugs then, isn't it?"

"Indeed. I'd not wish that on anyone. Happily, I've seen some brought to the Mederi in time. The Mederi are often members of the Fyuego as well as medical professionals, so they understand both sides of spiritual and scientific medicine—of the balance of nature."

"Nature is amazing," I said with honest feeling. If nothing else, I was sure of the truth in that statement.

"It is," Enya said, continuing to watch the enormous oasis. "This valley has always felt like home. As a girl I would come here as often as I could and hide from the palace. I would sit here, on the Tailfeather, and just watch for hours. Sometimes Wydgitta would fly me down, and I'd swim in the lake." She chuckled. "Father or Lord Byrne had to fetch me numerous times when my mother couldn't find me."

I laughed. "My mother lost count of how many times I disappeared into the woods or to the docks to see if I could stowaway on my brother's ship. Father got fed up with trying to find me, so in the end stuck me on a boat and left me there." I sighed. "The court didn't want the *Seventh Son* any more than I wanted it."

Enya's emerald gaze bore into me but I couldn't bring myself to look at her. I was too embarrassed and shocked that I had told her that, so I studied the rippling water below. When I eventually glanced at her, it wasn't so much pity but understanding that registered in her expression. It moved me but I couldn't cope with it. I needed to change the subject.

"How are you not sweating?" I said, wiping my brow with the back of my hand. The heat was genuine even if the accompanying chortle was not.

"Those marked by the Flame's blessing sweat less. The scales protect against heat." She watched me swat a fly away and laughed. "And against bugs."

"So you get to watch others overheat and be eaten by critters?" I met her grin. *That look could disarm an army.* A dragon flew over us, centring my thoughts. "Can I assume these Fyre Dogs are as tame as the ones in the palace?"

"No, these are mostly wild," Enya said matter-of-factly.

"What?"

"Those who are bonded with Fyuego normally live in the city, but many more live out here."

"But are they all human-friendly?"

"No."

"Oh."

"These rest close to the blessing of the Flame and guard it from any and all who they see as unworthy." Enya bobbed her head. "Although some wait for their pilgrim."

"Their—"

"Only the mature are ready though. It is very rare that a youngster accepts a bond."

"But it happens?" I asked, eyeing a smaller, comparatively less frightening dragon.

"I've only heard of one person bonding with a younger Fyre Dog in my lifetime." Enya paused, smiling. "And that was me."

"How old were you when you completed your pilgrimage?"

"Twelve. But Wydgitta and I met out here when I was eight."

"Eight?"

"Not alone. Father brought my brother, Aydan, and me here. It was magical. I stood on this very ledge and Wydgitta flew to me. There was something in her expression. We just knew we were destined for each other. Four years later, when I completed my trial, she was there, waiting." Enya chuckled. "She has grown a lot in the last sixteen years—way more than most. Father thinks she will outgrow Seraphyna eventually."

"What about your brother and mother's Fyre Dogs? I didn't see them?"

"Oh, they are equally large and impressive—as you'd expect."

"And Uryah's?"

"Cyrus is befitting of the Commander. Smaller than royalty, of course, but he is beautiful, nonetheless. Why do you ask?" She narrowed her eyes in my direction but didn't wait for an answer. "Don't go for the biggest Dog any more than the smallest when your time comes." Gazing across the valley, Enya shook her head. "Not that there are any young ones."

"Why? Where are they?"

Enya waved her hand as if brushing away her thoughts. "When up top, they will come."

"Come?" A new wave of anxiety made my skin itch. "What do you mean, *come*?"

She smiled. "You'll see. Just aim for a mature one, okay?"

"And how do I know if they are mature?"

"Size." Enya shrugged as though that should be obvious. "It's not an exact science, but Fyre Dogs roughly grow the size of one horse per year until they are twenty. Between ten and fifteen they are considered adults. At twenty they are full grown."

My eyes blinked as I recalled the size of Wydgitta and Seraphyna—and Dreygon as he flew over Benegnyem. "But there are bigger? *Much bigger.* Sera—"

"That rule applies unless of royal descent and potential sworn Protectors of the Flame—or direct heirs of the Empress' throne." Enya pointed to Liekke's Peak. "Do you see the black Fyre Dog up there?"

Following her direction, I couldn't see a black dragon, only the peak with a large dark boulder on the side of it. Then the boulder moved. "Mmm-hmm," I muttered.

"That's Adaryvan. He is the largest male in all of Benegnyem. He is the Chief Protector of the Flame—the Empress' Right-Wing and overseer of the Fyre Dog horde. If you can, avoid him."

"And if I cannot?"

"*Try.*"

Although *gladly* would have been my honest response, I was confused. "I thought the point was to meet a Fyre Dog up there?"

"Yes, but the only giant you need to impress is the Empress. There's no point pushing your luck."

Gulping, I asked. "Exactly how big is the Empress?"

Enya smirked, turning her hinny to leave. "Hopefully, you'll soon find out."

FIFTEEN

W e quickly rejoined our original pathway, weaving higher and higher up the mountain range. Every part of the view was beautiful, even when I spied creatures that frightened the living daylights out of me.

Enya had seemed confident in our timing, yet as the sun began to head towards the horizon, I began to doubt if we would make it before darkness crept across the hills.

"What's over there?" I asked, seeing a glow in the far distance.

"Dyana," Enya replied, barely glancing in the direction I was looking. "It is the largest city outside of Emberbyrg, situated on the edge of the Savannah. Dyana, along with smaller settlements, are in charge of maintaining the grassland herds of deer, cattle, and wildebeest for the Fyre Dogs."

"*For them?*"

"Of course. They have to eat. It is better to feed them in an organised fashion than watch a hungry or angry Fyre Dog burn a farm or village."

"Or a kingdom," I said, sadly. The lingering feeling of guilt that I had momentarily subdued rose in my stomach.

I could argue that I was still on my mission. I was trying to find help. The method just seemed really odd—and painfully slow as I tried to block out the screams of my people.

"My uncle's actions are unforgivable." Riding ahead of me, I could not see Enya's face as she spoke, but her left hand left the reins to wipe her cheek.

I wanted to respond, but I couldn't find the words. Apparently my silence was enough.

"Gryer left just before my fourteenth birthday but I remember my father's pain like it was yesterday. For years they had argued about the outer lands. Fed up with patrolling our borders for spies and thieves, he wanted to subject all to Emberbyrg's rule. He claimed that leaving them to their own devices discredited and disobeyed the Flame. Father said the Flame did not require blanket, imprisoned followers—only those who choose to follow and live in the light of the Flame."

"Yet you have almighty walls to contain yourselves?"

"We have walls to glorify the Flame and show that those who follow are blessed."

"However, something as simple as the wrong eye colour will see you rejected."

"From the city walls, yes, but not the blessing of the Flame—nor the protection and love of our city. All are valued members of Benegnyem."

I scoffed. "Tell that to the girl I met who did not dare lead me to the Kennel Gate for fear of reprimand."

Enya exhaled deeply. "There's nothing wrong with order, Niall."

"But there is in judgement for judgements' sake." We both paused for a moment. I should have continued in my silence, but I said: "Otherwise, why help a nation of marked people? A nation, by your measure, condemned for centuries."

"Because, although your world has lived without the Flame, the Flame has not forgotten you. By your own admission, whether you realise it or not, your nation has been given the key to enlightenment—and maybe salvation."

"How so?"

"A green-eyed son who traversed to another world in search of truth." Enya stopped. In the dim light I saw her smiling broadly as her glistening eyes panned upwards.

Following her gaze, the knot in my stomach twisted and the air rushed out of my lungs. There, carved into the mountain was a gigantic dragon head. Between the open, fang-filled jaws, a stepped-tongue stretched into the rocky beast's throat, ready to swallow a person like a whale does a tiny fish. From where I stood, the depth of the cavern was hidden from view, but ornate carvings leapt from the walls in ominous splendour. Staring at the looming skull, I couldn't decide if it was more awe-inspiring because it was twilight, but as I caught Enya's expression again, I knew that she was enjoying my astonishment.

Something moved above us—something big.

My heart thundered against my chest.

Enya giggled.

"Ah, Wydgitta, my dear friend. I should have known you would come before I called. How long have you been curled up there?" Enya paused, then bobbed her head in recognition as though the dragon had spoken aloud.

The head of the real dragon extended past the stone one, and I thought I might pass out. Her enormous amber eye captivated me and even though I felt like I might somehow fall into it, I could not look away.

"Not yet, Wydgitta," Enya said softly. "We will let Calcibus rest and start just before dawn."

"And I'll be able to see," I added.

"Right, that, too."

Something in her tone sent shivers down my back. "What don't I know?"

"Wydgitta wants you to kiss the Pilgrim's Toe," Enya explained, pointing to the claw-shaped rock sticking out in front of me.

"Pardon?"

"All pilgrims must kiss the Toe before they begin their pilgrimage."

"Begin? Have I not begun?"

Enya, Pynyt, and Wydgitta all laughed in unison, their combined voice and hisses echoing into the cave. Even the hinnies nickered.

"I'll take that as a *no*, shall I?"

"Dismount Cal and bow before the Foco Temple. Tomorrow you shall kiss the Toe, and *then* your trial will begin."

Sixteen

A torch protruded from the wall just inside the cave. Walking towards it, Enya clicked her fingers and a flame obediently materialised, followed by a dozen more torches further down the wall, lighting up the darkness—and illuminating the fiery, dragon-filled carvings.

"These are amazing," I said, cautiously running my fingers over the artwork. "Who did these?"

"The first pilgrims after the Dividing War." Enya walked to the back wall. "If you follow the carvings and paintings in both directions, you see the path of both worlds."

In the centre was imagery of the World's Divide. There was no mistaking the gleaming, opposing wall, even in still life, yet somehow the cave wall seemed to shimmer like scales—dragon scales—just like the Divide did in real time. Crashing waves were depicted against both sides, yet, as Enya said, the story from left to right varied greatly. A legion of dragons led by an almighty red beast blazed into the right side. Emerald green sparks danced amongst the red and matching shining scales outlined the winged army. However, they were not alone. Sailing the seas, below them were ships filled with men and women wearing blazing armour with swords pointing ahead while magical colours swirled around them. The flagship had a crowned man and woman standing on the bow. In their hands they held the chain of a green Amulet as a beam burst forward into the enormous wall.

On the left, a matching ship and crowned couple stood with an Amulet, yet the movement of the beam seemed to be in reverse, shining *into* the Amulet, as the rest of the fleet sailed away towards land. Each sailor had their back turned to the Divide. Only after I had silently observed the picture for several minutes, did I notice the rocks on either side of the Divide were not rocks. They were bones, piles and piles of bones—from both men and dragons.

Tears filled my eyes as I realised what we had lost.

The number of lives wasted on each side.

And for what?

More land? More power?

Because we could neither share nor agree.

"We had magic and lost it," I whispered without meaning to speak.

"Your side chose to live without the Flame or the partnership of Fyre Dogs. They wanted to rule their way. Disagreements became bloodier and bloodier." Enya pointed to a mural further down the right side of the cave. "The end came just after the Empress' firstborn was slaughtered. In her anger, Dragana invoked the blessing of the Flame and used the bones of the fallen to bind the Divide. In her benevolence, she granted each side an Amulet of the Flame. Should reconciliation be desired, communication may be sought, but the wall will only open properly if an Amulet is held on either side while the breath of the Flame is presented in unison. Until then, all who touch or fly over the wall will—"

"*Die.*"

"Yes," Enya said sadly.

My mind buzzed. "My forefathers erased this from our history. Back home, tales regarding the World's Divide are no more than folklore and legend. How? How could they have successfully blanked this much out?"

"If you forbid enough, long enough, and show wealth and strength another way..." Enya shrugged.

"Do all your people know of this?"

"Yes, of course. Naturally, the Fyuego have a more in-depth understanding, but as a huge part of the Flame's blessing and our nation's past, these carvings are universally known, even if not widely seen." Enya paused, gazing at the wall. "Concealing the truth helps no one."

My fingers wrapped around my Amulet. This was all my people had left from the history that shaped us all. The fact that history was repeating wasn't lost on me—but neither was the fact that my father must have had some idea, something passed to him through the crown in order for him to send his son, even his seventh son, towards a wall otherwise known only to destroy.

As conflicted as I was, I hoped I would be able to confront him on the matter one day. In the meantime, I would have to make do with asking Enya.

"Were both lands equal? Or has Virisinigne always been without Fyre Dogs?"

Enya immediately understood the real point to my question, and the anger that flashed across her face told me she didn't appreciate it. "Benegnyem did not invade or try to subjugate your land, Niall. Your people broke away and rejected the Flame. They didn't want to answer to anyone but themselves. *They* attacked the Fyre Dogs, seeing them as rogue beasts, not friends, guides, or links to a higher power."

The stubborn part of me wanted to refute her statement and point out her people would paint themselves as the righteous side, but in my heart I knew she was telling the truth.

It didn't make me feel any better though.

Leaving me to my thoughts, Enya led the hinnies to the far corner, weaving around a hidden opening to an inner chamber. When I realised she had disappeared, I followed and found Cal munching on a bale of hay while she untacked her hinny beside him. In addition to the gentle rhythm of Cal chewing, the sound of running water caught my attention. In the dimly lit room, I couldn't see where it was coming from, but as I was about to ask Enya pointed to the ground at the back of the room. "Only draw water from the left of the spring."

Glancing left and right, I couldn't understand what the difference was.

Smiling, Enya rolled her eyes. "Draw from the left, relieve on the right."

"Ah." A nervous chuckle slipped out of me. "Who brings supplies up here?"

"The Fyuego fly it up. It hardly seems fair to ask hinnies to carry us *and* their own food."

"Could pilgrims not fly up, too?" I said, gazing at Wydgitta's head as she peered into the temple, wondering if I wanted that.

"You seem to continually miss the point of a pilgrimage, Niall." Enya's face had returned to the more serious, official version that I was greeted with in the city. I was sorry for it, but I didn't know how to avoid it. Enya sighed. "Even tourists trek to the Foco Temple. It is part of the preparation of your soul—for pilgrims and citizens alike. Only those who pass their trial may fly."

"I see."

Viewing the walls, I could see why this place was referred to as a temple, not just a cave. It felt holy—and certainly required a degree of devotion to reach.

"What does *Foco* mean?" I asked, trying in vain to translate it myself. The knowledge that my ancestors would have understood these foreign words—some of which my people still used even if they didn't understand—really grated.

"Fireplace," Enya replied.

The ground began to rumble, forcing pebbles to dance from above and below. We dropped to the floor, huddling together as Pynyt sheltered under me. Fearing a cave-in, I anxiously looked towards the exit in time to see Wydgitta climb down from the rock dragon and curl up in the mouth of the temple.

"Don't risk trapping yourself!" called Enya. After a brief pause, she shouted again, "Yes, but if you are crushed then I cannot save you!"

The dragon's body didn't move, yet she extended a wing, turning herself into a living umbrella and repelled the falling debris from our backs.

Despite the danger, I was fascinated by the up-close view of Wydgitta's wing. Pynyt's were impressive, but the sheer scale took my already chastened-breath away.

"Crawl closer!" Enya commanded. "It'll put less pressure on her wing, if she won't protect herself!"

Enya didn't wait for me to answer, instead immediately heading for her companion's wing-pit. By then, I was so close I could see each scale rise and fall and smell the dry, sandy aroma coming off the dragon. Caught in fascination, I almost forgot about the quaking earth.

"See the scutes?" Enya said, redirecting my gaze. "There, the extra horned scales that stick out. The best route to the back is this row—" She waved at a vertical line of razor-sharp scales. "Then position yourself between the ones on the withers when riding. You can ride higher up the neck and on the head, but it is harder to stay on."

My mouth gaped, willing words to form while my brain screamed, *Why do I need to know that?*

Before I could collect myself, the rumbling stopped and Wydgitta tucked in her wing.

Standing up straight, Enya dusted herself off. "You must always save yourself first, Wydgitta. No ifs or buts."

"What did she say?" I asked, still not totally believing the enormous creature was talking.

"She says she was ensuring an escape route for us. Which—" Enya paused, throwing a dirty look at the dragon, "is all well and good, but she is as important as I am, so risking herself unnecessarily is *not* acceptable."

Wydgitta snorted defiantly.

"Yes, we will have to agree to disagree." Enya grinned, then shook her head. "The Empress' distress is increasing. She never used to rage and cause tremors like this."

"Why is she now?" I gulped. "And do I really want to go and see her? Is there no other—"

"None. Not for what you are asking. I can fulfil the Flame's request and present you for trial, but only the Empress can offer you what you seek."

Enya checked on the hinnies, then went to her saddle and rummaged in one of the pockets before producing two wrapped up parcels. Smiling, she sat crossed-legged in front of a circular iron grid in the middle of the temple. Once settled, she clicked her fingers, and again a flame sparked, this time transforming into a hearty blaze in the fire-pit below.

"Is this the fireplace?" I asked, slightly underwhelmed.

"No, no. This is just to warm weary travellers. The Foco is—well, you'll see."

My insides winced. "That sounds ominous."

"Here," she said, holding out one of the parcels. "Eat. The morning will soon be here."

Unwrapping the cloth, the smell of fresh fish and bread filled my nose. How it had travelled so well was a mystery and the aroma was a strange combination when mixed with humid rock and thin air, but the taste was amazing.

Pynyt watched each mouthful intently—too intently because I began to fear he would try to flame-grill the fish as it entered my mouth. Sharing was not my first choice, but I decided it was the safest. It came with a double reward though because not only was my Fyrewowwa-friend happy, but Enya smiled at me approvingly. I'd like to say I was too focused, too controlled to be affected by it, but that would be a lie.

Turning back to the remnants of my bread, I repeated to myself that she might be the younger child of the king, but she was still the anointed princess and was not going to want the seventh son of a kingdom under siege.

Seeking distraction, I asked, "Does your brother not journey up here, too?"

As Enya's face fell, I instantly regretted my question. "You mean instead of a girl?"

"What? No, of course not." My face flushed. "I only meant that he is your older brother, is he not? He must have—"

"Aydan has completed his pilgrimage, yes, obviously. He set out when he was fourteen—two years before I did. He scored very highly and completed his trial quickly. Some assumed he would be granted the role of Kennel Maid, but—"

"Surely *that* is for women only?"

Enya's eyebrows furrowed. "Why? It is a name of honour and respect, not gender. My father was the Maid before me. *He* is not a woman."

"Princess, forgive me." I bowed my head to her. "You take offence where I mean none. Please educate where I am ignorant and be patient with me, I—"

Enya laughed.

"Princess, I-I—" I couldn't find the words and her unreadable expression wasn't helping.

"You were right at Fort Fyuego," she said with a half-smile.

My eyes met hers. "Oh?"

She nodded. "About your chameleons. I have been thinking about it. I am not *Princess* on this mountain, not really. When it matters, I am the *Kennel Maid*, both high and low, but in the city, I am expected to be one thing or another. I dress and behave as required—with pleasure and pride—yet the mountain allows a certain freedom. It is the closest I come to being *just Enya*. Yet, I am not the only one who feels this way. It is for all who are blessed to visit the Liekke mountains. You must have noticed how Uryah and Rhys altered also?"

"I confess, I did." I chuckled. "The absence of Lord Byrne helped with that, though."

Enya's shoulders rippled as she silently chuckled. "The lord means well. He is loyal to a fault. The longer you know him, the more you will see that."

Absentmindedly, I bobbed my head. "I think he is hoping I will fall off the mountain into the Flame rather than achieve its blessing—or if he didn't before, he will when he realises Rhys was knocked off whilst escorting me. He seemed to like Rhys."

"Rhys is his nephew." Enya's smile slipped. "But we all love Rhys."

"What is it? He will be okay, won't he?"

"I'm sure he will, yes, yes." She waved her hand dismissively. "Sorry, I was thinking of Aydan—never mind."

"Your brother?" Suddenly Enya's parting words to Rhys and Uryah came to me. *My brother will never forgive me if you die, Rhys. See that you do not.* "Is your brother married to Rhys?"

Enya paled. "No."

"But they are together? A—"

"My brother is married to Princess Sonya. She is expecting their first child. He is very excited about it. He even cut short his annual sailing trip to survey wildlife on the Outer Isles to be back before her confinement. He is a doting husband."

She sounded like she was reading from a hymn sheet. In an attempt to settle her heightened nerves, I decided to reply in reverse order of interest.

"Sailing trip?"

It worked. Enya instantly smiled. "Oh yes, if you two spend more time together, you will probably get on very well. Aydan loves sailing and is also passionate about preserving our rarest species. Every year he spends at least a month at sea observing the breeding colonies of birds, fish, and mammals on the remotest islands of Benegnyem. He knows that fatherhood will reduce his ability to go for a while, but I am sure he will take his family with him when old enough. The work is important, so his team will continue without him, though."

"His team?"

"Patrols are necessary all year round." Enya rolled her eyes. "Savages from the east like to steal eggs and claim horns for their collections and false medicines."

"I see." I resisted declaring, *Huh! So you do have pirates then!* Instead I opted for a safer route of enquiry. "Do either Uryah or Rhys sail?"

Enya sucked in her bottom lip. She understood what I was getting at. Uryah was a decoy—well, mostly. I was curious if she thought of him the way he clearly thought of her—but I was sure there was more to Rhys and Aydan.

"You should understand. I thought you would, anyway." Enya said slowly. Holding her gaze, I didn't reply. I didn't want to risk saying the wrong thing and diverting the conversation in the wrong, silent, direction. My patience was rewarded. "The Prince of Benegnyem must marry a woman and produce offspring, no matter the direction his heart may initially lie. Crowned and anointed members of the Fyuego do not get a choice. The bloodline must carry on."

"Yet you are not married, Your Highness?"

"Yet."

That word stung more than it should and I bit the inside of my cheek, reminding myself on which side of the Divide I belonged.

Forcing a smile, I replied, "Can you not follow your heart *and* be loyal to the kingdom?"

"Not always, no."

"Then I return to an earlier point that was dismissed by Uryah. I believe both our nations can learn from one another." Enya scowled at me but waited for me to continue. "Would it surprise you to hear that Baran, the crowned Prince of Virisinigne, is married to a man and has three blood children?"

Enya's eyes bulged. "How?"

"My brother loves a man, but also lives with two women—both of whom have borne them children. It may not be a situation for all, but it works for them. Why should you or I or anyone else judge?"

"Hasn't it caused an uproar with civilians?"

"My eldest nephew is fifteen and not once have I heard reports that the people think of him as anything other than the heir to the throne." I groaned. "Until your uncle came along, that is."

We both grimaced.

Silence echoed off the cave walls.

The crackle of fire suddenly sent shivers down my spine as screams tormented my mind. Even with the Empress raging, as Enya called it, that cave was a thousand times safer than everyone on the other side of the Divide.

"I hope I am like your brother and manage to complete my pilgrimage quickly," I whispered.

"Have faith. Your path is yours to win."

Or to lose.

"We should sleep." Enya got up and collected our bags. "Unroll it, like this, and it is a cape-cum-blanket. Tomorrow, Cal will lead you so far, then you must remove the saddle cloth and carry it in your bag. Should your pilgrimage be longer, it is the only soft pillow you will find."

"How will I know when to get off?"

Enya grinned. "You'll know."

"What about Cal? Do I just leave him?"

"Yes. He will return safely on his own. That is why you are not allowed tack, including a bridle, beyond Pilgrim's Toe—tack gets caught if unattended. Naked, Cal can protect himself."

"Yet you have guards at the Fort for them?"

"A penned animal cannot run. A free one can run—or fight."

Unrolling my bag and laying on it, I folded the food cloth and placed it to one side. "Do you have food for me to take tomorrow?"

"The wilderness will feed you."

"I don't know your plants."

Enya turned on her side, facing away from me. "Then the Flame has answered you, and you'll die."

"Couldn't it have done that when I was comfortable on my ship—or at least at sea level?"

Wydgitta's tail slowly circled us both as Enya yawned. "That's not your fate."

SEVENTEEN

The Pilgrim's Toe was the cleanest part of the rocky dragon. Centuries of humble penance and pilgrimage had obviously kept the spot in shiny splendour while the rest was left to the whims of nature. Similar to the Tailfeather, tiny plants, like feathery-green moss, had taken up residence in the scales of the Foco Temple. Had I been hearing about it instead of seeing, I might have thought the moss made the statue less imposing. It didn't. It added to the texture, making it seem more alive as the breeze waved the minute foliage in the pre-dawn light.

Wydgitta sat above the temple while Enya serenely stood in the cave entrance, waiting for me to kiss the Toe. The claw. Internally I scoffed. It was less imposing to say, *Go to the Pilgrim's Toe* than *Kiss the dragon's claw.*

Almost on their own, my knees bent before the claw. When standing, I could look over it, but from my stooped position I could only see the sharp nail as it protruded from the scaly rock. As my knee hit the ground, Pynyt flew from my shoulder. His absence felt strange, even though he had only flown to one of the temple-dragon's spiky teeth. I considered raising my arm and calling him back to me, but he must have read my mind—or seen my hand twitch—as he flapped his wings and hissed impatiently. *Proceed,* he said.

Leaning forward in slow motion as though time had no meaning, my lips found the cold stone, and immediately the wind picked up.

A lightning bolt crashed upon the steps before me. The force was immense, but the rock wasn't marked. Frozen, I did not move. My eyes darted to Enya's, hoping to find reassurance in her expression. If it was there, I did not see it as another bolt hit the same spot and a green and red furnace filled the mouth of the dragon, blocking my view of her entirely.

Suddenly new colours burst forth, racing in fiery rainbows that consumed and fed one another.

Panic and calm crashed into each other within me. The conflicting sensations seemed to fight in my core. I feared the unknown. I feared the roaring furnace in front of me. I feared being separated from Enya. However, as I listed the third of my immediate concerns, it was quashed by a wave of inexplicable, other-worldly understanding that she was alright.

Walking towards the flame, my body absorbed the heat but it did not scold me.

It drew me in.

When I was about three metres from the blaze, a sound like thunder rang out.

Facing the sky, Enya stepped into the fire with her arms outstretched while her skin glowed with green, purple, and red scales. Wiggling her fingers, she released purple petals which sparkled and danced before they disappeared, filling the air with a sweet aroma that reminded me of a field of flowering herbs. When the last petal left her hand, Enya bowed her head, saying, "Oh mighty Flame, I, your loyal Maiden, present this pilgrim for judgement."

The thunderous sound, almost like a voice, rumbled again.

A third, louder, bolt of lightning flew out of the cloudless sky and hit the ground in front of me.

Then all went black.

My eyes blinked, desperately trying to focus on something, anything. I wanted to call out to Enya for help, but all sound choked in my throat. Every part of me shook with fear. My chest tightened to the point I thought it might burst. It felt like an eternity was passing—or my soul was slipping into it. As I was about to collapse, talons grasped my left shoulder through my armour and the hot, spicy breath of Pynyt wafted down my ear. My ears rang with white noise, but the rhythm of his breathing became my focus. With each puff, I took a breath. In, out, in, out. My heart began to slow to a less frightening beat. I could not see, yet I no longer felt like I was going to swallow my silently screaming tongue.

Warm fingers found mine, causing a new jolt of sensation to race through my body. Pynyt took an extra deep breath, reminding my heart that it needed to stay in my chest, allowing my hands to wrap around Enya's in a more calmed, orderly fashion. I was desperate to look at her. In my mind I could see her gorgeous eyes and melting smile, but only my hands worked. As if she understood,

Enya lifted our hands to her face, turning her grip so that my fingers wiggled freely in search of her cheeks. When I found them there was a hint of tears.

Does she cry because I have already failed? I asked myself. *Am I judged as unworthy and now have lost my senses?*

White noise buzzed all around me as I held Enya, yet in my head I could hear two hearts. The buzz increased. Suddenly I felt Pynyt's grip alter as he leant back. Turning to face him, a great wind slapped my cheeks, instantly blowing away the ringing.

Enya leaned in so close I could feel her skin against mine as she whispered, *"Open your eyes."*

Light raced into my retinas, and although the sun had not yet fully risen, I could see as though it were midday. Enya smiled at me and in her vibrant emerald-green eyes I saw mine reflected. I blinked, and the colour faded. They were still green, just less bright, as though I had to earn the joy of viewing hers again in their full glory.

Through a chastened breath, Enya chuckled. The corner of her lips curled upwards knowingly, but she did not speak as she held my hand and stepped towards the Temple.

Pynyt flapped his wings again, his voice commanding, but this time I did not need his instruction.

I would follow her anywhere.

EIGHTEEN

The light inside the Foco Temple was just as bright as outside, making the carvings and paintings come to life more than ever. There was so much detail to take in, but Enya gently pulled me along until we stood beside Cal. Lifting our hands, she placed them on Cal's withers and nodded to a sizable rock laying on the ground.

Using it as a mounting block, I swung my right leg over Cal's back. For a second my fingers moved away from Enya's and it felt wrong. Flustered at our separation, my sight faltered, but as our hands reconnected, I settled on my hinny's back in a much more dignified manner than the day before. Neither of us spoke, but reading her amused expression, I could tell that Enya was remembering my less-than impressive display.

Still chuckling, Enya passed me my empty bag-cum-cape and silently insisted on helping me put it on. My practical side knew that it would have been easier if my hands and arms were free to move without her assistance, but no part of me wanted to push her away.

Throughout, Cal patiently waited without moving, but as soon as I was still, his ears pricked forwards and he began to slowly walk out of the temple. Enya followed by our side, still holding my hand while Pynyt rode on my shoulder, and for a moment I marvelled at how bizarre my life had become. Exiting the Foco Temple, I searched for any kind of evidence of the almighty fire that had burned there minutes earlier, yet there was nothing. Even the moss remained intact and healthy.

Without even the slightest nudge, Cal methodically made his way down the steps, onto the open area in front of the temple, faced right up the mountain, and pulled himself to a halt. The spot we stopped at had no visible marking, yet Enya paused her stride at exactly the same position—just like a well-practiced marching army or on-stage dancer. Her eyes flicked up to Wydgitta and she nodded before turning to me.

"Follow the path. Be on your guard and listen. *Always listen.*" Enya stepped back a pace, still holding my hand, and took a deep breath.

My head raced with a thousand questions, yet somehow I knew that even if I could order them and ask, there would be no answers.

Not there, anyway.

Feeling her fingers loosen from my grip, I pulled her forwards and stooped to her hand, and kissed it. I had no idea if the rules of her world allowed for such an action. I knew the rules of mine, but regal decorum seemed somewhat lost on that mountain and it was but a mark of respect, thanks, and affection, nothing more dangerous—or so I told myself, even if my heart disagreed.

My doubt told me now or never.

My resolve told me it was time to test my worth.

Our gazes met.

A wind spiralled around us, reminding us of our duty.

Reminding me of why I was there.

As I sat up straight, Enya released my fingers, saying, "*Flamma vobiscum.*"

Immediately all colour faded and I was left in darkness.

Pynyt must have known what was coming because he instantly angled his nostrils down my ear, slowly counting my breaths in and out, reducing my sense of panic—and therefore preventing me from rolling off Calcibus' back. My fingers found the hinny's long mane and gently wrapped around two large tufts of coarse hair. Whether from approval or tender warning, Cal snorted, then slowly set off.

I'd never been afraid of the dark, but until then, I had never truly seen it. Moonlit waves or rippling shadows were not darkness. Tones always existed somewhere, but not then. It was as though the furnace had shown me all the colours and now I was allowed none. Not even grey.

Only then did I find my voice. It wasn't loud, and I had no idea whether Enya was still there, but my lips pronounced the foreign words, "*Flamma vobiscum,*" hoping that I would be found worthy to utter them by the unseen force that I could not deny.

As the breeze echoed the words back to me in the voice of the Maiden, even though everything else seemed lost, I smiled.

NINETEEN

The only reason I knew the sun had risen was because I could feel it on my face. Sweat trickled down my forehead, but I was reluctant to let go of Cal's mane, so I waited for it to really irritate me before wiping it away with the back of my hand.

The path we started on was relatively broad, but I had no idea if we were on a narrow pass or open valley. All I knew was the wind came from the left. Normally that would have been enough for me to gauge something of my position, yet nothing in this land followed the rules I had lived by.

What if this is permanent? No wonder Lord Byrne laughed at me when I asked for a guide or instruction manual—if they knew it was coming, who would willingly give up their sight? Silent, intrusive thoughts crept in, worming their way into my confidence. *Do the Fyuego have red eyes because they are replaced by fire when they pass? Do they die in darkness if they fail?*

If I fail.

When we awoke, Enya had reassured me that my crew would continue to be kept informed and treated well in my absence—however long that would be—but I found myself imagining what they would say if they were in my place. Not that I would have traded places. Scared to my core as I was, I was their captain, this was my mission.

Suddenly the intensity of the sun disappeared. Cal was still moving, but his footsteps echoed—my breathing echoed. All I could think of was that we were in another cave, but this one apparently led somewhere.

Are we supposed to be here? How am I supposed to know? I thought to myself. I yearned for vision, yet I had to acknowledge that even if I could see the path, I wouldn't know if it was the right one.

Be on your guard and listen.

That advice had been repeated to me, but was that always meant as a pair or were some trials separate?

Enya had said I would know when to get off Cal, but by then I was afraid to get off. He was my eyes. One false move and I'd crash into a bloody mess down a canyon or become eternally lost in a cave. At best I would be wild animal food. No sooner had I thought that than my brain started listing the animals I thought most likely to want to eat me—and the ones likely to find me in the cave.

If my negative thoughts had not increased my heart rate, the increased echoes finished the job. When they first began, they could have come from anything or anyone, yet now they sounded like steps, human steps, and they were closing in.

Pynyt remained still on my shoulder. His grip didn't alter. *If he is calm, maybe I should be?*

Concentrating on my breathing, I faced forward, praying that we were alone.

Jolting me forward an inch, Cal abruptly stopped as though something had blocked his path.

"If you're thirsty, I have water," said a voice unlike anything I had ever heard—or wanted to hear. "If you're hungry, I have food. But if you wish for vision, blood must be spewed."

"Who are you?" I asked, cautiously.

The voice cackled, sending every hair on my body on its end.

The cold blade of a dagger slipped between my fingers, shooting my meagre breakfast to the back of my throat. I gulped it down but could not speak.

"A prick won't do. I want the lot. A simple slit and that's it." The dagger jolted in my hand as the unseen figure poked it.

"You can't mean Cal, the hinny?"

"*Can't I?*" The voice scoffed. "Do it. Make the trade."

"But why? You ask for something with no explanation—no good reason. Why would I harm him on the off chance what you are offering is true?"

"I see. You don't." Malice filled their mirthless laughter. "Do it."

"Does loyalty mean nothing to you? He has carried me faithfully."

The sound of dragging feet, like two people wrestling, approached. "Tell him," muttered the gruff voice through gritted teeth.

A new sound echoed, like a fist landing into a stomach, followed by a grunt.

"It's him or me, Niall," said Raine through winded breath.

My skin bristled hearing my navigator's voice. "Raine? Is it really you? What's going on?"

"Yes, of course, it is. Don't tell me you'd choose a sterile donkey over me?"

"I was told you were safely on our ship. What happened?"

A second punch landed in Raine's stomach and we both cried out—one in pain, one in frustration.

"Leave him alone! What do you want with me?"

"I told you. I want blood. His or the beast's, but I want blood. Blood for sight. A simple trade if you want to complete your pilgrimage." The voice spoke as calmly as though they were ordering bread from a baker. No hint of irony or shame. Even the callous laugh was absent this time.

"Raine, talk to me. I cannot see. I am on my way to plead with the Empress for help. What happened? Who holds you?"

"There is no Empress! These people are sick! They get kicks out of tormenting us. We are all damned and they do not care—and certainly will not help us. They test you for fun, but we will fail if you do not understand their tricks. The offer here is real. You must regain your sight, but you cannot kill me, Niall. I am your brother—how can you even consider spilling my blood?"

"I am not! I would not! I will forfeit myself before harming either of you!" I declared, knowing in my heart that betraying those loyal to me, even if it meant ultimate failure, was a step further than I was willing to go. For all my other inadequacies, my soul would not allow this one.

"Kill the hinny and get back your eyes! Save us, Niall!" Raine's struggling feet dragged across the stony ground again, this time away from me.

Shuffling on Cal's back, I tightly gripped on the dagger and considered throwing myself in the direction of movement but feared losing Cal and stabbing my friend by accident. Instead, I opted for a panicked plea. "Stop! I beg you, stop! Where are you taking him?"

The voice tutted. "I am benevolent, so will give you one other offering. A prettier one."

More feet dragged, this time accompanied by the sound of sobbing—female sobbing.

"Enya?" Her name caught in my throat.

Someone scoffed. "Niall, have you already forgotten your sister? Has the witch taken your heart so soon that you forget your own kin?"

"Muriel?" I had not seen my sister for over two years but I would never forget her voice. "How? How are you here?"

Instead of answering, Muriel screamed. Her voice bounced off the walls again and again, ringing like a siren. In that moment I wished the Flame had taken my hearing as well as my sight.

"Why are you doing this?" My body trembled.

"Nothing worth having comes easy," replied the voice.

My world spun. Although all was black, the air around me whisked and I scrunched up my tear-stained face.

"DO IT!" boomed the voice. "You will fail all if you sacrifice nothing!"

"Niall!" shouted Raine and Muriel in blood-curdling unison.

Then it hit me.

The truth—or something resembling it—hit me.

I dropped the dagger, waiting for the inevitable sound of it hitting the stone floor, but the sound did not come.

Carefully leaning forward, I ran my fingers up Cal's neck. He was relaxed.

Sitting back, I lifted my right hand to my left shoulder, and found Pynyt's feet. Only then could I feel them—and only then did I realise that I hadn't registered his absence. Except Pynyt wasn't absent any more than Cal was stationary. Nor was Muriel or Raine in the cave. The real Raine hadn't called me *Niall* for ten years. Even late at night with a beer in hand, I was *Captain*. This creature, this spirit, this cruel deformation of my mind, was the lie.

"My family, I pray we meet again," I said with every ounce of my being, "but you are not here, and I am not playing."

Two open hands with bony, digging nails landed on my chest, thrusting me backwards over Cal's hind.

Spooked into action, Cal bucked and kicked out, propelling me upwards before I landed in a heap against a wall. Dazed, my fingers felt the back of my head and came away with a sticky substance. Logic told me what it was, but I smelled my hand anyway, and was instantly greeted by the classic metallic scent of spilt blood. In the near-distance, erratic hooves thumped again, followed by harsh snorts and bursts of fire. My mind told me to run, but my body flushed with pain so acutely that all I could do was lay there.

If the creature, whatever it was, was still there, I couldn't tell. No one spoke, no one laughed—although I would be lying if I said no one cried. Rising to a challenge had always been my thing, but crumpled on the ground, I felt utterly defeated. How long I laid there, I don't know, but the first thing that I was aware of besides my laboured breathing and shooting pain, was the sound of wings.

"Pynyt?" I whispered.

A wind channelled into my face. *"Follow."*

"I cannot," I whimpered.

"Follow," Pynyt repeated, this time adding a hiss.

"A creature—I don't think they were human—it attacked me. It pretended to have..." I choked on my own doubts. "I hope they were pretending to have—"

"Vampire Goblin," said Pynyt. *"Follow."*

A sharp burst of air stung my face as Pynyt took flight. I had questions—so many questions—but I was also desperate for him to stay with me. Until then, he always seemed to understand, yet even if I could see where he went, I was not physically capable of running after him. I couldn't even stand up.

Dragging myself onto my knees, sucking in the pain that was shooting from my right leg, I felt around in the dark. My hands found the cold, hard wall, and Pynyt hissed at me from further down the cave.

"I cannot walk," I pleaded.

"Follow."

Perhaps it was only metres, yet it felt like miles as I crawled through the cave, spurred on by Pynyt's continued hisses.

My body screamed at me to stop. I knew resting again would probably be a death sentence, but the battle of mind and matter was intense. Suddenly, the texture of the rock began to change from barren to inhabited, and my nails dug into tender sprigs of moss, while the sound of chewing filled my ears.

"Cal?" I said softly, afraid that he would run away.

Hooves moved and a soft muzzle nudged into my outstretched hand.

Patting him, my joy was so great, I fought for breath as it caught in my lungs.

"You waited for me," I sobbed. "Thank you." Cal nudged me a little harder. "We need to go, yes. But I don't know how to get back on—"

I was cut off by the sound of Cal's hooves scraping the ground followed by a gentle thump as he lay down beside me. He had already lived up to his name and I was afraid to be kicked again, but with no other choice, I reached out. Relieved to find his face, I ran my hand down his neck, and rested on his withers. Slowly, trying desperately hard not to lean on his legs or belly in case he took offence, I pulled myself upwards. Swinging my right leg was agony and the cave rang as I cursed through gritted teeth, but as I wrapped my fingers around Cal's mane, my faithful companion stood up—and my eyes simultaneously flooded with light.

Gasping, I took in the cave.

It was long, longer than my eyes could measure—even if my sight hadn't just returned—and multi-coloured boulders and spikes lined the ground, walls, and ceiling. Scuff marks from Cal's hooves decorated the stone floor, pointing in the direction that I thought I had just crawled from. The path had three options, the smallest of which appeared to have something smouldering hanging from one of the spikes in the ceiling.

Straining my eyes, I realised it was an impaled body.

A charcoaled, impaled body.

Only then did the smell hit me. Whether my sense of smell had been numbed along with my sight or simply frozen by pain and fear, I was never sure, but as it returned, my stomach churned. I wanted to look away, but seeing it validated my anguish. I was in a nightmare, but at least part of it was real.

About to praise Pynyt for his pyrotechnics, I turned to my left shoulder, and realised the wall was covered in paintings—but not of people. Although roughly man-shaped, the images were of bald creatures with bumpy, muddy-green skin, large ears, long nails, and fanged teeth. Some of them hung upside down from above while others peered around boulders with demonic grins. Below read:

Beware of hallucinations invoked by Vampire Goblins.

They are vindictive but defeatable—unless fed blood spilt by their silver daggers.

Don't do that.

Laying my hand on Cal's neck and facing my spirit guide, I chortled. "Did you two kill the Vampire Goblin for me?"

Pynyt chuckled. *"Time to go."*

TWENTY

Exiting the cave, the sunlight was glorious. Birds sang, insects chirped, and the wind gently fanned my sweating brow. It would have been idyllic had it not been for the thump in my head and the pain shooting up my right leg. Everywhere hurt to some degree, but in the unfiltered light, I could now see the state of my knee—and it wasn't pretty.

A ten-inch gash ran up the side of my leg, making a bloody, oozing smile. I was no doctor—or Mederi as they seemed to be called in Benegnyem—but I knew my way around cuts and stitches. This needed stitches. Lots of stitches. It also needed cleaning as pebbles and dust decorated the blood in a way that I might have found sadistically funny if they were on an enemy. Fever and infection would be hitting me soon, and I knew it.

"Can you take me to water?" Any kind of delay to my journey was too much, but my realistic side told me my journey would end on this mountain if I did nothing to help myself. At the very least, I needed to find the Empress and beg her for help before I died.

Cal's right ear twitched as I spoke. With nothing else to go on, I had to believe that was his signal of agreement. Seconds later, Pynyt flew from my shoulder, disappearing around the corner without as much as a cursory hiss. When we reached the bend he had taken, the path expanded into another valley—a really high up one, but a valley, nonetheless.

Despite the pain, I smiled. Every turn displayed new beauty and I wished I had a map to study. To count the number of peaks and valleys, to mark out the caves and streams or rivers. My eyes panned upwards once more, searching for Liekke's Peak. When with Enya, looking over Liekke Valley, it seemed close, or at the very least reachable. Now it just seemed further away.

Like darting arrows, Cal's ears whipped backwards and he broke into a gallop. Grasping his mane, I fell against his neck and squeezed as tight as I could with my legs to prevent me falling without giving him the idea that I was egging him on.

"Whoa-boy," I called with my head between his ears, but Cal kept running.

The pain began to border somewhere between unbearable and beyond recognition as adrenaline pumped around my body. Whether from luck, skill, or sheer-stupidity, I do not know, but I risked a glance backwards, hoping to see what had caused Cal to go deaf on me.

A glance was all it took to understand.

A rock bear was charging behind us at an alarming pace. Enya told me they were slow climbers but failed to mention how fast they were on the flat.

Everything wants to kill me, I pitifully thought to myself.

Ahead was a stream—the very thing I had been praying for minutes earlier, but I doubted it would stop the steaming advance of the enormous brown bear. Cal ran alongside the waterway. It didn't look too deep, but rocks lined the bank, inhibiting a hasty escape. In my gut, I knew the odds of the bear being able to cross faster than us, especially if Cal kept me on board.

"You're going to have to drop me," I called out.

Cal didn't alter his speed, but his right ear briefly twitched.

"I'm serious. I'm slowing you down." We were fast approaching a sharp incline up the next peak. There was no way Cal would be able to keep up this speed, and being able to loop back into the trees was far from certain as thick bushes of hibiyre, brambles, and fallen trees blocked our way. "Drop me in the brambles and then dash up and round. Without me I think you can make it." *I hope,* I silently added.

Cal must have been making the same calculations as he snorted, dipped his right shoulder, and suddenly took a turn, narrowly making it through brush to a spot he thought appropriate before dropping his left shoulder, sending me crashing to the ground, and running off as fast as he could—in the direction of the bear.

I knew that I was supposed to hide. I knew he was a hinny, not a person, but if I had learnt anything that day, it was the value of friends in whatever form they came. Watching him sacrifice himself was not on my agenda.

Searching around me, I grabbed the biggest rock I could find and launched it with everything I had. The pain that shot through my leg instantly knocked me to the ground, so I didn't see where my ammo landed, but an almighty roar told me I had hit the bear.

The ground rumbled and the roars increased, sending me rolling under the thick brambles as fast as I could—whilst simultaneously biting my vambrace as hard as I could to stop me crying out in agony.

I was too slow.

The bear's claws swiped across my right leg, dragging me backwards, and I screamed.

All pride, all hope, everything left me in that moment.

Suddenly the bear's roar altered—it sounded like it had a companion, like a duet.

The bear dropped me and I scrambled forward.

Roaring filled the valley.

Desperate for answers, I dared to look back.

Flames engulfed the bear's coat as it ran away with an orange fireball in its wake—a Pynyt-shaped orange-fireball.

Shaking my head, I chuckled, then collapsed.

TWENTY-ONE

The pain was unbelievable. Denial told me I just needed a minute, but when Pynyt flew to a branch and simply watched instead of telling me to follow, I knew my injuries were bad. When I finally dared to look at my leg, I cried.

I could not fail.

Not like this.

Nearby, the stream bubbled happily and I decided it was calling to me—it was either that or I was simply delirious. Keeping one eye on me at all times, Cal grazed close by. With each grunt or groan, his ear twitched in my direction, so I knew he was waiting for me to ask him for assistance, but the thought of climbing on him and falling off, even into water, terrified me.

I'd have to crawl.

The valley seemed peaceful, yet I knew other creatures could be lurking around any corner, so I forced myself to keep all expressions of pain to a murmur—maybe the occasional dull roar if I caught myself off guard. To aid with my stealth mode, I selected a small, sturdy stick and bit on it as I slowly navigated over the rocks and dragged myself into the water.

It worked for a few minutes, however, I underestimated the shock of water flowing into my cuts, so when blood and stream mixed, I slipped on a rock. Throwing out my arms. I saved myself from a full fall, but simultaneously bit down on the wood so hard that the stick splintered in my mouth, filling it with hundreds of tiny pieces of bark.

While I picked debris out of my mouth, blood trailed from my body, and I almost forgot it was mine as I watched the red streaks dance and dilute into the rippling water. Washing myself was an extra cruelty, but I did it until I was satisfied the dirt was out of my wounds. Honestly, I knew it wasn't perfect, but perfect wasn't on the cards that day.

Something splashed in a rockpool to my left, and I stared, waiting to identify the creature responsible. For a minute, my mind jumped between fearing what might be approaching, believing I was imagining things, and deciding it was simply a rush of water, but then the tail of a fish flicked above the surface, repeating the noise that had previously caught my attention.

Were I in better condition, I would have tried capturing the fish, but I had neither weapon, speed, nor energy on my side.

Relieved not to be under attack again, I pulled myself onto a large boulder beside the stream and stretched out like a starfish. It would have been incredibly easy to fall asleep and bake in the sun, yet my wish to live thankfully still overrode my desire to die—or more truthfully, my stubborn resolve to die trying was greater than my inclination to give up.

This is a trial, I whispered to myself. *Trials have solutions...*

A gentle splash, more like a plop or splosh, sounded next to me, causing me to sit up faster than my body would have preferred. My eyes danced, searching for the cause of the noise, but it wasn't until it started moving again that I realised I was next to a large tortoise.

She must have been observing me for a while because she didn't seem to share my need to stare. With a shell decorated like someone had painted a rockery on her back, the tortoise had the perfect camouflage. Back home, tortoises had beautiful patterns on their shells, yet I had never seen this variety before, so I added it to my list of things to ask about if I survived. The demonic Vampire Goblin had projected my sisters' voice, pretending that she was here, but in that moment—as I so often did when viewing nature—I thought how much Muriel would love this world. A soft chuckle bubbled out of me. She'd probably have pulled out her sketchbook and started drawing the tortoise and forgone her trial.

Totally unabashed by my presence, the tortoise made her way across the rock and into the nearest bush of hibiyre. Extending her wrinkly neck, she grabbed an enormous green leaf, and tugged at it, paused, then ceremoniously dropped it. Keeping an eye on me, she repeated the action. The third time, she waggled the leaf, then dropped it before moving to a blue petal and repeating the process all over again.

Enya's explanation of hibiyre suddenly replayed in my head.

"They're medicinal!" I declared, feverishly.

Seemingly satisfied that she had made her point, the tortoise grabbed a green bloom, yanked it from its plant, and proceeded to chew on it.

"Green fight infection, blue heal bones," I said to myself. As well as making a poultice, I remembered Enya talking about crushing them and making food with grass, but I had neither time nor skill to make the leaves more appetising. Ripping two green leaves, I ate them as quickly as I could. The tortoise might have liked them, but to me they were a little bitter and lacked appeal, but at least they weren't hideous to swallow.

Selecting the largest, most succulent blooms I could find on the bush, I collected green and blue flowers along with their leaves. All had exquisite patterns, like waves of colour drifting from the centre to the edge of each petal. None were smaller than dinner plates, but some were the size of two. My next problem was securing the leaves to me.

About twenty metres downstream, a tree dipped its roots into the water along with thick, hanging vines. *Nature provides everything,* I thought to myself with a smile—even if the inevitable pain travelling to the vines was nothing to smile about.

Screams repressed, backside dragged, and vines attained, I prepared to wrap my right leg in as much hibiyre as I could when the bright red blooms of another bush caught my eye.

Enya had been very clear in her warning about the red plants. *Too many have died looking for a quick cure* wasn't exactly a warning that most people would misinterpret. Yet I wasn't most people. Most people were not in the desperate, time-sensitive hurry that I was.

Red flowers will chase away fever faster, but you have to be strong enough to take their full, undiluted, effects. Enya's voice replayed in my mind and I wished that I had asked what the full effects entailed. Likewise, I wished I had asked how quickly they would work. However, quicker was quicker. Every second counted. City sieges would only last so long. The seventh son had to prove his worth...or at least test it.

Picking the red blooms, packing them under the green and blue, I doubted if I was strong enough. Oddly, I never questioned whether the flowers were actually able to do what Enya claimed. I'd never seen it, yet I believed it. I trusted in it. Possibly because I'd also never seen a horde of dragons, multi-coloured lightning that did not burn, nor had a tortoise, hinny, or Fyrewowwa guide me before either, yet all of those things existed here with apparent ease. Why would healing leaves be any different?

The leaves would work. I just had to survive them.

TWENTY-TWO

U nder the tree which overhung the stream, I took shelter from the sun but the fever—whether from my injuries or the poultice, I could not decide—was increasing by the minute. I had praised the Emberbyrg armour for being effective but light when I received it, however, by then everything stuck to me or poured from me horribly.

With nothing to cut through my leggings and totally unable to pull them down, I was double testing the abilities of my bandage although I had stuffed and wrapped hibiyre wherever I could. I even mushed up a leaf and squashed it into my hair, figuring something would find its way into the cuts. My boots were off—the left by standard means, and the right by gently undoing the straps the bear hadn't shredded and biting on a new stick to complete the task. My reward was paddling my feet in the running water.

After a while, fish began to swim close to me, causing my stomach to rumble. With a semi-sarcastic sounding hiss, Pynyt flew to a fallen branch and poked it with his foot before pulling on a vine with his mouth.

Half the members of my crew were better net-makers than me. Oryana, the girl Raine and I met when we first arrived, was certainly more skilful and I lamented not having her beautiful, fine net with me then, but I took the hint and made a vine net of sorts. Honestly, it was more of a panel, and any smaller fish would easily slip past it back into the stream, yet when a fiery red fish—a Fyre Fish—swam into my rockpool with three friends, I knew my efforts would be rewarded.

Pynyt flapped his wings with joy when the first fish panicked, landing itself on the rock beside him. He didn't require instruction, and promptly flame grilled and ate it. When the second fish popped out, I feared I was going to be the chef and not the diner, but rather than tucking in, Pynyt cooked it with a flash of fire, then stepped back, waiting for the next offering to jump out of the water.

By the time the fourth fish was cooked and laying under the tree, I was too tired to eat anything. My bag was going to eternally smell, but I placed two fish inside and stared at the third, willing it to slip into my stomach.

The sun was beginning to set and I was in a dangerous position for so many reasons, but none so lethal as the heat that burnt and ate at my leg. Whilst busy, I had tried to ignore the sensation, yet there was no denying it was increasing by the minute.

Sitting there, hoping for healing, fearing expedited judgement, my body battled itself. Giving up on eating, I slipped the third fish with the others, hoping that I would be able to eat something later. Pynyt sighed as I tied up the bag and I felt the weight of his disapproval almost as much as the gnawing furnace that my leg was becoming.

My clothes had dried, but I considered dipping myself back into the stream. I wasn't sure how that would affect the poultice, but if I didn't do something soon, I was going to rip it off anyway—or faint from the increasing drumming that was thundering in my head.

While I procrastinated, grumbling noises mixed with rustling branches in the trees behind me. Seconds earlier, holding my eyes open at all had been difficult, but now they flew open. Equally alarmed, Cal laid down beside me. I knew what he wanted—what we needed, but I was afraid to move.

Something hissed, yet it was not Pynyt. It was much bigger.

In his bid to distract the bear earlier, Cal had lost his saddle cloth somewhere in the jungle. By that point, it would have probably been more useful as a pillow, so when I used my last drop of energy to replace my boots and climb aboard my friend, I didn't even notice the cloth was gone—although that might have been because instead of attempting to swing myself into a sitting position, I laid across Cal like a dead body.

Honestly, it was the best I could do.

TWENTY-THREE

Dipping in and out of consciousness, I was vaguely aware of Cal's hurried pace and Pynyt riding my back like a jockey, whilst digging in his talons as he attempted to counterbalance my weight. Sometimes, I thought I saw the shadow of a creature behind us—or around a crevasse or hanging out a tree. They seemed to be everywhere. Sometimes they looked human and I thought about calling out to them, but the shadow man always disappeared as quickly as he came. Thankfully, so did the wild creatures that neither Cal nor I wanted to face.

Once darkness had covered the mountains, I had no idea of time, but I sweated like a block of butter in a hot pan. For a moment, I had rational thought: I felt awful. I knew I felt awful, but I also knew why. Then, in a blink of an eye, I forgot everything. The beast I was laid across had kidnapped me. Claws dug into every limb, tearing me apart, and my skin burnt as though someone had thrown me into a pit of fire. Desperation grasped my limbs and I thrashed out, completely lost my balance, and slid to the floor screaming.

Shadows danced around me. They wanted to eat me. They whispered their desires for foreign flesh. They argued on who would bite first while I cursed them using language so colourful that even old Alun, my ships' gunner, would have winced.

The shadow of a dragon loomed and the eye of a fireball formed in its mouth. From its shoulder a man with bright, green eyes looked down. His smile reached from ear to ear as he shouted, *Virisinigne is mine! Let the Flame cleanse the land of blue-eyed pretenders—and take their kin with it! Ignis pila!*

Sucking in one more breath, the dragon increased the size of the fireball in the back of its throat and released it in my direction. A furnace engulfed me. The intensity was unbelievable—too unbelievable.

Is this real? I asked myself, realising I still had clothes and skin—neither of which would withstand the temperatures my body thought it was experiencing. Not to mention the fact that death should have quickly followed.

"Cal?" I whispered. "Pynyt?" My limbs shivered and a cold sweat washed down my back. "Are you there? Please don't leave me."

A hiss whisked past my right ear, yet even in my state I knew it was not Pynyt—for he only sat on my left. My hand instinctively flacked at the unseen creature and my stomach immediately twisted. The hiss repeated in response to my touch. My arm recoiled, eager to get away from the smooth scales of the Pilgrim Punisher snake.

"Pynyt! Ignis pila!" I screamed, using words from my hallucination, somehow expecting him to understand what I did not.

A bright orange glow burst out, sending the Pilgrim Punisher backwards at high speed. Gasping for air, I watched its smouldering tail retreat just as a new shadow crept around a set of trees to my right.

Hallucination or real? was becoming a particularly exhausting game. I had no voice, no fight to give. Sitting back, for better or worse, I waited for the answer to present itself.

The new shadow broke into a run. The sound of hooves increased by the second and a body knocked into me, sending new bolts of pain through my frazzled nerves.

Teeth lifted me by the collar of my armour, swinging me into the creature's side—Cal's side. But, registering his hair and form too late, I missed. Cal snorted impatiently, repeating the action, this time skimming the skin of my neck with his teeth. Blocking out the pain, I caught myself, laying across him as fast as I could.

Approaching footsteps vibrated through the soil.

My shadow attacker was big—very big.

"Are they real?" I called out.

Wings flapped, sending air and words abruptly into my ear. *"Hold on."*

Cal raced towards the pitch-black hole of a cave. In any other circumstances, I would have got off or at least tried to reason with him before entering another cave, but the pounding roars were increasing and I didn't want to find out who they belonged to.

The ground began to shake.

Pebbles, then boulders bounced.

The looming shadow was gaining on us.

Now seemed like an especially horrid time for the Empress to rage again and it became a thousand times worse when, in the semi-moonlight haze, I saw a boulder dashing down the mountain towards us.

As the earthquake continued, more rocks broke loose, combining together to speed up their descent, while the approaching beast snapped branches and logs alike, making my empty stomach want to vomit. Cal's ears flicked, and in that moment I knew he had judged our odds and made a decision. Giving one final push, he galloped into the cave with the whoosh and clatter of falling debris sounding our arrival.

Screeching nails and frustrated roars echoed as the beast skidded to a halt. Then silence fell. Whether the beast stopped before, after, or during the rocks landing was impossible to tell because with no light, I couldn't even see my own hand.

There, in the total darkness, I was blind again.

My last hope was that this unknown hollow in the rock had another exit, but as pain, exhaustion, and anxiety mixed together, even being caved-in couldn't keep me conscious.

Twenty-Four

I woke up shivering next to a fire and my head resting against Cal's neck. In the dim light, I could see I was still in the cave, but I had no idea how long we had been there. Slowly pushing myself upright, I rubbed my bleary eyes and Cal stood up, vigorously shaking himself as though he had been desperate to do that for some time. A wave of guilt and gratitude hit me. Giving him pins and needles wasn't on my to-do list, but his unwavering care was appreciated beyond measure because without him and Pynyt I would have died several times.

"Where's Pynyt?" I asked, anxiously. Presumably my living box-of-matches had started the fire for me, so he must have made it into the cave, however, I couldn't see him.

In response, Cal nickered softly, but made no effort to point in any direction.

"We need to keep moving. I know I am a burden, but I must reach the Empress as soon as possible. Do you know a way out of here?" Only a few days earlier, I would have mocked anyone who spoke to animals quite so openly. I never doubted they had thoughts or feelings, but I would have whole-heartedly declared they understood less than humans—were less than humans.

How wrong I was.

Muriel, aged eight, whilst sitting amongst her bees, told me, *You don't need words to speak, Niall. You only need ears to listen.*

A chuckle rippled out of my dry mouth. *I am only now learning what my sister told me years ago.* My brothers mocked her for her sensitive ways—to my shame, so did I sometimes, even if I meant it less than they did—but Mother was right to push for baby number eight, for Muriel was worth more than all of us put together.

Cal's ears twitched, facing into what I thought was deeper into the cave. Straining my ears, I tried to focus on whatever he could hear, but all seemed quiet. My mouth opened to question him, but a wry smile spread across my face instead. *You only need ears to listen.*

When Cal relaxed, the tension in my body released a little. Part of me wished it hadn't because every inch of me began to quake uncontrollably—making the shivers that woke me feel comparatively toasty.

Covering myself in red hibiyre had seemed like an acceptable gamble hours earlier. In my mind, a great trial equalled a great, speedy reward. The reality was a great trial equalled a speedy decline in abilities, burning and frozen skin, and—if Enya's warning was true—death.

My resolve waned.

Ripping at the leaves, I tried to remove them.

Tried being the operative word.

The vines and outer, green leaves came away with relative ease. With a greater degree of effort, some of the green and blue blooms peeled, however, the red blooms held in place as though they were part of my actual skin. Attempting to cut into them with my nails hurt as much as it would if I had taken a knife to my own flesh.

In the fire light, the blue petals seemed to shine like ice while the red danced like the blaze in front of me. In response, my skin flushed hot to cold, cold to hot, and back again. The resulting sensation morphed from extreme numbness to agonising pain.

Bitterly, my mind repeated Enya's warning: *You have to be strong enough to take their full, undiluted, effects.*

Clearly, I overestimated myself.

Enya was strong enough, I was sure of it, but I was not worthy of her comparison. Groaning, I felt stupid thinking of the princess beyond my station, even if only briefly. She had held my hand knowing she broke through the darkness and gave me sight to climb onto Cal, that was it. An act of kindness. I was the seventh son, and she, as the anointed Maiden, was called by duty—maybe pity and curiosity too—but no more.

In every aspect, my actions were foolish, but my resolve to send meaningful, powerful help to Virisinigne had remained until that moment—until the moment when death and defeat seemed unavoidable.

Cal pawed the ground, flicking dust and loose sticks into the fire, making it crackle. I appreciated his efforts to warm me up, but my skin felt like a pulverised prune and I was pretty sure it had reached a point of withering beyond use.

Frustrated, Cal swished his tail, pinned back his ears, snorted, and pawed the ground again. Embers danced out of the fire towards me, fizzling out as they landed on my body.

"Hey!" I groaned, just in time for Cal to throw more fiery dirt in my direction.

There was a certain irony about me wrapping half of my body in leaves, being set alight, and then dying. Perhaps it was a method of burial in this world. *Wrap up and burn.*

More flecks of fire hit me—landing on the leaves and dancing into oblivion without remotely scolding the hibiyre.

The rest of Enya's warning came to me: *They are very hot, so are rarely used in their pure, natural state. Red hibiyre flowers will chase away fever faster, but you have to be strong enough to take their full, undiluted, effects. If you understand the balance and use any of the hibiyre correctly, they are a blessing, but too many have died looking for a quick cure.*

I had taken her words as literal, but in the wrong way—or at least missed the double meaning.

Pushing myself onto my feet, I struggled not to fall. My vision whirled as my head spun, yet my thoughts became oddly clear. The balance of any trial is to experience the effects but then rise above—to push through.

Or, as all in this world came back to Flame and fire, *to burn.*

Cal turned his whole head, pricking his ears forward as he paused to focus on something coming within the cave.

Interest, not fear struck him, but it didn't matter, my next step would either solve my problem or finish me.

Taking a single stride, I walked into the fire just as Pynyt came shooting around the corner.

He let out an almighty hiss, circling me.

Flames licked up my legs, creeping into every part of my body. I felt no pain—no extra pain, for I was already painfully numb. *"Ignis pila,"* I whispered, raising my eyes to the ceiling.

Hearing my request, Pynyt clicked his tongue, throwing out a single burst of fire into my face. Every cell on my body tingled, and I felt something fall away. Looking down, I saw the hibiyre leaves laying in the fire. As if in slow motion, they began to fade away, producing a sweet, spicy aroma as they went.

Stepping out of the fire, my energy renewed.

If given a million years and the language of every man, beast, and the Flame, I doubt I could amply describe how clean, how fresh, I felt.

My armour was still torn, but not burnt, and my skin was one. Only ripples, like waves, laid where huge gashes had previously been.

Swinging my leg over Cal's back, I sat up straight.

"Flamma nobiscum," said Pynyt, landing on my left shoulder.

Smiling, I asked, "What does that mean?"

"The Flame is with us."

TWENTY-FIVE

The cave was long and dark, but at that point I was so overwhelmed by what had happened, I didn't mind the blind faith required to follow the path that Pynyt assured me was there.

With my strength renewed, my hunger returned. Thankfully, despite the madness, I had held onto my bag and the three fish—although somewhat battered around—were still intact. How I didn't eat all three, I do not know. I was certainly hungry enough. Pynyt intensely watched me pull out the fish, so I passed half and expected him to be satisfied because it was bigger than him, yet after expertly swallowing it, Pynyt turned to me for the rest. Everything about this world was different, so rather than assuming Cal wasn't a pescatarian, I offered him a fish, too. The resulting snort was very close to laughter, so I took that as a no, and ate it myself. I could have happily eaten the third fish, but as this journey was unpredictable at best and I had no idea when I would see food again, I left it for later.

Fish had made up a large portion of my diet for over a decade and I was never sorry about that. In fact, when on land I would still choose seafood over most meat dishes, but the red-fleshed Fyre Fish was unlike anything I had ever tasted. Possibly it was the result of dehydration and starvation. Possibly a crust of stale bread and mouldy cheese would have tasted like it was a banquet by then, but I don't think so. Fyre Fish, just like everything else blessed with any kind of fire, was *extra*.

Extraordinary.

When light began to creep into the cave, I was almost sorry for it. I wouldn't miss the lingering fear that another Vampire Goblin was about to attack me, but my trust in my companions, coupled with the wonder of surviving red hibiyre hallucinations and acid-like burning had given me a certain level of reassurance that I hadn't previously experienced.

Colours springing from the walls caught my attention as paintings came into view. Had I unlimited time, I might have requested going back with a torch to see if I had been missing them all the way, but it wasn't to be. Forwards was my only option. I did, however, crane my neck so I could see as much as I could, for as long as I could.

Similar to the illustrations in the Foco Temple, the paintings told tales. The Foco Temple seemed to be focused on events around and during the Dividing War, acting as a history lesson, warning, and celebration all in one cavern. This cave, which was more of a tunnel, seemed to honour and celebrate the blessing and balance of life with the Flame—and dragons. Looking at the charred edges of the painting, I wasn't even sure that dragons hadn't either assisted with the production of the painting or given their seal (scorch) of approval afterwards.

While the first painting I saw depicted Mount Liekke, complete with wafting smoke, dragons circling, and humans dancing in the light at the foot of the mountain, the opposite wall was the reverse. At first, I thought it was Virisinigne, but the landscape wasn't right. When I saw Liekke drawn in the far-distance, I realised it was the kingdoms on the other side of the volcano. The ones in this world who live without the protection of the dragons and do not follow the Flame. The original artist didn't seem to be against their choices. If anything, light from the opposite wall seemed to be projecting across the tunnel pathway, blessing them anyway. However, a second, more recent artist appeared to have visited, adding dark rain clouds over the cities.

I was so absorbed in the images, I didn't realise we had reached the end of the cave until we were standing outside. The hot, heavy air immediately hit me, as did the view. Unlike the other side of the mountain, there was no sweeping valley and bubbling stream—not at our level, at any rate. Way, way below us were trees, but the path that we now travelled on was narrow and crumbled easily. Watching pebbles freefall into the canopy below made the fish in my stomach flip beyond the grave.

Gazing anxiously ahead, I hoped to see an end to this tightrope highway, but it stretched before me without end, winding its way around the mountain, linking to the next one until I could see no further.

The more exposed we were, the stronger the wind became—the gruellingly hot wind. Although I was thankful not to be feverish *and* trying to hold onto Cal for dear life, I am ashamed to confess how quickly my resolve waned again.

Keep your eyes on the path ahead. Only ahead, I repeated to myself.

Around the second mountain, a few trees bravely hugged the cliff edge, making a step of sorts to any creatures who could climb well, but for the likes of Cal and me, there was only one path available.

Pebbles scattered behind us and Cal came to an abrupt halt with his ears rotated backwards.

Twisting my neck, I glanced behind us.

Gulping, I turned forwards.

"Go, Cal, go," I whispered, nudging his sides with my heels.

Like a statue, Cal stood still.

Clicking my tongue, I nudged him again. "Cal, walk on."

He didn't budge.

My heart raced.

It made no sense. This hinny had unfalteringly carried me through everything, but now, when we were faced with undeniable danger, he stood still.

Then the possibility that this was another hallucination crossed my mind. Maybe this wasn't so undeniable...

I turned around again. How could I tell? Shout, *here, kitty, kitty,* and see what happens?

In the midst of my fear, reason slapped me. No, even if it was twice the size of any lynx I had seen in Virisinigne, I knew the creature behind me *was* a lynx—and Cal *was* watching it.

Enya said I would know when Cal had taken me far enough and I should get off. *This can't be it*, I muttered under my breath. It might have been me manifesting truth rather than believing it, but I had a point. The path simply wasn't wide enough. To get anywhere, Cal had to go forwards as much as I did, even if it was just to turn around. So, unless Cal was secretly planning to bring me this far so he could throw me off this mountain, I wasn't getting off.

Unfortunately, if the enormous lynx wanted to go up the mountain too, he was also going to have to use the path.

Where we were, there was no such thing as, *I'll just step aside and quietly let him pass.*

But gauging by his expression, *passing* was not on his agenda.

Dinner was.

The lynx's eyes were the definition of focused as it stalked up the dry, rocky path. Each paw was placed with perfect precision. It would stalk us until the end of the track or kill us here. With such agility, it wasn't going to fall before we were.

"Walk on! Trot on! Yah-Yah!—*Run!*" My mind charged through every known animal call to move I could think of. My mouth repeated them in a crazed loop, adding in clicks and whoops, while I twitched and wriggled my legs.

Still nothing from Cal, not even a snort.

Just ears back, body frozen.

"Pynyt! Do something!" I pleaded. "Scorch the lynx!"

Pynyt took flight, but instead of flying towards the golden-brown cat, he hovered in front of me. *"Fire is everywhere, but burning is not always the answer,"* he said, then flew off.

"What?" I gasped, equally astonished at Pynyt's full sentence as I was at his disappearance. Trying to kick Cal on, I pleaded with him again. "Move! Please, Cal, move! If not for me, save yourself!"

As it continued its advance, the black lines of the lynx's exquisite coat gently rose and fell with each, flawlessly calculated step. It was clear they were in no hurry. With size, strength, and speed on their side, not to mention location, they knew they had us.

"Hold on," said a new voice—inside my head.

My blood ran cold. "Cal?" I whispered.

"Patience."

Patience wasn't my strong suit, and this seemed like a monumentally bad time to exercise it anyway. Back home, everyone said that donkeys and mules were stubborn, and the thought that hinnies were no better flashed through my brain when every muscle in Cal's body tightened beneath me. The lynx effortlessly pushed off with its hind legs, springing into the air with such grace that I'm sure if I were not its target, I would have marvelled at its beauty. Instead, instinct made me cower whilst gripping Cal's chest and neck tighter—bracing myself for the oncoming claws which I had seen primed to dig into my back.

With a violent jolt, my hold was challenged as Cal flicked his hind upwards, squealing sharply as his hooves pounded into the lynx's chest. As his feet returned to the ground, he squealed again, and took three, jerky steps forward to catch his balance before stopping with a snort. It felt like fifty.

Shocked, I checked the path.

It was clear.

If it wasn't for the scuff marks in the dirt, I would doubt if any of it had actually happened.

With a gentle toss of his head, Cal recommenced on the path without a sound. My mind had questions, but my heart was still firmly lodged in my throat, so I remained silent as I desperately searched for the lynx. I needed to know where it was. Dead or alive. I couldn't rest without knowing if it was likely to come back or not. Obviously dead was the preferred option, but to my surprise, I felt guilty about that. It had attacked us, but I was in its territory and I didn't need to eat it. Captain Brooks, the first captain I sailed under, had instilled that respect in me.

"Be part of the circle of life, not the blunt edge," he said when I was a teen, clipping me around the ear for trying to catch more fish than we needed. "Only take what you must."

Captain Brooks' was long gone now, but his ethos remained etched into my soul. It wasn't the ethos of most princes, I grant you, but then again, I wasn't like most princes, was I?

Staring down into the canyon, I finally spotted the outline of a lynx laying across a boulder.

Sighing with relief that the ordeal was over, I leaned forward and patted Cal's neck.

Cal snorted, sounding rather pleased with himself.

"Thank you, I should never have doubted you."

He snorted again.

"Yeah, okay, I'm sorry," I said, continuing to pat him. "How was I to know you were going to kick him?" Suddenly laughter rippled out of me as I remembered Uryah translating Cal's name. "Ah, of course, the clue was there all along! Calcibus always *kicks*."

TWENTY-SIX

Pynyt returned minutes later. Gauging from the direction he appeared from, he had been watching from above. I wanted to chastise him for deserting me, but instead I chastised myself.

This was my trial, not his.

"Am I particularly bad at this?" I asked my companions. Neither answered, so I carried on, "If you graded me right now, do you think I'd pass?" I paused, hoping a voice would come, but in their silence I concluded they only used that ability on extra special occasions—which was preferable to me imagining they could talk. "Prince Aydan finished his trial in-record time and Princess Enya was only twelve. Do children have easier pilgrimages?"

"No," said Pynyt, giggling.

Deciding reptiles shouldn't be able to giggle, especially not at my expense, I wished he had remained silent—or I had.

For what I thought was about an hour, we travelled without uttering a word. The breeze and the occasional bird of prey was all I could hear beyond the sound of unshod hooves. My legs ached from sitting still for so long and my back was wet with sweat again, but I refused to complain after what Cal had done for me.

The track widened a little, but it was still a treacherous path of stone—beautiful, multi-coloured stone, but stone, nonetheless. Some of the mountains had patchy vegetation on their peaks or they rolled into another layer of jungle, but the one we were travelling up had a hard, rocky summit. Cal had proven himself again and again, but the way the incline increased above us, I doubted whether even he could safely navigate his way up it for much longer. I also doubted if gravity wouldn't claim me from his back if he tried.

Previously, a cave or new path or peak had presented itself and Cal had simply turned off, however, this time I couldn't see anything. In my heart, I knew that the point where Cal would leave me was coming. It had to be. In many ways, this cheered me, it meant I was a step closer to completion, to reaching the Empress and begging her for the help Virisinigne was so desperately waiting for.

But it also meant going it alone.

Although perfectly camouflaged with the mountain so it wasn't visible until close-up, a semi-submerged, circular boulder laid in the path up ahead. We had passed hundreds, if not thousands of rocks and boulders on the various paths, and although I was fascinated by the foreign colours and formations, none grasped my attention like this one. It was smooth—perfectly smooth—as though it has been rolled for centuries by the sea.

Cal circled the boulder, then paused beside it, brushing my left foot over its surface. Once above it, I could see the scorched flame emblem of Benegnyem with the inscription:

To achieve enlightenment, focus on the path, not the obstacles.

If animals had on and off switches, in that moment, someone switched Cal off. His bottom lip drooped and quivered, and he rested a hind leg, preparing himself for sleep—or taking a power nap. I couldn't blame him, he must have been exhausted, but I was reluctant to get off. And, gazing at the crumbly path which sprawled above me, I wasn't sure I wanted to climb.

A great wind raced around the mountain, howling as it danced around my head. Screams from home mixed in and the temperature rose to the point I expected to see steam rising. My limbs trembled as I tried to discern if this was a message from the Flame, from home, or from within. Realising the message was the same, regardless of the source, I swung my leg over Cal's back, landing two feet onto the blazing emblem, and bowed my head.

"I guess this is it," I said, affectionately stroking the side of Cal's face as he leaned into me. "Thank you, my friend." My voice crackled, and I was surprised by the level of honest emotion I felt.

Pynyt shuffled on my shoulder and I feared he was going to leave me, too.

"Are you off as well?" I asked, raising my free hand to pet his face. The contrast of hinny hair and Fyrewowwa scales wasn't lost on me, but neither was the appreciation of friendship in whatever form it came.

After a moment, Pynyt stretched his neck, bobbed his head, and took off. Simultaneously, Cal nickered and began walking back down the mountain.

"*Flamma vobiscum,*" I whispered, brushing a tear away. Two voices echoed in my head. "*Flamma nobiscum.*"

TWENTY-SEVEN

Afraid that my emotions would overwhelm me, I refused to watch my friends walk and fly away. Turning my back to them, I stretched out my muscles, took a deep breath, and began my ascent of the mountain. Pebbles crumbled under my fingers and dust wedged under my nails, but with a clear path before me, I slowly-but-surely made my way up the increasingly-vertical track.

When a rock tumbled down a harsher area to my right, I froze. My skin tingled as though I was being watched. Grasping my fingers into the rock to the point of it being painful, I was sure something—someone—was there, yet I couldn't see anything bigger than a beetle. Left with the choice of numb fingers or moving, I reluctantly dismissed the gut feeling of looming danger, and carried on.

After a few minutes, another rock tumbled. This time it was a little further away on an even steeper slope, but again I paused, desperately trying to focus on the blended white, grey, green, and blue layers of rock, searching for life. A breeze looped around and passed me, fluttering my hair as it went. Then, as their scraggy coats waved in the wind, I saw them, staring at me.

At first, I thought there were two, but the longer I looked, the more I counted. For me, it was an unexpected place to find a herd of goats, but as they seemed to be quite comfortable, I decided they were mountain goats and not in need of any kind of rescue. Not that I was in the position to offer them rescue had they needed it.

Why they chose to eat in such precarious places baffled me until I remembered the lynx and suddenly wispy plants in difficult spots became more appealing. I still felt judged as their climbing skills clearly outweighed mine, but as they were not trying to kill me, I gratefully continued without feeling the need to check over my shoulder every five seconds.

Hauling myself over the final ledge onto the summit, I wasn't really sure what to expect. I was fairly sure I wasn't on Liekke Peak, but I hoped it was close—or that the path to it was at least obvious because otherwise, without Cal, I was effectively travelling blind again.

Gazing around me, I was both pleased and disappointed. The positive was I could see Liekke Peak and it *was* the next mound over. The negative was, I had uneven, boulder-filled ground, shrubs, trees, the onset of a waterfall, and a number of dragons in between me and Liekke.

Quietly making my way towards a cluster of rocks, I peered around the corner towards the waterfall. As the faint rumble of water reached me, a map suddenly began to form in my mind, and I admired the gorgeous view of

Liekke Valley from a new angle—including the Tailfeather where Enya and I had stood two days prior. At least I thought it was two days ago.

It felt like a lifetime.

To my far left, in front of the wooded area, a slightly easier track seemed to wind up the mountain towards the other side of the waterfall. *The tourist route,* I thought to myself, remembering Lord Byrne's words to Rhys.

Shielding my eyes from the sun, I searched for the quickest route up Liekke. *There are many ways up, but only one good way down.* I wasn't sure if that thought was purely my own or a melancholy combination of Uryah and Enya's earlier discussion, but it rang in my mind anyway. Enya had said there was only one way to enlightenment, but in the glimmering heat, it was easier to imagine pilgrims tumbling to their deaths when they were found to be unworthy rather than anyone making it to the summit. Judging by the ominous expression of the enormous black dragon flying away from the far side of the volcano, I was certain he'd happily give any wayward travellers a one-way ticket to the ground.

As I saw it, I had two choices: carry on and climb through the night or find shelter near the base of the peak and climb at first light. Had I been with my crew, I would have opted for the latter. Rest, food, and fresh legs would always be preferable and any sleep would have been safe as we took turns to be on-watch. However, there I was alone, in a hurry, and as vulnerable in one scenario as I was the other.

As if to press my point, a dragon the size of a carriage flew over, angling its head with unnerving interest in my direction. Running was pointless. It would either catch me in seconds or chase me into the path of another dragon—which wouldn't be hard as they were dotted around everywhere.

The dragon kept going, but I needed a plan.

No, I thought to myself. *I need to keep moving.*

My mouth was drier than the rock I stood on and I could feel a disgusting layer of dehydrated spittle forming in the corners of my lips. With a solution to my immediate issue so close, I headed for water, hoping that no one took offence to my presence or felt the need to investigate my movements.

As a child, my long-suffering, ancient tutor always told me to walk with purpose. "Even if you are going nowhere, always look like you are walking somewhere. Remember, you have direction, you have rights. Own it."

At the time, he was trying to turn me into a presentable prince and I had no idea I would ever be heeding his instruction whilst standing in a foreign world surrounded by almighty, fire-breathing lizards, however, his counsel seemed to have value, so instead of skulking from boulder to boulder, I walked in the open.

Closing the gap between thirst and hydration, I found myself daydreaming of the cool, refreshing liquid that waved at me in the sunlight. The sound of flowing water grew louder and louder, hampering my ability to hear, but filling me with hope.

It wasn't until I was almost upon it that the waters' activity struck me as unusual. Waterfalls were busy places, they were loud, but they also tended to have rivers or streams running into them. This was a lake. A lake above the larger one in Liekke Valley. A lake with a natural fountain of water bubbling in the centre—plus a cloud of hot mist rising above it.

Virisinigne had hot springs, but nothing like this. Not on this scale. It was as though the volcano was filtering water from deep beneath the world's crust and throwing it into the lake specifically for its heat-loving companions to drink and bathe in.

Finding a quieter spot away from the waterfall, I ate my last fish by the shore before washing my hands and face. Despite the hot day making me think I wanted ice-cold water, it was the perfect temperature. Whilst dipping my head to drink from my cupped hands, I spotted movement behind me. Turning slowly, hoping they were small *and* friendly, I was greeted by rabbit-sized hairy creatures with rounded ears and incredibly cute faces.

Unlike rabbits, they walked instead of hopped, had short legs, and no tail. They also had no fear of me. Making high-pitched noises that sounded like a song, they chatted to one another, glancing at me, then back to one another.

Mesmerised, I didn't move, and before I knew it, twenty of the furry animals sat around me, chirping happily—or at least I think they were happy. Having drunk enough and conscious of time, I stood up, trying to map my next path out in my mind. As if the creatures had been waiting to direct me, the one with the longest, black, tan, and white hair shuffled up to me, poked my right boot, squeaked, and began walking towards some scrubs.

In hindsight, given all the strange things that had happened to me, I should have realised I was being guided sooner, but the poor thing had to repeat its action, each time walking away singing while I smiled, thinking to myself *ah, how cute*. On its fourth attempt, it walked up to my foot, bit my boot, and walked away grumbling. The bite marked the leather, but mercifully only pinched my toe. I didn't wait for the fifth occasion to find out if their teeth could penetrate leather.

Satisfied I was finally paying attention, the creature escorted me to a bush filled with purple, blue, and green berries. My mouth instantly watered. Had they been red, I would have been wary, regardless of how delicious they looked because over the years I had heard too many stories of hungry peasants eating red berries and either getting sick or dying. My own uncle, a man of great wit, but little industry besides hunting and wooing women who he should not, had the most disgusting diarrhoea after eating berries he 'found' on a walk. I was only eight at the time, but his description of the effects was so vivid that it remained with me twenty years later.

A juicy treat with natural sugars seemed like the perfect thing to set me off on what I was hoping would be the final leg of my journey, so I picked a purple berry and a burst of flavour filled my mouth.

Reaching for more was a no brainer.

Enjoying the flavour of the purple berries, I probably had a dozen or more whilst I continued to marvel at the multi-coloured creatures by my feet. Some of the fruit was low enough for them to reach, but I wondered if I was supposed to pay them for their services by picking a few. Plucking one, I offered it to the creature who bit my boot, and they immediately took it. Chuckling, I picked a few more berries, feeding each animal—or trying to because when I offered a blue berry, it was rejected. One looked as tasty as another to me, so I popped it into my mouth. Suddenly the creatures started singing in a higher, sharper tone whilst scuttling around my feet frantically.

"Hey! Quit it!" Rather than stopping, they just attracted more friends and I began to fear who or what else they might call the attention of with their chorus. "What's wrong?" I asked, collecting more berries and scattering them on the ground. "Here, eat!" I said, popping another berry into my mouth.

I expected them to be distracted by the food, but they continued their frenzied dance. My vision suddenly began to falter and colour flashed on and off as though day and night were controlled by the mere flick of a switch. As the colour faded away, the pattern of the dance made sense. There was no frenzy. It was distress. The purple berries were treated with glee, the green berries indifference—and the blue ones were rolled away.

Sticking my fingers down my throat, I gagged, trying my hardest to be sick. By the time I had reproduced anything, my eyes were streaming and my face was blood-red—or I assumed it was because I couldn't see my face any more than I could detect colour.

Everything was grey.

With no idea whether this was temporary or permanent, and my heart thumping so hard I thought I might be sick all over again, I made my way back to the lake and rinsed out my mouth. Would more purple berries help? Which *are* the purple ones? Would I go blind again? Without Cal, I would surely die. *Failure,* screamed my inner voice. *You are a complete failure. You were told to be on your guard and listen. What part of them screeching at you didn't you think was a message?*

The inner voice was mine but the tone sounded remarkably like my father just before he packed me off to sea as a teen. He had one son too many and wanted me out of the way—until he sent for me, asking for help, providing me with the call home that I had unwittingly longed for. Except I had failed that mission too.

The scenery around me jigged as though coloured by living, foggy particles. Even the stationary volcano peak buzzed with grey beads. Any and everything had lost its brilliance.

Close by—too close—a dragon hissed. It was answered by a roar. Unimpressed, the hiss intensified, and the roaring was accompanied by pounding feet. The little rodent-like creatures simultaneously let out a panicked *squueeee* and ran away.

They were surprisingly fast, but I stayed as close to the retreating animals as I could, hoping they would lead me to safety. We passed rocks, shrubs, and boulders alike—all of which they could have hidden underneath even if I could not—until we reached boulders lining the base of Liekke Peak. There, wedged between the ground and the rock, were multiple holes the size of my fist. My heart sank as every single one of my guides disappeared, leaving me in my monochromatic world.

Checking there wasn't a large tunnel entrance, I paced around the boulders. When my eyes landed on letters etched in the stone above more rodent-sized tunnels, I groaned at the message:

Cavernpigs will show you healthy snacks but heed their warnings and do not mix berries.

Reactions will vary.

Some are temporary.

If you're dead, they're not.

There and then, I vowed that if I survived my pilgrimage, I would vehemently complain to Lord Byrne. "A warning notice by the bushes full of toxic berries might be more useful than where these cavernpigs hide *after* they have given up on me!" I sarcastically declared as though he could hear me.

But I didn't need Lord Byrne to hear me to hear his answer. *If we gave you a guide before each test, it wouldn't be much of a pilgrimage, would it?*

Wiping beads of sweat from my brow, I gazed at my fingers, searching for colour beyond varying shades of grey. The best I could do was hope that my punishment for not listening was temporary as the sign said it might be. I wasn't dead, so that at least was a bonus.

The ferocious sounds of the dragons arguing rumbled again. Either disinterested in me or distracted by their disagreement, they hadn't followed, but waiting to see if either one found me wasn't on the cards. Nor was attempting to sleep through the night.

No, my choices were no longer left or right, black or white.

They were grey.

And the only way was up.

TWENTY-EIGHT

Although I had no idea how often pilgrims travelled up the peak, I was still surprised that there didn't seem to be a set pathway up it. There wasn't even any evidence of animals wandering beyond my current position. *Because only dragons dare go there and they fly.* I shuddered, trying to ignore the fact I was petrified of the idea of attempting to interact with a dragon, let alone with the Empress—who by all accounts was not only enormous, but was not in a good mood.

Climbing the first fifty metres up the peak was relatively easy. Ledges and holes were peppered all over the rock, and I was spoilt for choice. However, when I reached the first significant ledge, the rock type changed. Even with my altered vision, I could see it shine as millennia of dormant layers of lava rested resplendently—each displaying what was and what could be, were it not for the presence of dragons and the mercy of the Flame. Lower down the mountain range, the hardened lava and ash had given way to other rock types, soils, and plants, giving new life in different forms, but up here, at the top of the world, a beacon of the divine remained in all its fiery glory.

The temperature rose with every inch I climbed, and the air became thinner and thinner. Again, the idea that a twelve-year-old girl completed this unaided amazed and shamed me—but even though struggling wounded my pride, having spent the short amount of time with Enya that I had, my gut told me she was the exception, not the rule.

Whenever I could, I rested on a ledge and assessed the track I was on. Reliable visibility beyond a few metres was non-existent, making true planning impossible. The angle of the peak made it equally difficult to measure how far I had travelled—or how far I had to go. I only looked down once, and that was definitely enough, so when a ring of cloud descended around the peak, preventing my doubting eyes from faltering, I was grateful.

All I knew, all I needed to know, was I could not stay where I was.

The smooth appearance of the rock was deceptive because it made me think it would be kinder to my body. Every time I relaxed, random jagged pieces seemed to cut into me, reminding me to keep up my guard. By the time I had paused on the fourth large ledge, my hands, arms, and knees were a bloodied mess. As I set off again, my fingers began to protest with each new grip, forcing me to repeat the mantra I used to shout at new deckhands when they complained: *It's mind over matter...if I do not mind, it does not matter.* Shaking my head, I acknowledged the irony in chanting my own tease—which in truth, I had stolen from Captain Brooks. Over the years, my old captain was full of good sayings, but I was introduced to that one on my first day when I tried to play the *but I'm a prince* card.

"It didn't matter then and it doesn't matter now," I said, out loud. "I have to do what is needed of me. This is no place for doubt and inaction." Somewhere up that peak, my voice turned to Captain Brooks', and his command kept my arms and legs in rhythm as I powered upwards.

The next ledge looked unremarkable as I approached it. The rock was still the same smooth-but-not shiny set lava, but as I pulled myself onto it the stone began to shimmer as though living particles were trapped under a sheet of glass. Even in grey, it was mesmerising, but with full vision, I think I would have seen colours radiating into the sky. With no one to ask and nothing to do with my concerns, I paused for a minute, caught my breath, and carried on.

As if the wind wanted to test my resolve it suddenly changed direction and increased in speed. Within the accompanying cloud, shadows swooped and danced, disappeared, and swooped again. Being a step behind was becoming a regular occurrence on that journey, but when one shadow skimmed my shoulders, I realised I had been joined by dragons.

Wild dragons.

My heart raced, and my limbs sprang into action, eager not to be hanging on the side of a volcano when they decided to stop swooping and try to grab me.

Roaring bursts of fire circled the volcano. The sound alone was enough to turn my bowels to liquid and warp all my future dreams into nightmares—if I survived at all. Two heads poked out of the cloud below me, hovering as they faced one another. Pausing, I saw their mouths open and watched as leaping flames met in the middle, forming a dancing blaze which licked the soles of my feet. Crying out, I scrambled higher, and the dragons held their position, continuing to ignite the air below me—making me question whether they were spurring me on or trying to make me fall.

Both, my inner voice screamed. *Keep moving!*

When my fingers curled over the top of the summit, I didn't even realise I was there. The cloud was so dense I couldn't see, but the flames stopped, allowing me to hear the whistling wind and slowly flapping wings.

Enya had said they would come, but I expected to be able to see them—for one to gently come forward. No, not expected. *Hoped.* I had hoped that reaching the summit would bring clarity to all the hints and nods, to the half sentences, and the strange happenings that I had experienced on my way.

With all these things in my mind, what the top of the volcano looked like hadn't really figured in my thoughts. From the snippets of information I had heard of volcanoes, I presumed there was some kind of vent or crater, some place the lava flowed from when the volcano was active—and where I would find the Empress.

I was not expecting to be transported home.

The castle grounds were extensive and as a child I thoroughly enjoyed disappearing into them. I knew where my brothers, cousins, and their friends would be. I knew where I was expected to be. I always went the opposite way. Only my sister ever learnt the location of my favourite hideaway—and that was because I took her there. Just before I was shipped away for good, I made her promise to guard our secret and cherish it. Last year, she wrote me a letter telling me her firstborn had taken her first steps by our favourite oak tree. Sat in my quarters, I cried like a baby, imagining the scene, wishing I was there, if only for a moment.

Now I was.

Muriel and her daughter were playing on the other side of the pond, laughing and calling to me as though my appearance was the most natural thing in the world. Trick or not, I ran towards them, but as I approached, screams rang out, sending birds scattering, and instantly smoke billowed through the trees.

The sound of crackling, burning wood closed in as I reached my sister. Her eyes were wide with fear as I pulled her and my niece into a tight hug.

"They're coming," she whispered solemnly into my chest.

Then they were gone.

In a blink of an eye, I was in the castle, gazing out the tower window across the city of Tecta. The normally busy streets were empty, while soldiers stood on every corner and manned lookout posts. Archers prepared their arrows and guards sharpened their blades. The rooftops were all doused, presumably to prevent them from burning, but in the distance outer towns and villages smouldered next to the mighty army that my father had declared could never be formed.

"Staring won't help, boy." The king's voice boomed from behind me. My father rarely spoke in a lower tone. He could whisper, when he believed secrecy or discretion were necessary, or he could boom and project, reminding all of his authority. To him, there was no place for mediocracy. "Don't just stand there."

"What shall I do?" I asked, as eager to please him as I was to save the kingdom.

"You know your task," he replied, irritably.

The same sense of self-loathing I lived with as a teen hit me. Deep down, I knew my father loved me, but to him that was something to whisper. It should be known but never spoken of. Certainly not declared.

"Where are the others? My mother and brothers?"

"Doing their bit." The king bowed his head.

"Father, I am trying, I—"

His eyes bore through me, cutting off my words. At first, I thought there was no recognition, like he was talking to a complete stranger. Gulping hard, I tried to form words—either of comfort, regret, or query as I had so many questions for him—but no sound would come.

The sound of thunder shook the castle as a racing fireball flew by.

The king scoffed, turning up his nose. "Try harder."

Another fireball hurtled towards me. With nowhere to run, I covered my face with my arms, and braced for impact. An explosion of sound knocked me to my knees, but I did not burn. A dense vapour surrounded me, blocking my view of anything more than an arm's length away. However, scuffing my foot into the ground, I realised that I was back on Liekke Peak.

Bewildered, I questioned if I ever actually left.

With nothing else to do, I started walking. Everything was silent—even my footsteps made no sound. I appeared to walk on air and no wind, no wings, no fire accompanied me.

The feeling of being lost in a void petrified me.

The thought that lingered with me, echoed in my mind. *Have I already failed?*

My sister's anguish and my father's expression plagued me. For them—for Virisinigne, I would beg.

Falling to my knees, I declared, "I, Niall Beckett, your humble, ignorant servant, present myself. Please, if there is any way to save my people, please, judge me with mercy."

A great gust blew in front of me, pushing all of the cloud back so that it lined the edges of the volcano. But now the ground was neither bare nor simply made of rock. It was a graveyard of swords, spears, and axes. Some big, some small—all sticking out of the ground as though an army had left them there to hold their positions in a tournament.

Slowly, I approached the blade closest to me. Decorated with intricate, intertwining patterns, the hilt shone white in my otherwise grey surroundings. Just as I reached out to touch it, a voice ruptured out of the clouds:

"Choose your weapon wisely, for it may be your last."

TWENTY-NINE

There was literally nowhere to hide and no way to know which weapon might be the best one—nor what I would be fighting with said weapon. It occurred to me to ask, but instinct told me trials only had questions.

Answers were for the Fyuego—the blessed.

Bizarrely, the threat gave me comfort. *It may be your last* also meant I had not failed.

I had a chance.

I'd always been very particular about my weapons—my sword especially—so the hilt or blade could be as stunning as you liked, but if it felt wrong to hold, I would reject it. I had to. Grip was everything. Along with *The Leviathan*, my father had gifted me a sword when I became captain. It was an ornamental piece. Style over function. Had I been primed for a life of luxury, sat on a throne with little or no prospect of ever wielding it, the sword would have been perfect. But I wasn't, so I hung it on my wall and commissioned a more befitting blade in the first port I came to. I was so moved by the quality, I paid the blacksmith and swore to die with the sword by my side. My decision to leave it on board my ship was not done lightly, I needed Benegnyem to see me as a humble, non-threatening prince. I was right, but there and then, I also desperately wished my pilgrimage had allowed me to bring her along.

Unsure whether the command to choose allowed for me to pick up multiple weapons, weigh them in my hands, and then select my favourite, I was reluctant to lift any. All around me had intertwining imagery etched into the steel and leather, but not all the patterns were the same. Some of the pommels had snakes, others had dire wolves, dogs, dragons, bears, lynx, and lions, while the rest displayed a variety of ferocious mythical creatures. However, where they lacked unity in design in many ways, the grips unified them as identical, burning flames worked up both sides.

Even in grey, they looked alive.

Wrapping my fingers around a sword, I gazed at the next one, wondering if the shape might suit me better, but as a giant, angry Pilgrim Punisher snake dropped out of thin air beside me, I realised my choice had been made.

Expanding its hood, the snake coiled its body, and raised its head milliseconds before striking out at me. Dropping to my knees, I rolled away, immediately rising up again to its right with my sword ready to swing. I only needed two steps to get my footing right, but the snake flicked the tip of its tail in one, knocking me sideways into the flat side of another sword, sending it clattering to the ground.

With no time to think, I jumped up, again narrowly avoiding the snake's speeding fangs, and swung my sword at its retracting neck. Until that day, I rarely, if ever, missed, but the snake was faster than me. It saw my swing before I did.

With a toss of its tail, it had me over, jolting every bone in my body. Steadying myself, I put out a hand, but the planned rise to my feet was redirected as a second snake flew towards me. Drop and rolling, I collected the second dislodged sword, and braced myself for the snakes to attack.

Poised to swallow me whole in their cavernous mouths, they positioned themselves in perfect, terrifying symmetry before me. With my monochromatic vision, I couldn't tell if it was in the distance or coming from them, but light seemed to ripple and lick around them, adding to their menacing appearance. But I could only focus on the immediate threat, so with a sword in each hand, I waited. I couldn't outrun and I couldn't out manoeuvre, my only hope was to strike in unison.

It was a heinous game of patience.

They waited for me to move, while I waited for them to strike.

Someone had to give in first.

Abruptly shifting my weight on my right foot, I did a false start. Immediately both snakes thrust themselves forward, focusing on the direction I pretended to be aiming for.

Two-handed fighting was more my thing rather than fighting with two swords, but I swung them both, crossing and cutting to perfection. Beginners luck or not, my adrenaline soared as two heads flopped to the ground in front of me.

The snakes' tails eerily flicked as the last muscle spasms ran through their bodies, making me jump backwards, readying myself in case reincarnation was possible in this impossible world.

Nothing moved.

Panting, I slowly relaxed my stance. Only then did I realise that the two swords I held had identical snakes woven into the metal work. *Is this coincidence or design?* I wondered.

A new breeze rushed across the peak. It was mild, no more than a pleasant summer's day on the coast, but the moment the wind reached the corpses before me, they disappeared. It was as though the breeze had vapourised them.

Did they ever exist?

Against my will, my fingers released the swords, but neither made it to the ground before they too, vanished. Something clattered behind me. Whipping around, I faced a creature, an ogre of monstrous proportions with one enormous eye nestled amongst its wart-ridden skin. As our eyes locked, it grinned at me. Instantly, I preferred its solemn gaze—when its jagged teeth and abundant drool were not apparent.

Dropping its shoulders, it ran at me.

Grabbing the nearest sword, I ran away.

The ground vibrated every time the ogre's feet hit the ground. Risking a glance over my shoulder, my heart sank. I was faster on my feet, but it kept a steady, untiring pace. All it had to do was wear me down. There were no boulders, no trees, nothing to hide behind or slow its advance. All I saw was flat rock, dust, and a glimmering haze that highlighted the lumbering beast who wanted to crush me.

Glancing at the blade in my hand, an idea hit me.

There was only one way to win this. I'd seen it done—or at least I'd seen wild boar take down hunters like this.

Circling back, I raced at the ogre's legs. It's hands came down, grasping at me. Retreat was impossible, so I dropped to my knees. Skidding across the ground, pain shot through my body as flesh and blood smeared on the rock beneath me, but I made it past the trunk-like fingers with an inch to spare.

Landing under the ogre, the thought, *I should have grabbed a spear,* ironically rattled through my brain. Slashing at its left heel, then dashing to the right, I cut both legs twice, and ran again before I was crushed. Anxiously searching for a spear, I darted between weapons, but only swords laid before me—all of which had ogres on the pommels.

Do I get an opponent per weapon? I couldn't afford to find out. The sword I already had would have to do.

My slashes had slowed the ogre, but it was already back on its feet and heading my way.

Planting my feet, I took a deep breath.

Fly true, I whispered, thrusting the sword sky-high with every ounce of energy I had left.

Landing in the centre of its only eye, the ogre fell over backwards with such an almighty thud I thought it had triggered an earthquake.

The breeze returned, clearing the vibrations and battlefield in an instant—or so I thought. As the final particles of the ogre danced away, a foggy whirlwind spun, and a faceless figure stepped out. He—or at least I think it was a he—wore a full-body suit and mask. No part of his skin could be seen. The suit *was* his skin. Holding two curved blades, he somersaulted towards me.

A new sword laid at my feet and I grabbed it.

This one was heavier than the others—too heavy, like an overindulgent toy.

It's my fathers, I said to myself, swinging it for all I was worth. *I knew it would be useless in a fight.* But there was no time to lament my father's lack of understanding in swordplay. He had only known a time of relative peace. His father had died young, meaning he inherited the throne without having to occupy himself with anything as mundane as a job or proving his worth outside the castle. Sitting in a chair, drinking, barking orders, signing decrees, and listening to reports suited him just fine. He took his role seriously. He always did. But he was a diplomat, not a warrior, and in that moment, I couldn't help thinking that a little more fighting finesse would have been fabulous.

The faceless figure flicked back and forth with the agility of a cat. If they were not trying to kill me, I would have called it a dance of beauty. However, when my sword slipped, allowing my opponents' blade to slide into my left bicep, complimenting my assassin wasn't high on my to-do list.

Intending to search for another weapon, I leapt backwards. When I did, my feet landed on wood—planks of wood. As if recovering from a haze that I didn't know I was suffering from, my eyes focused—still in grey but clearer, like fog departing on an early winter's morning.

I was in my quarters on *The Leviathan,* my ship.

Staring at the wall were the empty brackets where my father's sword should have been. Next to it hung my beloved sword—the one I could fight with. As I snatched it from its holder, the door smashed open, and my masked assailant burst in along with waves of glimmering light. Slamming the door shut with one foot, he charged, immediately locking me into a powerful duel. My room wasn't small, but this fight would be easier on deck where obstacles and flying blades were less problematic—and where angry killers could be thrown overboard.

It was as though he read my mind because, try as I might, I could not reverse our positions to reach the door. If I pushed forward or tried to pivot, he countered me, pushing me back two steps for everyone I advanced. The best I could do was hold, but there was only so long I could do that—and he knew it.

The ship lurched starboard, finally giving me an advantage—even if it was only a minor one as the attacker was not as thrown by the waves as I might have hoped. It was, however, just enough for me to charge halfway across the room before he found his balance. Lunging forward, I staked him through the chest with my sword. A gurgling sound came out of him, followed by a patch of blood around his masked mouth. Victory seemed certain as I stepped back, withdrawing my sword, but as his chest stopped moving, no wind brushed him away.

Outside, I heard the familiar sound of sails blowing, and waves lapping around the ship, but no people. Suddenly afraid for my crew, I ran to the door, praying I would find them safe and well. As I wrapped my fingers around the handle, fingers dug into my shoulder, pulling me backwards.

Jumping to my feet, I grunted angrily as frustration and pain rippled through me.

Then I looked down.

The corpse was still there.

"How?" I screeched, rolling my shoulders, trying to shake away the feeling of being grabbed by a corpse.

Then I registered my selection of two swords.

A weapon for each opponent.

I groaned at my stupidity. Had I not already worked that out?

Yet I had no time to lament. Everything happened in split seconds. In flashes of thought and bolts of movement. Uninterested in explanations, the second masked man materialised in front of me with two blades primed. As he attacked, I realised this was the opponent for my sword. While Father's was impressive, it was heavier, and his moves comparatively more predictable. This one, although at a glance identical, was lighter on his feet and faster.

Were he training me, he would be the perfect sparring partner, but I was struggling to study his moves and keep out of the way of them. Every time I thought he had a tell, he switched it. My crew and I practiced regularly for this kind of fighter. I thought I *was* this kind of fighter, but the number of cuts and bruises I was accumulating suggested I was wrong.

Only racing adrenaline and the desire not to die powered me on—and that was beginning to falter. Even the ship lurching didn't stop him. It was like he had learnt from his twins' errors.

At sea, on The Leviathan is your home, use it! My inner voice shouted.

One creaky floorboard had annoyed me for years, but it never bothered me enough to fix it and eventually I simply avoided standing on it. Part of me had intended to use the cavity to hide goods if we ever came under serious threat, however, we always fought off pirates, and were never in possession of anything valuable enough to inspire them to collaborate and attempt a more forceful assault—until I inherited the Amulet of the Flame, of course, but that was only days ago, and it remained around my neck.

Letting the assassin push me backwards, I feigned a fall whilst stabbing my father's sword into the semi-rotten board. Seeing his chance, the masked man immediately came forward with his blade pointing at my neck—and placing a foot exactly where I hoped he would. Ripping backwards on the sword, I dislodged the plank, twisting it just enough to topple him. Releasing the wood-laden sword, I swung mine, slashing it against his throat.

Instantly my grey vision burst with colour.

For a moment, everything seemed red. Certainly there was a lot of it—including on me. My ears blocked and all around me was silent. I couldn't stop staring at the corpses beside me.

Suddenly, I questioned whether there was a face under the mask, and I leant forward, running my fingers under his chin. Just as I found the seam, the door burst open with an almighty gust of wind. Afraid of what the wind might have brought, I lost my chance to identify the man as the air whipped around my battered quarters, lifted the masked men, twisted, and disappeared.

Cries for help rushed in through the open doorway. I only had to hear the voices once to know they were my crew members. Alun's gruff tone echoed off the waves, swearing grim omens as the others rallied against an unseen foe.

"Captain!" called Raine as though he was being chased.

Reaching the doorway, I saw my crew had been herded onto the bow like sheep going to slaughter by three grey, horse-sized dragons. The sails were on fire, and the lookout post was set to tumble into the deck, ready to ignite the rest of the ship. Only then did I smell smoke, but it wasn't the typical scent of burning canvas. It was more pungent, more *breathy*.

Turning my head, I realised why.

Beside me was the head of a dragon that outweighed my men, the grey dragons, and my ship combined. Bordered with fiery orange and reds, every jet-black scale shone. His enormous amber eye watched me, waiting for me to make my move with delight. I am sure he wanted me to try something—anything—to save my men, so he could justify action. However, I knew my limits. Just one snort from the nostril that threatened to suck me in, and I would be blown away. One breath, one half breath, and I would be burnt to a crisp.

Glancing backwards, my father's sword remained in the plank of wood. Testing my right hand, I felt the once comforting weight of my beloved sword. I was better with one sword than two, but neither would take down this beast.

"Captain!" called Marino, standing bravely in front of the others. Our eyes locked, we knew this was it. Everyone stood like statues—waiting to be frozen in time, showing our valour to the last moment. This was our ship. We would die on it.

Normally that would be enough for me—to die with my family.

My found family.

But this mission, my appointed purpose, went beyond us this time.

And I needed the dragons.

I needed the blessing of the Flame to win a larger battle—for *all* our families.

The words on the boulder Cal left me on rang in my head.

To achieve enlightenment, focus on the path, not the obstacles.

"The dragons are not the enemy!" I shouted before I realised I had anything to say.

"Captain?" Alun's expression questioned whether I had lost my mind.

Baffled, Marino and Raine narrowed their brows in unison, but they waited for me to continue.

"We have come here to find the Flame." Stepping forward, I pointed to the three grey dragons. "*They* are the Flame's loyal protectors. They channel fire by the Flame's blessing. Today, my brothers, there is honour in defeat—in humbly bowing to make friends, not war."

The enormous dragon's head rose above me. It was magnificent. I had no idea if they would accept me, but as I approached the black dragon, the wind howled as though it was eagerly anticipating my next move.

Holding my sword flat in both hands, I bowed before the dragon, and reverently laid my blade on the deck.

Keeping my neck bent, with my heart inexplicably steady, I took a deep breath.

"I am yours. Do with me as you will," I said, relinquishing my spirit.

A circle of fire sprang up around me.

The ship burnt away, leaving me kneeling on rock once more.

Wings flapped from every direction, clearing the way to reveal a pitch-black night lit by a million shining stars.

"Arise, Pilgrim," said a thunderous voice. "Welcome home."

THIRTY

Standing in the centre of a horde of dragons should have been petrifying, but something had fundamentally altered within me, making me see them in a totally new way—and they knew it, because as my demeanour changed, so did theirs.

It made no sense and perfect sense all at once.

The fire before me still skipped and twisted as the dragons' fanned it, however, as they landed on Liekke's Peak, tucking their wings neatly behind them, the blaze continued to dance under its own power.

Surveying the reptilian circle around me, there were dragons of all sizes with colours ranging from steel grey to jet black. Each had a uniquely beautiful sheen across its scales, plus defining outlines as though someone had painstakingly highlighted them with multi-coloured ink.

Suddenly the arms of the fire rose to the stars, making me jump backwards a step. My cheeks could feel the intensity of the furnace, but they did not burn. Captured in absolute awe, my eyes held fast as bright red flames in the shape of a burning-spirit dragon burst forth.

She was mesmerising, but instinct told me to drop to my knees. Had I any doubt, as I peered upwards, I realised all the dragons had bowed their heads, waiting for the spirit to speak. When she did, she spoke with the power of a mighty warrior crashing out of a storm:

"Every pilgrim is born with the potential to be Charred—to be united by fire. To receive such a blessing, each individual must seek it, laying all they have at the foot of Mount Liekke, and proving themselves by accepting the balance and partnership that maintains this world. Once achieved, it cannot be broken. Step forward to find your match. Once bonded, together you will travel to me, the Empress, the anointed embodiment of the Flame's voice, and protector of the realm."

Out of thin air, a golden dagger with a green emerald in the handle dropped in front of me.

"Come, add your blood to the fire. Join the Fyuego and rejoice in the sovereignty and blessing of the Flame, the giver of all life."

Had I known about it earlier, I might have thought it the act of a cult but picking up the blade and cutting the palm of my hand felt like the most natural thing in the world.

Extending my arm, I reached into the fire with a balled fist, and squeezed. In slow motion, a drop of blood fell into the blaze, and instantly fizzled out.

Everything around me was silent except for the licking flames which crackled as though fuelled by wood although only rock laid beneath it.

Wings flapped, creating a howling wind.

In a flash, both the red spirit-dragon, the golden dagger, and fire disappeared.

Enya had told me the dragons would come. I didn't understand at the time, but in that moment, I equally understood what she meant and why she didn't try to explain.

Seeing *is* believing.

She also told me to go for a medium, mature dragon, yet the wind propelled me towards the largest dragon—the one I bowed to minutes earlier.

Enya's warning rang in my ears. *He is the Chief Protector of the Flame—the Empress' Right-Wing and overseer of the Fyre Dog horde. If you can, avoid him.*

Yet while my ears rang, my heart remained steady, pushing out all negativity. My eyes no longer dilated at the sight of him. My thoughts focused on him. My hand reached to him.

Once delivered in front of the dragon, all wind and wings instantly stilled and an eerily beautiful calm rested upon the volcano.

My fingers met the cheek of the giant beast and colour danced all around me—more than I even knew existed. Whether it was already day but I saw night, or time itself sped forward, I do not know, but the sun rose, illuminating the sky. All of my senses flared. Sight, sound, touch, smell—everything was more acute. I had never felt more alive.

Pilgrim, I am Adaryvan, said a deep, gravelly voice inside my head.

Gazing into the dragon's eye, I wasn't sure if I needed to speak or simply think my reply, yet I chose to play it safe and go with the former. "Niall, my name is Niall."

"Well, *my name is Niall,* it seems that destiny unites us." Adaryvan said out loud in a dry tone. "We need to see the Empress. Get on." He lowered his neck and body, making the angle of the scutes up his side more accessible—but no less daunting.

When Enya had shown me Wydgitta's scutes, I had been fascinated, but honestly never thought I would be climbing the horned scales. Gripping a hold of the lowest one and lifting myself off the ground, I gulped, but it wasn't until I had climbed a dozen steps that I felt light-headed.

Breathe. Adaryvan's droll chuckle echoed inside my head.

Opening my mouth to wryly tell him I was, I gasped for air and groaned, realising that I had automatically held my breath. We might have been destined and I may have had an inexplicable, almost instant feeling of trust regarding Adaryvan, but I had to acknowledge that my in-built sense of self-preservation had not quite caught up. Or perhaps it had—climbing up and sitting on a wild beast while it flew into a volcano wasn't high on any lists of *safe or sensible ways to travel.*

Again, Adaryvan laughed.

Great, trust me to be destined with the sarcastic dragon, I grumbled internally to myself.

"Oh, I think we are well matched," replied Adaryvan—simultaneously answering my question of whether I need to verbally reply. "We trust the Flame's judgement but question our choices."

There was no arguing his wisdom. "Maybe we are." I scoffed. "Can you hear everything I think? Like, *everything?*"

"When we are close, and our channels open, yes."

"How do I close the channel?" Adaryvan twisted his neck to look at me and narrowed his eyes. "I don't mean I want to right now, I just mean, you know—*if it was necessary.*"

"Concentrate on privacy, and a thought is solitary. Concentrate on communication, and I can hear." He snorted. "If you just rattle away to yourself, I can hear it, so you might want to consider what you are doing. I've no desire to hear every last detail of your day."

Impulsively, I muttered a sarcastic, not-so-flattering response.

"*Language,*" Adaryvan lightly growled. "You'll wound me with your sailor's tongue my flightless little gnat."

"Shall I take that as a term of affection?" I grinned. He could squash me with his pinkie-claw, but somehow his banter amused more than it frightened me.

A laughter-like grumble rippled out of him. "I would."

Reaching Adaryvan's back was another breath-taking experience. From there, I could see the other dragons sitting around us, but beyond them, beyond the edge of the peak, I could see the world in a way unlike anything else I had ever imagined. As he took flight, the wind bit into my face, threatening to push me backwards. Steading myself, I hugged the extra-large scales on his withers, but even my fear of falling couldn't stop me from gazing in every possible direction. My chest pounded. There on the corner of the world, was the World's Divide. My heart went beyond the living, lethal wall, and I, once more, renewed my promise to send help.

THIRTY-ONE

Adaryvan wasn't interested in taking me sightseeing. As soon as he reached an amazing height above Mount Liekke, he circled the ginormous crater, and then descended into it.

Inside the crater seemed like a whole new world—*another one.*

Layers of rock waved in colourful formation down the walls while great pillars rocketed out of the ground making islands, arches, and chambers in all directions. The closest I could think to describe it is akin to the intricate design of an ants nest but set to the most monumental scale imaginable.

Reaching the base of the crater seemed to take forever, but when the ground came into view, a strange white structure caught my eye. At first I thought it was the frame of a mighty ship with all the decks removed, yet when it came into proper view, its true identity was clear. It was a skeleton. An absolutely gigantic skeleton.

I was sure that Adaryvan was listening to my crazed thoughts, but he left me to marvel at my surroundings in silence. Landing with impressive delicacy, he settled on the ash covered ground next to the bones. From afar, I thought them pure white, but when close-up, images became apparent.

The style of the drawings was very similar to those in the caves, only these were etched by fire. They were beautiful, yet a sense of melancholy came over me seeing bones decorated this way.

"Whose bones are these?" I asked.

"Dragana's." Adaryvan replied in a reverent whisper.

"Why are they marked?"

"The First Empress' wish was to be laid to rest here and used as a reminder of all that was lost as well as all that was gained." Adaryvan carefully swung his tail, pointing at the mural on Dragana's shoulder. "The First Empress united dragons and humanity. It was her overwhelming strength of mind that searched for another way when all seemed hopeless—when peace seemed impossible. Despite her own grief, she begged for and was granted the extra blessing of the Flame. When she channelled it, she gave humanity a way forward, saving us all, and founded the age of civilisation you see today."

"I was told she used bones of the dead to form the World's Divide?"

"She did—including the bones of her firstborn who was brutally murdered. That was the end of the Dividing War. It literally named it."

"What started the war?"

"Humanity's desire to rule all and share none." Adaryvan twitched his tail. "Too many around the world wanted to live without the Flame, without magic, and especially without dragons. They feared our size, our abilities, and our closeness to the Divine." He snorted ironically. "As it happens, they only succeeded in driving us closer to the Flame, but that was not their intention."

"That which is willing to break, will be made whole," I said, reading the inscription that ran along the ribcage.

"It is a pledge pilgrims make when they join the Fyuego—both dragons and humans. To come together, we all must believe in more than ourselves. You did so, otherwise you and I would not be here, right now."

The depiction of the First Empress choosing to invoke the Flame's most prestigious blessing for good whilst surrounded by devastation, knowing that she could have easily turned that power to total domination, brought me to tears.

I truly felt broken.

Broken for the past.

Broken for the future—for there we were, fighting again. A different fight, but no less bloody or unnecessary. Gryer and his dragon, Dreygon, sought to dominate when they had been taught the way of peace. Of choice. Of respect. Of unity—even in the face of personal differences.

Without saying a word, Adaryvan began moving around the skeleton—which was approximately three times the size of him. More of the history of Benegnyem was displayed around the body, showing both events before and during the war, as well as the rise of the unified, resplendent age that Benegnyem now thrived in. The message was clear and I didn't need to ask Adaryvan to understand anything—until we reached the right shoulder of the skeleton.

"How long ago was this?" I asked, viewing an image of a ship passing through the World's Divide. *So, I am not the first ship to travel through?* I thought to myself, feeling irrationally disappointed not to be unique—and forgetting the dragon could hear me.

Adaryvan's body rippled as he chuckled. "Actually, it might have been fulfilled just a few days ago."

"What do you mean? Is this of me?" My eyes fixed on the picture. The image was too vague to have facial features, yet the ship was familiar.

"I believe so. Dragana left two Amulets of the Flame—you have one around your neck. She left those as ways for communication, unification, or friendship to be sought one day if it was desired by both sides. After her mother's death, Drayanna, the Second Empress, scorched the murals as reminders, but also as prophecy. The Flame told her, one day the Amulets would unite the realms and restore absolute balance of the world."

"That must have been centuries, if not millenniums ago?"

"Yes, but time to the Flame is but a blink of an eye."

"What about this one?" I pointed to another image on Dragana's neck. "This has the same ship with a black dra—Fyre Dog?"

"When alone together, the Fyuego are permitted to use our species name *dragon*. *Fyre Dog* is a term used to remind of our loyalty to the people, and as a lasting mark of respect to Dragana, both her name and that of her son, Drayon, are never uttered lightly. All three names are sacred." The tip of Adaryvan's clawed wing came forward. "But to answer your question, yes, it is thought the ship and sailor are the same. Certainly, the Amulet is present in both. Unfortunately, prophecies are not cheat sheets. We must live and decide our own path."

"But that—" I pointed to the black dragon flying above the depicted ship. "That could be you?"

"Quite possibly." He snorted. "At least, I've always wondered if it is."

"So that is why the king, the Fyuego, sent me here? Because they saw the sign of a prophecy?"

"It would be the decision of a poor king to ignore the arrival of the Amulet of the Flame."

"But I am no one. I am the youngest, most expendable son of a king—a messenger seeking help. You are the Chief Protector. Do you accept me? A humble foreigner seeking help for his kingdom?"

Adaryvan softened his normally gruff tone. "I neither question nor doubt the will of the Flame. I am the Right-Wing of the Empress. You are the emerald-wielding son of a king. It would seem that our destinies have always been intertwined. Now we must find out why."

My hand went up to the Amulet of the Flame. "My father only bestowed this on me recently. I am not—"

"Were you not born with emerald eyes?"

"Yes, but I am the seventh son, I—"

"Through the teachings of the Fyuego, it is known that in each royal generation, there are those who are born with the power to unite—should they seek it. Have faith.

The Right-Wing of Benegnyem and the Left-Hand of Virisinigne are meant to be."

Hope and belonging like I had never felt before filled me.

My smile must have been from ear to ear because it actually began to ache.

Adaryvan chuckled inside my head. It was bizarre, unnerving, and wonderful all at once.

"I wanted to show you this before you meet the Empress." Adaryvan's tone suddenly changed. It felt sad, almost repentant. "She is not who she once was. Great sorrow has engulfed her. She still follows the Flame, yet—"

Adaryvan paused but made no effort to continue. My entire body shivered. Only seconds earlier I had experienced true elation—a expectation of success and fulfilment. All of that had been blown away in a heartbeat.

"Yet, what?" I whispered, unable to find volume.

"It is not for me to say. The Empress must always speak first, I cannot speak for her. Come."

His invite seemed somewhat redundant when I was sitting on his back and would surely die if I jumped off with only a thin layer of ash on top of endless tonnes of rock beneath me.

"How is it that I am not burnt to death?" I asked as Adaryvan headed for the nearest chamber archway.

"Pilgrims are granted protection during their trial. Once Charred, the Fyuego inherit the natural resistance of their partner." I could tell that he meant this to sound reassuring, but I was still unsure of the particulars or process of *charring.* "You're right, I cannot tell you that either," Adaryvan mocked, reading my thoughts.

Entering the adjoining chamber, it looked like an alien art gallery. The walls were filled with stunning patterns that leapt and weaved from floor to ceiling. All of the marks were scorched black, but the rock was anything but monotone, resulting in the most fabulous display.

"Each Empress adds her own artwork throughout the Liekke chambers," explained Adaryvan. "They are quite beautiful, are they not?"

They are, I thought, too stunned to bother speaking.

Suddenly the ground trembled, followed by a whirlwind of angry, hot air.

Adaryvan's head and body dropped forwards. *Bow,* boomed through my mind.

Resting my knees into the scute in front of me, I bent my head, neck, and back as low and as humbly as I could.

The wind continued and brought an almighty roar—the same thunderous roar I heard from the fire.

The Empress had arrived.

THIRTY-TWO

Every bit as large, if not larger, than the bones of her predecessor, the huge chamber instantly felt small as the Empress entered. Straining my eyes upwards without moving my head, I was beyond awe-struck. No drawing would ever do her justice. Her entire body was as red as blood with bright fiery orange highlights lining each scale. She was meant to impress and there was no part of me that didn't quake in her presence.

"Arise," commanded the Empress.

Silently, Adaryvan and I obeyed.

"Adaryvan, *you* present this pilgrim?"

"I do, Your Imperial Majesty."

"Then he is already blessed."

"You honour me, Your Imperial Majesty."

"I simply state a fact."

Adaryvan dipped his head, respectfully accepting her compliment. "He carries the Amulet of the Flame—from the *other* side of the Divide."

The Empress hissed. *"What?"* Her head zoomed in on me. Adaryvan didn't move, but I felt his body tense underneath me. "You smell different, Pilgrim. Is it true? Are you from the other side?"

"Yes, Your Imperial Majesty. I have travelled a long way in the hope of begging for your assistance, for—"

"You have traversed the pilgrimage of the Fyuego, have you not? You have relinquished all to the Flame?"

I bowed my head again. "All that I have, Your Imperial Majesty."

"Then are you ready to be sworn in and receive your final blessing?"

"I am ready to be made whole, Your Imperial Majesty."

"So be it," said the Empress. "Come."

Following her, we were led through a series of chambers that seemed to descend and circle and descend again into the deepest depths of the volcano. Each room and passage was large and lit by torches which ignited as we entered, showing off an array of strange rock formations that were coloured by a combination of natural pigment and dragon fire.

Ahead was a huge archway that glowed with orangey-reds. Approaching the entrance, my pulse throbbed as shadows looked like they were dancing up the walls. When we entered, I saw why. A stream of flowing fire filled the centre of the chamber—upwards flowing fire.

Magma.

The closer she stood, the more the Empress glowed. By the time she was next to the stream, she was the brightest, most electric red I had ever seen, and her scales seemed to ripple independently from her body.

I didn't need to be told to know that this was the lifeforce of the world. The Flame's blessing might be omnipresent, but this was the hub of energy, the temple of that lifeforce. Whether for human affirmation or need, I couldn't tell you, but I knew that I was in the presence of holiness. Of absolute unyielding, unstoppable power. It was a sight I would be honoured by for the rest of my days. Instantly I knew why the dragons defended its authority and why they were the higher species. Humanity, at best, could ride in their wake, but to think we could or should own them, kill them, or subject them struck me as fundamentally wrong. The fact they join with us at all, especially after our bloodied history was testament to them, not us.

In the Flame and dragons' combined presence, I felt utterly insignificant.

The Empress spread her wings, sending sparks of fire around the room. While the flecks still floated on magical waves of air, she spoke in the most majestic voice I ever heard:

"Niall, I hereby Charr you, bonding you to my brother, Adaryvan, electing you, together, as Protectors of the Flame, each other, and the holy order of the Fyuego. May the blessing of the Flame be upon you, strengthen you, and commit your path to the way of enlightenment all the days that you shall live. *Flamma vobiscum.*"

"*Flamma vobiscum,*" repeated Adaryvan, the reverence in his gravelly voice sending shivers down my spine.

Swallowing the lump in my throat, I echoed their words. "*Flamma vobiscum.*"

The Empress took a deep breath, sucking magma from the stream into her lungs. Her face remained calm, but when her jaws opened, a racing ball of fire formed in her mouth. Reds ran into white, greens in yellow, blues into black, while a deep purple lined them all. When the ball filled the height and width of the Empress' throat, she roared, sending fire bursting forwards, and enveloping Adaryvan and myself.

Unable to cope with the intensity, my eyes scrunched shut. I saw nothing but felt everything. Fingers of fire held my arms, lifting me from Adaryvan's back. When they released, a torrent of air caught me. Screams flew out of my lungs as intense heat ripped through my body. My armour melted away, leaving me as naked as the day I was born, but my skin remained. I remained. My heart calmed, my body relaxed. The pain was in my head, not my flesh. But it felt different—stronger, thicker, as if my injuries were being healed and my bruises wiped away.

I was renewed—both in body and soul.

There was no guide because there were no words.

Describing this was impossible.

Opening my eyes, I found myself stood on the ground between the two dragons, facing the Empress. Seeing her, I bent my knee.

"You are a royal," said the Empress, somewhere between surprise and pleasure as the fire faded back into the stream. "The chosen heir."

"Not quite, Your Imperial Majesty. I am Prince Niall, the youngest son of King Ennis of Virisinigne. I have come to beg for your assistance on behalf—"

The Empress tutted. "I was not asking, Niall. The Flame is quite clear. Observe yourself."

Gazing down, I saw my body covered in jet-black scales like Adaryvan's. The only difference was while half of my scales had the fiery orange edging, the rest were emerald green. As I stared at my chest, the marks faded—or rather absorbed—into my skin, resting beneath the surface like armour.

The mark of the Charred, I realised.

"That is not typical Charring," Adaryvan added, listening to my thoughts.

I twisted my neck to look at him. "Oh?"

He nudged me with his wing. "Your arms—look."

Racing up my arms, the tattoos remained visible. Gorgeous patterns woven with black scales stretched all the way to my shoulders. *To my shoulders.* Not just my wrist or lower arm.

Just like Enya's.

"You are the Maiden's Fated Mate," said the Empress. "May you prove worthy of her."

THIRTY-THREE

I will not lie, the idea of being betrothed to Enya was not the worst idea that had come to me, far from it, but it was also far from the reason why I was there. Already my heart had skipped too much for her. I had only one mission of importance and millions of lives depended on me staying on point—and considering how Enya would take the news if she ever found out was not it. In that moment, I vowed not to tell her. "You honour me, Your Imperial Majesty, but, if I may, I have come to beg your ear, your assistance—" The Empress stared at me and I was suddenly conscious of being stark-naked. Covering myself with cupped hands, I blushed. "Forgive me, I—"

The Empress snorted, but her response was entirely serious. "I have no interest in the human form, only the heart and soul."

She gestured for me to look behind a rock. At first, all I saw was another, slightly squarer rock, but then I realised the rock had a lid cut into it. Sliding the lid away, I found a neat pile of clothes. Without delay, I dressed into the fresh armour and a sense of pride filled me as I viewed the Flame's emblem on my chest.

I am no longer the apprentice, but a marked member of the Fyuego, I thought to myself.

Waiting until I tied my boots, the Empress said, "So, what is it you wish to ask?"

Determined to succeed in my larger mission, I immediately answered her. "My world, where I come from, is under siege. Our once thought unshakeable kingdom will fall to the enemy if I do not rally assistance. I—"

"Your side of the wall declared themselves free. They wanted no part in our life or blessings. In fact they actively acted against us. They slaughtered us. Why should I interfere now?"

"That was not the generations who live today. We have no knowledge of the past or the part our ancestors played. Until I visited here, I knew nothing of this world or our combined history."

"Yet you miraculously got here?" The Empress' sarcasm was palpable.

"My father, the king, entrusted me with the Amulet of the Flame in haste. I can only assume that he has some knowledge, something handed down secretly through the crown that I am not privy too, Your Imperial Majesty."

"Indeed." She paused, slowly shaking her head. "I take no pleasure in hearing of your world's war or your people's likely doom, but *you* have been brought here. *You* have been blessed by the Flame, *here.* Perhaps your fate lies here, and here alone. I cannot help you." The Empress turned and began walking away.

"Please! You do not ask who has my father's kingdom under siege!" The Empress briefly froze, but ultimately continued into the next chamber. Without thinking, I ran after her. "Our invaders are Charred, they are *your* people, from *this* world. Together Gryer and Dreygon have formed an army and—"

The Empress whipped around so fast I thought she might trigger a volcanic eruption.

"*How?* They were lost across the eastern isles years ago—reportedly hunted down by remote tribes who care not for citizens of Benegnyem or our ways. It is not possible for them to have travelled through the World's Divide."

"And yet, respectfully, they did. For ten years they have hidden away, increased in power, and now Virisinigne will burn." My voice shook as I tried to maintain composure. "The siege can only hold so long. Without the Flame or your fire, *we will fall.*"

The gigantic red dragon paused, thoughtfully tilting her head. The prolonged silence was deafening. If it were not for the gentle swish of her tail, I might have doubted if she was even awake. I could not move—nor glance at Adaryvan who I knew was right behind me.

Everything rested on the words of the Empress.

Finally, she sighed and faced me.

My heart raced in anticipation.

"The Amulets of the Flame were made to give choice, not enforce fate. *I* will not enforce fate beyond my borders. Peace reigns here because we observe harmony. I am sorry,

Niall, but perhaps this is just the path your kingdom must take."

"Are you not the keeper of the Flame? Is the Flame not omnipresent? Do you therefore not speak for and reside over all?"

"I am—and I defend the Flame with everything I have. I respect the decision of my ancestors to separate the worlds and not intervene in the quarrels of man beyond this kingdom. We lead by example, not dictatorship."

"Dreygon—*your* kind— stands with Gryer. They attack purely out of selfish gain."

"And I am grieved to hear it, but my place is *here*. My kingdom is *here*. The concerns of afar are between them and the Flame—who, I might again add, your people rejected."

"Am I to blame for my ancestors decisions any more than you are bound by yours? Can we not start anew? Gryer seeks to destroy. I ask for peace."

"Your argument is sound, but my decision is made, and I am too tired. Virisinigne must fight its own way into a new age. The Flame has blessed you. If you insist on returning, maybe you can win a battle on your own? I wish you well, but I will not risk the lives of my family for the wars of a foreign land. That is my final word." The Empress turned, dismissing me with her tail.

"Do you permit me to ask Adaryvan to join me in that fight?" I called after her.

Taking flight, she threw a fireball at my feet. The heat was incredible. Any confidence or belief that I was now infallible withered as I realised I was still penetrable by fire—or at least I was by *her* fire.

"I do not!" The Empress bellowed in a completely different, and very angry tone. "Adaryvan is the Protector of the Flame. My Right-Wing. His place is in Benegnyem."

"Gryer will not stop in Virisinigne!" I screamed. "He and his dragons will spread all over the world if you do not stop them!" I *felt* Adaryvan wince inside my mind as I shouted *dragon*. Said in such a tone was akin to swearing in the worst way to them, but I could not leave the crater without the Empress' help. Me joining the Fyuego meant nothing without an army. Risky and impetuous as my tongue was, I preferred to die trying rather than remotely entertain a comfortable life in this world knowing that everyone else was dead or subjugated. "Simulinigne! That's what he calls his new kingdom! He is marked as a royal with scales up to his neck, like King Inygo."

The Empress snorted. "Not quite, his marks do not go so high."

"I don't know how else to say this, Your Imperial Majesty, but you are wrong. Is it possible for someone to add to their scales? Maybe Gryer and Dreygon have invoked the Flame's power in Mount Halo as well as breeding there?"

"WHHHAAAATTTTT?" Fire rose out of the ground like an almighty, wild furnace. The Empress glowed a deep, violent red and steam shot out of her nostrils.

Adaryvan grabbed me in his talons, pulling me into his body as the volcano rumbled all around us. Suddenly I realised I had a front row seat to what Enya referred to as *raging,* and I could only imagine the debris that was tumbling down the mountain peaks as a result.

I wasn't sure which part of my sentence had angered her more. I doubt any monarch likes being told they are wrong, but even so, I thought it more likely that Dreygon harnessing the Flame to bless Gryer without her knowledge was a greater offence. Terrified as I was, I had to use this anger to benefit my cause, no matter how volatile or dangerous it was.

Stepping out of Adaryvan's talon, I edged towards the Empress. "Surely, anyone invoking the Flame to such a degree has committed an unforgiveable sin? Surely—"

The Empress flexed her wings. "I am the voice of the Flame in *this* world. Once it was all, but the erection of the World's Divide left an empty volcanic seat and a land that we agreed to forego. Rightly or wrongly, Dreygon has the knowledge to draw power. The Flame takes no sides, it simply *is.* It mercifully provides for all. It gives signs and greater purpose for those who will accept, yet we must choose. Free choice is its greatest gift. The aim of our enlightened order is to choose peace, but if those faithful to the Flame choose to misuse it, then that is how it will be." Suddenly the Empress sounded weary, not angry, and the fires all fizzled out.

Her moods changed faster than I could blink. I didn't understand.

In Emberbyrg, King Inygo was quick to say the Empress was in mourning. Everyone seemed apprehensive to approach her. Even Adaryvan said she was not herself—that great sorrow had overtaken her.

Was this what he meant?

Or was it...

My brain charged through conversations—both said and unsaid. On the Tailfeather, Enya said I wouldn't see any small, younger dragons, but ignored my question why. At the time, I assumed they were elsewhere, but suddenly it dawned on me that maybe there weren't any.

Somehow, I had to ask.

"Your Imperial Majesty, there are at least four known dragons in Virisinigne, but Mount Halo could easily have younger—"

The fires lit again, rupturing out of rock, shattering artwork as it flared.

For better or worse, I had my answer.

Dropping to my knees, I put my hands together, and gazed into the Empress' eyes. It took every ounce of my being to hold my voice steady as I said, "Your Imperial Majesty, is there something wrong with the royal hatchery?"

With lightning-fast speed, the Empress' red talons surrounded me, snatching me from the ground and speeding me through the air further into the depths of the volcano.

In my head, I heard Adaryvan curse.

In his head, Adaryvan heard me scream.

THIRTY-FOUR

When the Empress finally opened her talons, I was so dizzy I didn't know which way was up. Only fear of her prevented me from vomiting. Until that day, I didn't think it was possible to be *too* afraid to be sick. I thought you were sick from illness, over-indulgence, poison, motion sickness, nervousness, or horror. Being squeezed half to death and whisked into the deepest depths of a volcano certainly felt horrific enough to induce vomit. However, I can now confirm it is possible to be so petrified that your body simply doesn't dare react.

Frozen to the spot but trying not to focus on the seething dragon glaring at me, I forced myself to take in my surroundings. The room was filled with shiny rocks, gemstones, various-coloured boulders, and lavacicles—like stalactites and stalagmites that I'd seen in caves in Virisinigne, only made from molten rock, not limestone and calcium carbonate. In the centre of the room, clusters of lavacicles jetted out of the ground and hung from the ceiling. At first, I thought it was a trick of the light, but beneath the surface of each lavacicle great blobs of red magma slowly swam up and down in an endless, gentle dance.

It was mesmerising.

Neither Adaryvan nor the Empress spoke. Perhaps they were talking silently to one another, but all I could see was them waiting for me to work something out—or say the wrong thing. I don't think the Empress minded which at that point. Beyond my heartbeat, all I could hear was the sound of steam blasting out of her nostrils. Each puff seemed to securely hold my confidence beneath a churning knot in my stomach.

Tired of waiting, the Empress roared. "Well? What do you say now?"

I desperately wanted to say something intelligent—something that wouldn't result in me being roasted where I stood—but I had no idea what I was supposed to be observing.

"Your Imp—"

"Don't *Imperial Majesty* me, boy! Answer the question!"

Again my eyes darted around the room. Rocks, rocks, and magma flowing rocks...

"Stop staring at the lava lamps like a hatchling!" screamed the Empress. "There are no hatchlings!" She began wailing and the sound of her sorrowful roars echoed off the chamber walls.

"This is the royal hatchery?" I whispered to Adaryvan. He nodded. Possibly I should have worked that out sooner, but how was I supposed to know what a dragon lair—a nest—truly looked like?

Anxiously scuffing my foot in the ground, layers of coloured stones and red and deep-orange crystals moved. *"What the—?"* I exclaimed without meaning to speak.

What? asked Adaryvan, inside my head.

Picking up a handful of crystals, I leant against a boulder. Immediately, the Empress flicked me away with her tail. "How dare you? Do you wish to die?" she growled, carefully curling her tail around the boulder. "I will not warn you again."

My body trembled. There were only so many death threats I could take in a day—especially when I didn't understand my crime.

"Forgive me, I don't—"

"Don't touch the eggs," said Adaryvan, pulling me away from the Empress with his left talon before releasing me.

Every word that came out of my mouth seemed inadequate. Every thought was dull. *"Egg?"* Turning back to the boulder, I took in its form. In my experience, eggs were small, usually a shade of brown or white, and laid by a bird. Sure, snakes laid eggs, but still they were small. They had shells. Smooth shells. They were clearly eggs.

They didn't look like dark-grey, armour-plated boulders.

However, standing at a distance with Adaryvan, the shape of an egg—albeit with an unusual exterior—was detectable. If produced by the Empress, I had to concede that it was probably in proportion.

"If there are eggs," I said, counting three dark-grey boulders, "then what, may I humbly ask, is the—"

"They are stillborn," Adaryvan said, sadly.

"They are *all* stillborn." The Empress' tone broke my heart. Dragons may not shed tears, but in that moment I knew without a shadow of a doubt they mourn. They grieve. They love. The Empress hugged her stillborn babies, wrapped in their shells, and I wept for her.

Dropping to my knees, I said. "What can I do to assist you?" I knew my home was under siege. I knew my father was waiting for me to send help. I knew fate had brought me here.

I chose to listen.

"We have searched for a reason for years, but each year, for fifteen years, it has gotten worse. The royal nest is now totally barren. *I* am barren—" Sorrow cut off the Empress' again.

"It has spread to all females, not just our beloved leader," Adaryvan quietly added.

My fingers again sifted through the substrate on the ground.

My brain raced.

"Do all females lay here?" I asked.

"No, only the Empress nests in here. There are several lairs within Liekke Peak. Why?"

Lifting my hand, I said. "Do all the lairs have this substrate?"

"Of course. Rubrunite is only found in volcanoes and is the prime mineral for our hatchlings," Adaryvan said proudly. "This has been known since the beginning of time."

"Liekke rubrunite makes the purest rubies and emeralds, the holy gems of the Flame. All the Fyuego's rubrunite and emerald, including that in your Amulet stone, was carefully mined from this mountain range," the Empress added. "Very few people have permission to visit, let alone take anything from there."

Despite the temperature being buffered by my new Charred skin, sweat poured down my back. I knew what I saw and I knew what I had to say. What I didn't know was if I would be burnt-alive for saying it.

"I am afraid you are both mistaken."

Two heads raced in, pinning me between their smoking faces.

Gulping, I hastily continued. "*This* is not rubrunite. It might look similar, but it is not it. I believe this is thanatonite."

"I have never heard of it," boomed Adaryvan.

"No, probably not—you wouldn't have cause to if Liekke hasn't erupted in over a millennia. Before Gryer and Dreygon moved in, Mount Halo used to have thanatonite around its hydrothermal vents. It's still there, just not as readily available since the vents have deactivated. Any thanatonite deposits here would be more hidden, you'd have to actively mine for it."

"There are no such mining operations. I would know." Adaryvan confidently arched his back.

"Precisely." I answered, trying to mimic his self-assured stance. I knew I was right, even if I felt minuscule. Next to him, I *was* minuscule.

"What are you saying?" The Empress narrowed her eyes.

"I am saying someone has swapped the minerals."

Adaryvan scoffed. "Ridiculous. Why would anyone do that?"

"Because thanatonite is toxic."

"Toxic?" Adaryvan spat the word at me. "How toxic?"

The Empress emitted a low, guttural rumble.

She knew the answer, but she was going to make me say it.

"Highly."

Adaryvan gasped, while the Empress' nostrils flared so wide I thought she was going to suck me into them.

"Your Imperial Majesty, I believe someone is poisoning—*murdering*—your hatchlings and potentially trying to kill you."

I had barely finished speaking when Adaryvan snatched me backwards. His wings wrapped around me with milliseconds to spare, shielding us both from the deafening roars of streaming fire as the Empress' rage exploded.

THIRTY-FIVE

The Empress' rage seemed eternal. She had every right to be furious, just as she had every reason to wail—which sounded like a higher, although no less frightening roar—but I began to wonder if grief and anger had not broken her mind entirely.

It was Adaryvan who spoke first. "Your Imperial Majesty, how can we assist you? Speak your order and it will be done."

Honestly, I thought him naively optimistic. Believing that the Empress could have formed a plan throughout her pyrotechnic display was simply too fantastical. However, the error in my assumption was apparent the second she answered.

"I would like to focus on the who and how—and bring them to a bloody end—however, the first task must be to clear the lairs of all toxic matter. Every able member of the Fyuego, human and dragon, must unite in this task. *Immediately.* The future of our species depends on it."

"If I may, Your Imperial Majesty—" I said carefully. The Empress tilted her head, consenting to me continuing. "You need to remove every speck of dust. While you were—" I paused, searching for the best word. "While you were indisposed, I noticed other minerals. Dust from any of these could also be toxic. Whoever did this knows their rocks. We need another expert to advise on the most efficient way to cleanse the hatcheries. I—"

"Adaryvan, you must visit King Inygo and summon him, the Fyuego, and all geologists here at once. I want this place analysed immediately. There must be someone who can—"

Sensing that the Empress was about to steam ahead without pausing, I cleared my throat and bowed, hoping not to incur her wrath.

"Yes?" the Empress glared at me.

"On my ship, *The Leviathan*, I think I have the man for the job." I couldn't believe that I was going to suggest bringing my foul-mouthed, blue-eyed, gunner to the most holy place in the world, but Alun, for all his faults, was a keen geologist and had spent hours over the years boring the crew with his knowledge of different formations. The only time I didn't mind was when we were submerged in a hot spring and he was listing every unique rock, mineral, and gem in the area. Coincidently, it was also the time I learnt about thanatonite meaning *death mineral* in our old tongue, so something must have sunk in while I snoozed. "Alun has been with me for a decade and despite his coarse ways, I trust him with my life."

"Why do you have a geologist on your ship?" Suspicion oozed out of her every word.

"It is a hobby of his, not a vocation. He is my gunner. He likes rocks and minerals. Sometimes he likes to improvise and make makeshift bombs, but mostly he just likes to know things." I couldn't help smiling as I recalled Alun's account of his failed experiments—one of which he refused his captain's command to halt, so he was evicted from his position and thrown onto my ship. Who was supposed to be punished more that day, I couldn't say, but we proved them all wrong. "I am sure he would be able to identify exactly what you have on the ground here and come up with a plan to get rid of the mineral dust."

"Can't we just burn it?" asked Adaryvan. "We can adjust our blazes to full power and—"

"No, I don't think so," I cut in, trying not to be disturbed by the idea that dragons have thermostats and I hadn't yet seen the *full power* option. "Thanatonite is fire resistant."

The Empress growled. "Then whoever put it here knew that even if we discovered the mineral, we would have to leave our holy home and flood it with lava to sterilise it."

"Is that an option?" I asked, not understanding the logistics of how the dragons' presence resulted in no volcanic eruptions.

"We would have to vacate for a year before Liekke fully mourned our departure and erupted. The devastation to Emberbyrg and Benegnyem would be catastrophic. Our treaty would be in tatters and the east would likely rise against us with more than poisonous rock. To live in peace, dragons would have to burn everything. The Flame would judge me a failure. I would be a failure to myself, my people, the Fyuego, and my ancestors. That is not the rule or legacy I want to my name—or a burden I want imprinted on my soul."

"We know you will not authorise that, Your Imperial Majesty, but the alternative means this generation is our last. Someone is undoubtably trying to lead us to extinction." Until that point he had kept his composure. Now it was Adaryvan's turn to rumble with anger.

"It is Gryer—surely you see it has to be Gryer?" I pleaded, slightly disturbed by their non-specific speech.

"The sight of Fyre Dogs is unwelcomed and feared in the east." Adaryvan groaned. "Niall, it could be—"

"Can anyone other than pilgrims sanctioned by the Kennel Maid or members of the Fyuego survive the temperatures in here?"

"No."

"Do the people in the east have access to mineral mines that you wouldn't know about?"

Adaryvan shook his head. "No, my siblings and I survey everywhere."

"Then there is only one place—*in your world or mine*—that Thanatonite could be sourced. And only one man who wants to dominate the world, has a Fyre Dog army in the making, the knowledge of the Flame, plus a growing human army."

The Empress sighed. "He lays your world to siege, not ours."

"Simulinigne."

The Empress twisted her mouth, exposing her enormous, white fangs. "Excuse me?"

"That is the name of Gryer's new world. Does it mean anything to you?"

She nodded. "Together in fire."

"Exactly. I am more convinced now than ever that Gryer means to unite the whole world under his reign. He is the only one outside of Benegnyem who not only understands but respects the fact that everything comes down to Fyre Dogs, the Flames' chosen ones. Without you and your connection to the Divine, kingdoms fall. Gryer, your enemy, knows this. He also knows his army is not yet strong enough to face you, so he conquers another, less defended, less blessed land. He will subject one side whilst silently weakening, disabling, and murdering the other with a more cowardly, yet highly devious attack." Both dragons hung on my every word. I had to keep going. "Please, Your Imperial Majesty, send an army with me to Virisinigne. Help me free my world but also wreak justice upon your enemies. Your enemy *is* my enemy, both now and always. I can—"

"No, Niall." The Empress' tone was slow but firm. "I will do nothing while my children wither and die in their shells. Without them, the future is meaningless. And if Liekke, our most sacred temple, has been assaulted, absolutely nothing will happen until that wrong has been righted. If you are correct, and two Charred members of the Fyuego have joined to rally against us, then to achieve what you ask, you will have to destroy one of my own. I cannot—*I will not*—sanction that lightly, not even out of extreme anger and betrayal. First, we must heal. I must heal. However, *I will* serve justice. Seek out your man, take him a sample. Save my children, and then I will see if you deserve the Blade of the Flame as well as the Amulet." Glowing like stoked embers, steam billowed from her. "If not, I will serve holy judgement and burn you all."

THIRTY-SIX

My new armour had both pockets and a satchel, and whilst filling the latter, I hoped I wasn't poisoning myself by carrying potentially lethal minerals. I had every intention of asking Alun when I found him but as the Empress' declaration of justice-cum-revenge rang throughout my body, I figured that failing her would be worse than any death the rocks could incur.

With my senses already overwhelmed, flying out of the crater into the full light of day was disorientating. I wasn't even sure how long I had been down there, or how long my pilgrimage had taken. From the number of days and nights I had seen, I counted three days, yet time on the mountain range didn't seem linear—not to mention that I wasn't always conscious.

Rising above the peaks wasn't any better.

Adaryvan soared effortlessly, cutting his way through currents and thermals way above the peaks and troughs of the jungle below. To begin with, only fascination prevented me from being violently ill, however, riding the airways was apparently similar to riding waves, so as long as I focused on the scenery, not the fall, I enjoyed my dragon's-eye-view.

Adaryvan must have been listening to me reason with myself because I heard his gruff chuckle as I calmed down. Oddly, his mirth helped. I still held on for dear life, but I released my grip enough for some blood to flow through my fingers—not that Adaryvan would have been particularly bothered either way, his skin was far too thick for my comparatively pathetic nails to leave any marks.

As we passed over the last edge of the Liekke's mountain peaks, Adaryvan tilted his head. Following his line of vision, I spotted a small sandy-orange creature speeding its way towards us and laughed.

"Pynyt!" I shouted as he approached. "Slow down for Pynyt!"

"I already have," Adaryvan replied sarcastically before releasing a semi-bemused snort. "You're either greedy, in big trouble, or truly blessed. Which is it?"

"Pardon?"

He chuckled dryly. "If the Flame has sent you a Fyrewowwa *and* Charred you with me, those are your only options."

As Pynyt landed on my left shoulder, a sense of completion filled me. We were possibly the most unusual trio I had ever seen or heard of, but nothing about their companionship felt wrong. The future still terrified me, I had no answer for Adaryvan's question, and I doubted if I would succeed or would be fast enough to save Virisinigne—or possibly all of humanity if the Empress' anger continued to increase. There was still so much I did not understand, yet somehow, none of that included my winged companions.

Gazing into Pynyt's eyes, I wondered if I needed to fill him in on our mission, but no sooner had I thought the question did he shake his head and hiss. "You already know?" I asked.

I know, he replied in my head.

My eyes boggled. "Can everyone read my mind?" I asked, feeling somewhat exposed.

"Technically, all members of the Fyuego can speak to any Fyre Dog, but only your Charred partner will hear and feel your call from afar." Adaryvan said focused on the horizon. "The bond and conversation between Charred partners is unique and unheard by others. Fyrewowwa's are different. Through the Flame's grace, they can choose to assist you as spirit guides. Both Fyrewowwa and Fyre Dogs *can* communicate at any time, but people will only truly hear us if we want them to—and they have accepted the Flame."

"As I have," I said, knowing it to be true but wanting to hear it anyway.

"As you have," repeated Adaryvan, humouring me.

When Emberbyrg came into view again, it was impossible not to be impressed by the scale of the city. It was beautiful from the ground, yet seeing the white stone walls and grand architecture shine from above was beyond anything I'd ever seen before. However, the splendour before me didn't prevent the pang of regret I experienced as I glanced back at the Liekke mountain range. As weird and unpredictable as my time there had been, it still felt freer, less pressured. Enya was right, out there was the closest to carefree independence any of us would ever feel.

When Adaryvan insisted on visiting the king before anyone else, I was annoyed. Listening to protocol could wait, I wanted to seek Alun's opinion as fast as possible and present my findings to both King Inygo and the Empress simultaneously. Adaryvan was uninterested in my displeasure, and when forced to reflect, I realised he was right. Triumph rippled through his scales when I conceded that, but even I wasn't obstinate enough to pretend my crew wouldn't freak out and attempt to shoot at an unknown, ship-size, fire-breathing dragon flying towards them. Any normal ship from my world would. Of course, they'd all burn for their efforts, but they'd consider it better to go down trying.

As we approached the city, an alarm, like an amplified roar called out. Within seconds, Seraphyna and Wydgitta rocketed out of the palace followed by half-a-dozen smaller dragons. I am sure that most dragons would be intimidated by being flagged, especially by so many large counterparts, but if Adaryvan's heart missed a beat, I didn't detect it. However, I didn't need to be able to read minds to read the surprise on their faces when they saw me on his back. In a strange way it made me proud, even if I knew it wasn't really thanks to any merit of my own.

I hadn't won over the most frightening, protective dragon.

The Flame had joined us.

As we came into land and the dragons began to communicate with rumbling hisses, imposter syndrome began to creep into my thoughts. How was I worthy of such a position? These ideas were not helped when Uryah and Prince Aydan stepped into the courtyard. Their combined shock was palpable. Actually, Uryah looked like he wanted to strike me down there and then. I couldn't wholly blame him. He had probably worked all his life and trained hard to complete his pilgrimage and earn his Charr. I had rocked up, winged it (in more ways than one), and been granted the biggest dragon available. If strength, manliness, and valour were proven by *my dragon is bigger than yours* alone, I won, but I wondered if Uryah was considering demonstrating how a terrier could pull down a mastiff. Neither sneering nor smiling, Aydan was harder to read. At best I thought he was undecided, yet their potential disapproval began to cement my fears of inadequacy until Enya entered, and one glance at her grin blew all other thoughts away. Blushing, I felt myself beaming and struggling for breath simultaneously.

"Decided to go big, huh?" said Enya, projecting her voice as she approached Adaryvan.

"Go big *to* go home, isn't that the saying?" I called back, smirking.

Still smiling, she shook her head and waited for me to descend.

I was inexplicably nervous. *How are you less anxious about abseiling down a dragon than talking to a princess? What an idiot.*

You need a rope to abseil, mocked Adaryvan.

Without meaning to, I sneered in response as I turned to meet Enya. Her smile dropped and my guts flipped. "Oh, sorry, oh, that wasn't meant for you. It was—oh, nuts, I—"

Smooth, Sailor, real smooth.

My eyes shot up to my silent companion and Enya laughed. "Trouble with the big guy?"

Groaning, I rolled my eyes. "Something like that. It's been an eventful few days."

She nodded knowingly.

"Everything feels different. The same, yet... I don't know how to put it." My mouth raced ahead of my brain, making me cringe inside. "Just different. Like—"

"I understand," Enya said, softly.

"I thought you would," I replied, holding her gaze.

Her smile, although more cautious than when we were on the mountain, melted me. Out the corner of my eye, I saw Uryah's jealous glare. My stomach twisted. I couldn't afford to be making enemies. I needed friends and favours. Allies. Alienating the Commander of the Royal Guard would be just as ignorant as making a play for the king's only daughter in front of her older brother. Blessed by the Flame or not, I was pushing my luck. The anointed Kennel Maid was not going to live on a ship in the Virisinigne seas. I needed to redirect my thoughts.

"He left me for a bit, but my spirit guide took pity on me and came back," I said, forcing a chuckle as I pointed at Pynyt.

Her face flashed with what I thought was disappointment, but she quickly smiled again saying, "So I see."

"Do you know if Cal got back safely?"

"Yes, I received word an hour ago that both our hinnies are resting at Fort Fyuego and then will return to Emberbyrg."

Genuine relief spread over me. "Good. I owe him my life. Without my friends, I wouldn't have made it, I—" My voice crackled as a wave of emotion caught me off guard. Gulping hard, I stared at Pynyt, willing him to rescue me once more. "I stand here by the grace and mercy of others. I know that."

Enya nodded towards Adaryvan. "*He* is more than the result of grace and mercy. What happened up there?"

I began to answer her when a herald called out, announcing the arrival of the king and queen. The pomp and ceremony was impressive the first time I met King Inygo, but whilst surrounded by dragons even the grandest humans seemed somewhat second rate. It did, however, have the desirable effect of organising the Throne Room and starting the meeting that I already wanted to be excused from.

The four royals sat on their thrones surrounded by their huge dragons, while the smaller dragons faced them alongside their Charred partners. Everyone present were red-eyed members of the Fyuego, but the only ones I knew by name were Commander Uryah and Lord Byrne—the latter of whom still regarded me with suspicion. Apparently even befriending the largest dragon in the land wasn't going to dispel that from his face. It occurred to me that perhaps Lord Byrne was simply a man who loved consistency and predictability. Such qualities made him perfect for his job, and in all fairness, I couldn't claim to live by either term, so possibly suspicion and distrust were all I was worth.

Adaryvan and I stood in front of the thrones and patiently waited to be addressed—well, semi-patiently, because Adaryvan internally told me to stop fidgeting twice.

"Adaryvan," said the king when he had finished conferring with Seraphyna, his dragon. "I am surprised to have the honour of seeing you here."

"No more than I, Your Majesty, no more than I," replied Adaryvan.

"Yet it is true? *You* present this pilgrim as an accepted member of the Fyuego and *your* Charred partner?" The king's tone was an odd mixture of disbelief, hope, and I thought, apprehension.

"The Flame and their holy vessel, the Empress, blessed him before my very eyes. Check his arms. He wears my scales."

All eyes turned to me expectantly. Releasing the straps from my vambraces, I exposed my lower arms, revealing my tattoos.

Are you not going to show the full length of your scales? Adaryvan said when I stopped rolling my sleeve just before my elbow. *You must show the king your upper arms.*

No. I kept my eyes on the king, watching him marvel at the marks on my skin.

I sensed Adaryvan's disapproval before he spoke. *You cannot lie, Niall.*

I am not lying. I am omitting detail. It is not the same.

Why? You should be proud.

I am proud, I replied, honestly. *I know these marks are a great honour.*

Then why—?

I am not sure everyone will see it as a blessing. Some here might see me as competition or a challenger. I am neither, but nothing should distract the Fyuego from the Empress' order at the moment. Please, give me time. Let us focus on one mission at a time.

Adaryvan paused and I feared he was going to disagree with me. Just as my brain began scrambling for a new argument, his gravelly voice rolled into my mind like a crashing wave. *Very well.*

Apparently having seen enough, King Inygo cleared his throat and said, "Then you are truly honoured, Prince Niall. I cannot pretend you receiving a gauntlet-size Charr instead of a cuff is beyond my expectations." The king's face was stern but not unwelcoming. "However, I have never questioned the divine will of the Flame and I am not about to start now." He stood. "Welcome, brother Niall. *Flamma nobiscum!*"

All humans echoed *Flamma nobiscum,* while the dragons all spat fire into the air simultaneously and I fell to my knees. I don't know if I was supposed to, but it felt right, especially as my body turned to jelly and I choked on tears I didn't know I was trying to swallow.

As soon as the flames fizzled into thin air, Adaryvan extended his body to its full height. "Now, we have a more pressing, life-threatening, world-ending matter to attend to, Your Majesty." His voice commanded and all eyes fixed on him. "The Empress has sent us to convey an urgent, mandatory mission. Niall must return to his ship immediately to do his part while we discuss how to destroy an assassin—and save the world."

THIRTY-SEVEN

A daryvan's scaled back was surprisingly accommodating but my body yearned for sleep, so climbing into the horse-drawn carriage and seeing an upholstered seat seemed like pure luxury. Had Uryah not insisted on coming with me, my journey to the docks would have been blissful, however, his piercing red eyes told me long before he spoke that he intended on probing me for details the whole way. Exhaustion ate away at my every cell and it took willpower—and the odd pinch from Pynyt—to prevent me from snapping. To be fair to Uryah, his questions were logical and on point, but I couldn't ignore the gnawing voice in my head that said I would have to repeat every detail as well as attempt to explain this world once I found my crew.

Uryah had watched me redo my vambrace straps with interest but he didn't ask to see my tattoos up close. Probably it was offensive enough to know I had marks to match his, seeing up close wasn't necessary—nor was telling him they were twice as long and the woman he clearly loved was supposedly my Fated Mate. Not that I really understood what that meant or why the Empress assumed it. Sure, I had full-length scales like Enya, but the king and queen didn't have matching tattoos, yet their union had been blessed by the Flame. I didn't ask the Empress and having dismissed it as soon as I heard it, I didn't plan to. Thankfully, with a more immediate issue before her, Her Imperial Majesty had also let the matter go.

As the carriage approached the Kennel Gates, I peered out of the window to see three dragons resting in the stalls next to the entrance kiosks. Bizarrely, they seemed less frightening this time. Still with the princess at the palace, Wydgitta wasn't there but even if these were smaller, only days earlier my heart begged me to run at the sight of any of the ginormous lizards and now I wore the marks of one and had ridden on his back.

Life really did not make sense.

"How sure are you the minerals have been swapped?" Uryah asked, pulling me out of my daydream.

"Pretty sure. In a world where stones are highly sought after and pirates love to prank, it pays to know how to identify what is a gem and what is poison."

Uryah raised his eyebrows. "But you think your man can answer without any doubt?"

"Yes. Alun is an awkward man, but he is rarely wrong." I laughed. "Please don't tell him I said that. I'll never live it down."

A smile crept across Uryah's face. He didn't say anything, but I had hope that my throw-away comment had softened his opinion of me, if only a little.

Guards approached the carriage door, took one glance at their commander, and waved us through the gates. From there, the horses should have had a clear run across Brindley Meadow, however, to my surprise we stopped a few metres beyond the gates.

"Why are we—" Uryah said irritably, sticking his head out of the carriage. A polite laugh rippled out of him as he swung the door open and stood aside. "Your Highness, I should have guessed."

A misplaced pang of excitement was replaced by one of disappointment when Prince Aydan's face appeared in the doorway. "Room for one more?" he said, leaping inside and placing himself opposite me.

Uryah sat beside him and knocked on the ceiling. Immediately, the horses sprang into action and I looked out of the window just in time to see Aydan's dragon take off.

"Coayl dropped me off," Aydan said, stating the obvious.

"Has your father's meeting with the Fyuego finished already?" Uryah said diplomatically, knowing full-well the main meeting would only now be commencing.

"No, no, but I heard what I needed to. Coayl will fill me in later, and the king and my sister can organise the Empress' request perfectly well. It was agreed that me accompanying Niall to his crew was more useful." Aydan sighed. "Anyway, there's only so much repetition I can take in a day." Pausing, the prince cast his eyes up and down me. "You've caused quite a stir, haven't you?"

"It was not my intention. I only seek—"

"Yes, yes," Aydan said, waving his right hand. "Don't look so petrified of me. If you have found the cause of our Empress' distress then your appearance—*despite the stir*—will have been Flame sent."

Taken aback and not knowing what to say, I bowed my head respectfully.

For a moment all were silent, but Uryah sent a chill cutting down my spine when he added, "Of course, if you are lying..."

"I am not, Commander," I answered without hesitation. Glancing between commander and prince, I couldn't decide who was the most dubious. I needed these men on my side. I needed their favour. I decided to start at the top. "How is Rhys, Your Highness?" I said in my most friendly, unconfrontational tone. "I sincerely hope he will make a full recovery?"

Instantly, the prince's face lit up. "I saw him yesterday. He is wrapped in a ridiculous number of blue hibiyre leaves, but he will be fine. Thank you for asking."

"Of course. I am relieved to hear it."

"As was I." He shook his head, then chuckled softly. "I obviously didn't mean it, but I did tell him he was an ass to fall off a hinny on a mountain." Prince Aydan's smile was infectious. Unlike his sister, who required several hours of sweat and high-altitude to get such an honest smile out of, Aydan made no effort to restrain himself around me.

Despite maintaining a more measured stance in my presence, even Uryah laughed. No matter how small, I took that as a win.

"I know it is not the point, but I am curious for your boat," Prince Aydan said, angling his neck to leer out of the window trying to glimpse the docks.

"Ah, yes, the princess mentioned you love to sail," I replied, instantly wishing I had left Enya out of my sentence as Uryah's smile dropped.

"I do!" Aydan declared. "I positively itch to get back to the open waters." His face grimaced. "My trips will be fewer for a while, though."

"For excellent reason," Uryah added, encouragingly.

Aydan lightly snorted. "Of course! The birth of my son is a cause to celebrate!"

"Your wife has given birth?"

"Yes, two days ago—while you were apparently conquering Liekke. Had Sonya not been so imminent, I would have accompanied you myself. But when duty calls, we must answer." Aydan nudged Uryah's arm playfully. "Anyway, Uryah here wasn't complaining, were you?"

Uryah nodded. "I rarely do, Your Highness."

Aydan chuckled at his own thoughts.

"Well, congratulations," I said.

"Thank you. Are you married, Niall?"

"No, Your Highness."

"I don't suppose your way of life lends to keeping house and home?" Uryah spoke kindly, but I didn't miss the extra message his eyes wanted me to take from his statement.

Holding his gaze, I replied, "Precisely."

"Are your siblings married?" Aydan asked, oblivious to any slight.

"Yes, all of them." I forced a light chuckle. Hoping to beat Uryah to any sarcasm, I added, "My father apparently tired of match making after seven weddings."

"I should think so," scoffed Uryah. "Even for a king, the needs and demands of so many would be tiresome. Emberbyrg has a two-child rule for good reason."

"Pardon?"

"What don't you understand?" Uryah looked genuinely baffled.

"You have a decreed limit on family size?" The expression on the queen's face when I said I was the seventh son replayed in my mind. If they could only have two children by law, it was no surprise she was gobsmacked.

"Emberbyrg is great and illustrious, but the city walls are finite." Uryah rolled his shoulders, stretching his already straightened back. If circumstances were different, I would have laughed and called him a peacock. "Surely, you see the wisdom in that?"

"What happens if a woman has twins on her second birth?"

"If she is a noble, she can apply for a special licence."

"And if she is not a noble woman?"

Uryah shrugged. "There are many towns and cities in Benegnyem without walls."

"Exile?" I said incredulously.

Aydan spread his arms out. "To live anywhere in Benegnyem is a blessing."

"But Emberbyrg is the greatest city?"

"Every mountain has a peak," Aydan said, dryly.

"For those with small families, the right colour eyes, and a partner of the opposite gender." Despite my irritation, as soon as the words came out of my mouth, I regretted them. My father had eight children and I was by far the worst diplomat. The irony of me trying to save them all kicked me in the stomach again. How I wished that Raine had brown eyes—or that we were already at the docks! *Flame, give me an enormous, sarcastic dragon any day over trying to say the right thing to a person, let alone a prince and his royal commander,* I silently sighed.

Aydan flushed red and Uryah stifled a gasp.

Sensing the prince's patience ebbing, I did my best to channel Raine's attitude and focused on keeping my timbre as even, humble, and honest as possible. "Forgive me, Your Highness, I mean neither you nor your world any offense. I am simply not accustomed to your ways and fatigue has marred my manners. I sincerely wish to learn quicker and pray you one day meet my eldest brother and his husband, for they are much more refined than I."

As curiosity spread across Aydan's face like warm butter on crumpets, I knew my effort had paid off.

Thankfully, I didn't have time to ruin my win as the carriage pulled to a halt and one of the coachmen called out: "All hail His Royal Highness, Prince Aydan, crowned and sworn defender of our esteemed kingdom and the almighty Flame!"

Stepping out behind the prince, I got to see the residents of Old Emberbyrg in a different light. While they originally met me with indifference, or even ridicule at my foreign accent, they greeted Aydan and Uryah with absolute respect. Pynyt flew off the second the door opened and I hoped it was lack of interest in crowds, not despair of me that made him go.

A dozen pristine guards stood to attention at the dock entrance. Stepping out of the office, the two guards I met on my arrival marched towards us. Although Cuykoo initially remained focused on the prince, Robyn's shrewd eyes quickly clocked my armour. Had there not been such a stark difference between the brothers' height, I am sure he would have muttered into Cuykoo's ear, however, where nature prevented discretion, sense also prevented tact.

"Blimey! I thought you'd been judged by the Flame, not enlisted!" Cuykoo called out, staring at me whilst pointing at the matching symbol on his chest plate.

Robyn sharply elbowed him in the thigh before saluting the prince. "Your Highness, how may we assist you?"

"Lieutenant, have you been watching the foreign ship and tending to the needs of the crew as requested?" Prince Aydan replied, trying to hide a smile. He was clearly well accustomed to the twins.

"Absolutely. My men and I have not let them out of our sight."

"Very good. I wish to see them. Lead the way."

THIRTY-EIGHT

s I approached *The Leviathan,* shivers raced from head to toe. Home was literally in front of me and it felt like a weird dream. When my crew began to line the portside of the ship, my heart pounded in my chest. Their smiles matched mine, and as Marino and Raine ran down the plank to greet me, I threw my arms around them with more affection than I would any of my blood brothers.

"We feared you were dead," whispered Marino as he embraced me.

"Apparently, I'm harder to kill than we thought," I chuckled, stepping back. Remembering the prince, and afraid I had forgotten myself again, I corrected my stance and turned to him. "Forgive me, Your Highness, I—"

"Not at all," Aydan replied, smiling. "It is quite right you greet your men."

Whilst bowing in thanks, relief hit me, but as I straightened up, it was Uryah's admiring expression that caught me off guard. He didn't say anything, and his sterner gaze soon returned, but I suddenly sensed that this was where we might find common ground. As a commander, he clearly knew what it was to be in charge and give orders, but also to have genuine affection for those around him. I suspected I let my crew get away with more than his soldiers, but that smile gave me hope that one day it could be possible to find more to unite us than to divide.

"Your Highness, Prince Aydan, may I present Marino, my first mate, and Raine, my navigator." Each side politely bowed. Turning to Marino, I asked, "Where is Alun? We must speak to him immediately."

Marino struggled to hide his surprise, but remained silent as he jerked his head towards the ship, sending Raine in pursuit of our uncouth gunner.

Alun grinned broadly as he approached. I wanted to believe it was purely due to the pleasure of seeing me again, but we both knew I was anxious about what he might say—and he was enjoying it.

"Alun," I said, after a brief introduction, "there is a lot I have to tell you all, but before any of that, I need you to identify some rocks."

Alun's grey, wayward eyebrows rose sharply. "Alright..."

Aydan cleared his throat. "Your prince tells me you are an expert in geology?"

I knew Alun would be bursting to retort the use of *your prince*. I was only ever a prince to them when it suited them on official visits or the crew wanted to mock me. Thankfully, for once, he stayed on point. "Aye, Your Highness, I know me rocks well enough."

Slipping the satchel from around my neck, I unfastened the buckles, opened the flap, and passed it to him. "Can you tell us what is in the bag?"

Peering inside, Alun rubbed his beard and grunted. "No rocks, that's for sure. These are minerals. Thanatonite, to be precise. Why are you carrying this around? Captain, don't you remember it's other names?"

"I do—or at least I think I know one of them. Please tell Prince Aydan though, not me." With Uryah's scrutinising eyes set on me, I was anxious the words came from Alun without it looking like I was feeding him information.

Alun held Aydan's gaze. "Death stones."

"You are sure?" Aydan said, taking a step towards Alun and the bag. "Could it not be rubrunite? We have a specific, unique quality of rubrunite in Mount Liekke that you may not have come across before."

"That may be so, Your Highness, but rubrunite is not in front of me." He jolted the satchel, making the contents move. "You have a few shards of orpiment in here, too. Someone likes their orange and red minerals. Why are you showing me this?"

"You call it *death stone*—why?" Uryah asked.

"Because they are highly toxic," Alun said, shrugging like it was blatantly obvious.

"How toxic?" I asked, again worrying whether I had killed myself by touching them. "I've been carrying them—"

"Did you hit them and then breathe in the dust?"

"No."

"Have you made some into jewellery and hung it on your person?"

"No."

"Did you lick them?"

"Alun!"

He grinned. "Then you're probably alright."

"So, it's not *that* toxic?" Aydan sounded relieved. "We can tell the Empress all is—"

"Oh, no, it's the worst mineral out there. Wear it on your skin or even sit around it for very long and you'll end up with various nasty effects. If you keep it around, the end result is always the same. It's a devious killer. *A Jeweller's Long Goodnight,* that's what me old man used to call it."

"Excuse me?" Uryah tilted his ear towards Alun as though that would help translate my gunner's gruff, foreign accent. "Did you say *jeweller*?"

"Aye. Story started way-way before I was born. Tale goes that a jeweller came to Tecta from the north with all kinds of precious gems and stones. You name it, he had it. He also had a neighbour with a thick tongue and wandering willy."

"Alun!" I wanted the ground to swallow me whole.

"Apologies. Not that I'm lyin', I just—" I waved him on. "Right, okay then. Well, the neighbour wandered into the jeweller's wife's knick—" I cut him off with a sharp cough. "*Bedroom.* The jeweller found out and was unsurprisingly furious. However, not wanting to go to prison for murder, he opted to lose a lengthy game of cards in which a ring with a lavish red gem was the prize. Of course, the neighbour mistook the red thanatonite for a ruby and wore it day and night with pride. Before long he was complaining of headaches, mood swings, and general weakness, and no doctors could understand why. Next thing, he was coughing up his guts and died in a pool of his own blood. It was the perfect murder. The jeweller got away with it, too."

"If he got away with it, how do you know this?" Aydan was not convinced by Alun's storytelling abilities.

"Coz when the jeweller unexpectedly died of a heart attack years later, the son took over the shop. He had learnt the family trade but knew nothing about his father's black-market range of *'til death do us part* jewels." Alun shook his head. "Story goes, the son had gone through all the stock, handling and shaping the thanatonite without a care in the world. He died of the effects a day after an old client had come looking for a *long goodnight*. Not interested in the business, the granddaughter found extra ledgers hidden in a secret draw when she sold up and so the whole story was slowly revealed."

Uryah and Aydan stared at one another, wordlessly assessing whether they believed Alun.

"You haven't answered why you want to know," Alun said abruptly, not bothering to wait on protocol—and jarring my fragile nerves.

Whether it was from surprise or just Alun's bizarre charisma, I don't know, but Aydan immediately answered, "Because if you are right, our Empress is in grave danger."

Sneering, Alun mouthed *Empress* at me.

That was a conversation for later. "Would thanatonite affect eggs?" I asked him, trying to stay on topic. "I mean reptile eggs?"

"Of course," said Alun, curling his bottom lip. "Remember the hydrothermal vent pools near the Magma Isles?"

"The hot springs?"

"No, not the hot springs. They are hydrothermal springs—they teem with life." Alun rolled his eyes as though I was stupid. "I told you about them when you were submerged *in* a hot spring. I can't believe—"

"Alun, you waffle on about a lot of things," I said gruffly, trying not to curse in front of the prince. "What about these vent pools?"

"The ones where death stones are found are void of all life. Nothing survives there. If anyone has put eggs in this stuff," Alun raised the bag of minerals, "they're wasting their time."

"If you had to remove thanatonite from a volcano chamber, what would you do?"

Pausing, Alun chewed his thumb nail. "Can any larger pieces be removed manually?"

"Yes," Uryah said, confidently.

"Do you have access to the main vent or is it sealed?"

"There are direct routes to gently bubbling magma."

Alun grunted. "Then I'd return it from whence it came and dump it in there. With any luck, it'll sink into the magma and that'll be that."

"So, we can deal with the larger pieces," said Uryah, "but what about the substrate on the lair floor? Does it all have to go?"

Out the corner of my eye, I saw Marino and Raine mouth the word *lair* while Alun's eyes boggled. There was only so far this meeting could go before I had to sit my crew down properly.

"Assuming you want something to survive living there...?" Alun glanced at me, and I nodded. "Then yes, every last speck of dust needs to be gone."

Aydan stared up at the sky. "Could we blow it out?"

"If you want to intoxicate those doing the blowing, sure." Alun scoffed. "Safest way would be to neutralise it."

"And how would you do that?" I asked.

"Lime? It would blanket it, anyway..."

"Would that hinder the eggs?" Uryah asked.

"Well, yes, you—"

"That's not the answer then," Uryah cut in.

After a moment's silence, a knowing smile spread across Alun's face. "I've always said that nature provides its own balance—ain't that right, Captain?" I reluctantly agreed. "So often the sting grows next to the cure, you just have to know your herbs."

My mind went straight to the hibiyre petals that healed my infected wounds and broken bones. A shudder ran through me thinking of the fever that accompanied the red ones, and I was sure an extra, untold magic had been involved as I stepped into the flames, but Alun was right: nature did provide.

"We need more than herbs," Uryah said, irritably.

"Aye, but creatures are the same. Tiny woodlice break down the most harmful things—"

"What are woodlice?"

"They're the small, armoured-looking creatures you find in moist vegetation; you know, like under rotten logs and leaves?"

Uryah sneered. "Pill bugs?" Conversation with Enya had already taught me that we didn't always name creatures the same way, but Uryah seemed honestly baffled that we would name them anything else.

"Well, we're not talking about pill bugs, are we?" Fed up with inconsequential details, Aydan slapped his hands against his sides. "We could collect every last bug across the land, but unless they are extreme-heat resistant or their corpses neutralise, we're no better off."

"What about the Empress? Can we cure her from thanatonite poisoning?" asked Uryah, not giving Alun time to respond. He was thinking though. I could see the cogs in his mind whirring—often that look made me anxious because it was the prelude to some crazed scheme or request, but in that moment, deep down, I knew that one of his wild ideas might just be the answer.

He did not disappoint.

"Do you have candlefly squid here?"

Aydan and Uryah stared at Alun blankly. "Excuse me?"

"They breed around hydrothermal vents and glow in the water, no matter how deep. Their ink is luminescent, like them. You'd know one if—"

Aydan's face lit up like a child solving a puzzle. "Ah, Fyrefly squid! Yes, of course, we rarely fish them though. Why do you ask?"

"The ink is fire resistant and can be made into a putty. If you use that to sweep your lair, it should collect any wayward minerals before you replace anything—assuming you want to add in fresh substrate for your-your, *reptiles*?" Alun paused, checking everyone's faces to see if he was using the correct terms. No one stopped him, so he carried on, "You could then feed the squid, especially the highly nutritious cuttlebones, to the Empress."

"Why the cuttlebone?" Uryah still eyed Alun suspiciously.

"It's absorbent and full of calcium. It will help balance and flush the system." Alun snorted. "I told you, nature has the remedy next to the toxin, if you pay attention."

Scowling, Uryah turned to Aydan, "Don't you think it is rather convenient these *foreigners* arrive waving the carrot and the stick, Your Highness?"

Aydan waved his hand, prompting Uryah to elaborate.

"I find it somewhat amazing that these men arrive from nowhere, supposedly knowing nothing of our world, yet are still able to diagnose what has haunted us for a decade as well as being uniquely positioned to tell us how to cure it." He paused but was apparently not finished. "And what is more, the ailment seems to come from their world, for we do not have thanatonite exposed here."

Mimicking his commander's expression, Aydan glared at me. "He has a good point."

"Why would I poison your world and then beg for assistance?" I asked with feeling.

Uryah raised an eyebrow. "Perhaps you seek to weaken us before luring us through the Divide?"

"Why would I risk my life completing your pilgrimage if I simply had to wait?" I understood the part of Uryah that wanted to test my merit and protect his nation from betrayal, but I had hoped we had moved passed such a level of suspicion. What was I supposed to do, lie? Say, *oh no, we*

*have no idea how to save your Empress—you know, the only
one whose order to assist Virisinigne you will listen to?*

"What utter rot!" spat Alun, narrowly avoiding a swear
word. "We didn't sail through that blasted wall looking for
enemies or corpses. We came to bleedin' well avoid them!
You say you have squid here, so you have the remedy. Suit
yourself if you listen or not. You'll need a tiny arse-net if
you do try." He chortled. "See, there's another bit of free
advice, but I ain't got a small enough net, so on that one
you'll have to save yourselves. Ungrateful bastards!"

Fearing Alun would continue his rant, I wrapped
my fingers around his old, but still well-muscled arm
and gently squeezed—simultaneously hoping my body
remained as strong as his in forty years' time.

"How do you know about the ink?" asked Raine, seizing
the moment to bring some calm to our storm.

"It's part of the jeweller story, ain't it?" Annoyed,
Alun shook his head. In all honesty, it probably was
something we should have heard either from Alun or the
grapevine over the years, but I didn't like the taste of squid
and couldn't see the appeal of blood-coloured ink, so I
apparently missed the finer details. "After the success with
his neighbour, he tried to off his wife. According to his
notes, he believed she survived due to a combination of
coincidences. First, the stone in the ring was very small,
but most importantly, it was eternally covered in clay, lime,
and red-squid ink because she was a potter with a fancy
for ink-coloured ornaments." Seeing Raine and mine's
surprise, Alun rolled his eyes for the hundredth time. "You
really should listen to history more."

Meeting Uryah's gaze, I expected him to continue with his doubtful comments, but somehow he seemed amused by Alun's *the devil may care* attitude. Or perhaps it was my lack of control over my gunner. There are few people who would think to make up a character as brash as Alun and even fewer who would dare present him to crowned royalty. This knowledge produced mixed feelings within me: I felt the weight of my unpredictable friend, but I equally felt a sense of protectiveness for him. Of all my crew. Rough around the edges as we all were, we were loyal and honest. Family.

Whatever his thoughts, and whether his challenge was merely a test, Uryah's curiosity had been peaked enough to switch him into planning mode. "What kind of net do we need?"

"Extremely strong, but also fine. Candlefly—or Fyrefly squid as you call them—can squeeze through most nets and have razor-sharp beaks. Or at least the ones in our waters do."

"I will send my soldiers out to get nets immediately," Uryah said, signalling one of his men from behind him to approach.

"The net is neither here nor there, Commander," said Aydan, seemingly rallying from deep thought. Knowing the prince well, Uryah silently waited for him to continue. "If we fish over the thermals, Ceytus will kill us before we pull them in."

THIRTY-NINE

The waters of Virisinigne were always teeming with life. For over a decade, I had witnessed creatures great and small swimming past *The Leviathan*, and although a few whales had given us cause for momentary alarm, none had truly come close to challenging our ship for its name. *We* were the sea monster as far as pirates were concerned, and wildlife—with the exception of fish we wished to eat—lived alongside us without fear.

Prince Aydan stood on the iron dock and described a watery menace beyond my imagining—but not beyond my belief. I watched my crews' faces twist with derision and turn to me, obviously expecting their captain to quickly dismiss Aydan's claims of a fanged beast who ripped apart nets and anyone who dared to cast them. But they had not seen what I had seen. For a moment, I both pitied and envied their innocence—and regretted that it would not last.

Fyrefly squid were not commonly seen back home. Fishermen had to be clever to find them, and often their nets would not reach deep enough to capture many—which of course added to their value—but to my knowledge they did not have any guardians protecting them.

Realising I was taking Aydan seriously, Raine asked, "Are the waters safe to sail at all?"

"Yes," replied Aydan. "I go that way every year on my surveys without any trouble. I have even seen the squid lighting up the sea at night, but knowing what lies beneath, I have never dropped a net near them."

"Are there no other populations of Fyrefly squid? There must be more than one set of hydrothermal vents in this world?"

"There are, but only one known source of the squid. It is possible the smallest vent to the east has some but those waters are no less problematic." Uryah glanced at Aydan, waiting for his approval to continue. When it didn't come, he shrugged his shoulders.

"Going to the closest known location makes more sense anyway," I said, breaking the silence. "We don't have time for scouting missions right now."

Aydan shook his head. "Agreed, but it is no good. Ceytus will sink you in minutes and the Dogs cannot land in deep ocean."

"I thought all creatures bow to the Flame and its divine protectors?" I asked, being careful not to sound antagonistic.

Aydan scoffed. "Yes, but Ceytus doesn't tend to stop long enough to hear commands."

"From a civilian, maybe not, but you are the crowned prince. Perhaps that is why you can safely sail passed, not because you don't fish there? Surely, given the stakes, the theory is worth testing? You could have Coayl on standby to airlift you if things get messy?"

Aydan puffed out his cheeks but said nothing.

"To be fair, we've never tried it with Fyre Dogs on standby. It's always unprotected fishermen who are lost..." Uryah left his words hanging in the air.

The sound of waves gently lapping against the side of *The Leviathan* set electricity through me. It was as though the sea was applauding our plan, willing us to find a cure for the Empress—and ultimately the world.

Everyone waited for Prince Aydan. For a second, I saw a flicker of amusement behind his eye and I felt like he had already decided to go ahead but he was enjoying the power for a moment longer. This man—this future king—was no coward. He would call for caution and plan for chaos.

Finally, he could hide his grin no more. "Go find suitable nets. We're going fishing."

Uryah viewed me with suspicion when I said I knew of a net maker. Possibly, given my short stay, knowing any tradesmen was unlikely, however, one glance at Raine told me he not only knew, but highly approved of my suggestion, so I continued without regret.

"When seeking directions to the palace, I met a deaf girl on a stall. Her name is Oryana and she makes exquisite nets. Do I have your permission to seek her out?"

"We'll go now," beamed Aydan. "Guard, turn the carriage!"

I still hadn't had time to explain anything to my crew and I desperately wanted to rest, but as Aydan placed his hand around my shoulders and propelled me forwards, all I could do was nod, letting them know I would be back. Truthfully, there was no need to voice a command to prepare for sail, I knew Marino would already have that covered.

"How fast is your ship?" Aydan asked as the carriage door closed.

"I can't say in comparison to yours as I haven't seen them sail, but *The Leviathan* has chased down many supposedly faster ships before."

"So your crew are good?"

"The best," I answered with pride.

"Perfect. I think we should take two ships," Aydan was so excited, he almost bounced in his seat. "I've always wondered if Ceytus objects to boats dropping anchor more than the nets, so I fancy trying to scoop up squid on the fly." His eyes danced as he anxiously waited to see if my foolhardy sense of valour matched his.

Honestly, what choice did I have?

Hadn't I already proven I was all in?

My crew had already chosen to follow me through a lethal wall into an unknown world. They weren't going to say no to racing through waters with a sea monster pursuing us—especially not if it served our ultimate cause of seeking help for Virisinigne.

"Very well. You set the plan, we'll do it."

Uryah cleared his throat. "Prince Aydan, if this is the plan, might I suggest you staying safely home and I—"

"Absolutely not! I might openly call for caution, but at no point will this plan happen without me being present."

"But if we are going for speed, there is no need to communicate with Ceytus. With any luck, we might not even *see* them."

"No one knows those waters as well as my crew, and my crew will not sail without my say so. No, Uryah—" Grinning, Aydan dismissively waved a hand in Uryah's face. "Our Fyre Dogs will shadow us and prevent us from being eaten. Have faith! I have a good feeling about this."

Defeated, Uryah sat back. I watched both men, trying to make them out. Oddly, I found Uryah the most consistent. He was loyal and sensible, possibly a little calculating, but being measured made him good at his job—and I was sure his regard for Enya made him colder towards me. Aydan flitted from reserved to uninhibited, from hesitant to adventurous. I stifled a sigh. Wasn't that just the prerogative of a prince?

"This net girl," Uryah said, changing the subject, "are you sure she has nets fine enough?"

"Yes, without question. I witnessed her weaving them myself. They are as fine and beautiful as she is—in net form, I mean." My desire to be certain sent me over the top, but gauging from their faces, I equally satisfied and amused my companions. Ignoring their winks, my mind started running through the practicalities of the task ahead. "Ideally, we want to catch the squid in one pass, but it might be wise to have spares on board or a repair kit. My crew can repair pretty well, but these require more finesse."

Aydan shrugged. "Well, let's just take the girl with us."

Had I told him we needed new shoes, I doubted whether Aydan would have been less flippant in his response. We needed assistance. The girl could assist. We would therefore take her. Never mind silly details like it being dangerous or she might not want to come.

"Certainly it would be good if she agrees to come," I said gently.

"Agrees?" Aydan looked genuinely confused.

I decided to try from another angle—one I thought him more likely to understand. "Her father may not—"

"Niall—may I call you, Niall? All this *Your Highness, Your Prince* stuff is fine for a show but it is tedious in times as these. Don't you agree?"

"Of course—" I paused, hoping this was supposed to be a two-way thing. "Of course, Aydan."

"Wonderful. Well, Niall, I don't know how you get things done in Virisinigne, but this net-girl's father is a subject of Benegnyem. A citizen of Emberbyrg, or Old Emberbyrg, it really is all the same. I, their prince, will insist, and they *will* obey."

Suddenly, I missed Pynyt's presence. His controlling talons gripping into my neck when he sensed I was going to protest or misstep had already saved me from several social faux-pas'. In his absence, I pinched the back of my leg. "Perhaps she might like to be asked—"

Uryah kicked me. "Sorry, cramp," he said, grinning.

The carriage stopped, saving me from the spiteful response that was threatening to spew from my mouth. Ignoring protocol, I jumped out, hoping to find Oryana first.

The stall was empty of life, but an array of nets lined the table and ground. Most where too big for what we needed, however, I instantly recognised the exquisite net that Raine and I had bought but never claimed.

Voices muttered from the surrounding stalls, dispersing like wind-blown whispers as word of the prince's arrival spread.

Realising his stall had a royal visitor, one voice boomed jubilantly, if not quite as respectfully as he imagined. "Your Highness," Oryana's father declared, bowing as he rushed in front of Aydan. "How can I serve you?"

"Are you the maker of these nets?" asked Aydan, pointing at the nets whilst eyeing the man's chubby, indelicate fingers.

"Not those particular ones, no, Your Highness. I am the owner of this humble establishment. As you can see, my name is above the door—" He swung his arm backwards, waving at the building behind the stall. I had not noticed it before, yet the sign clearly said, CONLEY AND CONLEY – NETMAKERS.

"So, your name is Conley?"

"Conley Conley, Your Highness." He smiled proudly. "My son has inherited the name, as I did from my father."

"Indeed," replied Aydan, masterfully brushing over the ridiculous double use of name. "Your son makes the nets, then? I thought it was a girl I was after, but no matter, I need—"

Conley Junior arrived at that moment, distracting Aydan. His gaze ran from the young man's stone blue eyes to his stocky hands.

"My daughter makes the nets," Conley Senior confessed. "She is the best netmaker in Emberbyrg. No hands are finer."

"Excellent. I require your finest, strongest nets and her presence at the docks at first light in the morning." Aydan stepped back, ready to climb back into the carriage.

"Forgive me, my prince, but may I ask why?" The father spoke while the son's mouth gaped like an oversized baby-bird.

"She is required on board my ship to mend nets." Aydan clearly thought that explanation enough as with one bound, he launched into the carriage without a second glance.

"Is it dangerous?" For a moment I was touched by the father's concern for his only daughter and lamented that she was not present to witness it. "I can't just let her go wandering off. Losing her would cost my livelihood."

Disgust twisted my lips just as Oryana walked out of the shop. Her shining blue eyes bore into mine, searching for the meaning of the meeting. Forcing a welcoming smile, I approached her, taking her by the hands. Confused, she let me, but turned to her father, hoping that someone's lips would move so she could read them.

"How much?" Conley Senior said, projecting his voice into the carriage.

My stomach dropped as I felt a quiver ripple down Oryana's arms.

"Excuse me?" Aydan said, leaning forward, scowling at the man's insolence.

"Of course, it is an honour to serve our prince," Conley Senior said, hastily bowing as he saw Uryah's hand grip the hilt of his sword. "But if you take her, I need to know she is coming back, or that I have compensation for—"

I scoffed. "You can't just—"

"Hang on there, Niall," said Uryah, staring at my hands as they held onto Oryana's increasingly trembling palms. "What would you need to retire, good sir?"

"It's not just me, Commander, I have my son. This business is his future, too. I cannot—"

Uryah smirked. "Perhaps that can be arranged. Maybe we could gift our visiting prince a beauty? What do you think, Your Highness?"

Prince Aydan tutted. "Fine, you are in luck, Mr Conley. Commander Uryah will see that you are handsomely rewarded to see you and your son to the end of your days. You can work or not as you see fit, but I have bought the girl. Satisfied?"

Conley and Conley glanced at each other, smiling. "Perfectly," said the father.

Aydan nodded, then sat back, signalling he was finished with the discussion. Oryana's grip on me tightened, but when I turned to her, her eyes were fixed on the lips of her father. No tears fell. No venom spat. Her breathing was calm and steady. It was almost like she had been waiting for this day. For this betrayal. The day that her family could make more money without her than with. I was ashamed of them—and of any part that I played in the scene.

Finally looking at me, she said, "Where am I to go?"

"You are to bring all your finest nets to the docks. We are catching Fyrefly Squid. We may need to make repairs."

Her eyes widened. "Fyrefly Squid? You cannot be serious?"

"We are." Uryah said, tugging on my arm and directing me towards the carriage. "Be at the docks before dawn."

A flash of orange proceeded the sensation of Pynyt landing on my shoulder. Oryana fixed her eyes on him. In any other circumstances, I might have jested that she was looking for intelligent conversation from my winged friend as the humans present had none, but nothing about this scenario was funny.

"She'll be there!" called her father. "Just don't forget our deal!"

"You'll receive payment on delivery in the morning," said Uryah, swinging the door closed. Smiling at me, he chuckled. "You're welcome."

"What for?" I asked, genuinely baffled.

"We just bought you a mistress."

FORTY

Laying my head on my own pillow felt like heaven. Facing the ceiling, I counted the planks, making note of each knot, each blemish, just in case someone had switched the ship and I was dreaming. Not that my method was foolproof though. Whilst on the summit of Mount Liekke, had I not thought I was on the ship? Had it not been so life-like that a long-standing dodgy floorboard had saved me? Curious, I got up, and walked over to it. Still there, unfixed, it creaked under my weight.

The lines of real and imaginary were too far blurred for me to understand. I might have thought I had imagined it all, yet my legs still bared the rippled scars where the hibiyre leaves healed me. Torn flesh had been made new, yet also crimpled with the Flame's wavy marks of remembrance.

My fingers traced the outline of the Amulet around my neck. Although cold and inanimate, I could almost sense life beneath the hard exterior. Silently, I mocked myself. Fatigue had made me fanciful. I knew it channelled magic, but there was enough mystery and wonder without me adding to it.

Afraid of someone waking me and seeing the extent of my tattooed arms, I slept in a shirt. There was nothing I would not share with my crew, but I had answered their questions long enough that evening and starting down that particular rabbit hole would have taken me until dawn.

Introducing Pynyt had been interesting enough.

"Since when do you have a pet, Captain?" Alun had said as I sat on a crate, surrounded by my crew.

Pynyt hissed, releasing a little steam for good measure. He seemed pleased at the resulting, collective gasp.

"Pynyt is not a pet, Alun," I said, calmly. "He is a Fyrewowwa. He has chosen to be my spirit guide and—" I paused, extending a finger to stroke Pynyt's cheek. "And, I believe, my friend." Pynyt stretched his wings, so I took that as him agreeing. "This world is full of things that we have never even contemplated. It is—"

"But will they help us?" cut in Alun. "As thrilled as I am to sail and investigate the unknown, it isn't what we came for, is it, Captain?"

"No, Alun, it is not." I was too tired to be angry at him for cutting me off, even though Uryah's disapproval ran through my mind's eye. "But they will only help us if we first help them. They live under the rule of a kingdom, but that is overseen by the guardians of the Flame, their deity." Suddenly I didn't know how to describe the dragons without my crew thinking I had either been drawn into a cult or slipped into insanity—or both. "Fyre Dogs," I said, slowly. Seeing their confusion, and knowing Alun's quick tongue, I knew I had to be careful to use the widely excepted name and not encourage them to say *dragon* in an irreverent manner. Pointing at Pynyt, I cleared my throat. "If you imagine a really big version of him, then you know what a Fyre Dog is. Here, they are everything—I mean *everything*. All rule, all decisions, all honour goes to the Dogs before anyone else. All in the name of the holy Flame. The king is head of this kingdom, but the Empress is the head of all, the voice and guardian of the Flame. Without her on our side, no one will sail to Virisinigne with us."

Feeling like my words were failing, I stopped. Even Alun was too confused to question me. Raine shuffled next to me. To my knowledge, he was the only one who had left the ship, who had heard the citizens' obsession with dogs like I had, but only I had seen the reason why. Apparently he understood the situation faster than I did—or by some mercy he understood me better than I did.

"Captain, are you saying these people are ruled by dragons? Like the creature we want help killing, comes from here?"

Taking a deep breath, I prepared myself for the inevitable barrage of questions that would follow my answer. "Yes, and now I have joined the Fyuego, their sacred order, and am bonded to a dragon, a Fyre Dog. He is huge. His name is Adaryvan, and whatever you do, don't try to shoot him."

Dawn came too quickly but it wasn't a human who woke me. At first I thought it was a voice booming on deck, then I wondered if Aydan had sailed his ship next to ours, but after what felt like a bell tolling inside my mind, I realised that Adaryvan was calling me.

"Where are you?" I groaned out loud.

We're outside.

"We?"

Four Fyre Dogs are joining you on this mission. The king wants us to take no chances with his children. If need be, we will lift the ship between us from the sea.

Pinching myself, I wondered if I was still dreaming as I imagined four dragons flying *The Leviathan*. Realistically, Adaryvan could do it on his own—although the ride would be less smooth. A boyish giggle rippled out of me as I thought of Alun's expletive laden response to either idea.

"Wait! Did you say *children*?" I bolted upright. "Surely there's no need for both Aydan *and* Enya to come?"

They both feel it is their place to oversee this mission. There was something about Adaryvan's tone that worried me.

"But why both?"

Adaryvan didn't reply.

Concentrating, I pushed Adaryvan's mind, searching for an answer. My feeble attempt made him laugh.

They don't trust me, do they? I asked, switching to internal-only conversation when I heard footsteps outside my door.

There are those who feel you are too new to be given such a task alone.

I grimaced. *That's just a polite way of saying* yes.

Prince Aydan is an experienced sailor and knows the waters around the Outer Isles well, it makes sense for him to lead the excursion, reasoned Adaryvan.

Try as I might to think of an argument, I couldn't. *Fine, but that doesn't explain why the princess has to come.*

The Kennel Maiden's responsibility is to watch over work for the Empress as well as Fyre Dogs. Adaryvan chuckled. *Also, she didn't seem too keen on her brother having all the fun, even if she did just escort you up a mountain.*

Oh. Ignoring any potential implications, I reached for my clothes beside my bed. Dressing in the dark had never been an issue for me, but as I picked up my leggings, a spark flew out of Pynyt's mouth, lighting a candle.

"Thanks," I said, nodding at my fiery friend.

Panicked voices called outside.

You better get out here, Adaryvan said wryly, before snorting loudly.

Suddenly I realised I heard him with my ears, not inside my head. "When you said that you are outside, do you mean, right outside the ship?"

Yes, obviously. Each word dripped with sarcasm. I had no time to respond as my door burst open.

"Captain, come quick. Please tell us this is your dragon—sorry, Fyre Dog—before Alun gets trigger happy!" Raine's normally calm exterior was sweating profusely. "It just rose out of the water next to us!"

"You can swim?" I said aloud, running out the door without explaining to Raine.

In shallow water, a little, but it's more holding ones breath and walking on the seabed than swimming.

Groaning, I ran towards my baffled crew who were frozen as they stared into Adaryvan's looming eyes. "Couldn't you have mentioned that while you were talking to me?"

Water dripped off his scales, pooling on the deck. *Where's the fun in that?*

Alun ran up the steps with his sword drawn.

"Put that down!" I shouted.

"Dammit, Captain, you said it was big, but that's ridiculous!"

Adaryvan opened his mouth, revealing the bountiful peaks of bone-crushing teeth and released a low growl. Ironic laughter bubbled out of me. Apparently even dragons took a while to get used to Alun.

I couldn't blame any of them for their fearful reactions. If anything, I was comforted by them because it mirrored my own response days earlier. Truthfully, I was more afraid of how quickly my response had altered. Was it normal to accept so much so soon?

There was no time to ponder though. Within minutes of me calming everybody, Raine called from the lookout post to say a ship was approaching with a dragon escorting it. Until that moment, I hadn't considered how the motion of dragon wings might propel a boat, yet thankfully the captain of the oncoming ship had as he dropped his sails long before I would have. *There's another skill I shall have to learn,* I lamented privately. It pained me to admit that Aydan was going to be better equipped to lead, but it pained me more to count the number of lethal traps I could unwittingly direct my crew into.

You're a fast study, Niall. Adaryvan's gruff voice was surprisingly reassuring. I hoped, if not whole-heartedly believed, he was right. In my silence, he sniggered. *Failing that, I can always airlift you.*

As the first glimmers of sunlight poked over the horizon, Oryana arrived on the back of a cart pulled by a hinny. Her worldly belongings were stuffed into a single time-beaten suitcase whilst her nets were neatly laid underneath her. As if they were going on holiday, her father and brother sat on the drivers bench, smiling from ear to ear without even glancing backwards.

Commander Uryah had arrived moments earlier along with his men and Princess Enya. Just like when she escorted me on my pilgrimage, she wore her armour, but this time her hair was beautifully plaited. It didn't matter what she wore or how she styled her hair though. She simply had the power to take my breath away.

As I steeled myself to speak to Enya, the pitiful sight of Oryana's family broke my gaze, switching me into captain mode. Strangely, I was grateful for it because distractions from my status were not helpful. The seventh son was no match for Princess Enya, but Captain Niall Beckett had purpose.

Raine bounded past me, taking Oryana's hand as she jumped off the cart. I searched her eyes, looking for signs of tears, yet I still couldn't find any.

"I am sorry to steal you," I said to her. "It was not my intention to—"

"You bought her, fair and square!" declared her father. "She's a good girl, she'll serve you well. Or will, once the deal is complete..." Conley Senior walked towards Uryah rubbing his fingers together.

Grimacing, I couldn't watch. "If you wish to say goodbye, do so now. When you are ready, Raine will show you where your bed is and help you with the nets."

A resilient smile spread over her face as I spoke. Turning to Raine, she passed him her bag, grabbed one side of a net, nodded for him to do the same, and together they started dragging it onboard.

"Looks like you've a feisty one there, Captain," chuckled Aydan as he approached. "You'll have trouble taming that one."

Over his shoulder I saw Enya's eyes narrow.

My mouth opened to refute his misogynist remark, but Uryah slapped me on the shoulder, making Pynyt hiss. "Come on, Captain, it's time to go."

FORTY-ONE

L eaving harbour and sailing into the open sea was exhilarating. It was my comfort zone. Yet it also felt wrong. It was the wrong direction. Everything seemed to be taking too long. When Marino told me we had been in Benegnyem for six days, I nearly fell overboard. Time really had warped for me. That was confusing enough, yet it also meant that my level of dread for Virisinigne's fate rose.

How long could the siege hold?

Had it held?

The idea that I would go through all of this only to return to a pile of rubble and my family's ashes blowing in the wind petrified me.

The faster this was finished, the better.

Aydan's idea of taking two ships had already altered. He claimed that he had conferred with his father and his captain, Captain Brandyt, and decided that *The Forging Fyre* should remain at a distance, acting as a backup crew, in case *The Leviathan* was attacked. Part of me wanted to question his trust in our winged friends' ability to lift us out of the ocean in time, but fearing my crew would lose heart, I kept quiet.

"We're fast, we have air support, we have nets that are the finest available. We've got this," I declared as my crew gathered around me. "Alun, you and your cannons must be on standby at all times. All other hands must be on deck with these nets. Speed is our friend. We haul up these little critters to save the Empress. Then we sail home."

"For home!" shouted Marino, towering above me with his arm held high.

The crew roared together. "For home!"

Out the corner of my eye, Liekke's Peak seemed to almost twinkle in the sunlight. Seeing it from this angle was strange, but the almost primal call *to come* that rippled under my skin was stranger. More unsettling. No landmark had ever had that effect on me before and I did not understand it.

Pynyt shuffled on my shoulder but said nothing. He had the ability to remain perfectly still for so long that I would forget he was there, but he also sensed when my thoughts threatened to swamp me and always adjusted his weight at just the right moment. Whether he did it to ground me or encourage action, I was rarely sure, but I found myself becoming reliant on him to snap me into the present. On this occasion, as my eyes met his they also focused on the scene beyond him—of Enya standing on the bow of Aydan's ship. Feeling my gaze upon her, she regally nodded. As I returned the gesture, she smiled, letting me know that she was excited by this adventure.

"Pity the commander put her on the other ship, aye, Captain?" said Alun in a mocking tone.

"Excuse me?"

"Just sayin' that the princess should have sailed with us." His grin spread wide around his grey beard and crooked teeth. "It's not every day I see you smitten."

"Aren't you supposed to be below deck, old man?" I said, half-heartedly pushing him away. "And I'm not smitten, so keep your thoughts to yourself."

"I'm a-goin', I'm a-goin'," Alun replied, laughing all the way to the stairs. Popping his head around the corner, he called out, "But I didn't get this old without learnin' a thing or two!"

"It's a pity manners weren't one of them!" If he heard my quip, I don't know because he disappeared, chuckling.

Insolent gunners aside, I felt prepared for what was coming next. Adaryvan, Wydgitta, Coayl, and Cyrus flew in formation around us. To me it was an awe-inspiring, bizarrely comforting sight. My crew anxiously glanced up at them every now and again, but trusting in my command, they maintained their positions. Alun had called me smitten, but Raine followed Oryana's every movement as she prepared the nets and then moved on to mending our old ones just to keep herself occupied.

"Watch the sea, not the mermaid," I said, joining Raine in the crow's nest.

He blushed profusely. "Sorry—I mean, I am, Captain."

Nudging him, I laughed, but staring out to sea, we fell into contemplative silence.

"Captain?" Raine said quietly, knocking his heel on the pole behind him.

"Yes?"

"Are you really going to take her as your mistress?"

My eyes darted to him while my mind went to Enya. "Who?"

"Oryana. Uryah's men said he'd bought—"

"I don't care what they said!" I rolled my eyes, scoffing. "Of course not! How long have you known me?"

"Twelve, maybe thirteen years, Captain."

"Exactly. And how many mistresses have I brought on the ship in that time?"

"On the ship? None, Captain."

"Then why do you think I am going to start now? And I'm definitely not into buying or gifting women!" Saying I hadn't fumbled onshore would be a lie, or that crew members hadn't settled with partners over the years—both on and off ship—but the one thing my mother had instilled in me was the sanctity of choice. Of respect. Aydan and Uryah might think nothing of purchasing a girl to make their mission simple, but I had no intention of copying them.

The relief on Raine's face was palpable. I'd never seen Raine so lovestruck. Not even Gem, the barmaid in the crew's favourite pub, *Run Aground,* could get that kind of smile out of him. "So, she is free?"

"Once we've finished this mission, yes. I will speak to her, but she can join us or not as she sees fit."

Chewing his lip, Raine laughed. "Good, because I was wondering if I was going to have to fight you for her honour."

"Twit." I rolled my eyes again, chuckling.

"What's that?" Raine muttered, peering into his spyglass.

All I could see was calm, shimmering water. Still wearing my Fyuego armour, I had left my spyglass in my quarters—a decision I instantly regretted. "What is what?"

"The sea. A patch on the horizon is sparkling, Captain."

A whistle blew from *The Forging Fyre*. They had seen it too.

"Drop your anchor!" Aydan's voice boomed across the water.

I did not want the royal party on my ship, but that is exactly what I got. To me, it would have been more sensible for them to observe from the safety of *The Forging Fyre*, instead of leaving a skeleton crew of rescuers should the plan go awry. Remaining on his ship, Captain Brandyt was clearly not stupid. He knew the odds of this mission and knew exactly which wheel he wanted to stand behind.

Marino had steered *The Leviathan* out of many storms—some so masterfully that I slept through them—but whether it was his hands or mine on the wheel, neither of us wanted the extra pressure of having royalty onboard.

We were still a few miles from the sparkling waters above the hydrothermal vents. With the wind on our side and the option of a boost from dragon wings, we were in position to speed through the open waters, drag our net, and still have ample time to choose our best escape route before drifting down one of the Outer Isle canals.

Everyone knew their tasks.

We just had to hold our nerves.

It would have been much easier to hold mine if Aydan and Uryah had stayed on the bow out of my way, but as we picked up speed, they joined Marino and me at the helm.

Uryah's red eyes bore into me. "You'll need to be ready to drop the net in a minute."

"We are," I replied as calmly as I could—with a little assistance from Pynyt's pinching talons.

"Just before the patch of squid, not when you get there."

"Believe it or not, this isn't our first-time fishing, Uryah."

"Relax!" declared Aydan, tapping Uryah on the shoulder. "Forgive him, Niall, my commander isn't used to leaving others to give orders. It makes him jittery!"

It struck me that one man was too relaxed and the other too uptight, but as I caught sight of Enya peering over the side of the ship, I suddenly felt an unbalance within myself. Hoping to distract Uryah at least, I said, "Can you not keep the princess below deck? Or at least away from the sides?"

Happily, his reaction was predictable. Even Aydan laughed as Uryah shot towards the main deck, but there was no time for mirth as Raine called from above.

"Squid dead ahead! Ready the net!"

FORTY-TWO

On my command, the crew cast the net. Taking the strain, *The Leviathan* ploughed forward with ease, but Wydgitta and Cyrus both hung back, adding an extra gust to counter the inevitable drag.

Unable to convince Enya to go below deck, she joined us on the quarterdeck. Leaning against a sail rope, her brother seemed so relaxed I thought he might nod off for a moment, but as we approached our target he burst forward, rubbing his hands together with childlike glee.

We're on perfect course, said Adaryvan from above.

"Excellent," I replied aloud, forgetting that no one else would have heard him. Enya grinned at me, making my cheeks flush red. "Sorry, I was talking to Adaryvan."

"I guessed." Enya nodded knowingly. "When we have time, you will have to tell me how you managed that," she jolted her head towards Adaryvan.

Despite telling myself to keep a respectful distance from Enya, her statement immediately drew me in. "What do you mean? Surely, you know how?"

"No one else has come out of their fear trial with *him* in tow." Chewing on her bottom lip, Enya grimaced. "A few have tried, but—"

"But what?" I asked when Enya made no attempt to finish her sentence.

"They never came back."

"Oh." Her original warning to avoid Adaryvan had suggested as much. "Hang on, you said *fear trial*? Don't you mean *pilgrimage*?"

"Members of the Fyuego often refer to the last stage of pilgrimage as the fear trial. Those final attacks were your fears. I know at least three pilgrims who were burnt to a crisp trying to go big. What did you do?"

Enya's eyes fixed on me as though she was examining every inch of my body and soul.

Were she anyone else, I might have been compelled to tell some heroic tale of valour, but totally under her spell, I felt no need to lie. "I laid my sword before him and bowed."

"Look!" called out Aydan, breaking mine and Enya's silent gaze.

Astonishment turned to awe as we followed his direction, watching the glowing squid filter into the net below the waves—or at least that was what I hoped was happening as their red flesh shone both within the projected confines of the net and beyond.

We didn't need to catch them all. I didn't want to. There was no benefit nor sense in decimating an entire population. We needed a bounty to save the Empress, not a haul to cause extinction.

Seeing the strain on the fine net increase, Aydan and I glanced at one another and nodded. We had risked our luck long enough.

"Lift the net!" I shouted.

My command rippled across the deck.

Incoming, Adaryvan's voice had lost its cocky edge.

Turning to my companions, their ashen expressions told me their dragons had spoken to them, too.

Remembering no one else would have heard them, I opened my mouth just as Raine boomed from above: "Starboard! Creature approaching starboard!"

The ship turned from organised industry to electric in an instant. Orders to heave up the net bellowed harder and faster. The shadows of dragons changing formation streaked across the deck. Two kept in position to lift the bow and stern if required, while the other two flanked us, posed to fire at anything larger than a squid that broke the surface of the water.

"Where'd it go?" Raine called to anyone that might have an answer—human or dragon.

Can you see it? I anxiously asked Adaryvan, keeping my expression neutral.

No, came the solemn reply.

Calm waters should be the sailor's dream. A lullaby. This calm felt like the prelude to a storm. Strained moans turned to questioning grunts as the weight of the net decreased.

Pointing out to sea, Enya shouted, "Look! The squid are swimming away!"

Dozens of eyes followed her finger. My heart sank when I saw the reality of her statement. Trailing behind us, it actually looked like the squid were laughing at us as their luminescent colouring flashed in the water before disappearing into the depths.

"What's happening?" said Uryah, standing behind me, to my right.

On my left, Enya trembled. She had enough sense to both understand and be afraid. "Call Wydgitta to get you out of here," I said, gently holding onto her arm. "Whatever comes next, you do not need to be on board."

Holding my gaze, her emerald eyes shone. "No, I am staying."

There was no time to argue as the ship suddenly jolted upwards. Screams rang out as equipment and personnel crashed across the deck. Before anyone could stand up, a second jolt sent the hull of *The Leviathan* flying into the air, simultaneously plunging the bow into a nosedive. Hurtling forward, I thrust one arm around Enya's waist, catching hold of the railing with the other as Uryah shot past us.

Hanging there, I glanced to my side. Marino was wedged across the wheel, while Raine dangled like a wind chime from the crow's nest. I couldn't see Aydan, but his cries above my head told me he was there. Everything probably happened in mere seconds, yet time seemed to be eternal as I observed my crew in various states of horror while the body of a monster zoomed past to strike again.

Wrapped around me, Enya tensed as an almighty crack sounded above us followed by a shower of splintering wood.

I got you, roared Adaryvan, using his talons to yank *The Leviathan* back into position.

Voices exclaimed as people attempted to catch their breath, but in the mist of the momentary relief, Aydan's desperate cry called, "Watch out!"

Turning, I was just in time to see a mast swinging at speed towards me. Pushing Enya back to the ground, I meant to drop on top of her, but the mast caught my right shoulder, propelling me straight into the sea.

Plunging below the surface, the sight of Fyrefly Squid lighting the way was strangely beautiful. On any other occasion, I would have stopped to admire the scene, but as I dashed for air, I was greeted with a scene that was anything but beautiful.

At least three men were tangled in the debris and another clutched a pathetic piece of driftwood, while caught on the edge of the net, an unconscious person bobbed in the water like a starfish. It only took a second to realise it was Uryah—and only took another second for me to decide to swim to him.

With Adaryvan shouting in my head to save myself, I wrapped my arm around Uryah's lifeless body and dragged him towards a more sturdy section of net. I knew without asking what the dragons were about to do. Adaryvan and Wydgitta were the biggest. Between them, lifting *The Leviathan* would be nothing. All we had to do was hold onto the net until they got us out of there. The crew could then finish hauling us in. *Simple*, I told myself, trying to ignore the cause of the enormous gashes in the net.

Hurry up! Growled Adaryvan, *It's going to come back.*

He was right. Even in my head, I didn't have time to argue. Concentrating on tying a twisted bit of net to Uryah's armour, I made sure he was surely fixed before I checked my surroundings. Hastily fastening themselves as best they could, the others in the water didn't need an order to mimic my action.

The current suddenly changed. It was like a whirlpool had opened up from nothing. Dipping my head under the surface, every fibre in my body froze as I witnessed the speeding form circling to create a watery vortex.

Thankfully, my mind did not freeze.

Lift up! Lift up NOW!

Are you secure? Adaryvan replied.

DO IT OR YOU'LL ALL BE SUCKED UNDER!

Around me, the silhouette of *The Leviathan*, my home, arose. Struggling against the increasing suction, I thrust out my hands, wrapping them around the first piece of net I could find, and held on for dear life.

Seeing the ship leave the water before their plan could work, Ceytus darted from its twister, spun around, and charged. The dragons were fast, but I doubt whether anyone would have foreseen the speed that Ceytus could leap from the ocean—even with two additional dragons primed to scold any marine life that tried to follow.

A mass of grey-blue scales gleamed briefly under the hot, Benegnyem sun as razor-sharp fins cut through the air. A flash of cyan marked a focused eye behind the blackhole of its mouth. Streams of flame burst forth, crossing under the ship, igniting the edge of the torn net as it fell away in Ceytus' mouth—with me inside it.

Crashing into the surf, I heard the flames fizzle out, but my senses were quickly overwhelmed by a combination of repugnant gigantic-fish breath and ever-increasing pressure coming from deep water.

Still clinging pathetically to the net as it hung from the monster's teeth, I gazed in wonder at the inside of the beast's mouth. It was a cavern—a living cavern. Giving a splutter, the tongue begun to ripple as Ceytus tried to swallow me.

Irony hit me. Of all the ways I thought I would die, death by sea monster was not something I had ever worried about.

Frustrated as though I was a chunk of roast caught in their mouth, Ceytus began grinding their teeth together. Panicking, I watched the fraying net, waiting for the moment enamel fully severed the rope and the game was lost.

As if time stood still, a bizarre realisation hit me. Deep beneath the water, inside a sea monster, I could see. The green tint was not the reflection of algae or bad breath. It was the Amulet of the Flame glowing around my neck.

Suddenly the speeding sensation stopped.

The teeth stopped grinding.

The throat ceased swallowing.

A new voice, like bells tolling in the distance, echoed around the cavernous mouth.

Speak, messenger of the Most High. Your servant is listening.

FORTY-THREE

ords evaded me. My jaw wobbled, desperately seeking audio, but to begin with the most I could produce was a pathetic *aaaahhh* noise. Ceytus was surprisingly patient. She neither repeated nor retracted her statement. With no Pynyt to pinch me or Adaryvan to mock me, I had to focus my own mind and steady my own heart.

Finally, I managed.

"I apologise for disturbing you, it was not our intention. The Empress has sent us to collect Fyrefly Squid."

Why? The word rumbled both inside and outside my head, making it impossible to tell whether I was hearing it through speech or telepathy.

"Someone has poisoned the hatcheries with thanatonite. We are hoping to remove all traces with an ink-infused putty and detox Her Imperial Majesty with cuttlebone. Fyrefly Squid have a unique—"

I know, said the voice. *That's why they feed off the coral in my garden.*

"Pardon?" I said, still holding onto the net in case Ceytus decided I wasn't worth talking to after all.

Is it possible you do not know the source of their blessing? Ceytus began moving again but we seemed to be swimming straight rather than descending further.

"I'm sorry to say that I do not. I am not aware that anyone on land does."

Yet you think it is okay to fish for them anyway? A snort, closer to a whistle rang out. *Curiously, this is the first time I have heard a request worth listening to.*

Tentatively, I took hope in her statement. *Listening* was not *granting*, but it was not abject denial either. "I only seek them now under—"

Yes, yes, you said. Ceytus replied, making a sharp right-hand turn, slumping me into a tooth which was larger than most flagpoles. *I am going to show you something. If you are not worthy of this knowledge, you will not tell another soul—*

"Of course, I would never give away secrets, I—"
She tutted. *You will not tell because you will not live.*

"Oh." I probably should have worked that out myself. Fearing that I would say something else stupid, I remained silent and waited.

It is a long time since I have felt the glow of the Flame's presence flowing through another being like it does you. Who are you? Do you rule in Benegnyem, little man?

"No, no I do not. Indeed, I am not even from Benegnyem. I am from the World's Divide, from Virisinigne, seeking help."

It is you who opens the Divide? Ceytus whistled again. *Interesting. Can it be the lost sheep wish to return to the warmth of the Flame?*

"We do not even know of the Flame. Or at least my world does not. Only now do I understand what we lost centuries ago. First, I seek to save my people from attack, but then I hope to introduce them to the—"

Divine, Ceytus said with melodic spirit.

"Precisely."

Then in that vein, I shall show you what you do not know.

The sides of Ceytus' cheeks puffed out and her body heaved. From the depths of her throat, a squelching sound echoed moments before a bubble formed, rolling towards me in a semi-translucent sphere as streaks of rainbow colours rippled over its surface. Although I had thought the conversation was going in my favour, being enveloped in a sea creature's belch didn't rate highly on my list of *ways to know when you're winning at life.*

With nowhere to run, I watched as the bubble came down upon and ultimately sealed around me. Instantly, Ceytus' jaws opened, and she flicked me out with her tongue.

We were so far below the surface, all around was black, yet the Amulet continued to emit a mellow green light—one much softer than the bright, intense green I had seen in the past. Blinking, my eyes readjusted and began to take in the elaborate flora around me.

"It's a garden," I whispered reverently.

In the near-distance, tiny bubbles rhythmically floated upwards from a crack in the seabed. Within each bubble, maroon smoke danced around rich, red sand—or what I thought looked like sand. As if that was not strange enough, around the bubbles were hundreds of thousands of tiny squid. Fyrefly Squid. Each one using their sharp beaks to clutch and consume the bubbles.

Apparently, they had been startled by my arrival and switched off their lights because after a few seconds, they relaxed, and one by one, their minute bodies transformed into luminescent beacons.

Whether directly or by proxy, all those who live in the Fyre coral garden are fed by the vent. It's very presence is a blessing from the Flame. Those who feed from it directly are granted a fiery glow—acting as a reminder that the divine cares for those below as well as those above.

I had no response.

What was there to say?

Speechless as I was, I understood why Ceytus defended the Fyrefly Squid and this underwater garden with such ferocity.

All I could do was observe until a question formed amongst my garbled thoughts. "Are you one of a kind? No one defends the Fyrefly Squid in Virisinigne?"

A melancholy mourn left the sea monster. *Long before the World's Divide, my ancestors guarded the vented waters around Mount Halo. As part of a purge of everything they could not control during the Dividing War, humanity tried to hunt and poison us. When the Divide went up, we made sure we were on the right side.* Ceytus scoffed. *Although the concerns of land seem to have been remembered more clearly even here. There was a time when the Empress herself would have told you that.*

"I don't believe she is herself," I replied, sadly. "That is why I am here."

The idea of history repeating itself made me sick. Again, I realised that a concealed or forgotten past only doomed the future. The circle of life only works as a whole—and the Empress is the link to it all. Without her, I was sure there was no hope for balanced scales.

Ceytus inclined her head but said nothing. It struck me as a particularly human action, but as I watched life bustle all around me, I realised I knew very little of the ways of any world.

"They are smaller in number, but a population of Fyrefly Squid still exist beyond the Divide. Does that surprise you?"

No. It is simply proof the Flame has not abandoned the other side. There is a beacon of hope in the darkness. She whistled again as though singing a hymn of praise. *I doubt the coral truly thrives without us to cultivate the sands, keep the vents clear, or protect the squid, but I am glad they are there.*

"*Us?* So you are not alone?"

Ceytus sent out a sharp tweet, like an alarmed bird. Ripples of oxygen bubbles shot around me as a pod of smaller Ceytus circled. Instantly, I realised humans had it wrong. It was not Ceytus, like a name, it was *the* ceytus, a species. A sea creature somewhere between a dragon, a whale, and shark. Like a whale, they sang to one another. Like a shark, they ferociously guarded home. Like a dragon, they worshipped and revered the Flame, the lifeforce of the world. Also like a dragon, the leader was significantly larger.

I am Chief Ceytus, she said with pride. *You may refer to me as Cee-Cee.*

FORTY-FOUR

As we approached the surface, Adaryvan's voice echoed in my mind, bouncing as though someone was shouting down a really long tube. At first the words were muffled, as if I had cups over my ears, but despite still being submerged, his gravelly call gained clarity. When I replied, he didn't try to hide his relief, making me feel oddly fulfilled.

Truly bonded.

Realising I had seconds until resurfacing, I quickly got to the point. *Don't attack Cee-Cee when she brings me up, okay?*

Who?

The Chief Ceytus. She is bringing me back. Let her drop me off without challenge. I'll explain once you've picked me up. Tell the others...

Confusion laced his voice, but Adaryvan agreed.

Metres before Cee-Cee reached the surface, I spotted a sandy-orange creature frantically circling. *I am alright,* I projected towards Pynyt, knowing that despite not being Charred to him, he would hear me. In response, a flame burst from his mouth and his circling slowed, but Pynyt remained in position as I rose above the gentle waves.

Cee-Cee released me from her mouth without popping the sphere on her teeth. Whether she practiced this trick or was simply extremely delicate, I do not know, but when she flicked her body and returned to the depths, I bopped on the surface, waiting for Adaryvan.

He was not delicate.

With one flex of his tail, he burst the bubble, sending me crashing into the water. Hovering awkwardly, he swung his tail a second time, offering himself as a ladder. When I reached his withers, I crashed against his scutes in exhaustion, and wished he came with a hairy pillow like Cal instead of horned scales. Hearing my unguarded thoughts, Adaryvan laughed while Pynyt took up residency on my left shoulder, hissing. It wasn't an angry hiss, though. He was relieved.

My heart pounded, matching his emotion.

Are you going to fill me in then? Adaryvan asked, impatiently.

Where's The Leviathan? I said, unable to see anything but water.

Adaryvan pointed his left wing. *By the shore. They are patching it up.*

What about the net? Are they fixing it, too?

I think the girl is trying. He snorted. *Why? It's not like we're going to get a second chance.*

A smile spread across my face. *Actually, we are.*

An almighty cheer welcomed me as I landed back on deck. Suddenly, almost drowning and being swallowed by a sea creature wasn't the most emotional thing I had done that day and I had to brush tears away from my eyes more than once. Pushing the lump in my throat down took multiple attempts, but I was doing okay until Alun's embrace broke me.

"Thank the stars for that, Captain," he chuckled affectionately into my ear. "For a minute, I thought all my years of training you were goin' to have been for nothin'."

All I could do was squeeze him tighter and laugh as tears fell.

"And now I'm all wet!" Alun jested as we stepped back. "What is that smell? How can you smell of metal, rotten egg, and fish?"

"Better than crap," I said, grinning.

"I'd not be so sure." Alun smirked, pretending to dust himself down.

"You ought to know," Marino said, patting Alun on the back with his large, coarse hand.

"What's the damage?" I asked, switching back into captain mode.

Instantly, Marino turned serious. "Two deaths—both Prince Aydan's men."

"The Commander?" I asked, fearing my efforts had been in vain.

"No, you saved him. He got seriously lucky," Raine said, running his fingers through his ear-length hair.

"There's twenty-three injured," said Marino, continuing his report. "The worst are down below being tended to as best we can. Would you believe it, the princess is wrapping people in petals and leaves? She sent a bunch of their men ashore to collect them." He raised his eyebrows, expecting me to share his surprise. When I didn't, Marino blew out his cheeks, somehow managing to raise his black brows even further away from his clear-blue eyes.

Deciding it was easier to show than tell, I removed my boots and rolled up my leggings, showing them my rippled scars. "These were gaping wounds a few days ago until I wrapped hibiyre leaves around them. I don't understand it, but I do believe it. Magic exists here. Actually, I think it exists everywhere—if you stop long enough to appreciate it."

"You don't have to stop long to see *that*," Alun said, nodding at Adaryvan as he landed on the shore next to Wydgitta.

Grunting in agreement, I thought about the inexplicable, magical bond I now had with Adaryvan. Running my fingers under my armour, I rubbed my tattooed shoulder. There was no discernible variation between skin and scale, but even without seeing it, every part of me felt different.

Focus, I snapped silently at myself. "What about the ship? Will she sail?"

"Aye, Captain," said Marino. "The talons piercing the bow and stern made a mess but nothing we can't patch up. In hindsight, we should have stopped to metal plate an area for talons to grab, it would have made less mess, but that's for another day now. We will make do and then make pretty later. The hull took the worst beatin'—thankfully not as bad as *The Forging Fyre,* though."

"What? What happened to it?" Aydan's ship was supposed to be safely positioned two miles away.

"She got attacked, too," Alun said bluntly. "The prince and his sister are downstairs with the injured, but his dragon apparently heard screaming so flew off and found the crew scurrying like ants coz they were taking on water."

"Are they all ashore now?"

"Aye, Captain. Say what you will about these dragons, but they are more efficient in a pinch than a tugboat."

A smile crept across my face as I imagined Adaryvan's disgust at being compared to a tugboat.

"*Fyre Dog,* remember?" I couldn't blame any of my crew for referring to them as dragons. It was the only name Virisinigne had for them and they *were* dragons, but I didn't want to risk offending anyone here or being forced to find out what the consequences were for coarse tongues pronouncing sacred words.

"Same difference," grumbled Alun, rolling his eyes, "but yeah, okay, point duly noted."

Deciding there was no point pushing the matter, I moved on. "Who attacked *The Forging Fyre?*"

"The sea monsters," Marino replied. "Sounds like smaller beasts than what got us, but no less vicious. Prince Aydan and the commander said there had been rumours of multiple ceytus, but until now no one had lived long enough to confirm it so they thought it folklore."

Internally, I cursed and questioned the wisdom of not mentioning that earlier, even if they thought it rubbish. "Captain Brandyt's note said there was a strange sound, like music, and the creatures just disappeared. Is that how you escaped, Captain?"

A memory of Cee-Cee singing and whistling came to me. The sounds varied. One noise was a call to come—or so I thought. Could it have been a call to halt attack instead? Or was that one of the other noises I heard her make? There was no point voicing my questions. My crew had no answers and they were already having to take on so much so fast. I couldn't stop to contemplate that because analysing their load inevitably made me think of my own. Acceptance was all I could cope with. Acceptance and dealing with one issue at a time.

"I'll tell you later. When will we be watertight again?" I asked my first mate.

Concern mixed with confusion spread across Marino's stern face when I didn't immediately recount my tale, but he answered without delay. "By morning, Captain. She should be sound by morning."

I would have preferred by nightfall, but I bottled my disappointment. "So be it," I said, stepping towards my quarters. As the sun dried my clothes, I could smell the sulphury-stench that Alun had so frankly mocked me for. "Let me get changed, then I will see all for myself and explain our next move."

With quick, but gentle bows, my friends let me retreat. In my rush to be inside, I swung the door behind me but the tilt of the ship as it sat in the sand prevented it from fully clicking shut. It was strange how the absence of that one sound unsettled me, but I had no time for routine or ritual. I needed to see the damage for myself, inform the crew of the plan, and finally collect the squid that the Empress was waiting for.

Whipping off my filthy clothes, I took fresh pants from a drawer, pulled them on, and opened my clothes cupboard. Instantly, my resolve for speed faltered. As if standing in polar opposition to one another, two uniforms hung before me. On the left were three versions of the clothes I had worn for a decade. One clean, one worn, one for washing. That was my motto for minimal work. Behind them laid attire for special use—both party-wear and armour. The clothing of a prince. Albeit a seventh son, but still a prince. I hated wearing them so kept them out of view. Gently flicking a jacket, the hidden splendour revealed itself for a moment. Only then did I remember leaving some of the clothes in the palace, yet apparently they had been returned while I was on Mount Liekke.

Slowly my eyes travelled to the right-hand uniform. The identical one to what I had just discarded on the floor. Behind it was a third set. One clean, one worn, one dirty.

Could I be the man to wear both uniforms?

I didn't know.

The door swung open.

Having been lost in thought, I would have jumped anyway, but Pynyt also startling and hissing from on top of the cupboard door made me stagger like a teenage boy caught gawping at a girl's chest.

"Princess Enya," I stuttered, unable to find any other words beyond her name.

"Oh, I'm sorry. The door wasn't closed, and I—" Her flushed cheeks paled as her eyes tracked from my face to my body.

For a second, I might have tried to fool myself into believing it was my half-naked, well-muscled frame that stopped her midsentence, but there was no denying it was my tattoos that took her breath away.

With each moment seemingly stretching for eternity, my hope faded that she might not share the Empress' interpretation of my scales, or even better, be pleased. However, unless body language in Benegnyem was significantly different to those from Virisinigne, I couldn't take her bloodless, ashen expression as that of excitement.

My heart thumped its way to my stomach and my jaw wobbled, gasping for air as though I were waking from a psychedelic dream.

I wished it were a dream.

"Why...?" Enya whispered. "Why didn't—"

"How's our—" Appearing behind his sister, Aydan's silhouette blocked out the streaming sunlight. Like Enya, the sight of my arm-length tattoos silenced him, but he recovered quicker. "Well, I, never," he said as a grin spread across his face. "And here I was thinking you were family through the Fyuego, only!"

Held in his gaze, I searched to identify whether it was a painted or genuine reaction. In my youth, my father had tried to impress on me that royals were supposed to be trained masters of emotion, politicians cloaked in mystery; however, as Aydan bound forward, grasping my right hand, shaking it enthusiastically, I wondered if Aydan didn't care for measured responses either.

Unfortunately, his sister remained rooted to the spot. Totally unprepared, all I could think was, *not like this.* Thoughts weren't even coming in formed sentences. No start, no finish.

Just, *not like this.*

Pulling me out of my stupor, Pynyt landed on my bare shoulder, pinching my skin. Controlling a wince, I reclaimed my hand from Aydan. "I've much to tell everyone but let me change into something less wet—and smelly," I added, forcing a relaxed smile.

Father would be proud, I lamented to myself.

He should be. Another time, I might have groaned at him overhearing my unguarded thoughts, yet the surprise of Adaryvan's three words of support gave me the push I needed.

Reaching into the cupboard, I took out my Fyuego armour and slipped on the shirt, hiding the marks that caused such a stir. Even out of sight, and with Aydan and Enya having gone outside, my scales felt like they were glowing.

Brushing the confused sensation aside, I dressed without delay. Stepping away from the cupboard, my eye caught sight of my captain's hat on the top shelf, and a sigh escaped my lips. I couldn't pretend to understand the future or what position others may try to impose on me, yet that hat was the symbol of the only constant I knew.

A mismatch of attire or not, I grabbed the hat, straightened my jacket, recalled Pynyt to my shoulder from the back of my chair, and left the room with my head held high.

FORTY-FIVE

Surveying my wounded ship and crew equally rattled and inspired me. Those unharmed helped those who were, while others worked on restoring our home. Brightly coloured blooms made leafy coats of armour, oddly suggesting a festivity more than a hospital ward. Very few people escaped cuts and bruises, myself included, and some injuries were gruesome; however, I noted the decoration was largely blue and green, with the worse wounds receiving a mushed-up red paste. No one was deemed ill or crazy enough to be covered in red hibiyre—or at least not the whole, raw petals that I so precariously used.

"It's a shame I didn't have a full herbal lesson before my pilgrimage," I said quietly to Enya, trying to break the awkward silence as I paused in front of a patient she was tending to.

"Oh?" she replied, raising an eyebrow.

"I used a bit too much red." I mock grimaced. "Not that I'm complaining about the scars, it saved me."

Her green eyes widened.

"My skin is rippled now," I said gesturing to my lower legs, deciding whether I should show her or not.

"Mmm-hmm," she said, nodding like a calculation had just made sense. "I saw. Apparently, you like collecting trophies." She rolled her eyes. "Some, anyway."

I knew I had to say something. Neither planning nor winging conversation had proven particularly productive for me to date, but as no plan came, I wanted to try the latter. "Enya, I—"

"Captain!" Alun's dulcet tones cut me off.

Seeing an easy escape, Enya moved onto another patient.

Semi-relieved, I turned to my gunner. "Yes?"

"Oryana has nearly finished with the net. It ain't as pretty as before, but her little fingers aren't half swift."

"Excellent." Following him onto the deck, I found Raine exactly where I left him: by Oryana's side, doing his best to mimic her technique. "It's no wonder it's not as pretty if Raine is helping," I laughed. Raine was a talented man, but finer artwork was not something I had ever seen him try before. Guilt hit me. At least he wasn't afraid to show his feelings. If Oryana accepted him, she wouldn't find a more loyal partner in any world.

"You're going to lose your gift," chuckled Aydan, nudging me with his elbow as he deeply inhaled on a pea-green coloured rollup.

"Pardon?" I replied, narrowly dodging the stream of smoke Aydan released from the right side of his mouth. Had it been anyone else, I would have mocked him for trying to mimic a dragon.

"I bought her for you, remember? Wives and mistresses need not mix." Aydan winked, taking another puff.

"Is that dog grass, by any chance?" I asked, breathing in the crisp, sweet scent.

"Yes!" Aydan's brows furrowed. "Are you familiar with it?"

"Not at all. On my pilgrimage it was mentioned and as I don't recognise the smell I thought it might be it."

"You've a good nose! Would you like one?" Aydan dipped his hand into his pocket, wrapping his fingers around a metal case. "I'm happy to educate you where others have not..."

"No, no, not at the moment, but I thank you," I said, gently holding up my hand. "I am also grateful for Oryana, she has been invaluable today, but am I right in thinking I can do with her as I wish? It is not a time sensitive gift?"

Aydan belly-laughed. "What kind of prince loans women? Ha! No, indeed, do as you wish with her—just don't tell my sister I said that."

Stifling a sneer, I chuckled. He was as full of crap as the dog grass between his lips, but checking cleared me of any potential social-misgivings.

"Other than marry, of course," he added, drawing on the cigarette again.

Had his statement not baffled me, watching his face melt with relaxation, I would have queried how addictive dog grass was. Instead, I kept to the point. "Why not?"

Aydan waved the cigarette in front of me, spreading his free fingers in astonishment, and shrugging for added effect. "Royals don't marry blues."

"Ah." I side glanced at Raine and Oryana, making sure he couldn't hear and she wasn't lip reading. "Play with blue, marry green?"

"For us? Absolutely. Red or brown, maybe, if just noble, not royal. But green wed a blue? Never."

"But blue and blue?" Talking about eye colour as if it had any meaning on a person's worth made me sick, especially as my crew were all amongst Aydan's idea of *play only*.

"What does that matter?" Aydan followed my gaze to Raine and Oryana. "You mean to gift her to him?"

I laughed. "I mean to let them decide."

He snorted, turning too many people's attention to us.

"The heart cannot be told," I said, softly. "I meant what I said to you before. Virisinigne is freer in some respects. My brother and his husband—"

"My *wife*, the *princess*, and I are very happy. My regard for Rhys is nothing I wish to discuss." Aydan stamped out his cigarette on the deck. "And I disagree. The heart is told how to beat by the brain every second of every day. Reason and sense lead, Niall, not fancy."

"And then sometimes, the Flame calls," I added, suddenly fearing I was opening a chasm that I could not close.

"Precisely." Gently gripping my upper arm, he smiled. "Though we may need to remind Uryah of that when he finds out *your* particular calling."

Having already been faced with extreme, dry heat, a new civilisation, a shared language with a different dialect, dragons, and an unheard-of deity, I decided that there was no point sugar-coating what happened on the seabed. I *was* swallowed by a monster, inserted into an air bubble and shown a new, watery world.

Part of me felt like a schoolteacher telling students tales around a campfire. The only sound beside my voice was the rhythm of waves—not even the wind wanted to interrupt me. Likewise, no one challenged the plan. I couldn't call it *my plan*. I was merely repeating what Cee-Cee had told me she would do. Neither man nor dragon verbally refuted what I laid out, although I was sure that more than one person was waiting to see it before they believed it.

When I dismissed everyone, those with a task returned to their work, and those without went to sleep. Unaware of my other revelation, Uryah found me on the helm and shook my hand with genuine appreciation. His leg was broken and his body bruised, but wrapped in blue hibiyre, he hobbled surprisingly well, and we both agreed that battered and bruised was far better than dead.

"The Flame has indeed watched over us," Uryah said, beginning to walk away. "Wary as I was, I cannot deny that the Flame has guided you here."

Hopefully, you'll remember that whenever Aydan tells you about my Charr... And Enya, I lamented internally.

Enya was still avoiding me, but I sent Raine on a diplomatic mission and made him insist that while she was on board, she would use my quarters. Few people, regardless of gender, can deny Raine when he turns on his quiet charm, and thankfully, Enya was no different.

The night was set to be short, and I was beyond exhausted, but my lack of a bed wasn't an issue. Propped against sacks or swinging in a hammock, my mind sparked in a crazed fashion, preventing me from any kind of slumber.

Wandering the deck, in the clear moonlight, I spotted a figure on the bow of the ship. Careful not to make her jump, I approached Oryana from the side, yet she must have sensed me coming because her gleaming eyes bore into me long before I reached her side.

She had worked tirelessly to finish the net and even managed to train a few hands while she did it. Not once had I seen her moan or complain. Neither had I seen her shed a tear. However, now the job was complete, now she had time to reflect on what her family had done, two steady streams worked their way down her face.

My heart wept for her. Our circumstances were different, but I understood the feeling of abandonment. The realisation that you have been cast out to sea for convenience. I was sorry to have played any part in her pain.

"Can't sleep?" I asked, feeling a little redundant.

"I tried."

"There's not many women in my crew, but—"

"They're all fine," Oryana said, forcing a smile that couldn't quite reach her eyes.

"It probably doesn't feel like it, but your family are not worthy of you," I said, reaching for her hand and gently squeezing.

"Thanks," Oryana whispered. "Do you know the worst bit?" Her eyes fixed on my lips, waiting.

"What's that?"

She scoffed. "I'm not surprised." Taking back her hand, she wiped her face.

Desperately, I searched for words of comfort, but instead found myself wishing Raine wasn't asleep. Each lost in thought, we leant on the rail, watching the waves. On countless occasions I had organised and assessed my life in this manner, but that day was the first time I tried to imagine what was going on in the depths.

"I need to talk to you about the deal," Oryana said, quietly but firmly snapping me out of my thoughts.

When I stared instead of replied, she continued, "I need to know what you expect."

Reflecting the moon and sea in her eyes simultaneously, Oryana struck me as a strange, serene beauty—even if her statement had the opposite effect on me. Aydan or my father would surely remind me that I was supposed to be calm and collected, not unnerved by direct enquiries from women, yet I was instantly glad that my flushed cheeks were shaded by the night.

Frustrated by silence, Oryana added, "You own me, I know that—"

Relief met my embarrassment. "Forgive me, I should have spoken to you directly instead of letting my mind wander. You are free. You owe me nothing and are indebted to no one."

The shock on her face was palpable. "Can you be serious, Captain? The prince—"

"There is no bind. It was wrong of me to steal you without asking, yet you have worked here with true skill and I am eternally grateful. *The Leviathan's* path is as yet unknown. I know what we hope for in the short-term but can make no promises on how the wind will take us. However, if you wish to join the crew—*our family*—as a free person, you are most welcome."

Her lips began to quiver, causing a wave of emotion to choke me.

Pushing it back, I added, "We take no slaves in our world and eye colour is not a marker of worth. Family comes in all colours, shapes, and sizes. Our manners may be rough at times but we stand together or go down as one. There's no rush to decide. The offer is there. Think on it."

Bowing, I walked away when her fingers grasped mine.

Leaning in, she softly kissed my cheek. "Thank you, Captain. I accept."

FORTY-SIX

Despite my reassurances, the tension onboard was tangible at dawn. Adaryvan and Wydgitta gently refloated *The Leviathan,* the net was primed and ready to drop, and Raine was in the crow's nest while everyone else anxiously waited for his call.

My stomach was a bizarre mixture of excitement and nervousness—like a child waiting for their birthday party. I knew today was the day, I just didn't know if the guests would show up. All I had to hold onto was Cee-Cee's word. I didn't even have the comfort of sending a sign.

According to her, there was no need for one.

She would see us.

She would signal us.

We just had to catch.

It didn't help that even Pynyt was on edge. Normally either stoic or sarcastic, I was surprised to see smoke spiralling from his nostrils.

"How can you escort me through pitch-black caves and past hordes of enormous, lethal creatures on a mountain, but a little fishing sends you into a frenzy?" I jested, trying to distract us both.

It worked, although the joke was quickly on me as he wafted a puff of smoke into my face.

I didn't waste my breath trying to encourage either Aydan or Enya to ride their dragons this time. Neither of them were going anywhere, and I needed the crew to see me calm, focused, and sure—not begging people to abandon ship. For a while, I held the wheel, but when Adaryvan's gruff voice mocked my white knuckles, I shot him a withering look and quickly delegated the task to Marino and held my hands behind my back.

Both Pynyt and Adaryvan hiss-laughed at me while Marino gave me a knowing smile, forcing me to question how I had ended up with an insubordinate crew both on deck, in the sky, and in my head.

Surely, the Charr-bond is supposed to help and build up, not ridicule, I said, inwardly laughing whilst subtly flexing my fingers.

I'd call it multiple-purpose, replied Adaryvan. *Focus. We're nearly there.*

No one else heard him, yet a silence befell the ship. No one dared twitch. Hands were posed over the net, ready to move it. Unhappy to be ordered away from his beloved cannons, Alun held his hand over the hilt of his sword. The crew were strictly commanded not to engage in any form of combat. I knew they heard me. They knew the consequences—but I also knew that after a lifetime of self-defence and battle, sailing straight into danger with our hands empty felt wrong.

A spurt of water flew into the air ahead of the ship.

It had to be my signal.

"Drop the net!" I shouted.

The command again rippled through the airways. The fair wind propelled us, but the dragons boosted it anyway. As my command moved forwards, a gasp suddenly made its way backwards.

I didn't need to ask why.

Cee-Cee appeared before us, then six, seven, eight, and counting smaller ceytus surfaced, all swimming in a large, uniform circle. In the middle, the water rippled and rived with small, red creatures. For a moment, I feared *The Leviathan* would plough into the speeding wall of ceytus, or their speed would create a whirlpool, yet with seconds to spare they expertly parted, forming a funnel that not only allowed us to enter safely, but also smoothly capture the Fyrefly Squid within our net.

As quickly as they had appeared, the ceytus disappeared, diving back into the depths without looking back.

Their job was done.

They had answered the Empress' call.

The rest was up to us.

FORTY-SEVEN

Processing the squid took time. Their sharp beaks, fiddly bodies, and tender ink pouches had to be handled with care. Not one was allowed to be wasted. Each one respected. Enya stood over the bounty, totally focused as she whispered a chant and released purple petals. She was in no mood to be asked, but I wondered if she kept a supply with her at all times, should her role of Kennel Maiden be required, or if she had just hoped to need them now.

They just appear, said Adaryvan as I watched the petals fizzle into thin-air.

What do you mean? I asked, briefly glancing up at him. *She put her hand in her pocket—*

So she might, but there's nothing in there. Sacred, purple hibiyre can be found, but as the stakes are so high, the princess is summoning holy matter, imploring the Flame to bless the souls of the squid as they return to the life stream, to maintain the safety of those transporting their bodies, and for longevity of Her Imperial Majesty.

As more of the petals ignited in a mix of violet and red sparks, the air filled with a rich, almost hypnotic aroma.

Without worrying whether Adaryvan could hear me or not, I added a prayer for Virisinigne.

For a moment, Enya's gaze passed over me. She displayed no emotion beyond serene focus to her task, her lips still almost singing words that I could not understand, yet while her eyes were on me, the petals she released floated against the direction of the wind towards me. As they reached the back of my hand, a warmth kissed my skin like the touch of butterfly wings, then disappeared in their beautiful, aromatic hue.

When I looked back up, Enya had turned her attention away again, letting me know that she would bless my cause, but not me.

What exactly is she? My breathless thoughts asked.

The Kennel Maiden is more than the title suggests, replied Adaryvan. *In your old tongue, I believe you'd call her* High Priestess.

Truthfully, I had guessed as much on the mountain. Both in Fort Fyuego and in the Foco Temple she displayed abilities beyond my understanding. *The Flame must be having a laugh, fating her to me,* I grumbled to myself, focusing on making my thought private, but forgetting to restrain my mouth from tutting.

Quickly, I followed it with a sigh, trying to make the two actions one. Thankfully, only Pynyt and Marino seemed to notice. With the rush of adrenaline fading and exhaustion increasing, I swayed on my feet. Leaving Marino in charge, I headed below deck, selected the first empty hammock, and threw myself into it.

As we approached the port of Vapyos, Pynyt took great pleasure waking me up. I didn't tell him, but his wings fanning my sweaty face was actually pretty nice. The impatient, smoky burp he followed it up with was, however, less pleasant.

Not unlike Old Emberbyrg, Vapyos was cut into the white cliffs that lined the shore. The port appeared to be as large, but the number of ships present was greater, and although the massive city wall was less apparent, the tip of it could be seen setback from the cliff-edge.

"So, this is another off-shoot town of Emberbyrg?" I asked Uryah, watching Adaryvan disappear inland.

"Yes," he replied, "but Vapyos is also home to our main shipyard. Over there—" Uryah pointed to a wide cave entrance, "is where the gunships live and are made. You'd be surprised how quickly one can set sail from that position." Although Uryah's general demeanour towards me had greatly improved since I saved him, there was a tone, a glint, in his red eyes that suggested that I had earnt a reprieve, maybe some extra respect, but not a complete pass from his suspicions. "Of course, the Fyre Dogs normally reach anyone unworthy first."

"So I've been told," I replied. "But as we're on the same side, that isn't—"

"Aydan told me." Uryah's flat tone cut me off. "About your Charr."

Ah, so not suspicious. Pained.

Pynyt darted into the air, disappearing into the seemingly endless clear blue sky.

"Where's he going in such a hurry?" Uryah asked.

Probably saving himself from an awkward conversation. "I've no idea," I replied, squinting.

Uryah sighed deeply. "Fate is still yours to lose, you know that, right?" Pushing himself off the rail that was supporting his weight, Uryah stood tall before me. "Nothing is a given."

"Then it isn't fate, is it?" I paused. "I thought fate was something you could not evade?"

"No, you cannot. But you can choose the path towards it."

Scratching my brow, I struggled to find the words to answer him. "You are contradicting yourself, Uryah. You say the Flame, the divine, guides, gives us the choice of paths to an ultimate goal. We can gain or lose. Follow or freefall. Choose light or dark. Yet you speak in the grey. If there are particular roles or goals predetermined, if prophecies exist for some, where the life or death of hundreds of thousands rests upon the few accepting the task they have been given, is it not their duty, their very purpose of existence, to rise up when called?"

A single tear trickled down Uryah's cheek, glistening against his tanned skin.

"Certainly the suggestion of *you* being fated to Enya is beyond divine benevolence."

"For what it is worth, I am sorry it pains you." Sighing, I puffed out my cheeks. "The news wasn't exactly well received by the princess. If asked, she'd probably call it divine malevolence."

"And you? What do you call it?" Although his fists clenched, hope simmered behind Uryah's eyes. Hope that I was the pretender who would choose to deny fate and take whatever consequences came afterwards.

What did I call it?

An honour? A blessing? My heart's desire?

Foolish. Mistaken.

Yet to be proven.

Too complicated to address.

"Unclear."

Suddenly, a shadow cast over the sun, granting a welcome break to our conversation as a stream of dragons led by Adaryvan sailed through the air. Pynyt's orange form dropped from the formation like a bullet, landing neatly on my shoulder with a scroll in his mouth.

Uryah took one look at the flaming red wax seal. "It's from Lord Byrne."

Despite it being delivered to me, on my ship, I decided not to risk upsetting the hierarchy by reading the message without first finding Aydan. As he had a fascination with watching the ink harvest, locating him didn't take long, but eager for news, I held my breath as he unrolled the parchment. Seeing what was in her brother's hand, Enya instantly joined us.

"Well?" she said, less than thirty seconds after he began reading.

"The Fyuego have removed the bulk of the rocks and minerals from within the hatcheries. Only the fixed formations and dust remain."

Aydan's twisted lips made me question whether I was missing something. "That's excellent—isn't it?"

"Yes, it is."

"But—?"

"But the Empress is still proving somewhat...erm ...*irrational*."

"Meaning?"

Aydan remained silent.

Enya gently reached for the letter. "Ah," she whispered before passing it to me.

As my eyes scanned the beautifully styled writing, my heart sank.

...The Fyre Dogs held Her Imperial Majesty back as long as they could, but her fury increases by the second and she insisted on overseeing everything. As suggested, we wore masks whilst removing the poisonous matter, yet she would not. This further exposure to toxic dust has expedited her mental decline. If you truly have a cure, I must urge your great haste before she summons Liekke's magma and destroys us all.

In the Name of the Flame,
Lord Byrne

FORTY-EIGHT

Depression quickly turned to action. Ink-filled putty was made, nets of cuttlebone were packed—and voices boomed in forceful encouragement until everything was complete. The crew could return to their usually cheerful songs when this was done. Their melodies were welcome to send Adaryvan and I on our way, but until that moment the only sound I wanted to hear was the industrial scale mechanics of squid flesh popping and ink mixing with clay.

Uryah reluctantly agreed his place was in the palace. His broken leg made him more hazard than help and none of my crew had skin to withstand the temperatures of Mount Liekke. Enya momentarily fought for the right to join Aydan and me. In the end, I couldn't decide if it was her desire not to be with me, her wish to cement Uryah's wavering decision to return to the palace, or her brother's insistence that only one royal should be risked for this particular mission that truly persuaded her. Her scowl at me made me fear the former.

"With the Empress as she is, even though you are the Kennel Maid, it is better for me to go with Niall. You have blessed us, now you must be safe. We will have Adaryvan and Coayl to assist us. Besides, taking too many bodies at once always annoys Her Imperial Majesty. If her temper is as bad as Lord Byrne says, taking more now could be the spark to ignite the volcano." Aydan gently laid a hand on Enya's arm. "The Fyuego, the Dogs, the people—they will all depend on you. You must be present to calm them, dear sister. Please, let me do my part, for Benegnyem."

Touched by his tenderness, Enya conceded.

Within minutes, the final preparations were done.

Adaryvan carried the net of cuttlebones. Coayl the putty.

"*Flamma vobiscum,*" Aydan said, turning to the ship one last time.

My crew didn't know what it meant, yet their voices still joined in when the others cried out, "*Flamma vobiscum.*"

Fearing that I might not return, or least not wanting to leave things with Enya on a bad note, I took a step towards her. Seeing my advance, she obviously called for Wydgitta through their Charr because a scaled tail immediately swung from the sky. Nodding at me with a glint in her eye, she grabbed the limb with perfect timing and was whisked away like a sailor on a rope in a storm.

My assent onto Adaryvan's back was less graceful, yet my technique was improving.

If we pull this off, you might actually get good at that, Sailor, laughed Adaryvan.

Just fly, will you? I quipped, settling myself into my 'seat'.

Over the whistle of the wind and the rhythm of wings, Adaryvan's gruff laughter filled the airways, but then cut off like the composer had forgotten the last sheet of his own concert. Peering around the giant scute, I realised why.

The sight of thick, black smoke billowing out of Liekke's Peak was enough to freeze even the darkest of humour.

With no time to spare, Aydan and Coayl flew straight into the royal hatchery to begin rolling the putty, while Adaryvan, Pynyt, and I went in search of the Empress. In the short time since my last visit, the evidence of her raging was impressive. Previously neat passageways were filled with rubble, the walls scorched with furious marks, and the air thick with ash and pain.

Visibility was poor, yet along with my new skin, apparently my lungs had also been enhanced. Less than a week ago, I would have died on the approach, let alone on entry to somewhere with half the amount of smoke in the air. I also wore a mask etched in ink—an upgrade on the miner's mask that Lord Bryne's team used—hoping to keep dust exposure at a minimum in order that the five who flew in, would fly out unharmed.

Hopefully, *six*.

Chambers echoed with eerie whispers as Adaryvan's wings navigated the mess. Every now and again he would pause, listening for any indication of where the Empress might be. Experiencing further earthquakes was not high on my wish list, yet I found myself praying for a roar, a snort—anything to guide us to her location.

Having wound our way deeper and deeper into the volcano, the heat increased exponentially. The tunnel forked and we turned right but halted when a soul-piercing roar called out to our left. It was the sign we had been longing for, yet it broke my heart to hear such a lament. Following the sound, we found the Empress gazing into bubbling magma, glowing the same colours as the deadly mass beneath her.

Disturbed by our presence, she faced us, but there was no recognition, no relief, only a flame-filled scream.

"Your Imperial Majesty," called Adaryvan, his gruff tone laced in sorrow, "we, your humble servants, return with the cure you—"

He couldn't continue as a ball of fire flew at him. At us. Thankfully, he dodged it, but the haul of cuttlebone was clearly slowing him down and I feared she would destroy our bounty, dashing all of our efforts into the furnace below.

"What use is a cure for them?" the Empress bellowed, pointing at the magma.

Only then did it occur to me that she or Lord Byrne had buried the dead eggs in the magma along with the thanatonite. One wasn't going to affect the other now, but there was an extra sense of sadness that ached inside when I thought about it.

The Empress twitched erratically. The toxin in her body was grasping at her, changing her mood, her thoughts, her movements by the second. If I found her difficult to approach before, now she was nearly impossible.

"We are treating the hatchery, Your—" again Adaryvan was cut off with an assault of fire. "Please, come outside and eat—"

"Poison!" screamed the Empress, throwing another fireball but this time following it, ploughing into Adaryvan with all her might. How I didn't tumble to the ground, I have no idea, but I both heard and felt the impact knock the wind out of my enormous friend. Pain, or rather an echo of pain, rumbled in my chest. As the Empress lumped into Adaryvan a second time, I realised the Charr connected us with more than thought and scales.

As if acting on their own, my fingers wrapped around the Amulet of the Flame. Was it not also a symbol of unity, of blessing, of second chances?

Heat began to increase under my fingertips and a green glow danced around the chamber as words, sang in a tongue I had never spoken, entered my mind. *Our minds*—for through the Charr, I knew Adaryvan heard them, too. As if pulled to my feet by an invisible force, I stood on Adaryvan's back, and together, we repeated:

"*Fidelis Defensor, audite. Hanc benedictionem. Manducare. Sana. Exsurgo. Iter nondum completum.*"

Inexplicably the translation rang in my mind: *Faithful Defender, listen. Receive this blessing. Eat. Heal. Arise anew. Your journey is not yet complete.*

The Empress straightened herself before us. Her eyes suddenly calm, yet her body still throbbed and glowed in fierce-red waves as she bowed her head. *"Omnipotens Flamma. Servus tuus gratias ago tibi." Almighty Flame. Your servant thanks you.*

Seizing the moment, Adaryvan reached for the net of cuttlebone and passed it to the Empress. Part of me worried the madness would grasp her again, but under the continued green glow of the Amulet, she began crunching into the tiny skeletons.

If I had somehow arrived at that point in my journey still doubting magic or the omnipresence of the Flame, all misgivings left me in that moment. Fire rose around the Empress in a circle, rising up and down as though commanded on strings. With each rise the colour changed from green, to red, to purple, and round again.

As though Enya were above us, scattering fresh petals, purple hibiyre floated from the ceiling, dancing as it landed on Her Imperial Highness, turning her scales lavender and violet like a patchwork quilt until the gentle glow of her healthy red returned.

There was no doubt, the Empress was the beginning and end of the natural order in this world, the guardian of the Flame, but being mortal, even she had to take a leap of faith sometimes.

Mesmerised, humbled, and honoured, Adaryvan and I watched. As the Amulet returned to its dormant state, the voice whispered to us once more.

Together, we repeated, *"Flamma nobiscum."*

FORTY-NINE

Leaving the Empress to rest in her own chamber, Adaryvan and I went to help Aydan and Coayl. Using his tail, Coayl had made short work of rolling out the putty, and they were already rolling it back up, collecting all the tiny fragments of mineral, dust, and dirt that had been left behind.

"Did you find the Empress?" Aydan asked, apprehensively. "The smoke is clearing—do I dare take it that you have been successful?"

We had no reason to omit the part about being spoken to by the Flame through the Amulet, yet neither Adaryvan nor I touched upon that detail as we reported our success. Such holiness was too private to speak of—and I didn't want anyone to misunderstand it as a boast.

"If you just have the last bits to roll up and dump, Niall and I can go collect fresh rubrunite, if you wish?" Adaryvan posed it as a question, but I could tell he wasn't expecting any opposition. "The king sent Seraphyna to oversee a mining team. They should be waiting for us to collect it."

"You go with Coayl, Adaryvan," said Aydan. "We'll be done faster if you both go. On your way out, just dump the large chunk of putty in the magma and leave the untouched ball in the next lair for later. Niall and I can collect the last of the putty in here and roll it into the passage before you to get back with the new substrate."

I was pleasantly surprised by how hands-on Aydan was. Some of my brothers had risen the ranks of their professions by a mixture of royal-status, arrogant privilege, and work, however, my eldest brother, Baran, had assumed his role of king-in-waiting with little intention of roughing his hands while he waited. Rolling potentially-lethal mineral dust would certainly not have been on his to-do list, even if he was one of the few people in the world physically capable of helping.

"Why do you smile so?" asked Aydan.

"Forgive me," I said, not realising that my face had displayed my thoughts. "I was musing on the difference between you and the crowned prince of Virisinigne. My brother would not be as proactive as you."

"I see," Aydan replied, raising an eyebrow.

His cool answer concerned me. Each day I was ticking off a task to reach home, but offending the prince was not on that list. My tongue failing me could not happen until Virisinigne was safe. Scrambling to make myself clear, I added, "I meant that as a compliment. I am sorry if that was not obvious. I admire your work ethic."

"If a job is worth doing properly, the best way is to do it yourself." Aydan chuckled. "Besides, I don't exactly see you sitting back with your fingers idle. You were gutting squid *and* shouting orders only hours ago!"

A wry, but proud smile spread across my face. Words again failed me, so I picked up an iron shovel that Lord Byrne's team had left, and started moving the thick, sticky putty.

"Am I right in thinking you don't get on with your brothers?" Aydan asked, after a few minutes silence.

"I've barely seen them for over a decade." I laughed. "Honestly, that has improved our relationships somewhat." It was said with humour, but Aydan's shocked expression told me to elaborate. "I was the youngest brother in a proud and busy family. I suppose it was inevitable that tension would flare and I would be the butt of their jokes. Like you, I was always close to my sister, though. You should be glad you've only one sibling to contend with."

Aydan matched my smile but I thought I saw something hidden behind it. The skin beside his eyes that normally crinkled, remained still. *Have I said the wrong thing, again? Say something else,* I pleaded with myself as silence bounced off the walls.

"I've been thinking about the thanatonite," I said, quickly changing the subject.

"That's hardly surprising as we're sweeping it up," said Aydan, lightly. "What about it?"

"Do you have any theories about how your uncle got it here? No one seems to doubt it was him, but equally no one knows when he did it..."

"Well, I'm guessing when he was banished—or just before."

"Maybe," I said, thoughtfully.

"It fits in with the increased infertility and poor health of Her Imperial Highness, don't you think?"

"I did…"

"But?" Aydan seemed curious, but not convinced there was a mystery to uncover.

"But that doesn't explain why the rest of the hoard were not immediately infected, too. It was as though someone topped up the lairs over time, starting with the royal hatchery, then the rest. Otherwise, although still toxic, the amount of thanatonite in here would eventually have been outweighed by the rubrunite."

"My uncle must have known the ratio he needed…"

"That's what I assumed until I spoke to Cee-Cee."

"The sea monster? How in the Flame's name would she know anything?"

"When I told her I came from the World's Divide, she said, *it is you who opens the Divide.*"

"So?"

"Opens, not *open.*"

"You could have misheard her, she is an oversized fish, after all," Aydan laughed.

"So that maybe, but the ceytus obviously feel vibrations in the water when the Divide opens—and Cee-Cee definitely said opens, plural." I paused, letting my words hang in the air before daring to continue. "Do you remember much about your uncle?"

"Gryer?" Aydan asked. I nodded. "Yes, I was devastated when he left. He and his wife, Idalya, my late aunt, were a huge part of my upbringing."

"It's a pity he didn't stay put," I said, without thinking, "we wouldn't be shovelling crap out of a volcano and my home wouldn't be on fire, if he had."

"True."

"Did they ever have children?"

"No." Aydan sucked in his bottom lip. "The only cousins I have are on my mother's side."

"You said, *late aunt?* Presumably Idalya died before Gryer left?"

"Yes, two years prior—in my uncle's arms after a botched burglary."

"I'm so sorry," I said, bowing my head. "If you don't mind me asking, what were they trying to steal?"

"Jewels. My aunt was a talented jeweller. She made the most exquisite pieces. Even now, they're extremely valuable—not as valuable as she was, though." A bitterness fell over his face. "The thieves, her murderers, drew the biggest Judgement Day crowd in living memory." Aydan smirked, curling up his lip as he spoke. "Carnyfex made sure they had a day to remember, too. It's a shame their families in the eastern states couldn't watch, but their crisp remains were dumped in Sabyloa town square afterwards."

Upon my arrival, citizens had repeatedly mentioned Judgement Day. With everything else going on, I hadn't stopped to question the details. Gauging from Aydan's expression, I still wasn't sure if I wanted to know, but my mouth went ahead anyway. "What is Judgement Day, exactly?"

"It is when prisoners' cases are heard by Carnyfex, Benegnyem's judge."

"Oh, I see."

"You must have seen the Atrium when you arrived?" Aydan sighed when I looked at him blankly. "It's just outside the Kennel Gate—it's pretty hard to miss."

Hope hit me. "The big, oval pit?"

"Exactly that."

"I thought it was a tournament arena," I said, grimacing.

Aydan laughed mirthlessly. "Sometimes, it feels that way. Actually, there is an annual sporting event and various plays are performed there, but once a month, it completes its most important role as a court. If crimes are proven false or are pardoned, criminals walk free. If condemned, they are marked and serve their time—or, well, you know." Aydan slowly passed an extended finger across his throat, mimicking the crackling sound of fire.

"By *marked*, you mean their eyes are turned blue?"

"Yes." Aydan shrugged.

"Is there any way to turn eyes back to their original colour?"

"Only through the blessing of the Flame—but few in this world would presume to try to revoke the judgement of Carnyfex. Once a convict, always a convict. The mark may speak of their past, but truly, once released, they cannot complain as they are usually still welcome, protected citizens."

I couldn't agree with that statement. The divide of rich and poor happened everywhere but not to the degree Emberbyrg had created, and certainly not with the lasting sense of conviction.

"Most of the Virisinigne population are blue eyed, so—according to the classification of Benegnyem—Gryer is trying to rule over a land of the damned?" It made no sense to me. If he was devout enough to form a Charr and invoke the Flame in Mount Halo, he surely had to believe in the rules of this world.

"Your world is full of generations of the ignorant—similar to the eastern lands here. I believe my uncle seeks to control all rather than leave heathens to rise above their station. Enlightenment may well bring more of your kind to the Fyuego in a new, progressive way." Aydan's cool understanding of his uncle bothered me although I couldn't put my finger on why. "My father had no choice in exiling him though. Gryer pushed every boundary and sought command when he had no power nor place to take it."

"Well," I replied bitterly, "he has certainly learnt from his mistake of trying to run before he can walk. Now he flies across my people with fear and fire." A lump formed in my throat. "I can only hope the Empress will now finally grant me the assistance I so desperately seek."

"You've done everything asked of you," Aydan replied, straining against his shovel. "I don't see why she won't."

Pynyt flew from my shoulder onto one of the lavacicles. At first, I thought he was simply fascinated by the lava bobbing within the rock, but when I didn't join him, he flew back to my shoulder, hissed *look*, and tugged on my ear.

Aydan chortled. "Really, you'd have to do something pretty stupid for her not to."

"Hmm, hopefully, not," I replied, distracted by Pynyt.

"Yeah, like trying to assassinate a prince!"

Shocked, I stared at Aydan, but seeing his mirth, I instantly joined in, "Haha, yeah, trying to kill the future king would go down really well."

Aydan glared at me, weighing up my words as though I were committing treason. It was *his* joke. How had it gone wrong?

"I'd never—you know that, right?" I said, maintaining eye-contact whilst walking in the direction of Pynyt's persistent yanking on my ear.

"Obviously," Aydan grinned, reminding me of my brothers when they tested me, but with nothing else to go on and his demeanour relaxed, I let it go.

As I approached the cluster of lavacicles that Pynyt was so intent on, Aydan pushed the last putty ball out of the archway, declaring, "Right, I think we're done! Let's get some fresh air."

"Hang on, I think Pynyt is telling me—" My eyes boggled. "Oh, nuts, there's loads of mineral deposit behind here. I'll just get a couple of blobs of putty and pick that up."

"Oh, that's annoying. I thought I'd checked back there." Aydan wandered over, peering at the dust as the moving lava illuminated his face.

"Never mind, no harm done, we found it." Gathering a chunk on my shovel, I threw the putty down and marvelled at how it still made a squelching sound. Whether it was Enya's blessing over it, predetermined divine intervention, or mystical properties of the ink keeping it wet, I do not know, but I was astonished by nature's provision.

"Do you want to live in Emberbyrg?" Aydan suddenly asked.

I had been asking a few impertinent questions, yet the directness of this one stopped me in my tracks.

"That's what is expected, you know that, right?" Aydan continued when words failed me.

"I am way beyond understanding what is expected of me, to be honest." Pausing, I rubbed my hand across my brow. "Before I can think of my future, I need to know my world is safe."

"But do you think of connecting the two worlds? Ruling both from one seat?"

"What?" I was stunned at the suggestion.

"Were you two commanders in agreement, you might delegate, but not as a married, ruling pair. Come, Niall, you feign surprise and mock my status, but it is clearly the wise move for any sovereign."

My mouth gaped. My heart raced. How had he misread me so badly? "I do not mock you, Aydan, and ruling, dominating is the exact opposite of my desires. Peace is all I seek. You say *sovereign* as though I am one. As though I am calculating the future with me at the top. I am not—"

Aydan scoffed. "My sister will be queen. You *are* her Fated Mate. If that doesn't make you a sovereign, I don't know what does."

My ears rang as though I had been in the firing line of a great explosion. This world was full of bombshells but this particular one made no sense. "Why would Enya be queen? *You* are eldest?"

Aydan screwed up his face as though I had slapped him. "A minor detail that the Empress chose to overlook," he said, waving his arms and slapping his sides.

My mind rewound to Enya and I standing on the Tailfeather, viewing Liekke's Valley. What had she said about her pilgrimage? Aydan completed his when he was fourteen—two years before she did, age twelve. *He scored very highly and completed his trial quickly. Some assumed he would be granted the role of Kennel Maid...*

"The Kennel Maid is the heir to the throne?" My words came out in an incredulous whisper.

Stone-faced, Aydan raised his eyebrows in acknowledgement.

Pynyt shuffled awkwardly on my shoulder. I wasn't sure if he was embarrassed by my ignorance or affected by the stern look that had set on the prince's face. My mind danced. Did I think this a better or worse system? Certainly, history had more than one example of the firstborn not making the best monarch and whether due to death, deposal, or divine intervention, the next in line had proven more worthy, but at least royal siblings knew the expected order. There was no coming-of-age trial or weighing character in a volcano, no public humiliation when you were not chosen, and therefore no disappointment when your plans were sent awry. Or, perhaps most importantly, no room for a dragon-born coup.

"Is your uncle the elder brother?" I asked, focusing on Aydan's almost swirling green eyes.

"Are you asking if he is the bitter older brother whose ideas for controlling a wayward world were ignored by the hierarchy in this city?"

"Is he?"

"My uncle's plans were sound. *Are sound*. A new age is upon us. Change is perhaps difficult at first, but once the dust settles we—"

"It was you." My words hissed as though pronounced by Pynyt, not myself. *"You* brought the thanatonite here!" I didn't know how, but one glance at his grin as he drew his sword, I knew I was right.

FIFTY

As I had been hoping to prove my worth and humility to the Empress and in turn be granted a new blade by her, signalling her blessing to return to Virisinigne with an army behind me, I had again left my sword on *The Leviathan*. Seeing Aydan draw his sword, my hand automatically patted the spot where my scabbard should be and I heard the despair of my childhood sword master echo in my mind.

Shovel it is, then, I groaned to myself, dodging Aydan's first advance.

Pynyt opened his mouth, blasting fire. Instantly, Aydan plunged forward, avoiding the blast as I threw myself back, jolting my left shoulder upwards, sending Pynyt to the safety of a lavacicle. His fire was only useful if he didn't die protecting me—and if I could position Aydan in his wake without also getting burnt.

Aydan plunged at me again.

Had the shovel a typical wooden handle, it would have been split into two. Instead, a toe-curling screech accompanied the iron and steel clashing into one another before I managed to push Aydan off and jump away.

"Not bad for a pirate prince," chuckled Aydan.

Suddenly the dual look in his eye that I had seen before made sense. He presented as calm and cautious, but the chaos, the drive for change and power had simmered beneath the surface—and now he had reached boiling point.

When I evaded a trio of swings, frustration flared his nostrils, but he had skill, and if it wasn't for the stubborn pig-headedness in me that refused to die holding a shovel, I think he would have cut me down faster.

Try as I might, I couldn't land a blow. Swords require skill to wield yet they are designed to cut air and flesh. Shovels are strong and determined, but in soil or stone, not in a fair fight—and I didn't think Aydan was going to switch his blade for a garden tool anytime soon.

I'd never seen him fight before, yet the way he moved felt familiar. The cold, concentrated expression was new, but the dance was not. The one step forward, two back, the struggle to guide him rather than just defend.

The edge of his sword pounded into the shovel, I pushed upwards, but the pressure was too great, my footing stumbled, and the blade sliced into my armour, finding flesh.

Pain shot down my leg and up my side.

A flash, a memory sparked.

When Enya asked what I had faced in my pilgrim's fear trial, I thought the answer had been clear: I feared the one who sought to stop me saving Virisinigne. Even after she told me the fights were fears, seeking a name hadn't occurred to me. He was masked, but by then it didn't matter, I thought I already knew who he was. Yet the figure fought, danced, like Aydan. I was accomplished, but he was better. Victory was only mine because the phantom version of my ship included the same weak plank that only I knew about.

Now every advantage was his.

Hearing my cry of pain, Pynyt swooped behind Aydan, ready to fire, but Aydan must have been keeping an eye out for my winged friend as his sword instantly swung at him. Diving forward, I blocked his strike with my shovel, saving Pynyt but leaving myself open to defeat as Aydan elbowed me in the face and pushed me down.

At least I die with honour, I told myself.

In a blink of an eye, wind slapped my cheeks.

Except it wasn't wind.

It was a gust of flames aimed straight at the back of Aydan's head.

"Woo-hoo! Ignis pila!" I called out as I rolled away.

Pynyt didn't need a *fireball* command any more than I needed to be told to grab the hilt of Aydan's sword as he screamed, trying to put out the flames that were engulfing his head.

Knowing it was a *me or him* moment, but doubting whether Enya would forgive me if I cold-bloodedly killed her brother, I turned my grip of the sword, ready to knock Aydan out.

Milliseconds before impact, a shadow cast to the side of my head.

I had no time to react.

The last thing I saw was a glimpse of speeding scales as they crashed into me, turning everything black.

Fifty-One

Waking up had never been so painful. Every limb hurt, my head pounded, and when my fingers explored the dryness on my face, they came away with a mixture of crusty blood and sand. Sliding my hand down my side, I grimaced, finding the gash Aydan's sword had made. It still oozed, but the main flow of blood seemed to have stopped. Had the blade not been buffered by armour, I was sure the cut would have sliced into my organs. As that thought made me shudder, I realised my armour was gone. Slowly dragging myself to my feet, I began taking note of my clothing which had been reduced to a plain tunic and leggings. No shoes, no jacket—and most importantly—no Amulet.

My heart sank.

Trying to centre my spiralling thoughts, I examined the room, hoping that against the odds the Amulet was still with me. The room was lined with white-grey stone, plus a dusting of white sand on the ground, so despite the uncharacteristically cool temperature, I decided I was most likely still in Benegnyem somewhere—but, given the absence of scorching heat and total lack of sunlight, that *somewhere* was probably underground.

The pale walls gave a less depressing feel than any other dungeon I had seen, yet I was still in darkness, save for a glimmer of light coming through a small, square window in a rusty iron door that had no handle—or not on my side, anyway.

Finding nothing, and feeling like a complete failure, I slumped against a wall. Without the Amulet of the Flame, I had nothing. No way home. Nothing to bargain with. They had just taken it—*Aydan had taken it*. A vision of him sailing to the World's Divide, opening the wall and travelling to Virisinigne to assist his uncle played through my mind. Everyone had been so focused—*I had been so focused*—on the mission to save the Empress, to right Gryer's wrongs and save Virisinigne, the idea that he had an accomplice, someone in agreement to his plans of domination, never occurred to me. Or certainly not quickly enough. I saw the boulder, not the avalanche.

And now I was buried.

My only shred of hope came from the fact I was not dead. There was a certain look, a void, in a man's eye when he intended to kill. The motive might alter, but I had seen the switch, the disregard for the sanctity of life, many times over the years. Aydan was not interested in simply teaching me a lesson or knocking me out. He had every intention of cutting me down in that volcano. Not only was I unwittingly interfering with and too closely questioning his plans, but I was competition. Benegnyem was supposed to be totally unaware. A sitting duck with infertile eggs from an ailing sovereign. I had to die.

So, the decision *not* to kill me had to have come from Coayl, his Charred dragon. Assuming, of course, it was Coayl who knocked me out. The speeding scales were dark grey-black, not jet-black with fiery scale-edging, meaning Adaryvan wasn't responsible—he might like to knock me out sometimes, but my body knew when he was around, plus he would have spoken to me, not attacked me—even if I was threatening the prince.

No, no part of me believed Adaryvan was involved.

Rubbing my arm, I focused on our Charr, hoping to sense his presence. We could only speak when close by, but he told me that he would hear my call at any distance. Internally, I screamed his name, but there was no answer. That frightened me more than the darkness.

And Pynyt? He had saved me from Aydan. What had become of him? My bond to him was different, yet his absence, my concern for his wellbeing, was no less great.

Rotting in a cell while so much was at stake was not an option.

I had to get out of there.

Reaching for the door, I peered into the dimly lit corridor where a candle flickered. For a while, I just listened, hoping the thumping in my head would dissipate and turn into approaching footsteps. It seemed to take forever, but when the steps finally came, I called out, pleading for attention, yet no one answered because no sound left my lips.

Panicking, I swallowed hard, checking there was nothing unusual about my mouth or throat. I'd checked everywhere else, but as I was so overwhelmed with internal thought, speaking aloud hadn't occurred to me. My lip was cut, my head bruised, yet my throat and tongue were fine.

Again, I shouted.

Nothing.

No whisper, whimper, grumble, or curse would leave my lips.

If it hadn't before, true, unadulterated panic raced through me.

Grabbing the two, thick iron bars that stood in the centre of the tiny door window, I rattled with all my strength. The hinges groaned and squeaked, but at no point did they give me any hope they would budge. I kept rattling anyway.

After a while, a face appeared in the tiny window. She was incredibly pale, so white that she almost blended into the walls, as though she was allergic to the sun and had lived her entire life in the shadows. She had a thick-set body, salmon pink eyes, and long, black hair that hadn't seen a brush for an equally long time.

"What?" she asked, gruffly. Until she spoke, I had struggled to guess her age, but she possibly wasn't as old as I first thought—which I had imagined was well into her sixties, yet her voice suggested she was half that age. Not that it mattered, right then, any voice, any age, was better than the silence I had had forced upon me.

"I said, *what?*" the woman repeated, more irritated than before. "Why rattle like an old sow on heat, then not speak when I bloomin' well come?" She cocked her head to get a better view of me through the window, then peered downwards on her side of the door. The scuffing sound, followed by a gently brushing noise suggested that she had lifted a sign hanging off the cell door, possibly a chalk board.

Anxiously, I watched as her eyes tracked across whatever she was reading.

"Ha! I see," she said, eventually.

What do you see? I said—silently.

"It ain't no good wobbling your mouth, boy. I can't lip read, and I ain't gonna try to learn it now." She paused, looking back at the board. "Pity, you're quite handsome."

"What's a pity?" New footsteps approached. "Ah, you talking to the false prince?"

The pale woman chuckled, stepping away from the door. "Yeah. He was rattlin' my nerves."

"Well, he don't want to rattle mine. I hate the night shift at best of times without whiner prisoners giving me a headache." A new, but almost identical face appeared at the window. If she hadn't plaited her hair, I would have said it was the same person. "What's the matter, false prince? *Dog grass caught your tongue?*" She roared with laughter at her own joke before walking away, taking her sister and the flickering candle with her.

A frosty chill slapped me across the face.

Dog grass.

Other than its origins, what had Enya told me about dog grass? It had multiple uses in different forms, was expensive, could be smoked—but if in the wrong balance, especially if injected, caused paralysis of the tongue...and sometimes death.

Aydan smoked dog grass, I knew that much, but it was presumably the good stuff. How easy was it to get an unconscious person to smoke? Pretty impossible, I decided—unless secondary inhalation counted? Then, as if called upon on cue, the inside of my left elbow throbbed. Squinting in the darkness, I could just about see a raised vein.

The bastard injected me.

How much had Aydan given me?

Didn't Enya say, if overdosed, the cure had to come quickly?

Slipping to the floor again, I cradled my head in my hands.

Flame, I whispered without sound as tears trickled down my face. *You are everywhere. Despite my ignorance, my failings, you have blessed and strengthened me. I do not profess to know why, but I have to believe it wasn't to see me die here. Not without saving Virisinigne. Please do not abandon me now.*

FIFTY-TWO

Assessing the passing of time was impossible. Five minutes felt like five hours. Hours could have been days. The cackling, burly guard wheeled a cart of unappealing bread and water down the corridor at one point but she made no attempt to enter or pass me anything. I heard the creak of iron hatches on adjacent doors, confirming there were other prisoners, but none of them spoke beyond the simple grunts of acknowledgment when passed food.

With no voice, I could not ask why I was not being fed. My fears told me it was because I wasn't expected to survive whatever came next.

"Hey, who are you?" spat the guard as she wheeled her cart back the way it came.

"Ah, hello. I've been sent to dress the wounds of the foreign prince," said an oddly familiar voice in a tone that I couldn't quite put a name to.

"Pfft, I doubt that very much."

"Why?" said the voice, unwavering despite the guard's disregard.

"From what I hear, the royal family are counting the minutes to his Judgement. Can't say I blame them. If he tried to infiltrate the Fyuego, poison the Empress, and murder my family, I'd cut him down, too."

Listening to the charges I was being accused of burnt a hole in my stomach, but I could almost hear the unseen women's shrug as she replied: "That may be so, yet my order came from the princess, and I'm not in the habit of querying the commands of royalty. Would you like to send for the Kennel Maid and see how impressed she is about being questioned?"

The guard snorted. "Do as you please. It's still a waste of time if you ask me."

"How so?" the voice asked with interest. "He is to answer to his crimes in the Atrium, is he not?" The speaker was careful to leave a slight inflection to invite a response whilst making a statement.

"According to instruction, yes."

"Then he has to be able to walk—or at least not die before Judgement Day. Sepsis will get him otherwise."

"Sepsis ain't gonna kill him before morning, Mederi, even I know that." The guard chuckled. "It's been a long time since we had two Judgement Days in a month. Last one I remember was when the King's brother tried overthrowing him." She scoffed, peering through the window of my door. "Treason does tend to piss them off faster, though, funnily enough."

"*Alleged* treason," the voice corrected.

"Humph," grunted the guard. "Though, Gryer escaped execution and got exile in the end—*in the end*." She grinned, clearly enjoying the dark memory. "Were you there? You aren't so young, are you, Mederi?"

"No, indeed, I was there. Everyone was there."

"Exactly. Tomorrow *everyone* is going to see this guy burn."

"Fyuego don't burn so easily," the voice said, with a hint of a smile in her tone.

"Huh! Tell that to Prince Aydan! Heat resistant isn't infallible—you should know that in your line of work. If a Dog, even a Fyrewowwa, sets their blaze to the right channel, it'll still take someone out fast as lightning." She cleared her throat, spitting on the floor in front of my door. "Carnyfex won't be marking his pretty green eyes blue tomorrow, that's for sure!"

"Well, that's nothing to do with me," replied the voice, obviously tired of talking to the guard, but trying to maintain a professional, yet non-confrontational tone. "I've just been sent to make sure he makes it *to* Judgement. How bad are his injuries?"

"No idea. I've barely looked at him." Keys rattled. "I don't have time to watch you. I've got the other wing to sort. If you're going in, I'll have to lock you in there with him. Your choice, but if he adds to his crimes and kills you, don't expect me to cry at your funeral."

"Very well," replied the voice, without hesitation.

"Fine. Okay, get back, foreigner!" boomed the guard. "Mederi's gonna help you, so don't be a knob. Stand against the back wall, pirate filth."

Fearing she'd change her mind, I did as I was told.

"Do you want me to tie his hands at least?"

"No, thank you, I'll take my chances," replied the Mederi. "It'll be easier to tend to him if he isn't."

"Right then, in you go." A key slotted into the door. "Shout loud when done. I'll hear you, *eventually*." She sniggered. "Oh, don't expect any conversation. He has been muted, thankfully. Traitorous scum."

The lock clicked, and the rusty door cried out as it swung open. Seemingly confident I would not attack her, the Mederi kept her back to me, watching the door close before turning to face me. The sense of familiarity of her voice had teased my overstimulated brain. I had hoped seeing her would instantly pull me out of my state of confusion. In a way, it did, but with clarity also came new uncertainty. Despite the pale blue tunic and head scarf, I recognised the beautiful young woman who stood in my cell holding a candle and small leather bag.

Oryana.

How? was the most prevalent, overriding question that rang in my mind. Her long, dark, flowing hair and sun-kissed skin were the same. Her voice had a slightly different air to match the part of a medic—Mederi—that she was playing but it was essentially the same accent that I expected from her. Her height, build, everything about her was as I remembered—everything, except her dark brown eyes.

Oryana had blue, crystal-blue eyes.

Not brown.

How? I asked, pointing to my eye, then to hers.

Oryana smiled, then pulled a face, gesturing her head towards the door. "Okay, prisoner, I am going to dress your wounds. I am told you have at least one significant gash on your side?"

My immediate thought was how does she know that? Then the answer came to me. *Pynyt.* She had to have been sent by Pynyt. Smiling with relief, I pointed to my side, and lifted my blood-stained clothing to show her.

Gently taking me by the hand, Oryana gazed up at me. "Remember, prisoner, I can*not* lip read," she stated, winking.

A wave of emotion flooded my eyes. *Flamma vobiscum,* I mouthed with every ounce of my soul.

"Flamma nobiscum," Oryana whispered softly into my ear whilst squeezing my hands. "The Flame is with *us both,* Captain."

Quickly pulling a jar of water, a clean cloth, and needle and thread from her bag, Oryana set about stitching me up. It was painful, yet her delicate fingers were perfectly accustomed to weaving and I doubted whether a real Mederi could do a better job—even if skin and net are not quite the same. I thought about making a joke about not turning me into a fishing net, but I didn't want to distract her from her work or in any way seem ungrateful.

The candle flickered and she paused, anxiously glancing at the door, showing fear for the first time. Tapping my ear, then jerking my head towards the door, I signalled that I was listening for movement.

For now at least, we were alone.

She nodded, holding my gaze.

I didn't try to kill Aydan, I said, desperate to tell her my story while I could.

Oryana nodded again, whispering, "I know, but what *did* happen?"

As briefly as I could, I explained that Aydan was working with his uncle and that he had attacked me for getting too close to the truth—omitting, in the name of both speed and my pride, how I had stumbled towards uncovering Aydan's plans rather than truly deducing them.

Full explanations could come later.

Hopefully.

So Pynyt is okay? They didn't get him, too?

Oryana shook her head. "He is fine. Fyuego guards came to the ship looking for him, but at the time we knew nothing was wrong, so after they outlined your alleged crimes, they declared the crew confined to the ship and left. Three hours ago, Raine and I were on the bow, watching the harbour, trying to come up with a way to get to you when Pynyt appeared, presenting me with a Fyreshroom."

A what?

"A Fyreshroom—or at least, that's what I hope it was, otherwise I was severely duped by your Fyrewowwa." Oryana let out a very quiet, nervous giggle. "Truthfully, I've never seen one before. Very few ever have. They grow in a treacherous cave behind the waterfall in Liekke Valley. Their red flesh supposedly comes from their roots—the mycelium—being linked deep into the world's life stream. Those that eat Fyreshroom are pardoned or blessed by the Flame—or granted extra strength, depending on which legend you listen to." She shook her head, rolling her eyes. "But I think the second part largely comes from the fact that Fyre Dog hatchlings eat Fyreshrooms to boost health when first out of their shells. Regardless of the truth behind the human benefits, I guess there are always those who see the blessings of others and think they should have it too, never mind if they will use it wisely or deserve it." She groaned. "It's no wonder that the Flame puts the Fyreshrooms in such an inaccessible place."

It is not just legend. Your eyes are *brown.*

"I know." Oryana smiled and her eyes truly sparkled. The sight of blue eyes had never bothered me before—they *are* beautiful—yet seeing Oryana in her natural, Flame-given colours was different. For a moment, I forgot that I was facing a judgement worse than being *marked by a Dog.* "It may sound odd, but I feel like me again. Whole."

But your hearing, it hasn't been restored?

"No." Oryana smiled. "You'd think I'd be disappointed, right?" I had to confess, I was surprised she wasn't. "But my hearing was lost through injury, not punishment. A bump in my life's road. Part of my fate—not a judgement, a conviction that was thrust upon me. Does that make sense?"

It did make sense. One was just an element of who she is, the other a label stamped across her, marring her identity. *Absolutely.*

"I can't say I've been the biggest fan of Fyre Dogs, for obvious reasons, but I will now be eternally grateful to your Fyrewowwa."

So, Pynyt spoke to you? I asked, eager to understand what had happened.

"Yes. He said, *Eat. Go to dungeon, Niall injured*, and then whipped Raine's side with his tail." She smirked. "I took that to be an indication of where you were hurt the most."

My eyes boggled. *So you thought, what the heck, I'll risk all for him? You're risking too much—*

Oryana coyly, but confidently smiled. "You gave me my freedom and offered me family when my own did not. I had to come for *my* captain."

Ignoring the pain in my side, and the need for urgency for a second, I hugged her.

Can you get me out? I asked, stepping back.

Oryana's face fell. "No, I can't."

Are you sure?

"Yes."

But how did you get in? Have you been here before?

A sadness crossed Oryana's eyes. "I know the route because I visited my brother here before—" She paused, momentarily unable to finish. Taking a quiet, but deep breath, she continued. "As a teen, my brother was regularly in trouble for being drunk or disorderly, but no one took him seriously until he started stealing. The Emberbyrg folk called him *Magpie*. Of course, eventually, he was caught. We hoped his crime would be heard by a human judge, but Conley stole from a spiteful elder who insisted on having his day in the Atrium. Mum bribed an old guard into telling her about a potential entrance via a cave on the cliff outside Old Emberbyrg. It's meant to be an air vent, but if you're small and a good climber—even better if you have a sturdy net, you can just about get in. Mum didn't dare climb, so she watched the net, sending me in. We got out, but my brother, struggling from alcohol withdrawal, wanted to stop at the pub. It was no surprise, but the guards soon came. We ran. My brother thought I was too slow, so pushed me into an alley. Later he claimed to have been protecting me, but I crashed into a moving horse and cart and was thrown into a wall. I haven't heard a thing since. Thankfully, the guards assumed that we had slipped out of the proper entrance, not the vent hole I used today, but we were all marked come Judgement Day, and Mum—" Oryana wiped away a tear. "She was petrified by Carnyfex. Everyone is. Her heart couldn't take it. She dropped dead in the middle of the Atrium."

My heart ached for her. It was a hideous story. Just standing here had to be torturous and I was humbled she would put herself through it for me.

Time was running out.

We both needed to leave.

What if I drop down the cliff into the sea? The crew could—

She shook her head. "*The Leviathan* has been surrounded by the navy. Raine managed to lower me into the water and I swam to shore. The ship cannot sail. The crews' lives are dependent on you being judged."

What about Adaryvan? Where is he?

Oryana dropped her gaze to the floor. "No one seems to know. The rumour is he is hiding after the embarrassment of your betrayal. Pynyt is looking for him."

Concentrating hard, trying to delve into the corner of my mind where our bond lived, I searched again for

Adaryvan's voice, calling out to him through it, yet my voice echoed, making my skull ache.

Hope for myself left me.

Then go, save yourselves however you can. If you can, save Virisinigne without me. Tell the crew about Aydan. He must be exposed before he and his uncle take over the world—or burns it. If you ever get opportunity, tell Enya I am sorry for the lies told and the words I should have said. Grasping both her hands, I gulped. *I thank you for this act of kindness. You send me to my grave with a full heart but—*

Reclaiming her hands, Oryana put a finger to my lips. "You mistake me, Captain. I came to patch you up, to buy you time, *and* learn what I can. Pynyt's Fyreshroom may have invigorated me and restored my eyes so the guard would not reject me, but I am not the chosen one. *You are.*"

Chosen to form a team, to beg for an army, not stand alone. I am not worthy of your sacrifice. In my heart, I added, 'On my own, I'm never enough.'

"Ssh, enough of that. Together is as one, for sure. One body, one goal, one family, yet all need a head," Oryana retorted. She was ten years younger than me but twenty years wiser. "I've stayed long enough. I know the time frame we're dealing with now. There's no time to return to the ship—and they cannot help right now anyway." With a determined expression set across her face, Oryana collected her things into her bag.

Gently holding her chin, I made her look at me. *What are you going to do?*

"What I haven't done for years." A melancholy smile spread over her lips. "I am going to knock on the Kennel Gate."

FIFTY-THREE

I gnoring my pleas to protect herself, Oryana left me in search of Enya. I both prayed for and feared her success simultaneously. Being granted access to Emberbyrg was one thing. It was still frightening, but in theory, as long as no one recognised her, it should be achievable. Yet being granted conference with the princess was on another level. Persuading the princess to listen to the friend of her brother's would-be assassin was yet another.

Coayl and Aydan had played the smarter card. I had to give them that. Killing me in the volcano would have been easier in one way, but returning me to Emberbyrg, declaring me a liar and a traitor, and convicting me before the masses and squashing all sympathy for my unknown world was better. Without the dog grass overdose, I would undoubtedly scream my innocence and Aydan's treachery in the Atrium. Cutting my tongue off or obviously gagging me would have made Aydan look like he was hiding something. Presenting me in one piece was far better. Most wouldn't know I was silenced, and even if they did, the mob would trust that Carnyfex could understand my moving lips or read my mind and judge me accordingly—some might even say, *fairly*.

I was afraid of the dog grass running through my veins. Understanding, or believing that I understood, Aydan's motives, I tried to reassure myself that the dose he gave me would probably not kill me. Giving a lethal dose, or even a dose big enough to cause wider spread paralysis would ruin the desired public humiliation he apparently had in store for me. Yet he had also persuaded my judgement to be brought forward to tomorrow. *The vocal coach*, that's what Enya said the so-called safer dose of dog grass was nicknamed. In the back of my mind, I remembered her saying tongue paralysis could last six to twelve hours. But that was if smoked. She failed to mention the duration of the injected form—or how quickly a lethal dose took to do its job.

Without meaning to, I found myself mulling over the benefits of each scenario: Die in the dark in a cell of stone and sand, alone. Or die in an arena, surrounded by eyes and what I could only assume was a large, fire-breathing, trigger-happy dragon. Either was pretty unpleasant, but burning to death with the jeers of an angry crowd all around me suddenly made the lonely option seem preferable.

But where was the high?

Surely the point of taking drugs was to mask oneself? To forget. To relax. To enjoy. I felt none of those things. *Lucky me,* I thought. *I get the side effect, but not the main attraction.*

Dulling my headache at the very least would have been nice.

Although I knew that Oryana would not return, I couldn't help listening for footsteps—or hoping this was nothing more than a cruel joke. Hoping, against all the odds, that Enya didn't hate me. That my family would forgive me.

Laying outstretched in the sand, I stared at the ceiling, watching the tiny flickers of light from the corridor come and go as the guard went about her business. I couldn't tell you if I slept or not. Perhaps at best I dozed briefly. Any detected sounds were not for me, yet whether real or imagined, I tensed at them all.

It was the longest day and night of my life. By the time a key clicked in my cell door, I disbelieved it. I didn't even turn to it. *I'd rather die at sea, if you please!* I shouted into my solitary void. It seemed impossible that anyone walked out of these cells with an ounce of desire for life, especially if they were here for a month.

Light filled the cell, highlighting what I had been trying to ignore, even when Oryana had her candle earlier. Food stains and flecks of blood decorated the walls, and scratches carved their messages in the stone. My favourite was on the back of the door:

Prepare to meet thy maker. The end is nigh.

"Oi! Get up!" The unbrushed guard grumbled, waddling into the room with a lantern in one hand and a spiked club in the other. I'd determined that her eyes were salmon-pink before, yet now they had a hint of faded red.

What's happening? I asked.

"What you wobbling ye mouth for? Get up! There ain't any questions you need answered now, foreigner." Kicking me, she scowled. "Get. Up."

Clearly she had no appreciation for my battered body—or my desire to move slowly and preserve my stitches.

"Come on!" screamed the other guard, somewhere down the corridor. "Don't tell me he is playin' you up?"

"Nah, we're comin'. Old boy is creakin' like a three-legged hinny, though." The guard by my side chuckled.

"Ah, we better cuff him! Remember Lord Byrne said to cuff him?" The voice approached, jangling iron cuffs. I didn't wait to be asked—or forcefully compelled. Wiggling my shoulders and wrists one last time, I took a deep breath and stretched both arms in front of me.

The sound of the clasp shutting felt like the final nail in my coffin.

"What about his feet?" the untidy guard asked.

Her sister laughed. "Nah, piggy's gotta run! Crowd loves a runner."

The two guards led me through a series of identical corridors that seemed to go on forever. Part of me expected to have to rise up at some point, yet neither steps nor slopes appeared. Eventually, however, natural light did begin to make its way into the depths. The labyrinth of tunnels did have an exit—even if I had no escape.

Six soldiers dressed in full, royal armour stood at the end of the path I was on. The dungeon guards had the flame on their chests, yet they apparently either didn't want or need to have the full Emberbyrg attire on. Maintaining their aversion to sunlight, both blanched-guards stopped short of the glorious sunrays, pulling me to a halt with them.

Stood behind me, with her club poking me in the back, the untidy guard cleared her throat. Two of the six guards were already facing me, yet at the sound of shifting phlegm, the man in the centre turned, setting his red gaze on me, scowling.

"Lord Byrne, sir," said the guard behind me, "we have brought the requested prisoner."

"Very good. We will take him from here. You may both go—or watch, as you wish."

"Much obliged, sir," she replied, bowing her head, side glancing at her sister. They didn't need to say it. They had every intention of watching me burn.

The sound of a gathering crowd increased with every footstep forward. I could almost feel their bloodlust. Sense might have told me to stay back, yet I wanted to see the Atrium. Upon our arrival, Raine and I had been impressed as we viewed it from above. Standing near the edge, I had gazed into it like a bird—free and able to fly away—and the rows and rows of seats had been empty. Now, they were filling by the second as people descended into the pit. Some seemed to be accessing through tunnels at the middle point—the Emberbyrg residents. Even now, in their joined delight at seeing punishment dished out, the brown-eyed citizens separated themselves from the working class, the damned, and the lowly.

If used for just sport or plays, the Atrium would be easy to praise. It's design was made to strike awe and it achieved it perfectly. However, as I was the chicken about to be roasted for a crime I did not commit while the chef, their prince, cooked up a much larger, world-altering banquet, my awe twisted into dread.

"For what little it matters now," Lord Byrne said, walking to my side, "I wanted to be wrong about you."

My shoulders drooped. *You still are,* I replied, silently.

Lord Byrne made no attempt to lipread, instead choosing to remain focused on an ornate platform on the right-hand side of the Atrium. The banners, sunshade, and thrones immediately labelled it as the royal box.

"Prince Aydan did well to trick you into smoking the dog grass. We don't need to hear any more lies."

So that's how he justified it.

Desperate to be understood, even if by the most suspicious person I had met in Emberbyrg, I tried to stretch my tied hands towards his arm. Instantly, I was blocked by the flat-side of a sword owned by a lower guard.

"Keep to yourself, vile pretender!" sneered the guard. "You are not worthy of the ear of anyone, let alone the Lord." His eyes caught the edge of the tattoo on my upper shoulder and hatred poured out of him. "You are certainly not worthy of the Charr. You are nothing but a stain on the Fyuego and the Flame."

No, innocent until proven guilty here, then...

"A stain that is about to be removed," replied Lord Byrne, nodding at the royal box as an unknown face peered over the front. "The king has arrived."

As if heard by the entire crowd, a silence befell the Atrium as King Inygo, Queen Brydget, Prince Aydan—complete with heavy bandaging—and lastly, Princess Enya appeared. A herald declared their titles as they were seated, yet I doubted there was a person present who didn't already know their names.

My eyes bore into Enya, hoping that she would feel it. That Oryana had found her. That she hadn't given up all regard for me. Her face was set—almost like someone had given her dog grass but instead of paralysing her tongue, it had frozen her features. The warmth, the care, had drained from her. She was angry. Really angry. So much so, she wouldn't even glance at me.

I had always thought myself unworthy of her. She was calm, focused, and obviously knew what she was expected to do and who she was whilst doing it. I bumbled my way through, leaning on my crew, my found family, to see me through thick and thin. They could rely on me to act in a pinch, to be the leader they needed because I knew they would back me up in a heartbeat. Together we kept the king's peace in western Virisinigne.

Whether alone or in company, Enya shone.

My gaze wandered to Aydan. He too, refused to look at me. Being high Fyuego, his wounds would heal faster, but it was clear he was battered, burnt, and bruised. I knew it wasn't enough. Unchecked, it was only a matter of time until he wreaked havoc on the kingdom. He was the snake in the grass. And these people, his family, would only see his betrayal after he had struck.

Flame, please don't let them realise too late, I prayed, almost forgetting about my own plight.

Another figure appeared in the royal box. Using a cane, his movement was slower, but Uryah kept his head held high as he approached the front rail in his fully-decorated Commander uniform. He glanced at Lord Byrne, waited for a short, sharp nod, then raised his sword towards the sky.

All were absolutely still.

A pin hitting the sand would have been heard.

"We are hereby gathered today to witness the Judgement of the man who calls himself Prince Niall Beckett of Virisinigne. We welcomed him into our great city. Our king listened to his plea for help, took pity on his words, and felt the guidance of the Flame in his heart, and sent his daughter, our beloved Kennel Maid, Princess Enya, with him to begin our holy pilgrimage—offering him not only an elevated, honoured place in our city, but also a place as a member of the Fyuego—being Charred with the Protector of the Flame, himself, Adaryvan. All this he was offered, yet he has thrown it in our faces. He has betrayed our trust, falsely projecting stories of poison, treason, and disaster upon us. And, worst of all, attempted to assassinate our prince when he unveiled his lies."

Uryah dropped his sword, and as intended, a gasp rippled around the Atrium.

"Bring forth the prisoner!" declared Commander Uryah.

A deep drumbeat beckoned my movement but it was the grip of two guards propelling me along that escorted me across the vast sandy arena. Boos roared from the crowd, joining with the drummer to play out my final march.

Even when I stopped, the jeers continued. I was the villain of their play and that was it. As everyone refused to meet my eyes, it occurred to me these people hadn't heard my sister's wisdom, for she always told me that she could read the truth of a person by simply gazing into their eyes. *They don't lie, Niall,* she said. *They are windows to the soul.* However, unlike Muriel, these people did not want the truth. They had their version and that was it.

King Inygo stood up, raising his sword, wordlessly bringing silence to the Atrium. Although a hundred metres above me, I could feel his hatred penetrating my skin. "Niall Beckett, of wherever you might come from, we hereby release you to the Judgement of the Almighty. May Carnyfex deliver that Judgement, swift and fair. May the Flame have mercy on your soul and return you to the life stream to be made anew."

Sheathing his sword, the king jerked his chin to someone standing on the far side of the Atrium. Although on the same level as me, the distance and brightness of the sun prevented me from seeing their features. However, when they ran to the side of an enormous gateway, activating its clanking metal mechanism, it wasn't the guard's features I was interested in.

For Carnyfex was blacker than any night, so black that sun didn't shimmer or reflect off his scales like Adaryvan's.

It was as though he had absorbed all the light he could take and it was inside, boiling, ready and eager to burst with hellish fury—*at me.*

FIFTY-FOUR

Running from danger is a natural reaction for any creature. If something is bigger, stronger, and highly likely to kill you, self-preservation should tell you to run. If you have nothing to fight with, it should definitely tell you to run. Heck, even the crowd wanted me to run—although me *saving* myself wasn't their motive. The fact I didn't produced screams of disgust from the masses above.

What is the point? I mouthed. *There's no exit. I'm not going to dart about to entertain you.*

If my hands had been free, I would have attempted some kind of sign language to Enya. Although if I had pointed to her brother and run a finger across my throat, that would probably have been translated to *I'm going to kill him,* not *he is trying to kill you.*

Look at me, I begged.

While his sister's stoney expression rested squarely on the approaching dragon, not me, Aydan's subtle smirk caught my eye. Sneering, I made no attempt to hide the hatred that filled me. *Traitorous bastard!* I shouted, much to Aydan's amusement.

Surely someone can lipread? I asked the crowd. The truth was, probably some of them could, if they wanted to. But that was the problem—they didn't want to. They wanted to believe they had been saved from my dastardly plan, not that there was a larger, much greater threat sitting before them.

In no rush, Carnyfex steadily advanced, swinging his tail in the sand with each methodical step. When first faced with Adaryvan, I submitted. Although I didn't know what the consequences would be, in my heart I felt that I had to lay my sword before him. This time I had no such compulsion. With my hands empty, I had nothing but myself to drop anyway. It occurred to me that it could still be the better way—possibly even the humbler way. Yet I was not guilty, so why should I be humble? The way I saw it, I had two options: die whilst refusing to engage or refuse to look away and die. What I couldn't decide was which option was more likely to communicate my innocence? Because that was all I really wanted to show. An ironic scoff slipped out of me. In the end, I would still be dead, so I would never know if I chose the right method.

I wished that I knew where Adaryvan was. His absence stung the most because I didn't understand it. Had he despaired of me? Or had Aydan got to him too? Concentrating on our bond hurt—like someone had torn it. Was he dead? I thought the Charr was unbreakable, yet if the Empress also believed the lies, maybe she had annulled our tender union?

It wouldn't take much to kill me. One stomp. One blast. But Carnyfex was the cat and I the mouse—and it wasn't just the crowd who was disappointed in my inaction.

He wanted to play.

To serve justice slowly.

Dragons could be delicate as well as brutal.

The flames had multiple settings: mark, maim, massacre.

If saving myself was not possible, I had to leave a message. Some doubt of the people's safety. If Virisinigne was lost, maybe I could save Benegnyem...

With speech and mime taken from me, my only other prop was the sand beneath my feet. My initial thought was to write *Aydan is a traitor*—or *Aydan with Gryer*, or *Benegnyem under threat*—but everything I considered would take too long.

I settled on four letters.

Digging my heel into the sand, almost toppling myself as I scuffled backwards at speed, I wrote:

L-I-A-R

At first, both crowd, crown, and guards were too curious to see what I was doing to stop me. To the former, I was finally moving, so that was something to cheer, while the latter simply gawped, waiting for someone higher up the chain of command to decide if my action was allowed or not.

When I reached the *R*, Aydan bellowed, *"Enough, traitor!"*

Instantly, Carnyfex whipped his body and tail around, swiping the sand clean and sending me crashing into it simultaneously.

The crowd roared with delight.

For a second, I will admit to questioning whether I wanted to save any of them.

Whether by default or design, my executioner had turned their tail so that the worst of the spiked scales were not facing me, however, I was still caught by the edge of at least two of them and I could feel blood trickling from my forehead.

Standing up while still concussed is difficult at any time, doing it with your hands tied whilst gazing up at a princess, is nearly impossible.

Her head remained still, but I saw Enya's eyes turn skyward. Her eyebrows gave a wry flicker as she briefly glanced at me. For a millisecond, I held her gaze. Desperately, I hoped she read my heart in that time because her eyes didn't stop long enough for me to mouth a word.

Thunder rumbled—or so I thought until I realised Carnyfex had changed tactics. Thumping his front feet, he was ready to dance again. When I remained rooted to the spot, frustration seemed to ripple the scales across his body. Extending his neck toward me, his enormous head lowered. His eyes were not like any other dragon I had met before. Everyone else had windows to their soul, almost like portals to another world, along with the life and power of the Flame behind them.

This dragon was a blackhole.

Clearly, Emberbyrg justified him as acting in the name of the Flame to keep the peace—or what they understood of it—but there was no justice, no hearing, and certainly no mercy.

Carnyfex flared his nostrils, sucking in my scent—which by then was mostly a mixture of terror-stricken sweat, tender resignation, and both dried and fresh blood.

His mouth stretched wide, displaying a furnace forming at the back of his throat.

Ignis pila came to mind and I almost laughed. The irony of learning their word for fireball only to be killed by it just seemed too much in the moment.

A roar filled the Atrium.

A shadow cast.

A dark green-grey shadow.

A voice filled my mind.

Hold on.

FIFTY-FIVE

U ntil that point, everything had been in slow motion, but what happened next was an absolute blur. Carnyfex's tail had already scattered sand into the air, yet the steady beats of incoming dragon's wings produced a sandstorm unlike anything I had ever seen before.

While the crowd cried out, shielding their eyes from speeding grit, a tail swung in front of me, catching the chain between my cuffed hands around a spiky horn with impressive precision as it jolted me upwards, leaving me no choice but to watch the ground, the crowd, and the Atrium disappear beneath me. I wish I could claim that I was not petrified, that I was used to heights, and I was just happy to be alive, yet all I could think was, *what if this chain breaks?*

A chuckle rippled in my head. *Then I'll catch you.*

Wydgitta? I asked, only then realising which dragon had scooped me up.

Yes.

What's going on? Why—

This is not the time for a Q&A. Wait, Enya has decided she is coming, too.

Twisting in the air, Wydgitta looped around, facing towards the city. Above the Atrium, running along the city wall with her brother in pursuit, was Enya. She had a decent head start, but if Wydgitta didn't get there before she reached the corner tower, either Aydan or one of his oncoming guard's would stop her.

Accelerating, Wydgitta streamlined, darting through the air, keeping her tail up just enough to stop me from slipping off. Approaching the thick, stone wall, Wydgitta's body blocked my view, but I expected her to pause briefly to collect Enya. She didn't. As we zoomed over the city defences, my eyes eagerly searched the spot where I had last seen the princess.

She was gone—but Aydan was there, screaming into our tailwind.

Hugging the scaled horn that I was linked around, I raised my middle finger. I wasn't sure that it meant the same in his world as it did mine, but the scowl on his face told me it translated well enough.

Remaining low, Wydgitta flew away from the city, over the jungle, and although we seemed to be circling the mountain range, I assumed we were heading for Mount Liekke. Looking back, I wonder why I didn't ask her, she obviously could hear my thoughts, but I figured she was talking to Enya and I didn't want to interrupt. Not yet, anyway. I also couldn't help anxiously searching the skies for more dragons. It seemed impossible to me that the king hadn't ordered someone to give chase.

No one will chase the Kennel Maid, Wydgitta said after a while, probably tired of listening to my repetitive thoughts. *No dragon, anyway.*

She pronounced the word *dragon* with true reverence—the same as anyone blessed, and worthy of the title, would not defy their chosen leader. It both comforted and concerned me.

What if they are just dog, not dragon? I asked.

Normally, I would say there was no difference. Wydgitta sighed so heavily that we dropped a few metres in the sky. *Yet now there is.*

Have you told the princess? Does she know I didn't—

I do. Enya's voice in my head, however brief, stopped my heart. When it started again, it pounded in my ears.

How, how can you—? I stuttered.

Enya didn't answer and I began to question if I had heard her at all.

Charred Fyuego can communicate with any Fyre Dog, if both parties are willing, Enya eventually replied.

Adaryvan had told me that much himself. Our bond was greater, but in theory all human Fyuego could communicate with winged Fyuego. But Enya wasn't answering the question. How could *she* hear *me*?

Because you are Fated, answered Wydgitta, bridging the silence. *Fated Mates can communicate through their dragons. I guess I am your amplifier.*

Oh, I replied, not knowing what else to say.

Wydgitta snorted. *We're nearly there.*

Gazing around, I tried to find my bearings. Although we had approached the Peak from an unexpected, unknown angle, we were over the Liekke mountain range. However, as Wydgitta suddenly began to descend, I realised, we were not heading for the Peak. We were heading for the Liekke Valley waterfall—and fast.

Why the speed? I said, feeling my blood still within my body.

Because, replied Wydgitta, *Adaryvan says Coayl is searching for us.*

Adaryvan? He is here?

Ssh, I need to concentrate.

Inside my head, something clicked, like someone had closed a door. Scrunching my eyes shut, I tried to find Adaryvan, but all I found was deafening silence. My stomach knotted as I reopened my eyes, watching the beautiful oasis come in thick and fast as Wydgitta dropped further from the sky, skirting against the flow of the river as it made its way to the lake. Before us was the waterfall complete with the jagged rocks that protruded from every angle. *No wonder so many died trying to navigate it,* I thought. *And my bones are about to join them.*

Wydgitta took a deep breath and released it, sending flames in the waterfall. A purple haze lined the red and I instinctively knew it was Enya. As if parted like curtains, the cascading waters parted, revealing a wide, yet unwelcoming cavern.

Only then did Wydgitta break—hard.

The moment her feet touched the ground, the water rushed back to its's normal position, filling my ears with its deafening roar, and casting us into semi-darkness.

The mouth of the cave was deceptively large, certainly large enough to accommodate a massive, speeding dragon, yet the further into the cave I looked, the narrower, steeper, and more lethal the way became—if a path could be more dangerous than riding a racing dragon while hand-cuffed as it thrust itself into a rock-filled waterfall.

The pressure in my head clicked, dispelling some of the thumping and buzzing I was experiencing but not making me feel any less sick. My legs gave way, making me slump into Wydgitta's tail.

Are you alright? she asked.

My manly pride begged me to lie, but I was beyond that. *No.*

The sound of feet landing on rock proceeded the echo of running. Wydgitta curled her tail, turning me towards Enya. With one glance at me, a word, perhaps a curse, slipped out of her lips, but instead of aiding my release, she ran off into the darkness.

FIFTY-SIX

A purple flicker of light shone in the darkness. As though in a weird dream, I watched it climb up the rock, navigating its way higher and higher, until it disappeared, leaving just a tender glow until that too vanished.

The cave was damp but warm, yet I shivered. My brain felt heavy and frozen. If Wydgitta tried to speak to me, I didn't hear her. I certainly didn't need to be told what was wrong with me as the crass guard's words rang intermittently in the silence.

What's the matter, false prince? Dog grass caught your tongue?

Previously, I had questioned the lack of a high to accompany my pounding head, throbbing arm, and speechless-tongue, but this was definitely the low. The slippery slope of death. Irony hit me. Hadn't I just been rejoicing my escape from the clutches of death?

There are some fates you cannot outrun, I muttered to myself.

The light returned, slowly but surely retracing its path. As it reached the cave floor and began a more straight forward approach towards me, through blurred vision I saw the purple glow coming from Enya's necklace. When she knelt beside me on Wydgitta's tail, cradling one hand behind my head, I wondered if the necklace hadn't altered the colour in her usually green eyes.

Hearing my slurred thoughts, Enya chuckled softly before wrapping her fingers around her necklace and slipping it out of sight beneath her clothes. When her hand retracted, the purple haze extinguished, forcing me to rely on whatever light filtered through the water, but I thought I saw another chain—until double vision took over, duplicating any and everything around me. Overwhelmed, I closed my eyes, praying it would stop.

With her now free hand, Enya raised her fingers to my lips. "Eat it," she said, pushing something soft and earthy inside my mouth.

Although beyond hungry, I had nothing to lose, so I accepted the morsel without much hesitation. It was surprisingly spicy, yet sweet, and before I swallowed it, I began to feel a warmth spreading throughout my body. Were it possible to fill a person with mist and fog, the heat pushed it all away like morning sunshine.

Satisfied I had eaten it, Enya let me go and leant back a little, watching me intently.

What was that? I asked.

"A Fyreshroom," Enya replied out loud. "Eating one is the only known cure to a dog grass overdose."

So that's why you said the people had to seek help from the Fyuego in time if they were to have a chance of survival?

"Yes. Fyreshroom only grow here and we cannot store them. Patients have to give us time to fly up here, pick a Fyreshroom, and get it back before the effects fully freeze their organs." Enya shook her head. "Were you not a Fyuego, you would probably have succumbed earlier."

Your brother presumably knew that. He wanted me silent, not dead before Judgement.

Enya's face fell. "My brother has been tinkering with the recipe for dog grass. It dulls or removes the high, but the poison is just as effective. He tried to pitch it to the king last year as a deterrent to poachers from the east." She brushed a stray tear away. "Father thought he had put a stop to that idea. He thought that my brother was—" She couldn't finish.

"I am so sorry," I said, in earnest. Aydan might have tried to frame me, a stranger, but familial betrayal was on another level. Suddenly, my eyes widened and a gasp caught in my throat as I realised I had spoken.

Through her sadness, Enya smiled.

Pressure on my wrists suddenly eased and the sound of sliding chain and clanging cuffs rang out as they hit the ground. Raising my freed hands forward, I rubbed my forearms and rolled my shoulders, groaning with painful delight.

"How?" I whispered.

"Fyreshrooms are a blessing from the Flame. They can cure those in need but can also exonerate the falsely accused or liberate the truly repentant." She coyly grinned. "One way or another, the Flame has not yet done with you."

I was beginning to lose count of how many times I had been saved, yet I was keenly aware that I couldn't assume continued rescues. Oddly, I was closer to assuming that another life-threatening situation was coming than I was presuming deliverance from it. The next time could be my last—so I had to make this count, even if I didn't really understand how I had gotten here.

My mind went to Oryana. The Fyreshroom Pynyt gave her had enabled her to visit me, but I needed to know what happened next. "How did Oryana convince you I wasn't lying?"

"She didn't," Enya replied. "I received a request from the Kennel Gates but I refused to speak to her." She read the surprise in my face. "Don't look at me like that. In my shoes, I am sure you would have—"

"Sided with my sibling," I said, finishing for her. "Yes, I probably would have too, especially as she came from the crew of the opposition—of the man who had avoided telling you everything." I waved my right hand down my left arm, indicating to my Charr. *Our Charr.* It was the closest I had come to acknowledging it, yet I still couldn't bring myself to talk about it. "If you didn't believe me, what changed?"

"Wydgitta," Enya replied, gazing up at the dragon's looming head.

Your friend, Oryana made a scene at the Kennel Gates, demanding to see Enya but she didn't realise that she was stood next to the very Fyre Dog she needed. Wydgitta snorted. I knew she was telling the truth because she smelt of Fyreshroom and there was no way she picked one without help.

"Pynyt!" I said. "Pynyt picked it."

Precisely. After listening to Oryana, I went in search of him, and found him outside this waterfall, hoping I would come.

"So you know *exactly* what Aydan did? What he means to do?" I spoke to Wydgitta but turned to Enya. Her light smile upended. "I don't just mean about me, about—"

"He wishes to rule. To join with our uncle and rule everywhere." Enya's voice remained steady, but only a fool would believe those words did not break her heart.

Risking rejection or overstepping my mark, I cupped my hands over hers. For a moment, all I could do was breathe in time with her, taking deep, solemn breaths when she did as I waited for my tongue to form a short, yet sincere sentence. A vow. "I am yours. Tell me what to do." She twisted her fingers, weaving them between mine as I added, "Together, we must bring peace to both worlds."

Deep in thought, Enya held my gaze. "We must present all this before the Empress." An urgency set into her expression. "Can you stand? The cure can take a little while to fully take affect..."

"One way to find out," I replied, letting go of her hands and pushing myself to my feet. A mild dizziness, like running with a half-filled bucket of water, sloshed through my head, but as it stilled, my body seemed to settle into its normal state—or rather, my new normal. A sense, like a consciousness of a nearby presence overcame me. "Is someone coming?" I asked, suddenly anxious.

Enya glanced at Wydgitta.

I can't detect anyone, but we should get moving, replied the dragon.

"Are you sure Coayl isn't there or that Carnyfex hasn't come to finish the job?"

"Carnyfex will not leave the Atrium," Enya replied. "He carries out the king's orders—"

"So the king's justice, *not* the Flame's," I scoffed.

Enya shuffled her feet. Apparently, she, too, struggled with the potential misuse of the Flame's name in the pursuit of human power. Shaking her shoulders, mentally dusting away any secondary concerns for the time being, she confidently answered, "My father will not put out an order for capture out on me." Pausing to observe me, she must have read my doubt. "*That* is initially why I came with you both. Wydgitta told me seconds before she arrived that she was coming but not why. Our loyalty to each other is everything, yet she defied my wishes and she risked her life to save you from the pit. I needed to understand why. Alone, my father might have ordered a military response, but with me here, he *will* wait."

There was no arguing with her tone or sentiment, so instead I asked, "Where's Coayl?"

Wydgitta gently shook her head. *He disappeared just after your Judgement began. I took a scenic route here and I believe avoided being tracked. Adaryvan said he saw him but—*

"We must go," declared Enya, impatient to end our stationary revelations. "We can discuss this on route now Niall has had the cure."

Agreed, said Wydgitta, lifting her tail up the side of her body. *If you could both ride on my back, I can use my tail without concern.*

Considering they had both saved me, any chivalry from me was probably weak at best, but I gestured for Enya to step onto Wydgitta's back first. Unfazed by the height, Enya skipped onto the withers, turned to grab my arm as I attempted to repeat the move with the same dexterity, and pulled me to safety when I almost failed.

Despite the size of a dragon and number of scutes, there really were only two ideal horns for a human to slot into. On Adaryvan, I leant forwards, hugging the one in front, knowing the one behind would support me if needed. Wydgitta was the same, the horn rose up on cue, but I wasn't sure if I was supposed to continue my gentlemanly behaviour and offer to take a lower, less perfect scute—or share. Suddenly, I felt like a confused teenager. It was ridiculous. The world as I knew it was on the brink of ending, yet my heart pounded at the thought of wrapping my arms around a woman.

While I procrastinated, something intangible, like a loose puzzle piece in the recess of my mind, slotted into place.

Aye, aye, Sailor, chuckled a gruff voice.

"Adaryvan?" I declared, glad not only of the distraction but also to hear from him. "Where have you been?" Conscious of Enya's gaze, I added internally, *I thought you had left me...*

No, Sailor, I just got detained.

Stop calling me Sailor, I said, feigning offence.

Adaryvan's mirth chimed like a bell. *I thought you prefer that to wingless gnat?*

Honestly, he could have called me anything and I wouldn't have truly cared at that point. I was just relieved to have him back in my head, and to know he was alive and hadn't forsaken me as a worthless traitor. Obviously, my sense of silly pride prevented me from properly expressing that. *Haha. Where have you been?*

Coayl tricked me. Laced in anger and frustration, Adaryvan's brief explanation came through loudly. *He told me Seraphyna had decided to mine the fresh rubrunite from a different cave, so I followed him instead of following my gut. The second I flew into the mine, he caused a landslide, knocking me out and blocking me in. Without causing a cave-in, I couldn't blast my way out.*

Why didn't you call me?

Adaryvan scoffed. *I did—when I came round, but by then you had been poisoned and our bond was blocked. Pynyt found me. He then tasked Wydgitta with saving me before she came for you.*

But why didn't you come for me? Are you injured?

Only a few bruises and my pride. Wydgitta was expected to be flying to the Kennel Gate, I wasn't, so we decided she would get you and I would escort your crew out of town.

Concern for my crew had been niggling at the back of my mind but I had been too afraid to voice the question. *Where you able to? Are they all safe?*

Yes.

As the chain of events linked together, I was struck by the unfathomable blessing of the Flame joining dragons all of sizes with humans.

"Is he alright?" Enya asked, sensing that I was lost in thought, not conversation. "Is Coayl visible?"

After listening to Adaryvan's reply, I repeated, "Coayl disappeared north somewhere. He didn't spot Adaryvan taking *The Leviathan* away from Emberbyrg."

"Then we need to get going before he returns. We can catch up on route to the Empress."

Sitting down, Enya shuffled forwards and quickly tilted her head, indicating that I should get behind her. Sliding into place, I hovered my hands over her sides, waiting to see if she would object. When she just stared forwards, I gently held onto her waist and was hit by a strange feeling of belonging.

How could something make no sense and all the sense at once?

FIFTY-SEVEN

The sight of Adaryvan and Pynyt flying just outside the waterfall warmed my soul. Together we headed straight for Liekke's Peak, only stopping when we reached the head of the First Empress's skeleton.

Everywhere was quiet, peaceful even. A total reverse of the day before when billowing smoke heralded the Empress' threat to invoke an eruption.

"Why are we not going straight in?" I asked.

"As the Kennel Maid, I feel that I should speak to Her Imperial Majesty alone first," Enya replied. Still in my arms, she turned, examining every pore on my face. "Do you mind?"

It struck me that it didn't matter if I minded or not, she was the anointed princess, and there was nothing to suggest she needed my permission. However, I also knew she wasn't asking permission, she was sharing—which she definitely didn't have to do, especially as I had withheld so much from her, but I appreciated it, nonetheless.

"Of course not," I replied. "It makes perfect sense." Gently releasing her, I got up. "I'll wait out here until you want me." Holding her gaze a second longer, I began the long descent to the crater floor. As soon as my feet touched the ash, Wydgitta set off to find the Empress, leaving me with Adaryvan and Pynyt.

I couldn't decide what to say to either of them, so instead I gazed up at Drayanna's skeleton. When first Charred, I had viewed the murals from Adaryvan's back, but now on the ground, they seemed to take on a new form. It occurred to me that they were only meant to be viewed from the back of a dragon—like an extra privilege or perk of being a blessed member of the Fyuego—but as my eyes travelled over the stories and prophecies, again taking in the details and pondering whether they truly depictured Adaryvan and I like he thought, I realised there was a mural underneath the skull that I hadn't seen before.

"What does this one mean?" I asked, pointing as a shiver shot down my spine. When Adaryvan didn't reply, a second icy-bolt ran through me.

Pynyt landed on my shoulder, taking up what I believe we both considered to be his rightful place, and tilted his head up at the image. I waited, hoping that he might respond if Adaryvan would not, but only a whistling wind filled the silence.

"Adaryvan? What is it?" I demanded. "You told me that Drayanna, the Second Empress, scorched the murals as reminders of the past, but also as prophecy. You said, the Flame told her one day the Amulets would unite the realms and restore absolute balance of the world—that you trusted in our Charr, our calling, so unquestionably because of a belief that we might be in these pictures—"

"I accepted because for the first time I felt called to do more than guard, yes," he replied solemnly.

"But what about this? Why didn't you show me *this*?"

"Because I needed you to believe in our power for good. In *our* ability to succeed."

"This shows destruction!" My tone was beginning to edge into shouting. "It looks like the Amulets are being used to dominate, to—"

"Yes, I know. While the Amulets are meant to unite, how that balance is restored is up for debate. Restored realms could be single domination, not friendship and understanding." Adaryvan spoke calmly, far more calmly than I listened. He, as ever, was resigned to do his duty. To play his role with honour. Come what may, he was steadfast in his belief in the Flame.

"Reading this, Gryer and Dreygon could easily see themselves as the bringers of foretold unification." Wiping a sticky layer of sweat off my brow, my heart sank. "They could genuinely believe they are acting for the greater good."

"The murals are not so clear cut." A deep growl rumbled from Adaryvan. "Look inside."

Walking under the rib cage, I realised there were more images. A light and a dark side of these prophecies, hidden from sight until viewed from the right angle. Then, beside where the heart would have once beaten, the most dramatic murals ran in fragmented pictures across multiple ribs. Two black dragons and riders with Amulets charged at each other in blazing fury. The final image showed one dead, one alive, surrounded by a bloody-red that was as bright as flowing magma.

Victory.

But whose?

Breath caught in my lungs.

Am I here to save or to be destroyed?

A roar echoed from within the volcano, breaking my swirling thoughts of despair. The sound was so deep, so guttural, it lingered in my ears long after it stopped. Adaryvan and I waited, anxiously preparing for a repeated cry or call to attention.

Neither came, but a gust whisked up the ash, twirling it around us and making it impossible for me to see beyond my own hand, yet when an enormous red figure approached, I knew it could only be Her Imperial Majesty.

"Prince Niall of Virisinigne," boomed the Empress. "My Maiden has told me all." At the sound of her voice, all dust fell to the ground, revealing her imposing gaze fixed upon me as she stood just beyond the skeleton's ribcage, while Enya and Wydgitta nervously waited behind her.

Instinct dropped me to my knees and closed my mouth. I would wait for a direct, unmistakeable question before I dared give any kind of answer.

Heat poured out of the Empress' mouth as she spoke, "Once, not so long ago, did I not tell you that I would serve justice? Did I not command you to save my children lest I serve holy judgement and allow all to burn?"

The Empress used inflections, yet I didn't feel like she was expecting a response, so I remained silent.

A deep, growling hiss emanated from her.

"I am grieved beyond words to hear of such betrayal. In truth, my initial thought is to serve justice, fire and brimstone on all and wipe the world clean. Let the Flame rebuild from our ashes." Sighing heavily, thick steam burst out of her nostrils. "However, I also told you that if you proved yourself—if you saved my children—I would grant you the Blade of the Flame. You kneel there now, next to the mark of a prophecy. Of a decree and promise to serve the will of the Flame. To protect the rightful balance of life—as well as the rightful balance of power. For with the rise of evil, must come the defender of good. Loathe as I am to defend a hair on his head, perhaps Gryer believes he is the good. It is rare that the villain truly sees themselves that way, yet when the understanding and drive of empathy is lost, *that* is when darkness falls upon us."

Opening her mouth, displaying her peaked teeth, the Empress extended her wings, stretching them towards the sky. Ash began to rise, as though rain had been reversed, and the ground began to quake. Grey specks became luminous sparks, and the lines between my scales began to glow purple, green, and red. In the near-distance, I saw Enya glowing too, our matching tattoos pulsing in time with one another. Then before me, a large rock rose from the ground, stopping a few metres before it pierced the spine of the First Empress.

The Empress, with a voice like thunder, declared: "Arise, Knight of the Flame. Wield this sword wisely. It will be your last."

Lightning hit the rock, shattering it into nothing, leaving a gleaming sword standing proud with no apparent prop. The pattern on the blade waved like streaming fire, while the Fyuego symbol rested above the guard. On the hilt were two racing dragons—their bodies joining in an endless, sideways figure of eight.

Any trepidation in me was overridden by a propulsion beyond description. A calling. My fingers curled around the hilt, testing the grip. It was perfect. No blacksmith could have shaped it for my hand better.

Lifting it, I felt a force, a hope, that I would be the light, not the darkness.

Bowing to the Empress, then Enya, I turned to Adaryvan. As on Liekke's summit, once again something deep within told me it was him I had to present my sword to. However, this time, rather than lay my sword before him and submit, I knelt beside it with the tip loosely in the ground and gazed into his eyes, appealing to his soul as I asked: "My friend, my Charr, without you I can do nothing. Will you fly with me to Virisinigne? Will you help me break the veil and be the light?"

A dry chuckle broke the tension. "Sailor, I thought you'd never ask."

FIFTY-EIGHT

When the Empress refused to accompany us, I was disappointed. She knew the murals better than anyone, she knew what was at stake, yet she would not leave Liekke.

"Whether this battle is truly the one foretold or merely a fragment of it, I do not know—after all, not all prophecies come as linear as they are depicted," she said without irony. "However, I do know that I am bound to this volcano. To this world. Until I have a hatchling to save, I'll risk nothing more. You saved me but the fate of my children is still uncertain. My legacy, the future and essence of this world is only intact if I or a descendant exists."

"With your health restored," said Enya, gently, "a hatchling might be possible. Time, Your Imperial Majesty, you must give yourself time."

"A royal egg was delivered this morning," announced the Empress.

My mouth opened to declare it wonderful news when Pynyt's ever-knowing talons pinched my neck. Grimacing, I tapped his body with my right hand—and received a nip for my efforts. *As usual, I was missing the point, but Enya understood.*

Keeping her body and voice low and humble, Enya asked, "What colour is the egg, Your Imperial Majesty?"

Even Adaryvan notably held his breath.

"Pink."

Enya gasped, choking back tears.

Is that good? I asked Adaryvan through our bond.

Dragons don't cry—or at least I didn't think they did until that moment, yet it turns out you don't need tears to share emotion. The normally gruff, sarcastic dragon slowly nodded his head three times, willing out a single, silent word. *Hopeful.*

My disappointment turned to understanding. Of course the Empress wasn't going to risk leaving the only sign of new life she'd had in a decade. Not when she had her warriors, her protectors, summoned before her.

"You must collect the Amulet of the Flame," said the Empress, "and fly to Virisinigne. Liberate the oppressed and enlighten all who you meet of the grace of the Flame. See if you cannot at last bring unity." She took flight, sending a sandstorm hurtling around the crater, however, none of the grains touched us. For a moment, I thought she had gone, yet my entire being jumped as her head burst through the whisking wind. "And if any reject or challenge the sovereignty of the Almighty, let them meet their maker."

Her majestic voice called out. *"Flamma vobiscum."*

"Flamma vobiscum," replied five very different, but unified voices.

It took a few moments for the reverence of the moment to dissipate but a sense of action came over me when it did. Adaryvan was undoubtedly on my side and Enya had already saved me, yet I had not asked Enya how far she was willing to go for me. *Where* she was willing to go for me. With everything hanging in the balance in Emberbyrg too, I couldn't assume anything.

"Enya, I-I—" I stuttered, approaching her. *How can I talk to a massive dragon but not a woman?* Incapable of talking about feelings, I went with facts. "Do you know where the Amulet of the Flame is? I cannot stay here any longer, but without it I am—" Her enormous grin cut me short.

Slipping her hand under her neckline, Enya lifted two chains. One with the purple sapphire that she used as a torch, and the other of the Amulet. Suddenly, my grin matched hers. "When the Empress told me to collect the Amulet, I was imagining a more difficult journey. How is this possible?"

"When Aydan returned accusing you of treason, my father immediately ordered your execution but also demanded that you be stripped of your armour, including the Amulet. I watched him lock it in his personal vault." Staring at the Amulet as it laid in her hand, Enya chewed the corner of her lip. "Something, like a niggling inner voice, told me to get it. I said that I came here because Wydgitta had risked herself for you, that I needed to hear why as much as I needed to understand what would make you go through so much only to throw it all away." Her eyes met mine. "That's true, I did need to know—even if

I told myself I was seeking closure. Yet despite the fact I thought you had tried to kill my brother, had rejected me, and were a lying, deceitful piece of scum, if I am honest, a part of me still hoped that I was wrong and you were not completely lost." Enya blushed, handing me the Amulet. "So, fearing that my father would be blinded by rage and not seek the full truth, I took the Amulet in case my hope was not ill founded... and my heart was not entirely mistaken."

Overwhelmed, my heart spoke volumes, yet as always, words evaded me and my mouth was left woefully silent. Turning the Amulet over between my fingers, it felt strange and unfamiliar in my hands, so I placed it around my neck, praying its magic would allow Enya to hear my unspoken thoughts, however, neither dragon nor princess acknowledged my frustrated conversation for one.

"We should go," said Wydgitta, probably too pained to wait for me to get my act together.

"Agreed, now we have the Amulet and the Blade of the Flame, we must go—but not to Emberbyrg." Adaryvan fixed his eyes on Enya. "I won't lie, I would prefer to fly with a Fyuego army, but even with your assistance, we don't know what Aydan has told the king and going to claim Niall's innocence will only provide a delay we cannot afford. The Empress' command for Niall and I was clear, but you must decide which direction calls you."

"If Virisinigne's fate also determines by brother's actions here," replied Enya, "then my decision is made. Right now, my brother may be planning and scheming, yet without my uncle's sway, I do not believe he has enough followers to stage an all-out coup."

"Your departure might be seen as siding with the enemy," I warned as my brain clicked into a more familiar grove of planning action, not tackling emotion.

Enya nodded. "Possibly, yet Wydgitta returned for me and I was seen going with her by choice. It is more likely my father is mulling on theories, not setting out—not yet, anyway. We need to see what we are dealing with, then we can call the true Fyuego to arms and flush out the false."

"Then it is agreed?" I said. "We travel through the Divide, assess the situation and strike?"

A calm resolution spread across Enya's face. "Fire with fire."

FIFTY-NINE

Perfectly hidden in a cove, *The Leviathan* was not visible until we were right above her. Adaryvan's dry chuckle rippled through me as I praised his skills, but it was the added steel plates on the bow and stern of the ship that made me laugh out loud.

"I made some modifications, Captain," Marino said, after embracing me. "We noticed the other ships in the harbour had them and once we, well, had first-hand experience." He jerked his head towards Adaryvan sitting on the shore. "We thought it might be worth adding a couple of handles before someone makes holes that we cannot patch."

"It's interesting you mention that," I said, grinning coyly, "because we are going to have to fly again."

"Alun will be thrilled." Marino's smirk was priceless.

Anxious excitement fluttered through me. "He might forgive me if he knows we're going home."

Marino's expression told me he felt the same. Although only days had passed, with everything seeming to take too long, to be too far, or the hurdles in between appear too high, it could easily have been years since we had seen home.

The crew had been largely confined to the ship, but their faith in me had been tested in every direction—including up. Had we been a less bonded crew, they probably would have abandoned me more than once, yet when I asked them to fly with dragons, fish with sea monsters, or accept the fact that I now possessed a sword to take down Gryer and Dreygon, they simply said *okay*.

I could not take that for granted. I would not. To move as one, to continue to be united, I had to treat them as equals. Sure, as captain I had command, but they deserved to know where and why we were sailing. Calling the crew together, with Enya beside me, I explained my vague plan.

After listening, Marino and Raine glanced at each other.

"What?" I asked, eager to hear their concerns.

"You say Aydan's Dog, Coayl, is missing?" Raine said. I nodded.

"Is it possible he has allies scanning the Divide?"

"Adaryvan says he saw Coayl flying north," Enya chipped in. "There's a Fyuego outpost in that direction, including a small Fyre Dog team who watch wildlife. As my brother visits there every year, it would now seem likely that he meets likeminded friends there."

"Well, although I am not keen on sitting about, I'd rather do it in this tiny cove then out there in the open in daylight." Raine jerked his chin, indicating out to sea. "It'll probably be another clear night, so why not use moonlight to navigate by and get Adaryvan to escort us to the Divide in the dark. With any luck, we'll slip through before anyone knows where we are."

Raising a quizzical eyebrow, I turned to Enya.

"Makes sense," she said calmly. "It's a few hours delay, but the benefits outweigh the risks—don't you agree?"

Without hesitation, I answered, "I do."

With the ship as ready as she was going to be, I ordered the crew to eat and rest in shifts, hoping that we'd make it to nightfall without being detected. Despite the recent inconsistency of my meals, my stomach was far from rejoicing when I forced food into it, but I did it anyway because the crew were observing me and they knew me well enough to detect the slightest hint of hesitancy. I had been honest about the difficulties of our mission but now set, I had to be their beacon of belief. Only a fool would have no nerves sailing into a war, yet we had come here seeking an army and I was sure that many would have preferred to wait for one. However, I also knew Adaryvan and Wydgitta outweighed any human army, and their fire power would easily match anything Gryer threw at us. "With them on our side, the balance will tip in the favour of my father's army," I told myself—and anyone who asked or would listen.

As long as that army is still alive when we get there, I added silently.

Oryana had stitched my wounds and the Fyreshroom had countered the poison, but I was extremely conscious of the dry, crusty dirt on my skin, plus the increasing odour coming from me—and if I wasn't before, Alun was quick to point it out while he and Raine lowered me in a lifeboat towards the sea.

Commander Uryah or Lord Byrne would probably have viewed me as lacking control, but Alun's jeers were welcome light relief from what was to come, so I just laughed.

"Where's my clothes?" I asked as I was hoisted back onto the main deck. Having lived together at sea for over a decade, the sight of a crew member in no more than a towel or even changing in front of me had become uninteresting. In my haste to be clean, I had only picked up a towel before washing and despite knowing the princess was on board, I couldn't bring myself to put my sand, ash, and blood infested tunic back on. To my eternal shame, I also assumed Alun would have collected something fresh for me.

"I thought you had them?" Alun grinned.

When Enya came up from below deck and her stern expression twitched at the sight of my bare, tattooed arms, my heart sank. With my mouth slightly agape, I willed by body to move as my brain desperately tried to find the right words to finally broach the subject. Clearly taking my dumbfounded expression as avoidance, Enya shook her head and continued towards Oryana who was mending a spare sail.

Perched on the rail, Pynyt flapped his wings. "Idiot."

Alun burst out laughing.

Scowling, I headed towards my quarters.

"He ain't wrong," sniggered Alun.

Retracing my steps, I faced my gunner. "Excuse me?"

Raine calmly wrapped his fingers around my tensed arm. "Ignore him, Captain. You know he enjoys winding you up."

Alun chuckled. "I was simply agreeing with your pet."

A small fireball flew past Alun's head.

"Bloody hell!" Alun shouted. "Sorry, not a pet. *Friend*—I was agreeing with your *friend*."

Pynyt bowed and hissed.

"Point taken." Alun stepped back. "Can I go, Captain?"

"Please do," I laughed.

"Funny how it can talk and laugh when it wants to, but spits fire if it don't," Alun muttered to himself as he headed towards the lower deck.

"Captain?" said Raine, once we were alone.

"Mmm?" I replied. "What is it?"

He cautiously glanced at Pynyt. "Don't spit fire at me, but Alun and Pynyt have a point. You do have to talk to her properly sometime."

"Who?"

"The princess."

A long, frustrated groan came out of me. "Not you as well?"

"Hear me out!" Raine held up his hands. Frowning, I waved my wrist, indicating for him to continue. "From what you've said—and a little from what you've not said—those marks on your arms are more than just acceptance into the Fyuego."

Rubbing my chin, I pretended to gauge the length of my beard instead of answering. "I think I need to shave." One look at Raine told me he wasn't buying my distraction. Sighing, I said, "I'm told we're Fated Mates."

"And you're not happy about that?"

"Until a few days ago, I'd never even heard the term! Arranged marriage, marriage for love, that's all I know. I didn't think I'd have either. I—" Lost in too many thoughts, I cut myself off.

"What?" Raine's blue eyes held mine.

"Have you told Oryana how you feel?" I asked, trying to deflect.

He grinned so broadly I thought his lips were going to fall off the side of his face. "I have."

I rolled my eyes. *Of course he has.* I should have known the man with all the right words wouldn't hold back when it mattered the most. "*And?*" I said, smiling, already reading the answer in his expression.

"She feels the same way."

Affectionately grasping his shoulder, I pulled Raine into a hug and whole-heartedly congratulated him. "I couldn't be happier for you—for both of you. You deserve every happiness." Walking away, I struggled with an enormous lump in my throat.

"You never know what is around the corner, Captain," Raine called to me, stopping me in my tracks. "Just because you didn't think something could be for you, doesn't mean it isn't waiting."

Unable to answer, I dipped my head and headed for the privacy of my quarters. As I went to close the door, fingers curled around the edge. Stepping back, I allowed the door to open and a blur of orange flew past as Pynyt came in followed by Oryana.

"Hi," I said, still marvelling at her newly-browned eyes. "Can I help you?"

"I thought I'd let Pynyt in before he scorched your door." Oryana grinned. "He doesn't like closed doors."

"Thanks," I chuckled. She nodded. "I think I owe you another *thank you*—I hear you calmed the crew when Adaryvan rocked up earlier?" I said, recalling Marino's earlier account of being removed from the docks. Apparently, they had all been searching for a way to get off the ship undetected in order to attempt my rescue, but when Adaryvan showed up, they initially thought they were being escorted to the pit to burn alongside me. When they then realised he was attempting to save them, Alun tried to load the cannons to bomb Carnyfex—or wherever he could hit in Emberbyrg, declaring that if they were all executed, they'd at least die laughing (his words, not mine). Thankfully, Oryana, Raine, and Marino talked him out of that one.

"Pynyt said Adaryvan was saving us," Oryana shrugged as though it was nothing. Suddenly she beamed. "I can hear him in my head, it's nice."

"I'm glad," I said warmly. "Ha!" I rolled my eyes, "but I hope he is politer to you than he is me!"

She chuckled softly, then twisted her lips as though she wanted to say something else.

"What is it?"

"I know what those scales mean, Captain." Oryana waited to see if I would reply. Unable to, I reached into my cupboard instead. "I also see how you look at her."

Whipping my head out from behind the door, I was about to deny it, but decided it was pointless. She and Raine had obviously teamed up against me. They had honest, open hearts and expressed them with ease. They also saw through me. She really was perfect for him.

A deep sigh slipped out. "What if she doesn't want me? Fate isn't always kind..."

"She's sailing to another world for you!"

"For the Flame. For peace and justice." I hid behind the cupboard door again, dropping my towel and stepping into fresh clothes.

"You keep telling yourself that," Oryana said quietly.

Remembering she needed to lipread, I stuck my head around the door again. "It's okay for you, you—" I stopped. Oryana had gone. "*Women,*" I groaned to Pynyt.

"Men," Pynyt replied, releasing a slowly meandering stream of smoke.

"We are going to war! The fate of an entire world potentially balances on my shoulders. I cannot worry about my heart when my soul—*when all our souls*—might be lost!"

What's one without the other? Adaryvan added through the bond. *And is love not the greatest, most noble, cause for action?*

If you're going to get all philosophical on me, love can also be the most dangerous, selfish thing to act upon. Wars and age-old disputes have started over the hand of one person or another. Jealous love is—

We are not talking about jealousy nor the love of power and you know it, Sailor. Adaryvan grumbled in my head. *Love, acting for others, for crew, family, nation, for right against wrong, for—*

Duty. A bitter sadness hit me. *I do not want to be forced on someone out of* duty.

Eager to get away from both of my scaled companions, or at least not be alone with them, I slipped on my boots, grabbed my jacket, and stormed onto the main deck before either could answer back. The sun was finally heading towards the horizon, and some of the crew were on lookout, but everywhere was largely quiet. On the tip of the bow stood the princess, gazing at the calmly rippling waves.

My eyes shot to the emblem on my chest, then to the sword hanging from my side. I looked every bit the part of a hero. *Fake it 'til you make it?* I asked myself.

With my hands clasped behind my back like I was cuffed, I joined Enya on the bow, only removing my imaginary restraints to grip the rail instead. In my head, I had approached fairly quickly, yet procrastination was either time-consuming or time-altering because the sun suddenly kissed the horizon, filling the sky with beautiful hues of pink and purple.

"Beautiful, isn't it?" I said gently. "It should be a clear night as Raine predicted."

Enya kept her eyes on the disappearing sun. "It's not just duty, Niall," she said as though I had started an entirely different conversation.

My stomach twisted around the meal I'd pushed into it. If Wydgitta could link our minds, it stood to reason that Adaryvan could too—I just didn't think he'd do it without telling me.

That's a violation of trust, I mentally gritted my teeth at Adaryvan.

Someone had to start you talking, he replied without an ounce of remorse.

You could have said she could hear me.

I didn't hide it. Adaryvan snorted. *You need to learn to pay more attention.*

Go away a minute, will you?

Okay, Sailor. A light but gruff chuckle proceeded a click in my head.

Hearing him leave didn't seem to be an issue, but I had to admit I was frustratingly slow at noticing his arrival.

"He isn't wrong," Enya said. "You'll talk about everything except what is literally marked on you. Why?"

"If you've been listening to my thoughts, you know why," I grumbled like an embarrassed teenager.

"You resent being told I am your partner." Enya still refused to look at me but her words stung as though she had slapped me.

"What? No. It's not *my* sense of duty I am worried about."

Her emerald eyes shot to mine, darting from left to right as she tried to read my expression. "You cannot doubt that

I am committed to duty?" Her tone was a mix of hurt and pride. "Have you not seen me do everything asked or expected of me?"

"Precisely. You have dedicated everything to the needs of others. You-you—" My tongue failed me and Enya's rising hope of an answer deflated in front of me.

"You want our help, you want acceptance and to prove your honesty—yet then hid the Flame-given blessing that achieved all of those things *and* might have obligated my father into more decisive action." The confusion in her face pained me. "*Speak to me*," she softly pleaded.

Irritated by my silence, my skin writhed and my ears rang.

"*Speak to me*," Enya repeated, gently waving her hands by her sides.

"I am sorry I didn't tell you about the Charr. I should have." I sighed. "I wanted to."

"Why didn't you?"

Gulping, I forced myself to answer. "B-because I was afraid you'd be disappointed." When she didn't respond, I dryly, but candidly added, "No part of me can imagine that the seventh son of a king you've never heard of is the partner you dreamt of. If we're being honest, someone who knows nothing of your world, fails to say the right thing at every given opportunity, and has lived at sea almost as long as he has on land is not exactly a major catch, is he?"

"I see." A faint smile crossed her lips. "Tell me truthfully, are *you* disappointed in Fate's choice?"

My heart thumped so hard I thought it might reach out of my chest and grab her. "No."

Enya released a long, deep breath.

"But have-have," I stuttered. "Have you never wanted something, someone, to choose you? I mean freely choose—heart and soul." I paused, not missing the irony of using those two words together as Adaryvan had suggested minutes earlier. "My crew have become my family because for one reason or another we have chosen to stay together. When I was originally cast out to sea, it was half punishment for not being *royal* enough—for being the seventh, most expendable son that my father couldn't be bothered to pair off. He had made enough connections to rule comfortably and I was deemed more embarrassment than asset in Tecta." I scoffed. "Only in his darkest hour did my father decide to call for me—when I was finally useful to the kingdom beyond peacekeeper and tax collector." Releasing the rail, I faced Enya straight on. "But I am still the seventh son who has made his life at sea when the land would not have nor hold me. Now I am not sure I belong anywhere else. Yet here I am, thrust upon a world, on a journey that I have to pretend to understand, only to be told that Fate connects me to this beautiful goddess that is surely worth more than I can offer—and who surely deserves to choose as much as I do."

Unable to take the intensity of Enya's gaze, I stared out to sea, hoping to get lost in the dimming colours on the horizon.

Enya's fingers gently wrapped around my wrist. "I believe the calling of the Flame to be an honour, not a privilege or free card for inaction. The call to serve, teach, or lead is a gift, however, you must still choose to do it. We all have choice. If this world teaches you anything today, let it be that the position of your birth has no weight on your merit, value, or destiny. *You* determine your path and the person you are or want to be—and *who* you want to walk life's journey with. You say your crew have chosen to stay together after destiny joined you. I believe it. I can see the unwavering loyalty and love that you all have for one another." Her voice wobbled. "I am sorry if that cannot extend to me."

Wiping her face, she walked away.

Afraid of never being spoken, words fired out of me. "It begins and ends with you."

Halting, Enya furrowed her eyebrows. "What does that mean?"

"It means I am petrified that the Flame will take it back and tell me this is a joke. That there is no way someone like you could ever be meant for me, but at the same time, if you are, and you want me, then—" I choked up, and try as I might, I couldn't find any more words.

Thankfully, I didn't have to.

Smiling, albeit cautiously, Enya stood in front of me with only inches between us. Taking my left hand in both of hers, she kissed the back of it, her lips caressing the edge of my Charr, sending new waves of emotion through every cell.

"I want you," she whispered, keeping her eyes fixed downwards.

With my free hand, I cupped her chin, gently turning her gaze to mine. My heart was so loud it could have replaced a marching drummer. It echoed throughout my body—through *our* bodies—as our chests heaved, taking slow, deep breaths in mesmerised unison.

As I leant in, Enya's arms held my sides. Electricity anxiously and eagerly soared between us, urging our connection, yet fearing I would break the spell, I moved slowly, drinking in her sweet smell before softly kissing her. Blown away, I pulled back slightly, allowing the dusky-night air to pass between us. Smiling, Enya tugged me a step closer, passionately reconnecting our lips, and melting time as we sank into each other's embrace. Soft remained tender, but polite distance became nothing as her arms wrapped around my neck, while mine clung to her waist and never wanted to let go.

Had Aydan or Coayl found us in that moment, I doubt I would have noticed.

SIXTY

With the fall of darkness, joy turned to duty. Wydgitta lifted *The Leviathan* while Adaryvan flew alongside us, ready to defend at a moment's notice should we be found. A bright half-moon aided our passage, and despite the increased altitude, the added wind was minimal. We had nothing to complain about, no obvious foe waiting to knock us down, or obstacle to block our path. It was perfect, almost *too* perfect—and everyone on board was on edge as we waited for our luck to run out.

In the distance, the World's Divide came into view. At first it was no more than a looming shadow, maybe a uniform mountain range or heavy storm cloud, but as we approached its supernatural, shimmering scales began to ripple in the moonlight. The sailor's beacon. The lighthouse of all lighthouses. *Stay away, for only death awaits those who try to tread here.*

As we were gently floated on the water once more, we raised the sails, praying the Divide would be as kind to us that day as it was when we first arrived.

The day when destiny called.

Knowing how petrifying the first time was and how many bruises we incurred, I ordered all non-essential crew below deck and to be seated. Part of me wished that I could hide in my cabin until whatever happened, happened, but I knew my place was on the helm, holding the Amulet of the Flame.

Of course, I tried to persuade Enya to take up a safer position, yet like me she knew she had to face this night head on.

The silence tore at me. Before we had the fear of the unknown, but now I had the fear of anticipation. I couldn't decide which was worse.

In an instant, the current changed. The calm sea grew angry, crashing waves against the rocks ahead, furiously spraying salty water that sounded akin to a cacophony of screams. As though a storm had risen from beneath us, the ship suddenly jerked forwards as the Divide's power claimed us. Wrapping my sweaty fingers around the Amulet, I extended it from my chest, waiting for it to once again heat and glow as it forged a gateway to the other side.

When it remained cold and inanimate, panic struck every inch of me.

"It's not working!" I shouted to anyone in earshot.

"What do you mean?" asked Enya with wide eyes.

My gaze shot to Marino as he stood by the wheel. Understanding my speechless command, he tried to gain control of the ship's direction but it was plain to see that *The Leviathan* was on a one-way course.

Again, I held out the Amulet of the Flame, praying that it was only timing, not method that I lacked. Nothing.

"Something is wrong—we're going to crash!" Whipping around, I focused on the dragons. "Pull us back!"

Adaryvan had heard my thoughts before I voiced them as within a heartbeat his talons sank into the ship, letting out an almighty roar.

Now perilously close to the Divide, there was no room for Wydgitta to safely grab the front of the ship, but somehow she managed to line up against Adaryvan's beating wings, joining him in an attempt to rescue us.

The continued roars and lack of sarcastic remarks told me how difficult their task was. Metal and woodwork groaned under the strain as *The Leviathan* was pulled in two directions and I began to fear she would be split in two. Out of nowhere, a howling wind arose and took shape, appearing like a pale blue dragon whirling around the ship with icy fury, fighting against the rhythm of the dragons' wings and chilling their senses.

"Hold on!" I called out as Adaryvan struggled to maintain consciousness. "You *can* do this!"

The wood beside Wydgitta's right talon cracked and splintered. Enya ran to her friend just as her enormous body dropped from the air and collapsed into the sea. "NO!" Enya's blood-stopping scream echoed. "Wydgitta! *Wydgitta!"*

In the chopping waves, the dragon quickly sank while the remnants of smoke wisped in the unnatural air. Pynyt flew from my shoulder, desperately circling where Wydgitta had disappeared.

Adaryvan groaned and I could see his talons slipping. "Hold on! Fight it off! Please, Adaryvan, you must hold on!" I pleaded, watching in helpless dismay as the ice dragon blasted him once more.

Pynyt began to glow red and turned himself into a bullet shape as he thrust himself towards our enemy.

My mouth opened to tell him to stop when my mind shouted, *Ignis pila!*

I couldn't tell you if Pynyt said it first and I was merely understanding his intentions, or if we were shouting it together, but the tiny Fyrewowwa released a stream of fire so great and so bright that even when I covered my eyes, I could still see the flames.

Exhausted, Pynyt plummeted towards the deck. Throwing myself forward, I caught his smouldering body in my arms, while the ghostly wind screamed like a tortured gale ripping through lofty caverns as it rushed back into the Divide.

Not waiting to see if it would return, Adaryvan immediately claimed full control of *The Leviathan*, yanking us away until the sea calmed once more. Satisfied we were safe, but too depleted of energy to be gentle, when he let go the ship rocked and groaned erratically as she balanced out. Either by choice or overwhelming inertia, everyone fell to their knees.

Scrambling to her feet, Enya again clung to the rail, desperately calling for Wydgitta. "I can't hear her!" she called to me with tears streaming down her face. I hadn't watched my Charr plummet into the sea, but when I was in prison I thought Adaryvan had either died or abandoned me, so I understood her current feeling of emptiness—of indescribable loss.

"Princess, can you warm me up?" Adaryvan extended his head towards Enya. "I need a boost."

"What? How?" I asked anxiously.

Enya laid a hand on his muzzle. Almost a spark, but nearer to a glow came from her palm and sank into his scales. *Flamma vobiscum*, Enya whispered through our combined bond.

Without a word, Adaryvan dived into the water.

Instantly, I heard the door of our communication click shut.

Now it was my turn to scream.

Losing one dragon was bad enough but if they were both gone...

It was too much.

I couldn't believe it.

Not knowing what else to do, I wrapped my arm around Enya's shaking shoulder and waited. Glancing around the ship, I saw that none of the crew were seriously harmed, yet in my heart I could not rejoice. None of us could. All I could do was wait as my impotency ate at me.

As pale as a peach, Pynyt took flight, darting over the surface like a swallow catching flies.

"What is it?" I called to him. "Can you see them?"

Air bubbles began popping on the surface and I had to fight the urge to dive in to see what was going on.

"Unless you've superhuman strength, you cannot lift them," Enya whispered. "If it's them, we're more useful out of the way."

Our eyes locked as we realised Enya had read my mind. At any other time, I would lament continuing to miss the opening of Adaryvan's connection, yet in that moment the fact Enya could hear my thoughts brought nothing but joy.

Beaming with hope, we clung to the rail, fixing our attention on the rippling water. Like a bobbed apple rising to the surface, a huge bubble splashed and rolled into view, simultaneously casting *The Leviathan* backwards with its undulating waves. In the centre of the bubble, Adaryvan beat his wings above Wydgitta's unconscious body, lifting them both high into the sky.

Either satisfied or out of power, Adaryvan flicked his tail, bursting the enormous pocket of air. The rush of new air mixed with an explosive *pop,* shocked Wydgitta's senses into consciousness, sending her charging into the sky with all the urgency of a hurried birth. The combined gasps, cheers, and whoops made the hairs stand up on the back of my neck and I could feel equal, if not greater electricity coming from Enya as she stood beside me.

Glancing back at the water, I saw the shadow of a ceytus lurking beneath the water. Once upon a time, the sight of those gigantic, watery eyes would have petrified me, but this time I felt only relief. "Thank you!" I shouted into the depths.

The tip of Cee-Cee's head poked above the surf. "You're welcome. It's not every day I see a Fyre Dog down here, let alone two." She snorted water into the air. "Careful your luck doesn't run out though," she added, deepening her tone. "The Flame might be with you, but had I not detected unusual ripples through the waves and then heard you screaming, I doubt the result would have been so harmonious. There's enough bones propping up that wall, it would be a shame if you were to add to them."

With both dragons frazzled, they returned to Liekke for a recharge. Like humans, under normal circumstances, food and sleep was all they needed to maintain or restore general health. However, there was nothing normal about that night and time was against us, so they left us under the unexpected guardianship of Cee-Cee and flew to the thermals of Mount Liekke for a turbo boost.

Once the initial shock of attack and failure had lessened, our combined concern was why the Divide hadn't opened. It made no sense. I knew I hadn't done anything differently, but that didn't stop me repeating events over and over, hoping that repetition would bring enlightenment.

"Maybe the Amulet is broken?" Alun suggested.

"Captain," said Raine, "didn't you say it glowed when you were in the sea with the ceytus?" I nodded. "So it was definitely functioning a couple of days ago."

"Yeah, but by all accounts he took a fair whack in that volcano." Alun narrowed his eyes, staring at the Amulet for imperfections as it rested on my chest. "Is it possible it was damaged then?"

A spurt of water flew in the air next to the ship. *You know that's not the Amulet of the Flame, right?* said Cee-Cee, her voice like a strange song.

Leaning over the edge, I gazed into the semi-moonlit water. "What do you mean?" Keeping the chain around my neck, I extended the Amulet from my body. "It's here, see?"

Land dwellers. Cee-Cee snorted. *You rely too much on sight. Down here we focus on sense and sound. Never mind what you see, what can you* feel?

Turning the Amulet over in my fingers, I searched its surface. There were no chips, no scratches, no nothing. In all honesty, I was more surprised that it hadn't been damaged after the number of beatings I'd taken whilst wearing it.

I didn't understand—everything about it looked the same.

"What's she sayin'?" asked Alun, wearily peering into the sea.

Ignoring Alun, Cee-Cee's words replayed in my mind. *Feel.*

The longer I stayed in this world, the more I understood—both about these people, the past, and myself. To many, the Amulet was an inanimate object, yet time had shown there was more to it.

There was a presence within it.

Distracted by the princess, the Empress, Aydan, my concern for Virisinigne, and not to mention the astonishing fact I was not dead, I dismissed the fleeting notion the Amulet felt weird when Enya returned it to me—but I *had* sensed something.

Realisation hit me.

"It's lighter," I whispered.

"What do you mean it's lighter?" asked Enya. "How can it be lighter?"

Racing thoughts froze my tongue until Raine gently held my wrist. "Captain?"

My gaze gratefully met his. He always knew exactly how to ground me. As if his released fingers simultaneously freed my tongue, I said, "We've been analysing the time when the Amulet was with me but that's not it. We need to know where it is now, because Cee-Cee is right, this *is* a fake."

Enya noticed the change in my expression as doubt and anxiety sped through me. I had just begun to open up to her, to believe that perhaps fate was not mocking me and that my future was by her side. *Surely, she had nothing to do with... she couldn't have... No, it must have been someone else—*

Enya scowled. "I didn't swap it, if that's what you're about to say."

"I didn't say that!" I replied, holding my hands up whilst mentally checking whether I could detect Adaryvan's open line of communication. In theory he was too far away, and it felt closed—but so was Enya as she glared at me with her arms tightly crossed against her chest.

Well, it didn't take you long to ruin that relationship, I lamented silently to myself.

Enya wasn't buying my feigned innocence for a second. "Why would Wydgitta or I steal the Amulet from my father, spring you from execution, side with you against my brother—*in front of the Empress, no less*—just to almost die on the Divide alongside you and then have to sail home empty-handed?"

Had I been given a few more moments before being called-out for remotely considering it, my pride declared that I would have come to the same conclusion, yet whether by my most amiable means or not, the answer did come to me.

"*You* wouldn't," I said with passion, "*—but your brother would.*"

"What?" Enya's arms dropped to her side. "He can't have. I don't see when—" she rubbed her fingers into her forehead, slowly pushing the skin upwards as she thought.

There was no doubt in my mind that Enya knew how to be strong in every role thrown at her—possibly too strong because she fought against displaying vulnerability in front of others. She'd been trained not to, just as I had been by family and court until I found a new family, one who celebrated my strengths, propped up my weaknesses, and laughed at me in between. In my heart, I hoped to be the shoulder Enya could rest all her hopes and fears on, but no matter how much I wanted to be her shield, I knew I neither could nor would force her into anything.

She still had to choose.

Trust was earned, not demanded.

And in this case, revelation must be discovered, not told.

Grimacing, the princess suppressed a groan. "We have been working on the assumption that my uncle has some unknown method of getting through the Divide..." Unable to speak, Enya shook her head, hastily brushing away a solitary tear as she was once again confronted with her brother's betrayal.

Picking up from her trail, I said, "Do you think Aydan has been letting Gryer through, not the other way around?"

"I cannot see any other way. The First Empress only made one Amulet per kingdom. Until recently, you clearly had the one from Virisinigne, my father has the other. How Aydan has such a perfect replica, I do not—"

"Your aunt was a jeweller, wasn't she?" I asked gently.

"How do you know that?" Enya kept her face stern, but suspicion flashed behind her eyes.

"Your brother told me. I didn't think much of it at the time, but maybe there's a connection?"

"I don't see how." Enya shrugged. "My aunt died before my uncle's exile."

"So I understood, yet Gryer may have knowledge, contacts in the trade, or acquired skills that assisted him?"

Enya pointed at the fake amulet. "Or she made this before her death and everything has been planned for years, decades maybe—including recruiting Aydan for the long game." She scoffed. "Aydan probably saw his opportunity to own both Amulets and took it. That would explain why he hasn't bothered chasing after us. He knows we can't get anywhere." Bitterness cut into her, twisting her face as she sneered.

"What now?" said Marino, gripping the wheel. "We can't just keep drifting, surely?"

Inaction and frustration gnawed at him—at everyone. In truth, I was out of ideas. I had completed their pilgrimage, joined their holy order, cleansed the royal hatchery, and gained the sacred sword, but without anything to aim it at, I was a fishing rod without a fish.

"You must return to the cove and wait," Enya replied.

Marino and Raine both looked to me, awaiting confirmation or denial of her order. A simple nod was all they needed while my heart said, *Let her rule.*

"Cee-Cee," Enya said, "Would you do us one more favour and escort *The Leviathan* to a safe cove?"

As you wish Your Highness, came the melodic reply. *Where are you going?*

Determination set across her face. "To face the crown and find the Amulet."

SIXTY-ONE

The sight of Adaryvan and Wydgitta returning filled my soul. Recharged by the grace of the Flame's thermals, they delivered Enya and I into the palace Throne Room before daybreak.

The lack of guards instantly had Enya on edge.

"Something is wrong," whispered Enya. "There should be two on this gate—and another over there."

"But you're the princess," I whispered back. "Do they need to—"

"That's exactly it—I am usually greeted on every corner. Someone always knows where the royals are when in the palace. Also, at least one Fyre Dog normally rests here day and night." Her hand hovered over the hilt of her sword. "Something *is* wrong."

An essential art of war is to never assume you understand the other side. For years, as captain of *The Leviathan* I had learnt to consider multiple motives as well as multiple angles of attack and defence. The fact that my ship still sailed and many did not was testament to mine and my crew's success. Sadly, for some inexplicable reason, that wisdom had failed me. We had assumed that we had unpicked Aydan's plan. We decided that he hadn't chased us because he wasn't ready to expose himself as a traitor. Instead, he had waited to take me down in a manner that portrayed me as the traitor and gained him the Amulet of the Flame perfectly. His only failing was not counting on my friends to find a way to save me quicker than he could publicly convict me. Seeing his sister run after me would have been problematic, but as he knew we were world-locked, we assumed Aydan would disappear with Coayl to rally a later assault, or most likely, feign innocence at home—waiting to see if Enya believed me once she returned, simultaneously keeping the king and the Fyuego on side because they would not attack the Kennel Maid without solid evidence.

Under unknown, hard to research circumstances, our assumption could have been advertised as *hoped* rather than *assumed*, yet either way, we judged poorly. When Enya ran along the city wall so Wydgitta could scoop her up, guards had attempted to stop her. On route to Emberbyrg, Enya told me she put this down to Aydan confusing the guards by bellowing *stop her, save my sister.*

Now, seeing the palace like a ghost town, it was painfully obvious that Aydan had allies in this city—and we had larger problems than reaching Virisinigne or the city of Tecta.

Stick together, said Wydgitta. *Adaryvan, you stay here. I'll circle the palace.*

It was the first time I had heard Wydgitta give such a forceful command, but I couldn't help smiling as I realised how perfectly the Flame had matched Enya. Gentle and kind, holy and respectful, fierce and direct, priestess and warrior—they were able to switch roles faster than masked dancers at a ball.

Through our bond, I sensed that Adaryvan would have preferred the more active task of flying-guard, but he agreed to Wydgitta as she took flight. Unwilling to delay, Enya led the way through the maze of identical, ornate corridors. Every turn was empty of people. It reminded me of my childhood when my brothers played hide and seek with me. Although servants would still go about their business, my brothers' cleared paths, guiding me into booby traps that they had so skilfully devised. After a while, I got wise to their pranks and refused to play, but no matter how loudly the alarm bells rang in my head now, I knew there was no turning back.

Given the time, it was logical that most people would be asleep, but the hush around the palace felt otherworldly, not dreamy. We opened each door with our swords drawn, waiting for the inevitable time when we finally found someone. Through my armour, Pynyt's talons nervously pinched every time a door creaked, but after the fifth empty room, he apparently tired of caution, instead choosing to fly in and circle erratically as he took in the scene.

On our way to the king's private chambers, we checked lounges, conference rooms, dining rooms, council chambers, and the library. All were barren of life, yet each room had been turned over as though a band of pirates had whipped through. The strangest thing was no ornaments, tapestry, or notable valuables had been removed. They had simply been tossed around. Enya's anguish was almost palpable when we reached the king's lavish rooms, finding them also upturned and empty of human life. To the right of the enormous bed, a velvet curtain had been pulled back, revealing an open vault.

Wandering inside, Enya stared helplessly at the scattered jewels. *This is not the work of thieves.*

No, no it's not. I answered. *What about your private apartment? Should we check there next?*

Fighting her despair, Enya shrugged. *Okay.* As she directed us down the dimly lit corridors, we kept our footsteps light.

Stopping outside a lavishly designed set of double doors with the royal flame emblem licking up it, Enya tilted her ear. Fixed on her expression, I watched her eyebrows furrow.

There's mumbling, she said. *I think I hear mumbling.*

Renewed fear struck us as Adaryvan's almighty roar thundered through us, but there was no time to return to him as a voice shouted from behind the door:

"Absolutely not! You can't do this!"

We didn't wait to identify the speaker. Throwing open the doors, we burst into Enya's bedroom. Pynyt shot ahead with his mouth wide and smoking, but we all froze in horror as we were faced with Aydan holding his blade across King Inygo's throat.

SIXTY-TWO

Fixed to the spot, I quickly assessed the situation. Like her father's chambers, Enya's consisted of multiple rooms, but in plain sight there was a reception room and an adjoining bedroom with a huge four-poster bed. Books, clothes, sheets, cushions, jewels, dresser draws, and even a child's toy dragon were dashed across the floor. There was a sizeable expanse between the door and lounge chairs which mostly faced out onto a balcony, but approximately a dozen paces from me was a beautifully decorated dining table with six chairs. Tied and seated opposite one another were the king and queen while Aydan perched on a chair, casually leaning his elbow on the table with his sword in front of his father. Disturbed from their raiding, six guards rushed into formation, shadowing the party with their blades drawn, while three deceased royal guards laid prostrate on the floor.

My eyes followed the trails of blood in morbid fascination as my mind attempted to replay the scene that preceded this strange state of still. Only then did I spot Uryah on one of the sofas. His face was pale but clutching his side, his hands were as red as his eyes. With his injuries he shouldn't have been on duty, yet in that moment I had nothing but respect for him. In times of peace, he was never off duty, so there was no way the royal commander was going to stay in his quarters on a night like this—even if it killed him.

Adaryvan's rumbling roar echoed like a storm but it was the answering war cry that truly sent bolts of fear into my heart. Not knowing what was happening was torturous, and I called down our bond multiple times before a single word, a name, came in reply. *Coayl.*

Hearing the dragons, Aydan's conceited grin fired my wrath. Nothing would have pleased me more than cutting him down there and then but knowing Enya had to lead and the king was in harm's way, I forced myself to remain silent.

"Little sister," Aydan gushed sarcastically. "I began to wonder if you were coming!" Turning to the six guards, he chuckled. "Had they been any slower, we might have missed breakfast!"

Dutifully, the guards laughed but neither monarch displayed anything other than stoic contempt.

"What are you doing?" Enya said, focusing on the sword across her father's throat. "Do you seriously think you're going to gain a crown like this?"

Aydan snorted. "Why not?"

"Neither the people nor the Fyuego are going to accept the rule of a regicidal, patricidal prince!"

He scoffed. "Of course they will. People are fickle. All they want is peace, food, and to be heard. To be safe and protected from wayward nations that you, Father, are too weak to control once and for all. It is naïve and reckless to simply watch as the feral, Flame-less, eastern lands grow in strength—and absolutely ridiculous how often they beg, borrow, or steal from us without repercussion." Aydan turned a deep red. "But no more! *We are the greatest nation!* They'll bend the knee or burn. I'll—"

"You're assuming the Fyre Dogs will obey you, brother." Enya stood tall beside me, refusing to let her voice wobble although I could sense how much this scene tore at her.

Smirking, Aydan shrugged. "They will when they hear of the traitor and his Dog attacking the palace and killing our beloved Kennel Maid in pursuit of the Amulet of the Flame."

"Have you no regard for your own beliefs?" I spat, baffled by how he could have studied the way of the Fyuego and the Flame but have so little respect for its order or his own kin.

"The Flame takes no side, Niall." Aydan spoke like a tired, disinterested tutor. "It simply blesses the faithful."

"*Faithful?*" Venom dripped from the word as Enya pronounced it. "What would you know of being faithful?"

"Look, a new age is coming and my uncle and I are, indeed, faithful to it. The world will be as one—just as the bones of the First Empress foretell—and finally, all shall know the name of the Flame."

A tear rolled down the queen's cheek. She understood her son's passion but felt every ounce of his betrayal.

"The greatest blessing is choice, my son," said King Inygo. Anyone hearing without seeing would have taken him to be at ease in a chair or standing on a podium, not awkwardly tied with a weapon against his windpipe. "Yours is to choose to do great things from the position already bestowed upon you. For even if you do somehow manage to take the world, I fear it will not be enough."

"*Worlds*, Father. I shall be the ruler of *worlds*."

The king scoffed. "If you believe Gryer will hand you the crown to anywhere, let alone everywhere, you are not worthy to be called my son."

As Aydan sneered, pushing his sword tighter against King Inygo's neck, the roars from fighting dragons were followed by flashes of fire through the curtains, making us all jump.

Releasing his blade's pressure a fraction, Aydan snorted. "It seems like the traitor's Dog is coming under some heavy fire."

Enya shook her head. "No one will believe Adaryvan is a—"

"Yes, they will." Aydan said slowly. "Patrolling Liekke like a tropical storm, he has always been the most aggressive Fyre Dog and everyone knows it. How many pilgrims has he sent home in bags of ash?"

"They were not worthy. They didn't follow their calling and attempted the wrong Charr."

"Or they simply were too pure, and Adaryvan was waiting for the right, dark partner in crime to play his part in the prophecy." Aydan waved his left arm at me like a director dictating a play.

From the angle I was standing, I couldn't throw my sword with the required accuracy at Aydan to save the king, nor was I close enough to ensure the life of the queen. Pynyt could throw flames, but not without catching both monarchs, and I knew Enya was calculating the same dilemmas from her position.

Whilst fighting him in Liekke Peak, I had decided against killing Aydan. No matter what he tried to do to me, I didn't want to be the one to kill my Fated Mate's brother. To say I lamented that decision was an understatement. Enya might have hated me and that pain would have been immense, but his death would have saved everyone else a much greater degree of distress. I hoped if we found a way out of this stale mate, whoever had a clear shot wouldn't hesitate to take it.

I'm going to kill him. Enya's bitter voice came through our bond. *Keep him talking while I come up with a plan.*

There was no point arguing, not now. *Okay.*

"Where is everyone?" I nodded towards the corpses between us. "Or have you killed everyone?"

"After Wydgitta stole you from the Atrium and took Enya with you, I hoped she would present you at Fort Fyuego to offer an explanation. The bulk of the Fyuego were ordered to convene there away from the public eye and bending ears of those who did not yet need to hear our discussions," said the king. "As for the staff, courtiers, and remaining Fyuego, they are either asleep or in the west wing." Pausing, the king read the query in his daughter's expression. "Your brother's people attacked through the east wing, killing and maiming as they went. On the agreement that Aydan's soldiers also disperse, I commanded my guards to stand down to avoid further bloodshed."

So, he has a traitor following beyond these six, I groaned.

Indeed, but how many dragons does that include, I wonder? answered Enya. *There must be more than Coayl otherwise they would not have moved from their positions in the Throne Room—and where are my parents dragons, Seraphyna and Sunniya?*

Can you hear Wydgitta? I asked. *Where is she? I can only sense Adaryvan fighting Coayl?*

I don't know. I can sense her, but not hear her voice so she isn't over the palace.

Disturbed by our conversation, but keen not to let on to Aydan that Enya and I were communicating silently, I decided to continue seeking answers whilst looking for an opening to counterattack.

"Where's my Amulet?" I said, focusing on Aydan's neckline. The only visible jewel on him was a ring with a pale blue stone, so if he had a chain under his armour, it was well hidden.

A flare of confusion whisked across his face but it was enough for me to read before his arrogance returned. "Ha! Wouldn't you like to know?"

He doesn't have the Amulet, I said to Enya, while Aydan rattled off some hateful nonsense.

What? she replied, keeping her eyes fixed forwards. *Are you sure?*

I think he is holding your parents ransom because he and his men can't find the Amulet. That's why the rooms are all a mess. I don't think he was waiting for us at all. He wanted to be gone before we arrived.

Flame help us, Enya reverently whispered in my head.

"Are you trying to run off to Gryer's aid?" I said, mirroring Aydan's smirk to goad him.

His nostrils flared.

"I'll take that as a *yes*, shall I?"

"Why did Gryer leave you with a fake?" Enya asked.

Aydan let out a cold, hard laugh. "Ask *daddy* that one."

For the first time, King Inygo squirmed in his chair.

"Father?" Enya's voice was so tense it almost squeaked.

"Go on, don't be coy," Aydan sneered. "Surely, it's time to confess your cowardly sins?"

The king grunted. "My greatest cowardice was exiling, not executing my brother."

Given his position, his words seemed like a curious choice, but King Inygo was clearly as proud as he was loyal. If he died today, he would do it with an unwavering conviction that he had ruled with the right intentions.

"Careful," spat Aydan.

Ignoring his son, the king spoke to Enya, "I can only imagine that your aunt's influence made Gryer listen to the tales of outlander jewellers. Otherwise, harvesting thanatonite to poison the Empress wouldn't have entered his head—even if he was searching for a way to seek revenge." He scoffed again. "It was his selfish, narcissistic side that compelled him to stray beyond the Divide in the first place though. He was always obsessed with more—seeing more, controlling more. *Being* more. Before she died, your Aunt Idalya was no better. I should have known she might forge a replica amulet and steal the real one. Underestimating them both is truly my greatest regret."

After a moment's reflection, Enya gasped. "Father, tell me *you* didn't steal Niall's Amulet?"

King Inygo took a long, deep breath. "My dear, peace and prosperity reigns here. I could not risk ruining that."

"Does that sound like *peace?*" I shouted, pointing my sword at the window as the screams of flames crashed outside.

"All of this started with *you*." The king's tone was hard, but even he winced as he spoke.

His embarrassment didn't stop my raging fury. "I only came because of *your* brother!"

"How could you?" Enya grimaced at her father. "You knew how Uncle Gryer was travelling back and forth but pretended to be ignorant. Rather than seeking justice, you chose to parade with a fake amulet to cover his continued deceit for a decade—even when you were presented with the reality, the magnitude, of his actions!"

"The people and lands of Benegnyem are my responsibility. Gryer is beyond—"

"You would rather an entire kingdom be reduced to ash than take responsibility for your choices!" As my admiration for his convictions shattered, my chest heaved with frustration and hatred. "What kind of king sticks his head in the sand and refuses to rule?"

"I rule over what the Flame gave me. Like all Fyuego, I have studied the Parchment as well as the holy murals. I did not want to be the king who broke, endangered, or lost the sovereignty, the blessing, or order that the Flame's grace and mercy has bestowed upon us."

"In fear of change, you allow things to stagnate and crumble." Aydan's grip of his sword was so tight, his fingers began to turn white. "Instead of seeking your place in history as the sovereign who oversaw unity, you are the chain that binds our great nation to dead-weights."

"It is not fear of change that stalls me, son. It is respect for what is meant to be. If your uncle has invoked more than he has the right to take, if Dreygon, a black dragon, has invoked more of the holy life stream than he is supposed to have, then judgement will come upon them. Please, stop this now. Stop the—"

"If he was not supposed to take it, why would the Flame allow it?" Aydan's mirth was unsettling.

A sigh filled with pain slipped out of Enya. "We all must choose our path." Still holding her sword, a faint glow pulsed from her hands as she collected them in front of her and quickly became a blaze. "And then answer for it."

"Too true, too true." Aydan spat. "And today is the last one that our paths shall cross."

Aydan's pale ring began to throb with a white-blue light.

Enya gasped. "Where did you get that?"

"It's a gift from Mount Halo." Aydan's handsome face twisted as he grinned and his green eyes glazed over as though frozen in a harsh winter's night. "Seraphina and Sunniya *ate up* my cryomagic. Would you like to try it?"

An almighty crash rocked the foundations as a dragon slumped into the palace followed by crackling blasts of fire.

"Open the curtain," commanded Aydan to one of his men as the light from his ring extinguished.

Pynyt twitched on my shoulder. I knew he was itching to add his own fire to this meeting, yet a fireball now would almost certainly see an eternal red smile cast into the king's neck and if any stability was to be claimed this night, it required the king to be alive by morning.

Rolling back on its ornate rail, a fiery display unfolded. The city had been designed to accommodate enormous dragons, yet apparently no one had allowed for two of the largest beasts to fight and now the beautiful gardens below were bearing the brunt of that oversight.

Adaryvan outweighed Coayl, yet Coayl had no apparent regard for property or fair tactics, enlisting the assistance of three smaller, yet still extremely large dragons.

There's your answer to number of dragon traitors, I lamented to Enya.

Momentarily distracted, Aydan turned to the window. Without hesitation, the queen stood up, reversing with all her might into the soldiers behind her and taking two to the ground. Pynyt wasted no time taking flight again, sending flames into the remaining four soldiers faces, setting them alight faster than any oil-drenched pyre.

Almost repeating our action in the volcano, Aydan released his father, swung out, aiming at Pynyt as I dashed forward, blocking his blade. It was just enough to deflect him as Enya sank her sword into the guts of one of the men knocked down by the queen. The other was quick to his feet, spinning around on me, engaging in a dance that could only end in death.

The balcony doors burst open and glass shattered as a dragon again rolled down the side of the building, while the light in the room increased tenfold as Enya flung fire from her hands at her brother. He dodged, and the blaze skimmed his shoulder, leaving a scorch mark on his armour before hitting the wall and setting the velvet curtains alight. Triumphant, Aydan's demonic laugh rang out and he lunged forward, clashing his sword against his sister's with every drop of energy he could muster.

Out the corner of my eye, I was vaguely aware of the queen working herself free and stealing the weapon from a corpse to free her husband, but concerned with avoiding death and tracking Enya's combat, the best I could do for them was to try and keep my fight on the opposite side of the room.

My challenger was skilled, but he was no master. He skipped on his left foot before thrusting with his right and in that moment I thanked my sword master for his years of patient persistence as he insisted I hone my abilities to not only fight well but read the tells of others. Once I understood his dance, all I had to do was wait for the skip and unapologetically run him through.

By then, Enya had pushed Aydan away from their parents and was heading towards the roaring night beyond the balcony. Although hyper focused on his opponent, Aydan was sure of himself. Perhaps they had trained together since childhood so he believed he knew his sister's moves. He certainly seemed to be anticipating a particular step in their dance before he did more than fence.

But then again, so was she.

Determination filled every cell in Enya's body and I knew she was waiting for her moment. If ever there had been a shadow of doubt that the Flame had chosen not only the most selfless, most faithful, and wise sibling, that moment also blew away all question of it having chosen the strongest. She was faster, smoother, and generally more skilled. Discarding her previous dance, she feigned weakness for a few steps and struck out on the next, changing the count each time so that Aydan struggled to block her.

Strangely, it was a thing of beauty, yet I couldn't help internally weeping for the burden she was about to bear. Not wanting that wedge or shadow between us, I didn't want to be the one to kill him before, but if part of my path was to ease her burden, standing by was not an option.

I had to do it.

Pushing and kicking shattered furniture and items out of my path, my stomach dropped in horror as I saw the king lunge forward and attempt to grab his son. Aydan twisted his body, turning his sword towards his father just as another blade dug into his side.

With dilated, fear-filled eyes, Aydan gazed down at Uryah as he remained leant into his sword from his weak, painful position on the sofa. Time crept by in tiny freeze frames as Aydan thrust his sword, striking Uryah with all his might across his chest, sliding off his armour and into his lower jawline.

"NO!" Enya screamed as Uryah slumped backwards, breathing his last.

Stepping back, Aydan stumbled on debris. Holding his side, blood seeped through his fingers as his chest heaved through pain and exertion. Gazing down, grimace turned to grin.

For a second, I thought lunacy or delirium was grasping him, yet as the king followed Aydan's stare, he obviously understood something that I did not.

"Leave that!" declared King Inygo. "He has the Amulet! Stop him! *At all costs, stop him!*"

Taking that as all the confirmation he needed, Aydan snatched the dark green toy dragon from the floor. Seeing the path to all other exits blocked, he took the only remaining option. Pumping his arms for all he was worth, he charged through the blazing curtains onto the balcony, navigated the rubble, and jumped as an enormous shadow darted past.

Without hesitation, I raced after him. *I'm coming off the balcony,* I desperately called to Adaryvan. *Catch me!*

If ever there was a test of faith in one's Charr, it was then.

Adaryvan's panicked plea for patience was too late.

It was all or nothing.

Only one prince would fly out of Benegnyem that night—and I prayed it would be me.

SIXTY-THREE

A rush of air rocketed past me as I hurtled towards the ground. Eight storeys high, the palace was tall, but in all honesty, I didn't know if Adaryvan was close enough to catch me.

Suddenly, I thumped into something solid, instantly forming bruises and refreshing old ones. A tearing sensation bit into my side as my stitches popped, making me cry out with pain, but as my fingers sank into my surroundings, I knew the cupped hand of my scaled friend had saved me.

Are you crazy? bellowed Adaryvan in my head.

Probably! I called back, peering through his talons. *Can you get above Coayl?*

Despite his obvious injuries, Coayl was in front of us, heading north as fast as he could. His left wing hung lower than it should and with a gaping hole in it, the right struggled to counter its drag. Risking leaning further out of his grip, I tried to assess any damage that Adaryvan might have taken.

I'm alright, he said, reading my thoughts. *Certainly better than Coayl.*

Where are the other royal dragons? Wydgitta disappeared and—

Seraphyna and Sunniya were hit by cryomagic—or at least that's what Wydgitta thinks it was. Before the remote eastern cave collapsed, it is said that there was a mention of cryomagic on its walls but until now no one in Benegnyem has ever seen evidence of cryomagic. Similar to fabled genies granting three wishes in children's stories, the Cryoring is said to contain the power of frost and grant its wearer the option to freeze three beings for eternity.

My mind boggled. *Why would the Flame's power be cast in such a way? Can those hit with cryomagic be saved?*

If reheated in time, yes. Wydgitta sensed Seraphyna's distress call when she passed over the city and freed them before their hearts froze.

Aydan has the Cryoring, I saw its strange glow. He said it came from Mount Halo.

If he has it, he has one shot left. Adaryvan hissed. *Charred or not, don't let him catch you with it. A human will freeze faster—and I don't know if you can be defrosted.*

I heard his warning but chose to focus on the wider picture. *In that case, or at least in theory, he will only use his last shot when he thinks it's a matter of life or death. Huh, so that's why he didn't immediately shoot it at Enya. He wanted to impress and threaten her but is actually waiting for a bigger target.*

Streaming past me in the night sky, a flare of fire shot out of Adaryvan's nostrils. *Well, regardless whether that target is me or the Empress, we must stop him.*

Where are the other dragons? I asked. *I saw more attacking you. Did you kill them?*

No, I broke their wings. Adaryvan's gruff tone was edged in sadness. Obviously, he took no pleasure in exacting punishment, even to traitors. *Wydgitta, Seraphyna, and Sunniya flew them to the Empress where they can await her judgement.*

In my heart, I knew there was only one judgement for Coayl, and as we finally flew directly above him, I knew, for better or worse, threatened with eternally-frosty magic or not, the Empress had given me the means to exact it.

A white-blue light began to glow and I knew it was now or never.

Adaryvan, do you trust me?

What?

Do you trust me?

Yes, Sailor, but...

Great! Bank right! I screamed, slipping through Adaryvan's talons.

Hurtling through the air for a second time, I barely had time to notice the speeding pressure or sting of the wind before I landed halfway up Coayl's back, jolting every cell in my exhausted body. Adrenaline alone powered me as Coayl roared, expressing his bloodcurdling anger, yet while I clung to his horned scale, I knew that without dropping Aydan as well, he was as powerless to remove me as Aydan was to use his blast of magic.

Holding the Blade of the Flame in both hands, without word or ceremony, I plunged it into Coayl's back. Fissures of fire spread across his body, screaming and echoing in a smoking blaze across the sky. Instantly we began to plummet. Wind and mist mixed with streaks of fire, slapping into my cheeks and blurring my vision as the ground fast approached.

My grip around the hilt of my sword was the only thing that stopped me tumbling overboard, and without that advantage, Aydan flew past me like a leaf in a gale, howling bloody-murder until he caught the tip of Coayl's tail.

Impact into the jungle was seconds away when Adaryvan's talons wrapped around my body, plucking me as though I were no more than fruit on a tree. Spinning around, I expected to witness Coayl thump into the oncoming rocks and trees with the force of an asteroid, yet instead his body burst open millimetres off the ground, releasing a storm of violent sparks and ash while a thick black cloud formed an ominous backdrop to the swirling display.

Sirens rang out in the still night from Emberbyrg as they tackled the rapidly spreading fires, but Adaryvan and I were too mesmerised, too overwhelmed to speak. Explaining the cause of raging dragons was one thing, but exploding ones was another.

Yet it was a treacherous prince who started it all.

And a foreign one who finished it.

Aydan is down there, Adaryvan eventually said, circling.

Landing, I couldn't decide if I wanted Aydan to be dead or not. Uryah's final act, slicing up under Aydan's armour, could easily have been fatal. Crashing from the sky absolutely should have been. He deserved to be dead—of that, I was certain—but a part of me also wanted to see him hunted down by Carnyfex.

As I walked cautiously towards him, it was not the debate of whether his soul had left him or not that took my breath away. Laying in a bed of ash, Aydan had no trace of metal or fabric on him as his armour had completely melted away. Although I knew that snakes shed their skin, I thought I understood that the Charr marks were permanent—tattoos of magical, divine, blessing. However, on the ground beside Aydan's naked arms, his Charr scales sparkled furiously as though they were dying their own, separate death—disowning the one that they once clung to with their last drop of life.

My own scales wiggled uncomfortably on my skin, almost begging me to look away from the awful sight, but I couldn't bring myself to move until the last embers faded away.

It is done, Adaryvan said stoically.

What now? I asked. *We lost the Amulet of the Flame.* Just thinking the words broke me. I had been so close to gathering help for Virisinigne but now they would all burn.

The only thing we can do, Adaryvan replied. *Return to the palace.*

Having had the sense to keep back until it was safe, Pynyt landed on my shoulder. I was used to his long tail tapping my back or shoulder, but as he settled, something clanged against my armour.

"What have you got?" I asked, twisting on myself unsuccessfully.

Contradicting his previous, depressed tone, a low, amused rumble came out of Adaryvan.

Tired of turning, I stopped, instead tracing my fingers over my shoulder around Pynyt's feet. In his left talon was a chain. Working it into my palm, I began to feel the weight—the correct weight—of the Amulet of the Flame, and I released the breath I didn't realise I was holding.

Amazed, I could only manage one word. *"How?"*

Pynyt shrugged his wings. *Aydan dropped a toy in the air. This fell out.*

On a less stressful day, I might have asked why he didn't bring it to me sooner, but overjoyed, I kissed his scaly head and laughed as renewed hope surged through me.

Let's go, chuckled Adaryvan.

Stepping to climb his shoulder, I paused. *What about Aydan? Dead or alive, surely we must return him to the king?*

He is dead. He needs to be seen and reported by more than us in this Flame-forsaken state. Those that sympathise with his rebellion must know it has no legs, no scales, and certainly no blessing from the Almighty.

As if summoned by wishes alone, Lord Byrne and five Fyuego riders came into view. Obviously understanding the night's events, the Lord's previously suspicious glare turned sorrowful, perhaps even apologetic, as he ordered the removal of Prince Aydan's lifeless body.

Beyond a brief account, Adaryvan and I watched in silence, waiting for our time to leave. Departing wings blew dust and ash back into the atmosphere, disturbing the clear-blue sky of an oncoming dawn as well as wafting the remaining debris of the Flame's judgement.

A tiny glimmer caught my eye.

Retracing my steps, I lifted Aydan's ring from the ash between my thumb and finger. Set in a platinum band was a smooth, almost glass-like stone. Interchanging from white to blue, it felt alive as though a storm raged beneath its surface. Cautiously peering at it, I startled as a bolt of frost, like a fierce spear of ice, thrust itself from left to right.

Whatever magic that contains, we want no part of it, Sailor, Adaryvan said, narrowing his eyes at the tiny ring. *The Flame is the life stream, the giver of life, the passer of death, and all that lies between. There is nothing else, no devilish tricks nor selfish pursuits—in this world or yours—that I wish to entertain. Are we agreed?*

Undoubtedly, I replied. *What shall we do with this? Destroy it?*

We cannot destroy what we do not understand. Adaryvan sighed, sending a smoky gust of air across my cheeks. *But also, we cannot allow such a thing to fall into the wrong hands. Pocket it, keep it safe, and we shall worry about it another day—for now we must make haste because this is not the only kingdom under unjust fire.*

SIXTY-FOUR

As if awoken from their stupor, the residents of Emberbyrg had turned into a hive of activity. The previously empty palace bustled with life and dragons flew back and forth extinguishing the last of the fires.

When we arrived, the royal dragons met us, demanding answers. Happy to only repeat our story once, I left Adaryvan and Pynyt to fill them in while I went in search of Enya. Through my Charr I knew she was close, and my heartbeat in double time as I climbed staircase after staircase to reach her apartment.

Unsure of the reception I would receive, despite the guards permitting me to pass, I lingered down the hallway. Suddenly the double doors to her room burst open and Enya hastily stepped out. Both at a standstill, her tearstained eyes searched mine while our hearts spoke what our mouths could not. Her lip quivered, and I could take no more. Rushing forwards, we met halfway, immediately wrapping our arms around one another. Her face neatly sank into my neck and I pulled her to me so tightly, feeling her essence filling me so completely, that I was sure her heart and lungs were keeping time itself.

Despite the weight of events that led to that embrace, despite questioning my place, my right to aspire to be by her side, I knew that I loved her. Her presence alone was more soothing than any medicine, so with all my being I hoped to be able to find a way to both deserve and claim her when all of this was done.

But I knew my mission was not finished. While my crew were waiting and a nation bled beyond the Divide, I could not rest.

Leaving a lingered kiss on her forehead, I arched my back and neck so I could gaze into her eyes. She knew what I had to say.

"Come, my parents are waiting inside," she said sorrowfully. Taking me by the hand, Enya led me into the room I had jumped out of two hours earlier.

The room smelt of burnt fabric and the hot sun had already begun to stream through the open doorway, but most of the thrown items had been collected—including the bodies, although red pools marked their previous positions. The stained sofa was the saddest sight. I knew Uryah was dead. I knew he had died with honour defending the crown. But I also knew that he had died for love—albeit unrequited, or least not in the way he dreamt of. For his was passionate, hers platonic. However, I was indebted to Uryah and his loyalty.

We all were.

Although I couldn't help thinking that if the king had held his nerve a little longer, the mess at the end of that encounter could have been lessened—even if Uryah's original wound was already potentially fatal. Without time travel, we'd never know.

"I see," said King Inygo with a trembling voice, holding his wife's hand, after I told them the news that no loving parent ever wants to hear. The battle between grieving father and affronted monarch was clear, but finally it was the latter who spoke next. "And the Amulet of the Flame?"

"I have it, Your Majesty." Keeping the chain around my neck, I laid the jewel on my palm in front of my chest.

The king fidgeted. "You must give it to me."

Enya knelt before him. "Father, you cannot doubt that the Amulet is meant for Niall to use? That we are meant to—"

"Knowing your brother and his raiders were searching for it, I sought a new hiding place. Your grandmother loved putting pockets in things, and I remembered the toy dragon with three woollen eggs laced into its chest that she made for you as a babe, so I tucked the Amulet in there, hoping it would be safe until the invasion was squashed. To my eternal shame, I thought I could talk down your brother." Shaking off his thoughts, King Inygo's resolve set in. "Emberbyrg, nay, Benegnyem, is only safe while I, the king, have an Amulet—*and the Divide remains unbreeched.*"

"Your Majesty, please," I declared, "Gryer will not stop if you do not help."

"But he will—or at least with only one Amulet he can only come with one ship."

"What do you mean?"

"One Amulet of the Flame will only admit one vessel. Now we know to look, we can defend against and destroy one ship. After all these years, Dreygon will be too large to sail onboard, so he either cannot travel here or would have to come alone. Neither he alone nor any Fyre Dog small enough to sit upon a ship will be a match for the full Fyuego army." The king saw my expression and shook his head. "I see your pain, Prince Niall, but if you sail home with an Amulet and fall, even without my son's help, Gryer *will* find a way to come for us all."

"Forgive me, Your Majesty, but even with the best intentions, your desire to rule unchallenged has left you open *to* challenge. Your son lays in a cold testament of that—as does your brother still. You say the Amulet permits only one ship at a time, yet it was designed to join with its twin—to open a pathway of communication between worlds." I scoffed. "Alien to all history, I was sent without explanation by my father. The more I have learnt, the more I have questioned his choice, but now I know it was not my father's choice or even wisdom. The Flame *has* brought me here. Fate *has* brought me here." Softly smiling, my eyes held Enya's tender gaze before returning to the king. "And although not as aptly or eloquently as I would have liked, I have done everything asked of me—and must continue to do so. I cannot wallow in fear of failure." Kneeling before the king, I drew the Blade of the Flame and laid it at his feet. "Your Majesty, if you truly are the Flame-fearing king you claim to be, rise up and answer. Send your army with me. This is your calling as much as it is mine."

King Inygo scrunched his eyes shut, forcing a tear to fall down his cheek. Standing, the queen clicked her fingers, producing a purple flame. To my right, Enya mirrored her mother. Exhaling deeply, the king arose, igniting another. Joining their hands, the flames danced, purple turning to red, to green, to white, and back to purple again.

"I hereby pledge, in the name of the Flame, if you find the second Amulet and open the Divide, as blessed by Her Imperial Highness, the power of the Fyuego will fight alongside you." The king bowed, placing his palm upon my breastplate, extinguishing the flame as its essence absorbed into my being. "Arise, Prince Niall, for the healing of two worlds rests upon your shoulders."

SIXTY-FIVE

In my dreams, I had envisaged returning to Virisinigne with Adaryvan flying beside *The Leviathan* and a fleet of both ships and dragons behind us. The realisation that multiple ships and dragons could not enter Virisinigne using one Amulet was an almighty blow. An anger unwittingly simmered within when I considered that the king had withheld that piece of information, but I forced myself to remember that he had told me the truth now—and hopefully time would prove his confession to be better late than never. Afterall, I *had* persuaded an army to follow me. I *had* found myself beyond the World's Divide. Now I just needed to find the other Amulet and open the Divide to let them through.

Just.

Flying out of Emberbyrg filled me with emotion that I didn't realise a city could produce from me. The tolling of bells added to my sombre mood, for while I prepared for yet another battle, they had to mend what was already broken and mourn those lost. Traitors or not, lives were lost. Families, including the royals, had to grieve. And Carnyfex may have missed out on judging me, but I was certain that the coming Judgement Day would be a busy one.

Adaryvan collected *The Leviathan,* escorting her to the World's Divide for what I hoped would be the last time—or at least the last time under such circumstances. Ships were meant to sail. Dragons were meant to fly.

With no impending danger, we had no reason to wait for nighttime on this side of the Divide, yet when Marino questioned whether it was easier to scout in the dark, I agreed.

"Captain, you need stitching again," said Oryana, pointing at the red patch on the edge of my shirt. "What kind of mess have you made of my work?"

I couldn't help grinning as I received her reprimand. Gone were the meek clothes of a netmaker, a girl made to sit in the scorching sun whilst her lazy father and brother barked orders. There stood a woman, an equal, who would mock me like the rest of my family and sail with me anywhere.

"Sorry, milady, but splitting them was not my first choice." I winked. "May I beg you to work your magic a second time?"

"I better. I don't want you running around Tecta dripping blood, do I?" Oryana rolled her eyes. "Go inside then, I'll get my kit."

I dutifully went into my quarters, leaving the door open as I stripped off my top half. Gazing at myself in the mirror, I was impressed by the number of bruises I had acquired, but I also marvelled at the effectiveness of my armour because I had no doubt that if I'd been wearing the blues of Virisinigne, not the Flame of Benegnyem, my injuries would have been a lot worse.

The door closed behind me and I turned, ready to greet Oryana, but instead found Enya with a bowl of water and needle and thread in her hands. It was the third time she had seen me without a shirt but the first time I wasn't embarrassed about the marks up my arms matching hers. I didn't have all the answers, but the lost feeling that gnawed at my soul was gone.

"Have you volunteered to patch me up?" I grinned, hoping she would be as light fingered as Oryana, but not wishing for them to swap for anything.

Silently, Enya walked to my dresser, resting the bowl in the middle before she picked up my chair, dragged it to the door, and propped it against the handle. *She's done that before,* I chuckled to myself.

Not with the same intentions, I have not, she replied.

Dammit, Adaryvan! Can you not tell her everything I think? I groaned.

His gruff chuckle rippled in my head until a click indicated he had mentally stepped out.

When her fingers touched my bare skin, every inch of me tingled. The euphoria made up for the fact she was lacing me up like the hem of a dress. Honestly, she could have signed her name on me in thread, and I wouldn't have cared—but she didn't need to. I was already tattooed as hers. Charred, bonded, as Adaryvan's, but destined for her.

In another life, that might have sounded oppressive.

But not now.

"Come back to me," she whispered, setting her tools on the table. "Promise you'll come back to me?"

"Enya," I said, taking her by the hand and pulling her back to the corner of the bed where we had been sitting. "Look at me, Enya." Holding her cheeks in my cupped hands, I forgot she was royalty. There and then, we were just two people with reasons to fear being left or betrayed, daring to take a chance. "Come what may, my heart is always yours. As long as there is breath in my lungs, I will use it to return to you. Only the Flame will stop me and even then, my spirit is eternally yours."

Leaning in, I kissed her, tenderly lingering my lips on hers.

"I love you." Caution be damned, I needed her to know. "I should have told you earlier, but I love you."

Wrapping her body around mine, Enya smiled. "I love you, too."

As we kissed, a heat emanated from our arms, like the scales were moving and aligning, holding us to our declaration in whatever was to come. My lips travelled down her throat, caressing the mark of a fiery crown licking up her neck. The black marks came alive, like a mirage waving under her skin.

Staring at me, Enya gasped, twisting her body as though she were tracing movement from my arms to my back. I was about to ask what was wrong when I glimpsed myself in the mirror. Images of fire and water rose up my back. Stormy waves came from the left, while blazing flames swept from the right. In the centre they twisted together and formed the head of a dragon.

"What does that mean?" I asked through a chastened breath.

"It means I am yours and you are mine," she said, kissing my neck and nibbling on my ear. "And you better take me now to prove it."

SIXTY-SIX

There was never going to be enough time to hold Enya, but with the fall of darkness, I kissed her one last time before ascending onto Adaryvan. Wydgitta hung back with *The Leviathan,* ready to grab hold should we have underestimated what a safe distance was, but whilst joining in Enya's call of *Flamma vobiscum,* the crew's faces were filled with concern for me, not themselves.

There had been some heated discussion regarding our plan. Many were disappointed not to return with me immediately and worried that my idea to claim the second Amulet of the Flame without them was too sketchy. To be fair, it was dependent on a lot of ifs and buts and maybes, but my resolve held as the Empress' command stuck in my mind.

Fly into Virisinigne.

Some, mainly Alun, argued that her use of *fly* instead of *sail* could have simply been an off-the-cuff choice of wording, not definitive instruction, but I knew it wasn't. The images burnt onto the First Empress' bones stayed with me—and called to both Adaryvan and myself.

Come what may, whatever side of the mural was us, the Right-Wing of Benegnyem *had* to travel with the Left-Hand of Virisinigne.

As we approached the Divide, the wind picked up, warning us of impending, imminent danger. Struggling against the current, I held out the Amulet of the Flame, and for one agonising moment my heart stalled when nothing happened. With an amazing flash, like starting a fire on a cold night, the Amulet activated, sending a bright, hot beam straight into the World's Divide—striking it with such force that the newly formed, multi-coloured archway of light rippled and groaned. Waves roared as they crashed against the rock, spraying high and wide as the shimmering, magical scales undulated across the length of the never-ending mass.

It was strange because no matter how much time I had wasted in my life procrastinating, I never doubted that Pynyt would accompany me through the Divide. Honestly, I wasn't sure when that truth had sunk in, but by then I understood that we had a unique, unspoken, yet very real friendship that would last. My only anxiety was our collective and singular longevity.

Clutching Adaryvan's horned scale, I held Pynyt against my chest, bracing as we were propelled by a wind that howled like a horde of angry dragons. It was as though the Divide wanted to test Adaryvan's skill before agreeing to admit us. Banking left and right, it took every drop of Adaryvan's strength to fly true. I could feel his sheer grit and determination through both my body and mind, but I remained silent, focusing on the goal instead of distracting him from the all-encompassing task. Then with one almighty jolt, we were sucked forwards. Bright colours dazzled, before turning out. With my head forced into a bow, I saw neither rock nor portal, although I was certain that the mercy of the Flame had transported us through the impenetrable.

The following still darkness felt ghostly, like we had been delivered into a spirit world, not one I used to call home. Then as I realised my ears were blocked, I stood up, rubbing them in an attempt to regain my full senses, and realised Oryana lived in a world of silence all the time. A world where you learn to listen another way—through thought and deed and action.

Through heart—something this world all too often lacked. But in the moment, my hearing returned, I wondered if it was even possible for my heart to be reclaimed. For over the calm waves, I heard the shrill cry of war and saw the distant glow of blazing fire.

Flamma nobiscum, I prayed. *Please tell me we are not too late.*

SIXTY-SEVEN

A lush, green land with numerous rivers, islands, rolling hills, abundant crops, and fertile seas, Virisinigne was a kingdom of beauty. The western isles had hotter, drier climates, and the north a mix of everything, yet there was a balance in nature, if not in humanity. The capital city of Tecta had grown complacent and now they were paying for it.

The long familiar scent of salty water mixed with cooked fish, baked goods, and perfumes had been replaced with a singed, lifeless musk. The sound of bustling industry that used to waft out of the city, hailing merchant ships, had dimmed to a fearful murmur. And the canal system—the one I had so proudly championed as elite when I saw Emberbyrg's open harbour—had crumbled into the water alongside the charred, half-sunken remains of my father's fleet.

Similar to Old Emberbyrg, the edge of Tecta reached the shore, rising into the expansive city, yet unlike Emberbyrg, only the City Keep surrounding Tecta Castle was walled. Along with the castle and its grounds, the court and high members of court, the royal guard, and general barracks were hidden behind those walls. From the ground it was unbreachable. From the air all its splendour and glory would fall in minutes. However, as Adaryvan skimmed around the coastline, I could see the siege there still held. Gryer's army had spread like wildfire, waiting triumphantly in their camps and commandeered houses, but they had not burnt everything.

Gryer wants a throne to sit on, grumbled Adaryvan. *I am sure he would rather burn it than lose it, but if he can avoid the hassle and expense of rebuilding the City Keep, it makes sense to do so. All he has to do is wait.*

It is a shame he does not regard the civilian houses with the same reverence, I replied, losing count of how many rooftops were either charred or on fire.

It had been years since I had used my escape routes from the castle. The grounds were extensive but the call of the woods or docks—of anywhere non-royal—was strong and I quickly found that where the servants could disappear, so could a lowly seventh son.

No one expected me to be desperate enough to use the sewage route, but before the final hammer of my father's dismissal came down, I found a way through there, too. The tunnels were man-size, gated, and guarded. However, the guards were a jolly couple in their late sixties who's diligence to protocol was easily distracted. A quick stop in the kitchens or a slipped bottle from the royal cellar, and they were only too happy to turn a key and a blind eye. It was their continued existence that I was now counting on. I needed them, or at least someone like them, to let me in.

Having looped the city coastline twice, my scaled companions and I decided we had seen enough. We couldn't risk going inland and being seen. Not yet anyway. Deciding Gryer's army were firmly watching south, not north, Adaryvan suggested an attack from behind was the way to go. I agreed wholeheartedly, but none of that would matter if we didn't have the numbers. As fast as he was, there was no way that Adaryvan could escort an entire army from the court to behind the sieging encampment without being seen.

We needed more fire power.

We needed both Amulets of the Flame.

After dropping Pynyt and me under the jagged rocks below the castle sewer exit, Adaryvan took off into the night. Even at a distance I could feel his anger seeing Dreygon and his dragon army. In a one-on-one fight with Coayl, Adaryvan should have been the victor. Here with Dreygon the same size and three smaller dragons, it felt like we were preparing to repeat the assault we had fought in Emberbyrg. As a species, dragons had accepted the name *Fyre Dog* to express their loyalty to both the Flame and peace with humanity. Joining the two together in the Fyuego was the ultimate declaration, honour, and blessing. As devoted keepers of order, I knew that it would take an enormous push to make a dragon turn on a dragon. The Empress' reluctance to serve justice on one, even one who had attacked her, was testament to that. Me being granted the Blade of the Flame really was the expression of how badly these dragons had gone astray. I felt bad referring to them as *Fyre Dog* or *dragon*, even if only in my head. One was the name of affection, the other of sacred blessing. Dreygon deserved neither.

Climbing the rocky path in the dark, with shrubs and brambles covering each ledge, I struggled to find the track that had obviously been long forgotten. The wayward son had gone and no one else wanted to travel through excrement to get in and out of the castle. Why would they? In times of peace, the gates were manned but freely opened, and in war, the enemy could swoop in from above. Simply put, clean shoes and fresh air would win every time.

A bramble waved in Pynyt's face, making him hiss and threaten to burn it, but a quick *ssshh* reminded him of the need for stealth. When the path seemed to have disappeared completely, I considered breaking that requirement in favour of removing the tangled brush and illuminating the way, but just as I was about to suggest it to Pynyt, a shriek cut across the airwaves. Panicking, I dropped and rolled on the tiny ledge, entwining myself with thorns in the name of remaining hidden. Had I been seen, the patrolling dragon would have had to take a significant clump of bramble with me if they wanted to rip me from the cliff, but thankfully the beast kept flying.

With renewed fervour, I continued clambering up the cliff, heading towards the hardest, most barren stretch of grey-brown rock which housed the opening I sought.

The tunnel was flowing as usual, but luckily not as heavily as it did after heavy rains, meaning I could pass through. I liked to imagine that my father would be pleased to see me, but with the extra demand for water to douse fires, I wondered if he would have preferred a bumper rainfall.

A shorter person could have run at their full height with ease, but being tall and muscular, the narrow tunnel was not as well suited to my twenty-eight-year-old body as it was my teen or pre-teen self. Adult me also didn't remember how long and disgusting it was down there, but I managed to run along the ledge and not in the sewage, only pausing when a gruff voice called out: "Who goes there?"

"Who are you?" I replied, carefully stepping forward.

"The king's guard," the voice growled. "Who. Are. You?"

"State your name now or die here in the shit," another voice said. "They're your only options."

"I don't suppose either of you are called Wade or Fisher, are you?" I asked, taking a tentative step closer towards the faint glow of their light. "I used to be friends with them."

The first voice grunted. At a guess, I thought these voices were too young to be either of the men I remembered years ago but it was worth trying. Realising we would soon be highlighted by their torch, Pynyt instinctively slipped down my back, pinching the leather work to steady himself without needing to flap his wings. Before travelling, I had deliberated on which armour to wear. Eventually, I chose the Flame's because it was lighter yet stronger, and more likely to protect during a firefight.

It was also bizarrely homely.

Wearing it, I felt complete.

How others might view it was open to debate though. To my family, it would be the sign of a promised army. To the enemy, a sign of incoming judgement. However, to these men it would simply be a foreign curiosity until they saw my miniature dragon—the symbol of their oppression and loss. Hiding Pynyt as long as possible was undoubtedly wise.

Muttered voices came from up the tunnel and then the sound of footsteps approaching.

"How do you know Wade and Fisher?" asked the remaining guard. His familiar, quick tone made me smile. It seemed like an eternity since I had heard the drawl of Tecta civilians. I had taken it for granted. Discarded it as nothing. Now it was something I wanted to protect.

"A long time ago, they used to let me pass through here when I should not," I said with a smile.

"There was only one person I ever let through," replied an elderly voice from down the tunnel. "Why did I do that?"

"For the love of cake, cheese, and wine, good sir." I chuckled. "And maybe the desire to give a young man a little reprieve."

"Prince Niall?" A wobble hampered the clarity of his words. "Can it really be you?"

Approaching the iron gate, I stepped into the light.

The old guard gasped. "We thought you were dead." He reached for his belt, pulling on a chain filled with keys.

"Nearly, but not quite." I shook his extended hand with affection. "I feared you would not remember me."

"Or I'd be dead." He scoffed. "You ain't the only one lost or thought lost, my prince. My husband, Fisher—" Wade grimaced. "It's me and me grandsons down here now. There's more guards in earshot, you know, in case of an attack, but—" He paused, searching my face for information. "Please, my prince, tell me you come with good news?"

"I come with hope, but I must reach the king." It was my turn to wince. "Tell me straight. Is he still alive?"

SIXTY-EIGHT

s Wade led me out of the sewers, he filled me in on the siege. Battles outside of the castle had been bloody and displays of firepower overwhelming. People either submitted or died. A civilian army rising up to defend Tecta was not going to happen without a significant show of force from an outside army.

From me.

Wade was vague regarding the whereabouts of my brothers, however, I was relieved to hear that my parents and sister were inside Tecta Castle.

Entering the City Keep for the first time in years made my heart thud horribly. It was a strange mixture of relived childhood trauma, the fear of failing my blood family and nation, plus the hope that I could potentially bring them salvation.

Could.

For I still needed Gryer's Amulet.

Without it, I was just adding my body to the royal pyre.

"Before I go any further," I said, keeping my back to the wall. "Can I just test your reaction to meeting someone?"

"Of course, my prince," said Wade, shuffling on his arthritic legs.

"Don't freak out," I said, patting my left shoulder, "but this is Pynyt."

He swore heavily, then flashed bright-red, pointing. "Forgive me, my prince, but you've a baby dragon on your shoulder—aah!"

Arching his neck, Pynyt hissed.

"He is a Fyrewowwa, not a dragon—baby or otherwise," I said, stroking Pynyt's head to both calm him and demonstrate to Wade that he was friend, not foe. "He has helped me no end in my pursuit to return to Virisinigne and I am hoping the citizens of Tecta will accept him."

"Given the times we are livin', that might be a hard sell, my prince." Wade shrugged. "But if people see it is your shoulder that he is sitting on, well, stranger things have happened lately."

Keeping one eye on Pynyt, Wade continued to escort me. Courtyards which were once open and richly decorated now housed tents and shacks as civilians tried to escape the dangers beyond the Keep walls. Observing their drawn, sorrowful faces, I couldn't decide which residents were better off: the ones being starved within the walls or those being subjected outside. Either way, they were under the constant threat of being killed.

As we passed by each set of guards, whispers of my arrival spread and I heard my name repeated almost in a chant. That sense of wonder, hope even, seemed to protect Pynyt and I from being challenged by the ever-increasing crowd that followed me to the Castle gates.

Attracted by the hum of gathered people, Lord Calder appeared within minutes of my arrival. Head of castle security and longstanding, extremely loyal friend of my father's, Lord Calder had known me since an infant. Or perhaps, more accurately, known *of* me since I was an infant. He, like the rest of my family, was baffled by my character and couldn't see why I would try to slip away from his guards or the splendour of the castle. My reappearance with a beast (of any name) on my shoulder just added to his confounded expression. Had I a patch on one eye and a parrot on my shoulder, he would have looked at me less suspiciously. *He'd get on well with Lord Byrne*, I thought to myself.

"I hear you claim to be Prince Niall," he said, narrowing his clear-blue eyes as he observed my armour.

"Lord Calder, you know perfectly well it is me. You gazed at me for sixteen years like that so don't pretend a change of clothes and a beard has made any difference to your ability to name me."

"Your tongue is certainly still as sharp. I would say *welcome home*, however, you can see that home is somewhat *unwelcoming*." He opened his arms, obviously meaning the siege but I struggled to stop myself pointing out the double-meaning in his remarks.

Behind me the crowd peered through the gate, eagerly waiting to see what kind of reception I would receive. The younger residents would not recognise me at all, but many would only remember the boy and would be forgiven for failing to connect the dots. To the left, a door burst open, sending startled guards into a tizzy as they were not sure how to respond to the woman darting across the yard.

I, however, had no such dilemma.

Opening my arms as wide as they would go, I caught my sister as she flung herself into my embrace, sobbing my name as she sank her head into my chest.

"Is it you? Can this day really be so blessed? Let me look at my brother!" Muriel declared, holding my arms and leaning back.

Her emerald green eyes blurred with tears of joy and her chin quivered, instantly melting my hardened manners. Her dark auburn hair was twisted loosely into a knot, leaving beautiful curls to frame her face which had the signs of worry etched into it, yet in essence she was the same, sweet sister I remembered. The heart of the family in every way.

As if blinded by her excitement, Muriel only then noticed Pynyt. Watching her jump reactivated the childish joy of teasing one's sibling, but remembering why I was there, I bowed, saying, "Allow me to introduce you to Pynyt. He is a Fyrewowwa and without him I do not exaggerate when I say I would not be alive today."

Muriel's eyes boggled, but her astonishment did not outweigh her kind, warm spirit because she immediately smiled, saying, "Then it is my pleasure to meet you, Mister Pynyt." Still the girl who would sit with bees and sing, she extended her right hand to him, laying her palm flat. "Any friend of my brother's is always welcome."

Pynyt sniffed her hand, then leant his chin on her fingertips. Taking the hint, Muriel scratched him, apparently hitting just the right spot as he curled his tail while little puffs of smoke wafted out of his nose.

Although tears threatened us both, an awestruck chuckle accompanied Muriel's smile, and for a moment, time stood still, briefly allowing us to just be reunited, loving siblings, sharing the blessing of meeting a new friend.

Lord Calder cleared his throat. "Princess Muriel, we should—"

"Immediately escort my brother to the king? Absolutely, make haste, Lord Calder, make haste!" Muriel fluttered her eyes at the Lord and grinned at me.

Not bothering to wait for his response, she took me by the arm and marched me inside without speaking. As the entrance hall opened before me, a knot dropped from my throat to my stomach, making me extra grateful for her swift, non-verbal action.

Thoughts of Enya came to me. I knew Muriel would like her and one day I hoped they would meet in peace. But a new realisation hit me as I entered the castle. All this time I had struggled with the notion of Benegnyem calling me—of prophecies tying me to a foreign land and a princess way out of my league. I thought home was here. This land. I was wrong. I didn't fit in because I was destined to leave. My found family sailed on a ship and we could sail that in different waters. We could dock in a new harbour.

I would save my roots but my wings would take me elsewhere.

SIXTY-NINE

Approaching King Ennis as he sat on his throne was difficult. I had questions, lots of questions, for my father. Part of me said they could wait, yet the other part told me that if my destiny was to fall, not confronting him was one regret I did not wish to take to the grave.

Muriel didn't leave my side while our mother anxiously sat beside the king. In her eyes I could see that she wished to greet me properly, but with the High Council watching and Pynyt perched on my shoulder, she couldn't bring herself to break protocol and hug her youngest son.

I was, however, taken aback by the note of affection in my father's voice. "You have returned, my son."

With my head bowed, I bent my knee as expected. "I have, my king."

"And were you successful?"

Standing tall, I replied, "Do I have permission to speak freely regarding my time away?"

The king nodded at the guards and waved his hand. Dutifully, everyone except the four royals left, closing the mighty oak doors as they departed. Designed with grandeur in mind, the elaborate thrones were up high, while rich tapestries hung from the ornate ceiling and carved pillars lined the room. Five hundred courtiers and councillors could easily be seated, yet the throne room was a far cry from the open, sandy one in Emberbyrg, making it feel small. Or perhaps the task ahead just felt too large.

King Ennis cleared his throat. "Gauging by your unusual dress and er—"

"Friend," I quickly added, eager for Pynyt not to throw a flame at my father should he call him a pet or baby dragon.

"*Friend*," my father repeated. "Can I assume you were able to breach the World's Divide?"

"I was."

"Yet you have returned alone, so found no mercy." He posed it as a statement but was obviously hoping I would contradict him.

Where was I to begin with what I found? Mercy, grace, knowledge, fear, friendship, hatred.

Love.

With the crackling of fire and a jeering army outside the City Keep beginning to ring in my ears, there was no time for a description of all I had seen and heard. Hopefully, that would come later. I needed to understand the more imminent and work out how to get the second Amulet.

"I have an army." Hearing those four short words, my father straightened on his throne. "But I need two Amulets to bring them here."

"Two?" My father scowled. "You have one, they—" Although lacking in many respects, my father was not normally a slow man. Proud and arrogant, making him too quick to dismiss rumours, certainly, but not slow when faced with an equation. "Our invader is not a mystical being from Mount Halo, is he? He is one of theirs."

"Gryer stole their Amulet and dragon eggs." Spite could easily have made me add, *which you ignored in the Halo region for the last ten years.* Sorrow could have added, *and I had to kill the guy who helped him.* Instead, I said, "I will explain all later, but now I need you to tell me about his army so I can obtain the second Amulet and save our world."

It was then that I learnt of the death of five of my brothers and the capture of my eldest brother, Prince Baran. The idea that I had taken too long ate at me as my father spoke, soberly detailing the speed in which they were taken from their various posts, executed by fire in front of the city gates, and left on stakes for all to see.

"How are the defences? When did this happen?" I asked, trying to piece together the time frame of events, both for my own torture but also to assess how long we had until Gryer tired of waiting.

"Defences hold now as well as they have for the last fortnight," Muriel answered when our parents would not. She clearly understood my confused look because she added, "They died two days after you left, Niall."

Even with all the will in all the worlds, my father cannot have expected me to return with help so quickly. No one could have. Yet even with that knowledge, I did not feel relief. My burden was no less and the outcome of war was no less bloody.

My father saw confusion and anger flash across my face. "Gryer had formed his army and marched quickly. I misinterpreted his intentions."

"You thought he would threaten with fire but not burn your door so soon." My tone was laced in disapproval, but I could not help it. Staring into his blue eyes, I struggled to understand why he acted so slowly—or why he chose to send for me, knowing waiting for my return from the west would delay appealing for help when six sons were within his reach. "Why did you send for me, not one of my brothers?"

King Ennis' expression changed. "Because the prophecy rests on your shoulders, not theirs."

His confession was something I had begun to suspect, but hearing it hit me hard, like a wave of sound or a wind so harsh that it cut through to my soul.

My eyes watered and my jaw set. Blinking to clear my vision, I couldn't bring myself to brush any tears aside.

"What prophecy?" Muriel asked anxiously.

"One that has been the burden of monarchs for centuries," replied my father, "passed from crown to crown under the strictest secrecy. Each king or queen praying that they are not on the throne when history, prophecy, and conflict meet—or that they are worthy enough to rise to the challenge if it does come." Deeply exhaling, he shook his head.

"So you know of Benegnyem and the Flame?" I asked.

The king shook his head again. "I know of a land that was once connected to ours. A land rich and varied, where people connected to an otherworldly power, a magic, supposedly gifted from the Divine. It is said that there were those who opposed the use of magic, the sovereignty of the Divine, and the partnership of fiery beasts. Rather than seeking a peaceful solution, some sought independence with violence, resulting in a bloody war. I do not know the details, yet my father told me, as his father told him, that although the world believed that peace was won, and is maintained, by our merit alone, the truth is that in her grief and benevolence a Divine Messenger left a gift—a way to reconnect should unity once again be sought." As I thought of the First Empress, my father pointed to the Amulet of the Flame hanging around my neck. "Legend has it, when that Amulet is passed from one ruler to the next, so does the burden of knowledge of our past and the potential for ruin in our future. For it is said that only the chosen holder of the Amulet can champion a nation, bridge the Divide, and seek unity and friendship. *Or mercy.* For it is also said that a challenger will one day rise in our great kingdom. A challenger evoking unimaginable power, seeking to subject and destroy our way of life, and build a new one on our ashes."

"If you knew this, why did you ignore Gryer?" I asked. "Why not crush him long before—"

"Because it is easier to repeat fables and satisfy the whims of old men than it is to realise that fairytales are in fact, fact. By the time I registered that the rumours had merit and I took my head out of the canal, it was too late. I wanted to be the king who reigned over peace. Who continued prosperity and passed his crown to the next generation without opposition like those before me." He scoffed.

"Even when I struggled to produce an emerald heir, I did not see the full signs. I didn't want to."

"An emerald heir?"

"Your eyes, son, your eyes," my mother said, holding my gaze with her own green eyes. "Only an emerald heir can wield the Amulet in front of the World's Divide."

"That is why you had so many children?" The words shot out of me before I had hardly thought them.

The king nodded. "According to instruction, all monarchs must produce two emerald-eyed heirs. If the eldest does not possess green eyes but takes the throne, they must marry one of noble, blessed blood in order for hope of salvation to continue."

"Why not just tell everyone this?" Muriel asked. "If this noble, emerald line that you speak of is so important, why not make it known?"

"Our ancestors wanted a world without magic, without curses, prophecies, dragons, or the mention of the Divine. They wanted to simply do their own thing and make their own rules." The king snorted. "Hearing that eye colour had become a sign of divine presence was *not* what they wanted."

Statuesque, I listened with my mouth agape but my mind was anything but still. *The seventh son was not surplus.* "All my life, I felt like the extra. The unnecessary, redundant child... You sent me away—"

"I sent you away because you were not like your brothers." My father grimaced. "It pained me more than words can express, but I knew that when the day came and I had to tell Baran that he inherited the throne with a proviso, that his birthright under our law was not truly whole, I feared what he would do. He was already a jealous, power-hungry man, and my great-great grandfather had had to kill his brother when he challenged him after discovering the truth of our royal legacy. I didn't want history to repeat."

Internally I lamented that, in a way, it still was. "Does Baran know now?"

"Not yet. As he opted to marry a man and two wives, two of whom have green eyes, it allowed me to delay."

"What colour eyes do their children have?" Everyone fidgeted but no one answered. I scoffed. "Blue, right?"

My mother nodded.

"Why two emerald heirs? Why is one not enough?" Muriel said, barely making a sentence from her understandably confused thoughts.

Suddenly, I knew the answer. "Because the Flame chooses on merit, faithfulness, and spirit, not order of birth."

"The *what*?"

Adaryvan was close enough for me to feel his presence, yet too far to question, but I desperately wanted to hear his thoughts. Enya had told me that Aydan had completed his pilgrimage in good time and was predicted by many to be announced as the Kennel Maid. However, I hadn't thought to question *when* that declaration took place. The Charr must have been granted there and then, but now I realised that the title was only bestowed when both siblings had presented themselves in front of the Flame on Mount Liekke.

Pynyt poked my cheek with his nose and grumbled quietly. I decided this was him listening to my internal monologue and agreeing. Had I been wrong, he would have pinched my neck with his foot.

"Why is no one answering me?" Muriel scowled. "You can't tell me this much and then refuse to speak!"

"The Flame is the omnipresent lifeforce, the Divine power and being of both worlds. Virisinigne was named by the founders of the post-war world using the old tongue they presumably then outlawed. *Green without fire*—that's what it means, yet whether we know it or not, there is nothing without the blessing of the Flame." The conviction of my words surprised even me.

"So *you* are the true heir of this kingdom?"

As Muriel stood before me with the same grace and beauty that I loved when we were children, the truth hit me and made me smile. Her heart and soul were both strong and pure. There could be no calling that would make me turn on her. All my life I had wondered why my family seemed so split. I wondered why I floated the sea only to then have a foot in two kingdoms. Without key knowledge, the answer was hidden, but now it blazed through me with crystal-clear precision. I could have argued that another role was yet to be laid upon me, that the Flame simply hadn't tested us both yet, but as Muriel's emerald eyes shone, I knew when that day came, the Flame's blessing would reveal the extent of her path.

"No," I said, taking her hands in mine. "The Flame has not chosen me to reign."

She tilted her head. "How do you know?"

"Because I am the bridge between two worlds. *You*, dear sister, are the corner post."

SEVENTY

Standing on the top of the castle tower, I watched Dreygon in the distance. There was no denying he was magnificent. Jet-black, he was the perfect illustration of a shadow monster that children dreaded and nannies used to coerce their charges into submission. The Flame may only guide, not dictate; push, not propel, but my body still ached from taking on Coayl and the thought of facing his older, more determined cousin did not fill me with joy.

Neither did the idea of asking my sister to leave the City Keep.

There was no one better suited or more likely to trust me purely because I asked than Muriel. Even though it meant leaving Talia, her daughter, temporarily behind, she understood the gravity of our task. We both did. If we failed, none of our bloodline would survive.

It was that simple.

By all accounts, Douglas, her husband, was a good man and had risen the ranks to Royal Commander through merit as well as family status. Although sorry to commandeer his wife and keep information from him, I told myself that if we succeeded, he would have all the time in the worlds to understand—or reprimand—my actions later.

Talia shared both her parents' emerald eyes but had her mother's dark-auburn hair. She was only two years old, but in our brief meeting I was struck by the gaze of a much older, wiser person. Either that, or the sight of Pynyt has stunned her into behaving for the uncle she had never met. But no, she had inherited another of her mother's traits, her ethos—the one that had come to me on my pilgrimage. *You don't need words to speak. You only need ears to listen.* Talia, just like Muriel, listened to the natural world and people alike. In my heart, I knew that if I could clear the way of Gryer and Dreygon, I would be able to rest easy knowing that Virisinigne had at least two future rulers worth following.

Surrounded by shielded guards, the king approached my lookout position.

Taking a spyglass in his hand, he exhaled deeply as he scanned the span of the sitting army. "I believe many of those fighters are there for self-preservation, not necessarily belief. I cannot wholly blame them for going with the one who shouts the loudest, especially when he calls out the things they want to hear—things they probably should have heard me say." He put away the spyglass, tutting. "For too long I stayed in the comfort of Tecta, ignoring the lands and islands beyond the southern shires."

"There's still time for change," I said, walking him back to the safety of the stairs. More than once I had seen the dragons eyeing the tower. One well-timed, well-aimed fireball would see this siege concluded if they took out the standing monarch, and even Pynyt—who had remained indoors—twitched anxiously until the king was off the roof.

"Virisinigne's zest for so-called freedom has made us forget our past. Change comes hard. The fulfilment of this prophecy means opening this world to change, but I hope it will eventually be for the better—and that you will forgive me for my part in hampering the transition." He laid his right palm on my chest plate. "May your Flame be with you."

Covering his hand with mine, I replied. "With us, Father, with *us*."

Gulping, he gently nodded his head, neither trying to hide nor expand on the sentiment, the raw emotion, of the moment. His eye caught the edge of my Charr tattoo and he gently lifted the edge of my vambrace, raising an eyebrow. "My father once told me in passing that Mount Halo has paintings that only the scaled can read. He said his father had uttered the words like a quiet whisper in the wind on his deathbed, so neither man was sure if they were repeating the information correctly. Goodness knows how many elements of the prophecy have been lost in such a manner." He peered at my wrist again. "Until now, my grandfather's half-heard words seemed like madness, however, I believe Halo holds paintings that you can visit. You may want to go there when this is done."

When this is done.

It was such a quick sentence for such a mighty, all-consuming task.

The inscription Adaryvan showed me on the sacred bones came to me.

That which is willing to break, will be made whole.

It was time to fulfil something else on the First Empress' bones. To find out which image is Adaryvan and I, and which is Dreygon and Gryer.

"I'd like that," I said. "When this is done."

SEVENTY-ONE

Gryer would either see me coming or he would not, so there was little point waiting for nightfall. And, with a combination of dread and excitement electrifying my senses, I was beyond sleep and food. Trial and procrastination had taken too long, now I just needed to act.

When I explained my plan to Muriel, her shock quickly turned to determination. I was undoubtedly asking a lot of her, yet when she returned, having donned her armour, she looked every bit the warrior princess.

"To the untrained eye, Adaryvan looks similar to Dreygon," I said, watching her features freeze for a moment. "But I trust Adaryvan with everything, including my favourite sister."

Instantly laughing, she mock hit my arm. "I'm your only sister!"

"Mere semantics, I assure you!"

That was the last joke I told her that day, but I had broken the tension and it was enough to push her over the metaphorical edge as we wandered down the stinking tunnels towards Adaryvan's rendezvous point.

No matter which direction we were spotted in, we would engage with the enemy. Turning away was not an option, however, our preference was to loop around and catch the camp from behind. If nothing else, it would keep any returning fire facing north, not at the city.

Time would tell if that idea was successful.

A sharp gasp sucked every drop of oxygen from Muriel's lungs.

She's seen me, Adaryvan said, standing with his back against a moss-covered rock adjacent to the sewage exit.

"Muriel this is Adaryvan—Adaryvan, Muriel." I gestured from one to the other. "Are we good to go?"

Muriel delayed for half a heartbeat, but both of them nodded so I stepped onto Adaryvan's back, holding out my hand. Muriel gripped my palm and took the leap of faith, smiling behind her chastened breath. Not wanting to linger, I led her to Adaryvan's withers, and ushered her to sit down. Gracefully, she took her position, all the while marvelling at the glorious display of finely decorated black scales that surrounded her. Seeing her reaction, and knowing how it compared to my own, I really could not understand how my ancestors had chosen to be wholly without these magnificent beings.

Partnership not subjugation.

Friends not foe.

Fyuego.

I had tried to warn Muriel about flying but as we had spent our lives with our feet little higher than a horse, it was no surprise that her initial reaction was to turn green.

However, something within her clicked. An adrenaline rush. A calling. An appreciation for life.

Just like Enya, Muriel really was born for this.

The crisp sting of slightly damp sea air whooshed passed my cheeks, coupled with the almost primitive need to see everything while I could. Fishing villages, woodland, and farmland alike whizzed past on our left while on the right the tide ebbed and flowed as it always did. If anyone saw us, we were gone too fast to be concerned. Whether for Gryer or not, they'd never send word to him fast enough. Not now.

The towns and villages who had submitted quietly versus those who did not were obvious. According to reports, some were not given a choice, they were merely burnt to make a point, but as Gryer came with the proposed name of Simulinigne—*together in fire*—proclaiming the rhetoric of uniting all the forgotten people, he neither wanted nor needed to use force on everyone. With sadness, I viewed the scorched remains of a once thriving market town, and in my heart understood that whether truly converted or simply avoiding death, for many citizens, joining the incoming army made sense. My father was going to have a lot of healing to oversee if he survived this onslaught.

Knowing that we had only minutes until reaching our destination, I tapped Muriel on the shoulder. Wiping her face, she turned to me. Like me, she had viewed the war from the castle tower and heard reports, she'd lived for weeks under the screams and cries of death and fire, knowing that one wayward dragon could scorch them all, but she hadn't seen its expanse. She hadn't seen the bodies of incinerated men, women, and children as they laid in the ash-ridden streets.

Removing the Amulet of the Flame from around my neck, I balled the chain into my palm and securely cupped it into Muriel's. "You must keep this safe at all costs. When I get the other one from Gryer, regardless of whether I make it or not, travel to the Divide and let Enya in. You'll love her, as I do, and together you'll make the worlds better. I know you will."

My neck felt empty without the Amulet of the Flame, but I was happier knowing that by giving it to my sister, I was attempting to retrieve one Amulet, not risking losing two.

"I thought you were coming to the Divide?" Muriel said. "I thought I was to take—"

"I hope to, but it is more important that you get there with both Amulets. You must promise me to go either way." Holding her gaze and hands, I couldn't let go until she answered me.

Muriel nodded. "I promise."

"This ends today," I whispered into her right ear, hugging her. "The coming battle may be big and bloody, but in the name of the Flame, I believe we *can* do this. It ends today and tomorrow, we start anew."

"*Flamma nobiscum,*" said Pynyt, stressing my point.

"What does that mean?" Muriel asked, recognising foreign sounds as words, not Fyrewowwa noises.

"The Flame is with us," I translated.

"That sounds, almost *feels*, familiar, like an inherited memory long forgotten," Muriel said. "Is that even possible?"

"Like a calling?"

"Yes," she smiled. "Exactly that."

I nodded, knowing in my heart precisely what she meant, despite having no time to dwell on it. Shooting away from the coastline, Adaryvan headed out to sea towards a cluster of uninhabited islands situated within a short distance of the World's Divide. In addition to the mainland, Virisinigne had numerous islands, large and small. Some of the small were used by fishermen, but some were just too awkward to be useful—until that day.

While I met with my father, Adaryvan had scouted the coast, looking for a boat and somewhere to hide it. His choice was perfect. Not only was the island uninhabitable to anything other than birds, or perhaps a young dragon seeking a solitary perch, there was a small cave, more like a rocky hollow, cut into the far side where a rowboat could sit out of sight. And, although birds were welcome to visit my sister while she waited, I hoped to keep all enemy dragons distracted.

Muriel glanced at the boat tucked securely under the ledge and gulped.

The boat was a basic one-man rowboat. The idea of my sister being pulled through the World's Divide on such a craft sent shivers through me, yet I was not aware of any requirement for vessels to be grand—just singular. Glancing inland, seeing nothing but water and knowing how long it would take to row, my brotherly instinct was further rattled.

She really was a sitting duck if I failed.

I didn't voice my concerns though. I needed her to believe—for us both to believe—in our coming success. "No one on land can see you here. Hold tight until one or all of us returns. I know you can fight, but that is your last resort for now, so if anyone else comes, hide behind that rock." I pointed to an odd-shaped boulder which had been carved out by millennia of sea erosion. "See you soon."

She kissed my cheek and steeled herself. "Okay, Adaryvan. Let me get off."

SEVENTY-TWO

From the air, the path of destruction to the once-green landscape was clear. Had my father asked for a precise map of the incoming army's movements, I could have easily drawn one. There was certainly no need to stop and ask for directions to Gryer's camp.

It pained me to see the wafting smoke where clear skies, fields, and treetops once marked the edges of settlements. However, while we soared towards the outer regions of Tecta, the moment for sentiment or sight-seeing came to an abrupt end as three dragons darted towards us in an arrowhead formation.

It was time to dance.

Each of the three dragons were about the size of ten horses, making them about ten years old according to the scale Enya had once taught me. In varying shades of green-grey, they might not quite possess the same level of ominous impression that Adaryvan or Dreygon instilled, but their screeching calls and fire-filled mouths certainly struck me as awe-inspiring.

Adaryvan held his course, refusing to deviate even an inch from his flightpath as the three dragons hurtled towards us. Their eyes were locked on his, narrowed in a game of dare. But they were challenging the wrong dragon. Adaryvan was more than ten times larger and he knew it. One of his wings could cover all three of them, and on that day, size absolutely mattered. I half expected him to open his mouth, even if only to threaten to throw a fireball, but when they realised impact was inevitable, not even a puff of smoke was necessary to send them shooting up in the air and around us in a beautiful, if not lethal, aerial display.

In my head, Adaryvan chuckled. *Hatchlings.*

Inexperienced and comparatively undersized or not, they were not giving in though. They were terriers going after the giant's tail—this time flying in a straight, keenly-focused line.

Keeping his head ever-so-slightly tilted so he could see their location, Adaryvan waited, maintaining a fast, but I guessed not top, speed.

A sense of glee flashed across the middle dragon's stern expression as she saw Adaryvan's tail coming into her reach. Her mouth opened wide, baring her teeth ready to sink into scaled flesh.

Hold tight, Adaryvan's matter-of-fact instruction growled through my head. I had no time or right to question him, instead tightening my arms around his scute to counter any sudden moves he might make. Adaryvan's wings suddenly twisted like sails, pulling him to a halt like a rearing stallion amongst the clouds.

A trio of thunderous thuds rang out as the dragons impacted the thick, iron-like frame of my Charr. His tail swished violently, whipping the middle dragon with his spikes, instantly slashing open an enormous cut across her face and left wing, sending her hurtling to the ground alongside her unconscious sisters.

Are they dead? I asked, peering down at their lifeless bodies as dust and dirt billowed into the atmosphere.

Adaryvan circled the field below.

A pool of blood oozed out of the middle dragon's mouth.

Even I could see that she was dead.

Her sisters, however, I was not convinced about. One had felled a tree as she landed and her body laid awkwardly over the stump, but the other simply laid still amongst the crops. Through our bond, I sensed Adaryvan's sadness. For decades he had played the part of the impenetrable beast, but I felt honoured to know his true heart. He was the Chief Protector of the Flame, the Empress' Right-Wing, he would do what needed to be done, but that didn't mean he always enjoyed it.

Pynyt descended lower, cautiously poking the one flopped over a tree. When she didn't move, he landed on the ground and checked underneath her body. Within seconds he took off, returning to my shoulder, shaking his head.

Dead, he said.

Smoke rose out of the third dragon's nostrils.

Land, I said, tapping the hilt of my sword. *Let me help.*

An almighty roar reverberated across the sky. My head whipped around to see Dreygon coming at us with Gryer upon his back while a huge furnace of fire crackled between us.

Now you can help, Adaryvan said, shifting sideways to avoid the blast.

A new level of determination surged through Adaryvan. Unlike the younger dragons who were effectively victims of their own birth, Dreygon had chosen this life, this fight. All sadness and sympathy packed away, deep, deep into the recesses of Adaryvan's mind, and I felt him focus on the increasing sense of rage inside him.

Then I realised what he was doing.

He was channelling the Flame.

Not just drawing its energy like all life does. Not even taking extra to feed their fire-breathing abilities. Channelling. Invoking. Drawing on the Divine in the solid belief that we are on the right side of history.

We are your champions, bless us.

Although I was loath to speak for the Divine, I did feel strengthened by Adaryvan's silent petition. Now, we just needed a target.

Unlike Benegnyem's often clear, scorching skies, Virisinigne's weather was variable. Clouds blew in and out at will. Rain came long and often. That day, however, the sun shone, charging both dragon's from above and below, although clusters of light clouds dotted the blue expanse just enough to provide a moment's cover for Dreygon as he spun around, ready to attack again.

Fixed on every shadow, I knew that Adaryvan was waiting—watching and waiting.

Flames cut through the cloud, blasting all around us. Growling, Adaryvan dodged the worst of it but kept his course as though he had planned to take on fire.

Remember I can't take the same level of flames as you! I called into his mind, recalling the day he had shielded me from the Empress' raging blast, while his scales glowed like an active fire beneath me.

He didn't answer, instead he released the energy he had accumulated, spewing magma-like fire across the sky, into Dreygon's face, forcing him to crash-land.

Adaryvan dived, zooming towards the edge of Gryer's camp. I hadn't even noticed we were above it. I had been pleased that we had drawn the fight away from the camp—and therefore the city—yet somehow we had turned around.

We had *been* turned around.

Those ignorant people, I said to myself as soldiers and archers sprang into action. *They follow a man who is willing to use them as cannon fodder for his cause, rather than fight one-on-one combat to end this all.*

With no choice but to defend himself, Adaryvan fired into the camp, setting their tents ablaze instantly. Screams rang out as soldiers jumped back. It would have been easy to wipe out the whole camp, but satisfied he wasn't going to be pestered or I wasn't going to be struck by an arrow, Adaryvan held his fire. *Literally.*

Unfortunately, Dreygon didn't.

Having had just enough time to recover his senses, Dreygon threw himself at Adaryvan with his mouth wide open, biting into his neck. Unable to retaliate, Adaryvan roared with pain while his body writhed horribly beneath me.

Guilt hit me when I realised he wasn't thrashing as much as he could because he didn't want to knock me off. A thrum emitted from the Blade of the Flame as it called to me. There, before us, was its main target.

The reason I had been granted it.

Pynyt, I screamed, scrambling to my feet, *burn Dreygon's eye once I've crossed over!*

I had neither time to think or plan fully but a strange memory popped into my head. After Cal and Pynyt delivered me to the final stage of my pilgrimage, the Fyuego stone had read*: To achieve enlightenment, focus on the path, not the obstacles.*

It had helped me then, so rather than being distracted by my path chopping and changing, with scales, teeth, and fire rotating with alarming speed, and a moving canyon between the two dragons' shoulders, I focused on the path that took me to Dreygon and Gryer—and jumped.

The palms of my hands cried out as I grasped the first scute on his shoulder, feeling every fibre of my strengthened skin tested by the thick, horned scale. Hauling myself up, I steadied my balance just in time to witness Pynyt thrust a fireball into Dreygon's eye.

Instantly, Dreygon released Adaryvan and both stumbled backwards, flattening tents and trees as they went in opposite directions while I desperately clung on. On the ground, humans ran as dragons roared, each sending out another wave of fire as they lost their tempers, but when Dreygon levelled out, regardless of the height I stood to fall, I didn't hesitate to lift my sword to end his tyranny. The moment I plunged down, Gryer leapt from behind a horned scale, crossing his sword with mine, holding us in a close-range standoff.

Although both red-faced and trembling from the pressure, I watched his green eyes examine me, travelling from my face to my clothes, to the sword in my hand. A strained chuckle rolled out of his mouth as he sneered. It struck me how similar to his brother he was in appearance, even if they differed greatly in character. Gryer was taller, more muscled, and had grown a thick beard like many in Virisinigne did, but even their dark hair was peppered with grey in similar places, so no one who met Gryer and King Inygo could doubt they were siblings.

"You're not of this world," Gryer said, keeping two hands on his sword, thrusting me backwards.

"Funny," I scoffed, catching my balance, "neither are you."

Smiling conceitedly, Gryer grunted. "How'd you get here?"

"The same way as you, I'd imagine." I tutted gruffly, focusing on his neckline.

"You know of the Amulet." Confusion, or perhaps displeasure, briefly marred his arrogant stare, but it soon returned along with unbridled disdain. "Fine, let's say you have breached the Divide—or at least know how to do it. You don't sound or look like a citizen of Benegnyem, so don't pretend you are. How did you recruit Adaryvan to your heathen cause?" Even after a decade's absence his Emberbyrg twang was noticeable. Glaring at me he added, "And who did you kill to get that armour?"

I scoffed. "You unjustly tar me with your own brush, Gryer. I know of the glory of the Flame, the honour it is to wear this armour, *and* the disgrace you bring upon both worlds."

Anger etched every line in Gryer's face as he snarled. "Who are you?"

"Your Judgement Day," I said, swinging my arm to drive the Blade of the Flame into Dreygon's back.

From nowhere, a speeding mass knocked me sideways. The propulsion swept my feet off the dragon, over his back and down his side so quickly that I didn't have time to cry out. Despite flying through thin air, my instinct was to hold onto the sword for all I was worth. Then, as if in slow motion, I saw the form of the injured grey dragon topple from the spot I had just stood. Apparently too weak to fly in a controlled fashion, she dropped, freefalling above me as though gravity had decided to reclaim her too.

If the fall doesn't kill me, she's going to crush me, I winced.

A talon wrapped around me, catching me a matter of metres before I was dashed upon the all-too solid ground.

Grabbing the smaller dragon with his mouth, Adaryvan bit into her body and threw her at Dreygon. Screeching, she furiously tried to flap her wings, but concussed, she had no control over her movements so rolled up and over Dreygon's withers, taking Gryer down with her.

Dreygon's wing shot out like an extending hand, breaking Gryer's fall, but the level of propulsion was great enough that he still tumbled to the base of a pine tree on the castle-side of Gryer's camp.

Put me down. Quick, put me down! I cried out.

The second my feet hit the ground, internally shouting, *Distract Dreygon!* I sprinted towards Gryer.

Adaryvan didn't need telling twice, blasting off the ground with such force that a cloud of dry soil and ash erupted into the atmosphere, tackling Dreygon in a spiralling tube of fire as they went out of sight.

With dragon-induced thunder crashing in the distance, the sound of the castle gates opening rang out. The small moat bridge cluttered and clacked as it came down, followed by the rhythm of marching feet and drums as soldiers crossed. Silently, I questioned the wisdom of my father sending foot troops into such a fight. The ensuing clash and grind of metal from the hollering armies told me my opinion was both unwanted and too late, however, I guessed that my father had seen Gryer's burning camp and scattered soldiers and—having watched them wreak havoc for weeks—wanted to finish them off. The trouble was, he hadn't accounted for the fact they had waited just as long, if not longer, for their moment with the Tecta army.

There was no way they were surrendering without a fight.

Gryer's face was grazed and bloody as he lifelessly laid in a crumpled heap. Grabbing his collar, I fumbled with the chain in my shaking fingers. My heart throbbed erratically, willing the clasp to come undone whilst my eyes darted left to right. Twice, I had to stop and defend myself from attackers, each time feeling the buzzing power of the blade as it sliced through armour and flesh as though it were no denser than butter. Finally, I worked the Amulet of the Flame free, and held it in my palm for half a second in celebration. It was all I could afford as the battle-cries around me echoed and howled in a manner unlike anything I had ever heard before.

Running through clouds of dust, I screamed, *Pynyt!*

Suddenly, the dust parted, like someone had a small but strong fan in their hands. A bright shadow formed before me, and I exhaled deeply as I realised the cleared path was thanks to Pynyt's beating wings as he aimed for my shoulder.

Flamma vobiscum, I whispered, passing him the Amulet.

Flamma vobiscum, he hissed softly, grasping the jewel in his talons before looping the chain in his mouth as well for good measure before flying away,

Flame's speed, I uttered reverently—just as Gryer's sword landed against my side.

SEVENTY-THREE

G ryer's blade bit into my armour, slicing into leather and metal before hitting flesh. Lingering for a moment, he grinned before tugging it away, ready to swing again. There and then, as pain spread over my body like barbed threads of a spiders' web, I decided that if he wanted to dance to our graves, so be it, but I would take him down with me.

He fought like Aydan—or rather, Aydan fought like him. As Enya used similar techniques, they clearly had the same royal sword masters, but I also wondered if Aydan had had yearly lessons with his uncle as well as war meetings on his so-called nature watching expeditions. Strong, forward, calculating with each step, each defence, each attack, Gryer made an interesting adversary, and despite the cut on my side, I was grateful to be able to drop and roll away a few times without the added concern of tumbling hundreds of metres.

Both armies seemed to form a bubble around us, somehow knowing to keep their own battles out of the way. The space was appreciated, however, Gryer's skill level was not. *Marino would knock you out,* I lamented, ducking away from yet another swing of Gryer's sword. *Or Raine would defuse you with words.*

Or you can. Adaryvan's voice was tired and distant, yet still as strong as ever. *Believe in yourself. Fight on, Niall, fight on.*

Having grown accustomed to him calling me *sailor*, the gesture of using my real name was keenly felt and spurred me on in my moment of weakness.

Finally, I was gaining ground on Gryer, pushing him backwards rather than being pushed, and I sensed victory within my reach as he visibly weakened with each clash.

Soldiers to our right suddenly stumbled and fell to their knees. Had they been cutlery on a table, I'd have said they had the cloth removed from under their feet as the line of disturbance rippled towards me.

Then I felt it.

The wave-like tremor that then tired of rippling and moved to a full-on earthquake.

The throng of war ceased as confusion spread.

Distancing myself from Gryer, I feared what the continuing tremors could mean. When I was a boy, such an earthquake meant Mount Halo was erupting, however, now with resident dragons, it was less likely to be the cause, but with a sigh, I knew it was almost certainly nothing good.

"What have you done, Gryer?" I yelled.

"That's *King* Gryer, boy." His tone dripped with contempt, but the dilation in his eyes told me this wasn't his trick.

I called to Adaryvan down our bond but got no reply. *Adaryvan?* The thought of losing him frightened me more than the quaking. *Hold on, Adaryvan. Wherever you are! Hold on!* I waited, hoping for a grunt, hiss, or growl. *If you can hear me, bring Dreygon here!*

The quaking ceased and fighting reinvigorated, but Gryer kept back, reaching into his pocket and hesitating before pulling his hand back out. At first, I couldn't see what he had, but as he shook his head, he dropped a small, white vial, and crushed it with the tip of his sword.

Instantly, a white fog shot high up into the sky in the shape of a mushroom.

"What's that?" I shouted.

"Insurance," he grinned, lunging forward once more, pushing me towards the castle moat. The scales on my arms twitched and the blade in my hand glowed. It made no sense, but the fire within seemed to be pulling me to the water.

Fire and water don't mix, I said to myself—or to the Flame, I was never entirely sure.

You are *the bridge,* whispered a voice as if it came from the sword. *And remember, the Flame is as above as it is below.*

The ceytus came to mind. Had Cee-Cee not told me of the Flame's blessing below the surface of the sea already? The blessing and power of the Flame *is* everywhere.

It *flows* everywhere.

Concentrating on the water, I felt something shift and heat, then an invisible force rose up, shooting scalding water at Gryer and his foggy beacon in a harsh, penetrating stream until he was on his back.

Water droplets fizzled as they touched the lingering fog, breaking off into frozen flakes before fluttering to the ground in an otherworldly manner. Suddenly dizzy and transfixed, it felt like I was dreaming—or concocting phenomena from my concussion—but my hazy doubts were smashed aside as Gryer struck me again, forcing me to drop and roll over shards of glass from the vial he had broken. As it crunched under my weight, screeches carried on a flurrying wind taunted those below. Eyes turned to the sky, searching for the source of the ear-piercing noises until six young dragons swarmed the battlefield, blasting all signs of the strange, frozen display away with their fiery breath.

With dragons hotly pursuing anything that moved, screams of gurgled blood came from all angles, but with Gryer charging me again, there was no time to reflect.

"Party tricks are all well and good, but that's all your water feature is," Gryer said with blistered cheeks. "Surrender now and spare what lives you can, even if yours is forfeit."

"That's rich," I jeered, "I'm not the one summoning hatchlings to a grown-up fight. Plus, I told you, this is *your* Judgement Day, not mine." My words, for once, came out without me worrying whether they were too much or too little. "The Empress has endured enough."

Gryer balked.

Standing several feet apart while war whirled around us, time seemed to slow down. I was conscious of everything, yet the action danced in a blur, the roars echoed in the wind, fire crackled out of reach. It was the most bizarre parley imaginable.

"Look at how much you are destroying!" I commanded, adding the sense of a plea to my tone and spreading my arms wide—whilst making sure I remained out of striking distance. "And for what?"

"No war was won without a little bloodshed and the new world will thank me in the end. One rule rather than many. One—"

"Such arrogance in oneself is beyond comprehens—"

Gryer chortled. "Says the man standing in the Flame's armour. If you earned that, you know the teachings, the one true way. *I am* doing what my brother is too afraid to do!"

"There is a difference between being afraid to take action and choosing a cloak of ignorance because you fear challenge or change," I replied. "Your brother, at times, may be guilty of both, but I do not believe his motives are wholly selfish. Cowardly, perhaps, but not entirely selfish. He does care for the lives of those beyond his gates. It is a pity his son didn't listen to him more."

Gryer narrowed his eyes. "My nephew and I share a goal."

"Your traitorous nephew is dead." I shouted over the increasing roar of dragons, soldiers, and metal as they lunged for one another. "Poisoning the Empress and plotting against the king will do that to a man. So, if you are counting on him raising you an army, you are out of luck—*in both worlds.*"

Enraged, Gryer's face turned deep red. "You'll pay for his blood," he snarled venomously. "His death will not be for nothing and a mighty kingdom will still rise. It is written in the bones of the First Empress. I have seen the prophecy! I *will* lead a new world!"

"The Empress is the Imperial Leader. The *only* one. You know that—that's why you tried to kill her because you cannot invoke another or stage your coup while she lives."

"I have settled Halo." Gryer almost pouted like a child.

"Yes, but that's the most you can do—get dragons to quell the magma and nest there so you can draw on the life stream and take more energy than you should. You could have brought friendship to Virisinigne, yet instead you chose mutiny, bloodshed, and violence."

As if to prove my point, a stray fireball flew between us, crackling as it went.

"You must have been sailing through the Divide for years, feeding Aydan's mind with hatred and false claims," I said, grimacing through the ever-increasing plumes of smoke. *"And for what?"*

"Destiny." Gryer stood proud. "We all must play our part in it. I am certainly not afraid of mine."

"Destiny has not given you a crown. You have twisted one from brambles and called it golden." There and then, I realised there was no reasoning with Gryer. He believed his path was righteous, and clearly he had groomed his nephew for years. For Enya's sake as well as my own, I was glad to have drawn out a little more information, but now I was in a loop of deluded rhetoric. Shifting my stance, I raised my sword, ready to pick my moment. "You are driven by your own greed yet call the cause holy. It is not the same."

Gryer's arms twitched. "What can I say, I'm an *all or nothing* kinda guy."

"What does that mean?"

"You'll see." Gryer curled his lip. "Or not. I doubt you'll see another day anyway."

Rather than striking, he let out a short, sharp whistle. Two of the closest hatchlings turned, halting their fiery attacks on the Tecta soldiers. Gryer whistled again, this time a little harder whilst pointing at me.

The Blade of the Flame hummed in anticipation, almost swinging itself as they rocketed towards me. The first hatchling was downed with a single cut, and a blaze ignited from the steel as though it had been fed by the life of its victim. The second hatchling's shrill cry was deafening, yet upon seeing the young dragon dissolve into nothing, it was Gryer who again came for me, not the beast.

It felt like we were travelling the breadth and width of the camp, each as determined as the other despite the growing number of injuries we were both sustaining. Blisters on his neck and face glared as angrily as his eyes, while my blade chipped at and cut through his armour, however, each time I made contact—just like the wounds inflicted on me—the damage was only enough to wind and bleed, not kill.

"Where did you get that sword?" He spat.

I was sure he knew the answer by now, but I humoured him anyway. "Her Imperial Highness."

"Why would she favour you?"

Although it crossed my mind that winding him up was not wise, I was past heeding caution. Grinning, I triumphantly replied, "Destiny, I guess."

Frustration ate at him. "It is my birthright to lead! *I* am the eldest!"

"And *I* am the seventh son." I shrugged, finally realising that order of birth meant nothing. Life is whatever an individual makes it. "My birthright is to *serve* the Flame in the capacity bestowed upon me—as it is yours."

"Prince Niall?" Gryer smirked, clearly ignoring every word or meaning beyond my identity. A devilish chuckle rolled out of his mouth as he pointed to my left. "Do look upon your brothers, I saved you a spot."

The remains of my brothers on spikes lined the moat. Reluctantly, I gazed upon them and my stomach churned. For a brief moment, my mind blanked out the activity around me. There were no dragons, no soldiers, no fires, and no sound.

Bodies in various charcoaled states stretched over the line of the moat, but I counted five on the spikes, not six, causing a glimmer of hope that Baran was still alive. However, until this fight was over, attempting to find or rescue him was pointless.

As if he read my thoughts, Gryer said, "You know, the crowned prince was my prize, but as birthright is clearly ignored here too, Baran may wish to join my cause when he sees you."

The irony of his threat was not lost on me. Maybe my father's fears had not been quite this, yet if his words were true, he had sent me away to avoid the potential for Baran's jealousy to turn murderous.

Channelling every ounce of childhood trauma, rejection, and confusion, I focused on the path to ending this. The blade responded, licking flames up my arms without burning me. Gryer's eyes dilated, reflecting my blaze, but as I stepped to attack, Adaryvan's panicked growl burst into my head.

Get back!

Looking up, I saw him barrelling through the sky towards the unsuspecting armies. With hardly a moment to curse, I retreated, glancing over my shoulder in time to see Gryer set off in the opposite direction.

His calculations were better than mine, because Adaryvan skimmed over his head, hitting the ground meters from me, throwing up dust, dirt, people, trees, and structures with earth-shattering force as he buried himself into the ground.

Immediately picking myself up, I ran to the edge of the almighty hole. Looking down at Adaryvan, tears sprang to my eyes. Through our bond, I called to him with laboured words as though I were actually speaking.

Talk to me! Please Adaryvan! Don't you dare die on me!

No words came, but I sensed a faint heartbeat as he projected the only thing he had left to communicate with.

Stunned, I had no idea what to do.

A string of gasps rang out behind me. Spinning around, I saw Dreygon's talons metres from me and coming in fast. Dropping onto Adaryvan's back, I landed, twisted, and as Dreygon descended, ready to crush me and drop onto my friend, I sprang upwards, thrusting the Blade of the Flame into the air.

Despite the thick, seemingly impenetrable nature of the dragon's skin, the blade slid into him like a knife in a wedding cake. Instantly, glowing cracks lined every scale on Dreygon's body, illuminating the battlefield so brightly that I thought the sun had crash-landed.

Then, with the loudest explosion I have ever heard, Dreygon scattered like confetti.

The flakes of ash landed near and far, yet those which settled upon Adaryvan melted into his scales, beginning to mend the enormous slash across his right eye and healing the bites upon his chest and neck.

Seeing their leader and father destroyed, the surviving hatchlings dropped to the ground.

Soldiers on either side solemnly stood in a bloodied standoff.

Gryer, however, flung himself on top of me, knocking me off my feet and my blade from my hand, whilst immediately raising his arms to cast the final blow.

A bolt of fire came from the heavens, throwing Gryer off Adaryvan and back at least twenty feet.

Blinking, I wondered if I was dead or dreaming, yet my heart skipped when Enya's glorious smile greeted me as she rode on Wydgitta's back with Muriel by her side and Pynyt on her shoulder.

Behind them flew the army of the Fyuego I had longed for.

The friendship, the salvation, the possibility of new beginnings.

Then, as if my joy was too great, my aspirations too lofty, the sun blocked out, turning the land an eerie grey, lit only by the flickering flames of spreading fire. Smiles turned to frowns, whispers of relief to confusion, while murmurs of an apocalypse and damnation spread out into the pseudo-darkness until each individual's eyes adjusted.

Peering up, the cause gradually became apparent.

The shadow took shape.

The grey turned a magnificent red.

Muttered trepidation morphed to silent, terrified, yet reverent awe.

Enormous wings fanned the fires, conducting them to perform an angelic chorus, heralding the arrival of Her Imperial Majesty.

Inside the volcano she was impressive, yet here, where all scale and size was lost, she was the most spectacular creature that ever was.

Her voice resounded across the sky.

"I am the Empress, the keeper of all that is sacred, the bringer of justice and peace, and the Guardian and Voice of the most high Flame who gives you all life. It is time to cease the age of separation and find common ground—for the divided to seek unity, grace, and mercy. For this current path only leads to eternal judgement." Beating her wings in a melodic rhythm, she waited, giving people time to absorb her words before laying down her ultimatum: "To all those willing to embrace change, drop your weapons now. For in the name of the Flame, I entreat you to choose your position wisely. I shall not ask again. Bow now or burn."

Lips trembled and hearts raced, yet every knee and head of both human and dragon bent.

All except one.

"So be it," the Empress declared. Opening her mouth, she released a laser-like furnace, hitting Gryer with perfect precision between the eyes.

The blast was so great, so unyielding, his body didn't even have time to drop to the ground before it disintegrated, leaving no more than a sprinkling of ash to mark his misguided existence.

SEVENTY-FOUR

The Empress could have easily reigned by subjugation but she remained true to her word. She had no interest in slaves, false declarations of belief, or domination. Instead, she came to unify, to open the line of communication, and forge a world of peace without thought of merging kingdoms as Gryer intended.

The following hours were only a prelude to a long road to finding that balance, yet when my father, King Ennis, joined us on the blood and ash torn battlefield, he greeted our saviours with all the humility and respect that they deserved.

Although beyond grateful for her impeccable timing, I was curious about what had changed the Empress' mind. Before I spoke to Enya, I assumed it had been her influence, yet when I was finally able to draw her aside, I quickly realised I was wrong.

"After you went through the Divide, Wydgitta and I asked for the Empress' assistance again, but she said we had all we needed for victory and she would not sway the outcome further—nor leave her egg who continues to turn a darker, healthier red by the minute. After Muriel and Pynyt came through the Divide, they gave Wydgitta and me an Amulet and returned to Virisinigne." An awe-struck smile crept over Enya's face. "You must have felt the almighty earthquake that accompanied us opening the archway in the Divide?" Only then realising that was what had distracted the fighting, not Mount Halo, I nodded. "The archway is glorious, truly glorious. Five ships can sail side by side under its shimmering lights without touching—certainly, the Empress can fly through without an issue, but when the Fyuego and your crew entered Virisinigne, there was no sign of her joining us. We were as surprised as you were to see her suddenly appear."

The knowledge that the World's Divide now had a lasting passage in it hit and overwhelmed me but having planned for the required two Amulets and two messengers of fire to open it, and desiring the long, if not rocky road to unity, I understood that phenomenon better than details regarding the egg. "I thought it was pink?"

"Pink is the first colour of a living dragon egg. Normal dragon eggs then turn dark grey or green, but royal heirs turn red. For a decade, the Empress' eggs have arrived in varying shades of light grey and changed to black." Tears lined Enya's eyes. I knew she was thinking of her brother, the cause of so much death, yet smiling, she added, "There is finally hope of a healthy future."

Her expression alone summed up my heart.

My greatest desire was to remember and learn from the past but somehow be able to move forward, to remain moving forward, with that hope—and this love.

"If you didn't persuade the Empress," said Muriel over-hearing us, looking none-the-worse for her debut as a dragon rider, "who did?"

"Not *who, what*," bellowed the Empress, cutting off her conversation with my parents and the Tecta high council—including my brother who had been recovered severely beaten but alive.

"Your Imperial Majesty?" I said, bowing.

"Your sister—" the Empress paused, lowering her head to sniff Muriel, whose body froze but her countenance showed no real fear, just respect. "Hmm, you also need to walk the path of the pilgrim, my dear. The Flame is strong and the blessings numerous for the faithful."

"It would be my honour, Your Imperial Majesty," Muriel replied, dipping her head.

"Princess Enya will see to it when you are ready," the Empress replied, retracting her head a little.

"Of course, Your Imperial Majesty," replied Enya, squeezing my sister's hand affectionately.

In my soul I already knew that Muriel was special, but my brotherly pride swelled seeing her acknowledged and my heart skipped seeing the women I loved the most beginning to form a friendship.

Before me, I was sure I was witnessing the journeys of two future queens—two strong queens who would lead their kingdoms firmly but fairly into a new age.

...Even if we did have the detail of my eldest brother, Baran, to contend with.

Pynyt nipped my neck. *What,* he said, reminding me of my original line of thought before I had time to complain about being attacked.

"Your Imperial Majesty, if I may ask, what made you fly to our rescue?"

The Empress shuddered. "I felt the chill of ice fog."

She made no attempt to expand or explain. In winter, ice, fog, and snow fell in parts of Virisinigne, but not now, not in the summer. Tecta's temperatures were cooler than Benegnyem's, so a draft through the Divide was potentially detectable—but even so, the Empress wouldn't be able to feel that whilst inside the depths of the volcano.

Adaryvan shuffled behind me and I heard him clear his throat through the bond. Turning to listen to him, a wave of sadness hit me as I took in his face. The open wounds were gone, yet a scar across his right eye remained. It added to his ferocious look, but it wasn't fear that the tooth mark instilled in me. It was regret and relief. Regret for him being harmed, but relief that he was still there beside me.

The Right-Wing of Benegnyem and the Left-Hand of Virisinigne *had* held on long enough for the true champions to arrive.

A body is made of many parts, Niall, Adaryvan said, reading my thoughts. *Each is as important, as valued as the next. For the Flame, the Empress, the Fyuego, and you, I will always do my part.*

And I, you, I said, laying my hand across my chest.

"Good," said the Empress out loud, obviously having gate crashed our conversation. "Because if you find anyone using ice fog, kill them on sight."

Her words hung in the air for a moment before my mind clicked into gear. "Gryer had a small vial, a glass jar filled with fog. He pierced it with his sword, and a mushroom of foggy cloud sailed into the sky. Before I knew it, hatchlings arrived."

A deep, guttural groan rumbled out of the Empress.

The five remaining hatchlings had been detained by the Fyuego in the hope they could be gently persuaded to see a calmer, less violent future in the Liekke Valley. Gauging the Empress' reaction, it was perhaps providential they were not within reach at that moment.

Adaryvan nudged me with his tail. *Show her Aydan's ring.*

Fumbling in my pocket, my fingers found the jewel. Reacting to my touch, I felt the strike of a cold bolt across the glass surface before I witnessed its frosty, threatening movement.

"Your Imperial Majesty, before Aydan died he used this ring to freeze Seraphyna and Sunniya."

"Cryomagic," she winced, flicking her tail in the dirt. "Do you know where he got it from?"

"He could have been lying, but he said Gryer found it in Mount Halo."

"Mark my words, neither cryomagic nor any kind of ice fog or wind magic is ever to be used." A growl rippled from her. "Is that clear?"

As the Flame was supposed to control everything, I didn't truly understand, yet her accompanying roar was enough to compel complete compliance.

"I must return to the royal hatchery," she declared, "but Adaryvan and Niall, you must explore Mount Halo and seek reassurance that nothing ancient has been disturbed."

"And if it has?" I asked, softly.

"Then your mission, I fear, has only just started."

Although smaller than Liekke, the Halo mountain range had numerous caverns dotted throughout. They would all need investigating, but Adaryvan, Pynyt, Wydgitta, Enya, and I headed to the crater first because it was inaccessible to those not Charred, making it the most likely to hold secrets.

Unlike Liekke Peak, which had had centuries of care and maintenance, Dreygon and Gryer had a comparatively small—tiny even—network of usable chambers. Having little to go on from the Empress, who seemed to prefer to keep details of what she feared to a minimum rather than share secrets unless absolutely necessary, we decided to venture into the tunnels together.

The smell and air in Halo was thick and unsettling. Wydgitta said it was because the resident hoard was not stable, and they hadn't learnt how to properly maintain or channel the magma flow, but whatever the reason, it made my dragon-skin itch and weighed heavy in my lungs.

To the right, we found Dreygon's lair. Gauging by the debris, Gryer had slept there too at one point, but the more recent activity seemed to be located in the next lair where the younger dragons had lived. We could only assume Gryer had summoned the smallest ones as a last hurrah—yet it was also possible that he had hoped revealing the progeny of his stolen eggs would be a demonstration of extra strength and potential longevity to the citizens he wished to rule over. No one in Virisinigne would have known where he got the older three from. To them it was all magic, so stealing eggs from beyond the World's Divide would not have entered their head—and Aydan, the unknown prince, claiming them from the last of the hoard's unpoisoned batch certainly wouldn't have been in their minds at all.

With relief, we returned to the crater floor. The air was still dense to breathe, but finding nothing was definitely preferable, and I just wanted to join my crew for a big meal, sleep with my arms around Enya, and then begin to decide whatever the future holds next.

As Adaryvan escorted us to the left tunnel, I almost protested, like a sixth sense was telling me all my plans for peace and love would be shattered down the long, winding track. Rocks jutted from every angle, leaving only just enough room to squeeze an enormous dragon down. Apparently Dreygon was a minimalist, even if he was huge and redecorating would have been to his benefit.

Not that it mattered now. He was gone forever.

The tunnel split into two. Left led to the heart of the volcano and the only chamber that looked remotely as grand as the one in Liekke. There, magma bubbled and a stream of fire flowed up and down in a translucent rock into the ceiling. Again, no one spoke. We knew the room above would be the hatchery where strange lavacicles continued the flow of magma, but with no inhabitants to appreciate its rhythm, it all seemed rather pointless.

The three dragons that had been old enough to lay eggs had clearly been successful, otherwise six hatchlings would not have come to the battle, but it made no sense for Gryer to summon babies if he had any interim dragons, so we knew the hatchery would be as empty as everywhere else in this forsaken pit.

Where the Cryoring had originated from, we could only guess. Over time, I would make it my mission to investigate every cave for clues, including the blocked one in eastern Benegnyem that Adaryvan spoke of.

But that was for another time.

Now was a time of warmth and love.

Flying into the hatchery, a sharp hiss stopped Adaryvan in his tracks so quickly that Wydgitta nearly crashed into him, yet apparently sharing his surprise, she didn't complain.

An unnatural, icy wind cut across and stung my face. Gazing at Enya, her cheeks were pale and her eyes dilated as she stared forwards. Following her line of vision, I saw the lavacicles ebb and flow with pure, white snow. My brain shouted *how?* but my senses were too frozen to communicate with anyone. A crack sounded from a rock—no, not a rock, an egg, a white egg, laying in a bed of rubrunite which had been precisely positioned around the lavacicles, now icicles.

The wind increased, but rather than blowing, it felt like it was drawing us in—feeding off our energy.

Thank you, said a voice.

Chills struck every inch of my body.

An explosion of fog shot from the egg, clouding the room immediately.

Adaryvan and Wydgitta threw fire across the room, pushing back the thick smog just in time to see the long tail of a white creature shoot out of the egg, burrow into the ceiling as though it was made of feathers, and disappear out of sight.

"Was that a white dragon?" I said, barely above a whisper.

"No," Enya said, leaning on Wydgitta's scute whilst rubbing her forehead. "It was a white wyvern."

"A wyvern? What's a—"

"A messenger of Ventus," Adaryvan said solemnly.

"Ventus?"

"The Guardian of the Frost."

Through our combined bonds, I could hear five hearts throbbing. The answer was obvious, but I had to ask. "I take it neither Ventus nor Frost are someone we want to meet?"

Adaryvan scoffed. "Not unless you enjoy seeing deities fight in an endless cycle of war."

"I thought the Flame was the Divine—the *only* deity?"

"In these two worlds, yes."

"Wait, what? There's more than two worlds?"

"The frozen kingdom lies dormant, boxed away many millennia ago after the Flame and her loyal champions combined to seal the Frost away along with her wyvern minions and cryomagic."

"Is that when the Flame and dragons bonded?"

"Yes, in our combined desire for peace, we formed a pact that has lasted."

"So, this Frost is the nemesis of the Flame—the lifeforce of everything as we know it?"

"Yes," Adaryvan winced, "and we've just woken her up."

If you liked this book, please consider leaving a review on Amazon, Goodreads, or any other social media that you use. Honest reviews are invaluable to any author, but especially independent ones like Alexia.

If you would like to join Alexia's newsletter and be the first to receive updates on forthcoming novels as well as read exclusive short stories, please visit:

www.alexiamuellerushbrook.co.uk

ALSO BY THE AUTHOR

Dystopian trilogy:
THE MINORITY RULE
BEYOND THE FENCE
INTO THE FOG

Paranormal mystery with romance
THEY CALL ME ANGEL

Dark psychological thriller
YOU

ACKNOWLEDGEMENTS

How I have written six books in four years after saying I couldn't write for over three and a half decades, I will never know, but if you have taken a chance on a shy, independent author who finally realised her passion for storytelling, THANK YOU. Whether you are a beta, ARC, or post-publication reader, you are amazing. I hope you love my stories as much as I do and will stick with me on whatever adventure runs through my head and makes it to ink next!

There are a few people who I simply cannot finish this novel without giving extra thanks to because their support means the world to me—on all sides of the Divide.

To Sergio, my alpha reader, best friend, and soulmate. The man who listens to me ramble, champions my stories before anyone else, and who doesn't complain when he walks in and I refuse to talk until the chapter I am writing is done. Sorry, but also thank you. I couldn't do it without you.

Booktok and Instagram seemed like such unlikely places for me to frequent, but finding friends as well as readers on both platforms has been a massive highlight for me. If you have found or supported me via social media, please know how much I appreciate you, but I must mention a few extra special people here because their support has gone above and beyond my wildest dreams. David W Adams, C L Adams, Iain Benson, C K Andersson, Emma, and Iona. To say I am grateful for your friendship is woefully understating the fact, but your encouragement and wonderful feedback spurs me on every day. (Dear Readers, They also write amazing books if you're looking for new authors!).

As always, I am incredibly grateful to both my editors, Belle Manuel and Jessica Netzke. Regardless of the genre I present to them, their work is fantastic.

Although some of my previous novels have fantasy elements, In the Name of the Flame is my first high/epic fantasy and I knew that by stepping into this territory, I had more scope for commissioning artists. In particular, I really wanted the cover to be special. Pantelis Politakos took my rough design, embellished it, and completed it to perfection. The cover is stunning, and I cannot thank him enough.

For the chapter headings, I knew I wanted to have dragons in the infinity symbol, and Hannah Zoey is the wonderful artist who made it happen.

M.T Zimny, a fellow indie author and cute character illustrator extraordinaire, designed stickers for Niall, Enya, and Pynyt. They aren't included in the book but if you follow me on Tiktok or receive a book directly from me, there's a chance you'll end up with one—or three!

Shade of Stars painted portraits of Niall, Pynyt, and Enya. Without question, she has brought them to life and there aren't enough words to adequately express the detail and beauty of her work. Again, her portraits are not in the book, but gorgeous prints are likely to be shared as well as seen on social media.

And finally, I must say thank you to Carol. I dedicate this book to you, my old friend who I see far, far too little of these days, but you are always the first person I think of when dragons come to mind. Mine aren't Welsh, but hopefully you'll forgive me and love this book anyway—and even if I have spelt Wichita and Peanut's names wrong, please know I had them in mind all along.

In the Name of the Flame—or maybe the Frost?

Alexia

About the Author

Alexia Muelle-Rushbrook is a multi-genre author who has spent her life daydreaming in the English countryside whilst surrounded by her animals. A self-confessed geek, she loves sci-fi and fantasy and has a passion for the natural world—thankfully a joy which her husband shares, otherwise the number of pets she has would drive him crazy!

Stories have always run through Alexia's head, but it wasn't until one voice really wouldn't leave her alone that she realised her dream of being a writer. That voice turned into dystopian trilogy, The Minority Rule, but now unleashed, the voices refuse to be boxed in—or stick to one genre—meaning Alexia can still be found daydreaming with her dogs but the narrative now gets recorded!

www.alexiamuellerushbrook.co.uk

GLOSSARY

HUMANS:

Niall – Nye-all
Enya – En-ya
Uryah – Yoo-rai-uh
Gryer – Gree-er
Aydan – A-den
Oryana – Or-ree-an-a
Marino – Ma-ree-no
Alun – Al-un
Inygo – In-ye-go
Brydget – Brij-et
Rhys – Rees
Lord Byrne – Lawd Burn
Muriel – Mur-ee-ell
Raine – Rayn
Ennis – En-is
Talia – Tah-lee-uh
Remi – Rem-mee
Conley – Con-lee
Baran – Ba-ran

Douglas – Dug-las
Idalya – A-dar-lee-ya
Lord Calder – Lawd Cal-der

DRAGONS AND OTHER NAMED CREATURES:

Adaryvan – Add-a-van
Pynyt – Pea-nut
Empress – Em-press
Wydgitta – Wid-gee-ta
Coayl – Co-al
Calcibus – Cal-ki-bos
Seraphyna – Ser-a-fee-na
Cyrus – Sy-rus
Brytt – Bret
Sunniya – Sun-ni-ya
Dragana – Drag-gan-a
Dreygon – Drey-gun
Drayanna – Dray-an-na
Ceytus – See-tus
Fyrewowwa – Fi-er-wow-wa
Carnyfex – Car-ni-fex
Ventus – Ven-tus

OTHER:

Virisinigne – Viri-see-nine
Benegnyem – Ben-egg-ni-em
Simulinigne – Sim-u-line-in
Fyuego – Few-way-go
Emberbyrg – Em-ber-burg
Tecta – Tec-tur
Liekke – Leck-kay
Thanatonite – Than-a-tone-ite
Rubrunite – Ru-bron-ite
Ignis pila – Ig-nis pe-la *(fireball)*
Flamma nobiscum – Flam-ma no-bisk-cum
(Flame be with us)
Flamma vobiscum – Flam-ma vo-bisk-cum
(Flame be with you)